A LEARNED ROMANCE

A Sequel to Pride & Prejudice

ELIZABETH RASCHE

Quills & Quartos
PUBLISHING

Edited by Debra Anne Watson and Mary McLaughlin

Cover Design by Carpe Librum Design

ISBN 978-1-951033-87-3 (ebook) and 978-1-951033-88-0 (paperback)

"She had been forced into prudence in her youth, she learned romance as she grew older: the natural sequel of an unnatural beginning."

— JANE AUSTEN, *PERSUASION*, CHAPTER 4

One

By all rights, George and Lydia Wickham should have been destined for a hovel, cheap lodgings, or a debtor's prison. The fact that after only a year of marriage, the two were ensconced in a fashionable London town house seemed to spite the divine order of things, or so Mary Bennet thought. Her sister Lydia's foolishness in running away with Mr Wickham was equalled only by his unscrupulousness in refusing to marry her without being paid, and Mary had predicted a dark reckoning to come. If any weighty punishment was due them, however, it had not yet fallen; the Wickhams lived in reckless enjoyment and dazzling wealth. Though the two coveted the position of courtiers at St. James, they could not expect to achieve that without patronage, and so far, their wealth and fashion had not allured anyone to sponsor them in so great an endeavour.

No one knew the exact cause of the Wickhams' sudden ascension to wealth. Some rumours posited a distant relative, whose grasping hands had been so tightfisted in life that rigor mortis had, comparatively speaking, loosened them and spilled gold into Mr Wickham's lap. Others pointed to a shrewd investment in a coal mine in Wales and an even shrewder decampment before news of the flooding of the mine became public. Though Mary had asked her brother-in-law how he was able to afford a luxurious town house, a transfer into an elite London regiment, and Lydia's unmanageable spending, Mr Wickham had never given her a straight answer. Lydia claimed it was all due to her husband's cleverness, an infinite source of good things in her mind, and Mr Wickham only smiled.

"Ladies never understand business, and I shall not bore you with it," was the most he would give to Mary's pressure, and then he would excuse himself to perform his duties. Those duties were light—the business of an exclusive London regiment appeared to be mostly dressing in uniforms better suited to ballrooms than battlefields and marching in formation. Lizzy Darcy called those uniforms 'England's best incentive to pacifism,' and certainly the soldiers who wore them were careful not to soil them with wearisome, useless tasks like practising shooting. Their gloves were unspotted with powder; their boots knew no mud. Mr Wickham's regiment marched in docile formations like ninepins for a portion of the day and bowled themselves over with drink and play the rest of it. Mary often wondered what would happen if the regiment faced a real battle with the French. Their skills seemed to consist mainly in turning smartly from left to right and wearing well-shined boots.

Mr Wickham's professed business in life was the regiment, but Lydia's was something more tender and filial: she intended to please her mother by helping all her sisters get married. Jane and Lizzy had pre-empted her plan, making not only sensible, but also loving, choices of their own before Lydia could even look about her. And by the time Lydia had written to invite Kitty to stay with her, Kitty had found a hot-headed lieutenant on leave in Meryton. That impetuous gentleman had marched off to Spain shortly after marching Kitty down the aisle, and Kitty had settled in to wait for him at Longbourn in surprising cheerfulness. Now Kitty scoured the papers for news of her particular officer with as fond a heart as her mother had once had for the general class.

That left only one sister to benefit from Lydia's generosity: Mary. At first, Mary had hardly thought of efforts towards marriage. Hertfordshire had few prospects for her, and although she had the same girlish hopes of a love match, she had long since tempered them with a more realistic appraisal of her chances at any match at all. Though London bettered those chances, Mary still thought more of her role as a sister or churchgoer than the idol of devoted swains. She had agreed to stay with the Wickhams, who by that time had bloomed in wealth and glory in London, in full expectation of some dramatic revelation and catastrophe, after which she would support poor Lydia with her own piety and quiet sisterly comfort. Surely no good could last for the Wickhams.

And yet, Mary had to admit that so far, her premonitions of disaster had been disappointed. The worst she had seen was Mr Wickham well into his cups in the evenings and regular squabbles between the couple that made Mary cringe. The squabbling discouraged Mary from being too eager for a marriage for herself.

"But dear Wickham, it is only natural that I wish to change the drawing room a little." Lydia appealed to her husband by widening her brown eyes and giving a little shake of her dark curls. As a girl in Meryton, her tastes had been showy, but a Season in London had refined them into a studied careless- ness, adorning her with the finest of Indian muslins in the most sumptuous (yet proper) of designs. The coral lips she used to pout at her husband displayed the prettiness he had chosen to reign in his household, but Mr Wickham admired them without falling in with her wishes. He had grown used to her charms and frolics soon after their marriage.

Not as used to them as I am, Mary Bennet thought, *but then, I have had a lifetime to adapt.* Mary's own curls were not fresh from a maid's touch, nor were they mahogany-coloured like Lydia's. They were mouse-brown and as mousy as everything else about Mary. In another family, she might have counted as pretty, but arrayed against her sisters—especially the eldest, Jane—Mary did not impress. Plain brown eyes, dull brown hair—the only features in which Mary could compete with her sisters were her delicate skin (a mouse stayed huddled at home) and the elegant dexterity of her hands, skilled in home pursuits like embroidery. She used them now to spread butter over her morning toast, tapering the moist- ness perfectly to the edges, but her eyes remained on Mr Wickham. Even after two weeks of living with the Wick- hams, Mary felt uneasy at their incessant quarrelling. *Good- ness knows there was enough arguing at Longbourn.*

"The drawing room was refurnished before we moved in, my dear," he said. Mr Wickham's trim figure and handsome face had only benefited from their change in position; he looked as dashing as he always had, but the sheen of gold gave him a needed air of respectability. His attitude towards his wife was indulgent, but Mary suspected that indulgence stemmed less from desiring his wife's happiness and more from indifference to her. Even Mr Wickham's cosseting had limits, however, and the two often quarrelled over how to divide the spoils. Mr Wickham preferred the gambling table and neat little dinners out with his comrades. Lydia preferred hosting routs and shopping. Mary could not say Mr Wickham had ever denied her sister anything she really needed, and he gave her a great deal of leeway as to her desires. Lydia's white muslin bore ribbons of the finest silk, and a generous garland of hothouse flowers poked from Lydia's curls. The Wickhams' London home boasted shining china, glittering candelabras, and polished mahogany—everything bright and new that ought to be new, everything impressively old that ought to be old. No one doubted Lydia's taste. It was simply that Lydia's desires to make herself and her home the objects of envy in the Season of 1814 were expansive indeed.

"Perhaps—" Mary tried to think of something to say that would curtail Lydia's pleas, but in the end, she faltered and dropped her gaze back to her toast. Lydia had not heard her soft voice any way.

"Before we even moved here! They are ancient ruins now, as far as I am concerned," Lydia said, as if Mr Wickham's admission completed her case. "Lord! I shall have to tell the draper to be sure to bring a shovel when he comes." She laughed, and although the disagreement still unsettled Mary, the trill of Lydia's laughter reassured her a little.

I daresay all married couples argue, Mary reassured herself. *It is not really any different from Mama and Papa, or the Lucas boys tussling in the garden.* But those battles had always made her cringe as well, and how she hated the thought of her sister's life becoming like that of her mother, where arguments were replaced by snide asides and sarcastic wit. The thought spurred her to try again to distract her sister.

"Lydia," she said, "I thought you were going to...um, teach me a new dance." Mary's face flushed, although she had no reason to be embarrassed.

"Oh, of course," her sister answered, scanning Mary's face. "Why, Mouse, you look positively abashed! Nobody was scolding *you*, you know." She reached down the breakfast table to pat Mary's hand. "Mr Wickham knows perfectly well that I need to redecorate—"

"Actually, I know perfectly well that you *did* redecorate every other room on that floor—"

"But not the drawing room! And it is *my* drawing room—"

Mary held herself still. *If I stay quiet, it will all blow over like a storm over the sea.* Arguments in Meryton had whipped up and misted away in that way, and however unpleasant they were, she could at least reassure herself that she had not caused them or made them worse by interference. *Except that once, with Harry Lucas.* Regret sliced through her, and she pushed the memory back. She waited until the debate died down enough for her soft voice to break through. "Lydia, you were saying? About the dance?"

"The dance?" Lydia looked perplexed for a moment at the topic. "The newer dances. Yes, I will teach you—tomorrow, perhaps, or the day after. Just imagine being in town for the Season without knowing all the latest dances! Mama should have had you taught. She cannot expect you to get a husband without dancing."

Mary was beginning to think her change of subject was not to her advantage. "Perhaps she does not expect me to get one at all this Season."

"Of course she does. I got a husband pretty quickly, didn't I, Mr Wickham?"

Mr Wickham smiled. "You did, my dear. A very willing husband."

"And even Lizzy got one, same as I. Well, not the same husband—that would be against the law—but at the same time, almost." Lydia refilled her teacup. "And you know she was practically an old maid, while you are only twenty."

Mary grimaced at Lydia's heedless reference to her age, though honesty demanded she correct the error. "One and twenty."

"Are you really?" Lydia deposited the teapot on the table hard enough to make the cutlery rattle. "You had a birthday last week, didn't you? You sly thing! I forgot, and you said not a thing to remind me."

"There was not any reason to do so. I do not wish for any special attention," Mary said.

It was true, but Lydia was hard-pressed to believe it. "Well, now I must take you shopping or something. Poor little Mouse! I forgot Mama had a whole *slew* of babies in January. Jane one year, and then Lizzy—"

"Lizzy's birthday is in May."

"—and then you a couple after. She must have found April a most romantic month."

"Lydia!"

"Well, she or Papa must have. Oh, I know, I am awfully vulgar today. It is all on account of that drawing room. One cannot help feeling vulgar every time one goes in. It mars one's character."

Mr Wickham's tone was placid. "But you are not in it now, my dear."

"Vulgarity *permeates*, Mr Wickham. It goes through the walls. Now, as I was saying, Mary—one and twenty, is it? Whatever the age, once you know all the dances to conjure with and speak the right words to charm a man, you will ensorcell him as a husband—"

Mary tried not to laugh. "That sounds almost demonic. Is that how you won Mr Wickham?"

"Present company is always excluded, Mouse."

Mr Wickham drew the teapot, the surface of its china misted from the wintry air, towards him with an unruffled air. "My dear, you had no need to ensorcell me. There is no refuting your allurements."

"There! And people have the audacity to say we are all at sixes and sevens in our marriage. I defy anyone to find any other husband who says such pretty things—to his wife, I mean—and *meaning* them." Lydia dropped her voice to a whisper, but it was plainly audible across the table any way. "Captain Roarke no doubt says such pretty things, but I doubt whether Lady Lucy hears a word of them." It was moments like these that endeared Lydia to Mary. The stage whisper signified propriety to Lydia. "Society has a great many rules about what one must not say," she had told Mary, "but I find you can break all of them if you show that you know you ought not to say it!" Certainly Mary could not reproach her sister.

"I have no desire to—ensorcell anyone," Mary said. She could imagine happy homes, couples leaning on one another's arms, doting on each other and cooing at infants, but she never could picture herself as the beloved bride in such a scene. The maiden aunt mending in the background, perhaps, or a wife wed for convenience. However sweet a dream a loving marriage might be, it was more realistic to focus on what she could obtain—a peaceful home. So long as she found a quiet nook, Mary would make herself content. And she had adapted herself for such a purpose, as Lydia's next words confirmed.

"You know you are welcome here as long as you like," Lydia said. "I thought you would scold me and frown at me, but I find you are a perfect mouse."

"Very agreeable," said Mr Wickham with a nod firm enough to shake his dark hair.

Mary's heart warmed. She had made an effort to omit her usual topics of conversation: the stiff, sententious quoting of scripture and sermons. Though such thoughts still ran in her mind, Mary knew Lydia did not like such talk, and she suppressed it as much as she could stand. It made Mary silent most of the time. Lydia did not understand what it was to be shy, to hate to offer one's own opinion unsubstantiated by anything weightier. Mary had much rather repeat what *Fordyce's Sermons* said about a thing than state her own view. Who should care what Mary Bennet thought about anything? Offering an authority's opinion seemed safer and wiser, and could there be any greater authority than that of God, or Fordyce?

But Mary had tried to keep her mouth shut rather than quote religious sources, and here was her reward: Lydia and Mr Wickham did not mind her so much now, and even spoke warmly to her together. If it was like this always! Peace and harmony, kind words and quiet. Even the little nickname Lydia had given her, 'Mouse'; some might have seen it as less flattering than she did, but it conveyed a familiarity, a sister-liness that Mary had always missed at Longbourn. It was all she wanted. But though they had a few minutes of silent chewing, Lydia soon turned to a subject that stirred the depths again.

"Mouse, you simply must come with me on Wednesday to Mr Cole's lecture. You will learn a great deal, I assure you."

"A lecture?"

Mr Wickham's dark brows had lowered at the name of Mr Cole, and now he supplied the explanation in a terse tone. "He is a scientist of some sort, although he seems full young to be anything such. But he gives lectures to ladies' groups, and Mrs Wickham patronises him."

"Oh, yes, I find him most entertaining," Lydia said with an eagerness that disturbed her companions.

"What kind of scientist is he?" Mary asked, wondering what manner of young man could make a lecture sound appealing to her sister.

"It was something ending in -ology, I know."

"Biology?"

"No, not that one."

"Archaeology?"

"I do not think so. Botanology, perhaps."

Mary's lips twitched to hide a smile. "That is not a word, Lydia. Do you mean botany?"

"That has not got an -ology. Well, whatever science it is, Mr Richard Cole is *quite* proficient. You will adore the lecture and learn so much." Lydia's assurance did not go for much with Mary, and apparently not with Mr Wickham, either. He shifted in his seat.

"Perhaps you would do better to visit Mrs Holt on Wednesday instead, my dear," he said.

"But she will want to go to Bond Street together. And did you not say I should visit the shops less? Except today—I must go today! Mary, you can go with me, and I will buy you something nice."

"I do not need anything." Mary hesitated. "I would rather stay home, if you please."

"Home again! You have not gone to the shops above twice with me since you arrived, and heaven knows you need new gowns. You cannot wear my old ones forever. Indeed, you should not be wearing them at all." Lydia gave a pointed look at the neckline of the muslin morning gown Mary wore. Lydia's bosom had filled it out admirably, but it drooped on Mary's bony frame. The waist hung similarly; Mary and Lizzy had always been the thinnest of the family. "At least let Addleby take them in a little. You look a fright!"

"She is so busy. I would not like to bother her."

"She is paid to be busy. Isn't she, Mr Wickham?" At his amused nod, Lydia continued. "If you will not come to Bond Street, at least get Addleby to work on those gowns. And— oh! I must hurry to the shops. It is almost time. For shopping, I mean." Lydia's rosy cheeks turned redder with some unexpressed emotion. "Mouse, you can help me choose a bonnet. Hurry now!" She pushed her chair back in an unladylike fashion, jostling the teacups as she moved.

"My dear, your sister has not even finished eating," Mr Wickham said in protest, but Mary hurried to defend her.

"I am quite full, really," she told him as she rose, though her fingers traced the edge of her toast longingly. With one last look at her half-finished meal, Mary followed Lydia to her bedroom.

Two

When Lydia had finally completed choosing her bonnet and run off to Bond Street, and Mr Wickham had trotted off to his own business, Mary passed Addleby in the hallway. The odour of dog hair hung in the air, trailing the lady's maid. Addleby had one arm around a mussed ball gown and the other around Prince, Lydia's pug, and from the way she held them apart from one another, they had already run afoul of each other.

"Addleby." Mary's gaze flitted over the torn stitches in the silk and Addleby's grim expression.

"What is it, miss?"

The weariness in the maid's voice reminded Mary of her sister Jane when Mr Bingley had been driven away from her, or her father after a long morning of Mama's tedious talk. "Um, nothing," Mary said. *Lydia can tell her to fit the gowns later. Or perhaps I can fix them myself.* Mary had made up gowns before at Longbourn. The result was not likely to look as trim as a lady's maid would produce, but perhaps it would pass muster. She entered her bedroom—an elegant display of Lydia's taste, all cream silk, gilt, and mahogany—and pulled out a gown to work on, seating herself in the chair in the far corner. The chair, too, bore the gilt and arabesques that Lydia favoured. Indeed, the only things that marred the style were the rag doll perched on the bureau and Mary herself. And even the rag doll looked like she was making an attempt to conform to London elegance; despite a faded face and tufts of stuffing poking out one shoulder, she modelled the attire of a white silk gown and a bonnet stylish enough to be Parisian.

Mary took out stitches and separated the pieces of Lydia's old merino. As she worked, maids passed in the hallway outside her door and chatted with each other. Mary found the relative quiet soothing. When Jane, Lizzy, and Lydia had married, Longbourn had lost most of its noise and bustle, but it had still been chaotic enough with Kitty chattering about her lieutenant and Mama pouring forth her woes to all who would listen. Mary had, then, thought to dedicate herself to music, but her concertos, it seemed, were exceedingly trying to her mother's nerves. It had been difficult to establish herself amongst the five sisters, being neither the most beautiful, the most witty, the most sickly, nor the most lively. The most of nothing, she chose to become the least of everything.

Sitting still and mending had been Mary's retreat, a way to be useful and to allow her fingers the movement they craved. Her father had seldom taken notice of Longbourn's Mouse, but when his eyes did fall on Mary, she could almost *feel* her father's sense of impatience. She had tried, like Lizzy, to establish herself through the absence of silliness that marked her younger sisters, but the subjects she preferred—mostly theological and historical—were too often met with vexation. She soon recognised that they all liked her best when she was quiet. Mary was of little use in the house, but she had the virtue of requiring little from her parents. She could not make her father laugh like Lizzy could, nor please the eye so well as Jane, but she could prove her worth in being clean, neat, and obedient and by restricting her practice on the instrument to times when the rest were away.

Out of sight down the hallway, the voices of the housemaids drew Mary's attention. "Mrs Wickham is out chasing that man again."

"No!"

"She is. Not that I wouldn't chase him myself. Have you seen him?" The voice was saucy and sure.

The other sounded scandalised. "Hannah! You ought not to talk like that. Supposing Mrs Forrest heard you gossip about Mrs Wickham and Mr Cole?"

"I'd say it to her face, housekeeper or no. I'd say it to anyone." From the way the voices dropped into silence as Mrs Forrest's slow tread approached, the boast was an idle one.

Mary tried to focus on her sewing, but a shred of discomfort remained. *Idle gossip*, she told herself, and though a spike of fear went through her, she tried to ease it. Lydia had always been wild, but she was devoted to Mr Wickham. Devoted at sixteen might mean bored at eighteen. Mary had always believed that her sister had married far too young.

Perhaps she had a mild fondness for another friend; gossip fed and grew fat on less. But so long as one kept quiet, most things blew over. In a few days or weeks, no one would even remember this Mr Cole.

A housemaid entered Mary's room, adjusting draperies and dusting a few spots. Mary watched her graceful movements in silence. When the maid picked up Mary's doll and examined it, Mary drew in her breath sharply.

"Oh!" Startled, the maid dropped the doll. She turned around and spied Mary in the corner. "Oh, miss, I'm sorry. I didn't know you were here! I meant no disrespect." The voice had sounded saucy in the hallway, but now it was scrupulously polite. Wisps of blonde hair poked from under the maid's cap. A multitude of lines indented the woman's face, but she was young for all of that—no more than twenty, probably. She bobbed a curtsey and then bent to pick up the doll.

"I will get her," Mary said, setting her dress aside. She was not quick enough though; the maid scooped up the doll and started to put it on the bureau, only to notice the stuffing protruding from the shoulder.

"Shall I have this mended, miss?"

"No." Mary tried to keep irritation from her tone. "I do not want it mended." At the maid's perplexed look, Mary felt obligated to say more, though she wished she could have been left alone in her quiet. "My mother made her for me." For most daughters, such a statement would have signalled only happy memories. Mary had plenty of those—dressing her doll under her mother's eye, carrying it about, and even once spending her own pocket money on a new doll bonnet rather than treating the Lucas boys to candy or giving it to

Lydia for ribbon. But her first memory of the doll was not so cheerful.

"That is very sweet, miss." The maid settled the doll onto the bureau. Her hand rubbed at her back through her uniform, and she sighed. "I am sorry I did not see you. Indeed, it is hard to tell anyone lives in this room. You keep it very neat, miss. I have not had to do much with it since you came."

"Your name is Hannah, is it not?"

"Yes, miss." Hannah repeated her curtsey, and Mary found herself forgiving the maid the gossip as she saw the exhaustion tinging the pale face with colour. A moment of idle talk was probably the only break the woman got in a busy household like Lydia's. *Besides, it does not mean anything.*

Hannah waited a moment to see if Mary would say anything further, but Mary remained silent, and at length the housemaid bobbed another curtsey and exited.

Mary shut the door behind her and returned to examine her doll. The shoulder was unchanged; neither more stuffing, nor less, stuck out from within, and the gown sleeve bore no smudges of dirt. Satisfied, Mary propped the doll against the wall and went back to her dressmaking, pushing thoughts of the gossip away. Her mind focused on the doll instead, centring on the day she received it.

"New doll, new doll," Mary sang, dancing around the drawing room. Mama's stitches continued to line the patchwork doll, pulling the stuffing inward, giving the figure a recognisable shape.

"I cannot see why you are so excited for a doll like that," Lizzy said, sniffing with the disdain that came with entering her teens. "Mr Hampton sells dolls far nicer than Mama can make."

"But she's making it for me." In truth, Mary was growing a little too old for dolls, but the prospect of her mother's attention focused on her gave a new allure to the idea. "Just for me!" Mary thrust her arms upward and spiralled. It would have been a full pirouette, but Jane was sitting nearby, and Mary caught herself before buffeting her just in time.

Kitty and Lydia paused long enough in their quarrelling to gape at the dancer. "How come Mary is getting a new toy, Mama?" Kitty asked, pushing her sister's head aside to get a clearer look at her.

"Because you took the orange from her Christmas box," Mama said. A hint of testiness had entered her voice, but Mary could not tell if it was because of the toys and mending strewn all over the floor, or the noise of the girls' quarrel, the crash of a falling teacup, or the acrid smoke warning that the cook had forgotten something.

"It was not me; it was Lydia."

"'Twas not!"

"Well, whoever it was, that is why." Mama sewed on, despite the noise, and Mary gleefully watched the doll take further shape. Soon she would be all neat and tidy, just as Mary loved *all things to be. Not that their home ever looked that way in its common rooms—apparently, large families just laid things here and there—but her own blankets were pulled tight over her bed, even though Kitty and Lydia shared it, and she kept her toys lined up, unless one of her siblings took them to play with. Mary knew that in a large family, awkward things were bound to happen, like her sisters taking her orange. But Mama and Papa always found a way to make things right somehow, and she felt compensated. A large family might mean many mouths to feed, but it also meant many hands to push her on the swing, many smiles to reassure her when the neighbour's dog barked, and many eyes to watch in admiration when she balanced on the fence post.*

And many ears to hear me sing. "New doll, new doll!"

"Oh, Mary, do be quiet!" *Mama's voice sounded shrill, and Mary was startled enough to stop the dance. She watched uncertainly as Mama threw an angry look at Kitty and Lydia.* "Stop your squabbling and pushing, girls. You are wearing out my nerves! Lizzy, cannot you see I have my hands full? Take Kitty and Lydia outside."

"But it is snowing, Mama."

"So much the better; they will use up a little of that energy keeping themselves warm. Go on."

Lizzy dutifully snapped her book shut and trudged out the door, pulling coats and scarves from the strewn clothing as she went, and Kitty and Lydia followed, albeit with the zigs and zags of chasing one another. With the comparative quiet, Mary dared to approach her mother.

"She's going to be a beautiful doll, Mama. Will you make me a dress for her, too?" She peered over her mother's work.

"Just be glad for what you get, and do not ask me for more." Mama's tone still held the testy note. The smoke from the kitchen was growing thick enough to smudge the ceiling. "What on earth is Hopper doing? Just because we owe her a little, she is determined to burn everything we eat and the house with it. Jane, go and see what she is doing. Move out of my light, Mary."

Mary shifted. She wanted to sing some more, but something held her back. "She is almost done, Mama. Look how pretty her eyes are!" They were only buttons, but Mary admired them all the same.

Behind her, Jane returned. "I think Hopper needs help with the dinner, Mama. Everything is smoking again, and the new girl is not much use yet."

"Oh, here." Mama thrust the doll at Mary and got up, sighing with an emphasis meant to attract sympathy.

"But Mama, she's not finished." Mary looked at the left shoulder, where stuffing poked out of an unsewn gather. To her, it looked ghastly and deformed, like her neat and tidy little doll had become part hunchback instead.

"I ran out of thread, Mary." Mama said it firmly, as if that decided matters. Mary did not understand.

"Where is more thread?" When Mama didn't answer, Mary repeated it. "Where is more thread, Mama? When will you finish her?" She tugged at her skirt. "Mama, when? Her shoulder is bulging out."

"Oh, hush, Mary! You would think you were the only child on earth who needed something. Cannot you see I have enough to do already? My nerves are nearly jangling! Your father says we are in serious difficulties, that some of his investments—"

Mama shrugged her shoulders, giving up the topic, as she usually did when pecuniary matters confused her. "Don't be selfish. I'll finish it some other day."

Mary shrank back from her. As Mama stalked towards the kitchen to scold the cook, Mary remained silent. I shan't ask again, Mama. I shan't ask for anything. *The sickly feeling in her gut made the whole world feel unsafe. What did serious difficulties mean? She had never really thought there might not be enough for all of them—not enough oranges, not enough money, not enough love.* You won't have to do anything for me. I shall be good. *Mary studied the doll's figure. The face was still good. Most of the body was workable.*

Probably even Mary's ten-year-old hands could sew up the rest of the shoulder, but she didn't want to. She preferred thinking someday Mama would finish her.

In the distance, Mary could hear her mother's angry voice and Hopper's irritated one lifting to match it. Her hand slid over the broken cup that had landed next to Jane's upended sled. Did they have enough money for a new cup?

Hesitating, she finally picked up the pieces and deposited them. Then she dragged the sled to the spot near the door where it belonged. The mending had to be corralled from a thousand places, but in the end, Mary got it into one round pile. I won't be any trouble to you, Mama. I won't talk back like Lizzy. I won't fight like Kitty and Lydia. I promise. I promise. You'll hardly even know I am here.

Three

A few hours after Mary's musing, Lydia returned, her face flushed with a triumph that soon dwindled when their sister Lizzy Darcy was announced. Mary sat with Lydia in the much-maligned drawing room to receive their sister. Although the walnut chairs and thin rugs were not much to look at, they were serviceable enough in welcoming their sister.

"You can come sit here, in our little purgatory, Lizzy," Lydia said. "Mind the chair backs—there may be nails coming loose."

"I think not," Lizzy said, amusement twitching her lips. She had the same dark hair as Lydia, and although it was not coiffured in the latest style as Lydia's was, it was done up with elegant curls and a jewelled comb, a mark of her characteristic taste, rather than Lydia's more slavish adherence to the whims of fashion. Her square-necked, white wool gown showed the same calm, independent style. "I take it you have some resentment against these chairs, that you malign them this way?"

"Lydia wishes to redo the drawing room," Mary said. Though her tone was soft, Lizzy caught it.

"More redecorating! I thought you had had enough of that sort of thing." Lizzy embraced each sister and seated herself with a grace heedless of any nails. "Mr Darcy will come with me tomorrow and pay his respects." Though she did not say so, probably she was ensuring her husband would not have to meet Mr Wickham face to face. Though the old enemies were civil enough to each other when they met, no one wanted to test their civility unnecessarily. "We will not be in London long, I fear. Just long enough to tempt me with London's dissipation and not long enough for me to fall into it." She made a wry smile. "Luckily, Pemberley has its own attractions to harden my moral character."

"Oh, do not speak to me about being hard, Lizzy. I am all compassion now that we are rich. Did we not take in Mary? And I have half a hundred charities asking me for money every day," Lydia said.

"I do not think their *asking* you is a sign of your compassion," Lizzy said, smiling.

"Well, it's true that I do not give them anything if I can help it. But sometimes I must, because there is someone standing by that I particularly want to impress—so there you are!" Convinced she had proved her compassion to their satisfaction, Lydia tossed her dark curls.

They chatted a few minutes longer in a way that seemed aimless, touching on Jane's confinement and Kitty's husband requesting leave, but Mary sensed an undercurrent to Lizzy's drifting conversation, and it soon turned to Mr Richard Cole. "I hear he is a friend of yours, Lydia," Lizzy said, her voice sounding carefully neutral.

"Oh, yes! He is a delight. I shall introduce him to you if you like, but you must not monopolise him."

"We will not be long enough in London to monopolise anyone," Lizzy said, "but I had heard you tend to monopolise him yourself."

Lydia looked rather pleased than otherwise at the rumour. "I told you, he is great fun."

"But any rumours of monopolising are unlikely to do you any good." Gentle hinting seldom did any good with Lydia, so Lizzy moved on to more directness. "You may be married now, but that does not mean your reputation is inviolable."

"Mr Wickham does not think I am doing anything wrong." Lydia's brows drew down in annoyance.

Mary dared to correct her. "I do not think he was pleased with your saying you would go to Mr Cole's lecture. Perhaps you had better not go."

"What, slight my friend because of people and their ridiculous talk? Nonsense! I should lose all my friends that way."

Lizzy's compressed lips suggested she thought that discarding all of Lydia's friends might not be much of a loss. Certainly, Lydia did not favour good sense or decorum in her friendships. "Had you not better focus on helping Mary find a suitor instead?"

"I can do both." Lydia's tone was sour. "Seeing as I have been a married woman longer than you, I know more of what things are all about. None of this is your business."

"When it comes to our family's reputation, it is a business that belongs to us all." Lizzy's gaze turned to Mary as if to suggest something, and Mary shifted in uneasy incomprehension. "Think on it."

Rising, her own tone shifted to one more light-hearted. "Mary, perhaps you would like to come with me to Bond Street?"

Lydia seized her reticule and stood up. "Mary never wishes to go, but I will go with you."

"I have invited Mary, Lydia. She can help me select some books."

Lydia sat down again. "Oh, a bookstore. Never mind." She tossed her reticule onto the sofa, the coins in the muslin bag jingling faintly. Mary accepted her sister's invitation, sensing Lizzy wanted more than a discussion of what books to purchase. Sure enough, as the Darcy carriage launched into the flood of coaches and carts swelling the road, Lizzy's brow furrowed with worry.

"I want to talk with you about Lydia. She is as heedless as usual with this Mr Cole. If she goes any further, her respectability as a married woman will be at serious risk."

Mary twisted the strings of her reticule on her lap. It was nice to feel her sister deemed her worthy as an ally, and Mary felt a small satisfaction that her predictions of grave results might yet prove true, but in her heart of hearts she dreaded interfering. She liked the idea of being the patient consoler in the aftermath of a great scandal, but she had no desire to be an active participant, not even in preventing it. "I fear the same, although I do not see what I can do about it. Lydia does not listen to me."

Lizzy's tone was sympathetic, but firm. "You are living in their household. Should Lydia be deemed less than respectable, you will share in that judgment more than the rest of us. That is a great disadvantage—but being in their household also means that you are uniquely placed to help avert a catastrophe."

Mary slouched a little in her seat. "I cannot do anything. Lydia always goes her own way. She will not do anything just because I tell her."

Lizzy took her hand. "I have thought of that. You cannot disassemble this flirtation of Lydia's from her side. Anything we do to try to persuade her will only spur her on more recklessly."

"Then what?"

"You must work on Mr Cole instead."

Mary blinked in surprise. "But I do not know him. Why would he listen to me?"

Lizzy leaned back a little. Her increased ease made Mary wary; it meant Lizzy thought she could bring Mary round to her way of thinking. *And Lizzy is usually right.* Mary squared her shoulders and tried to look imperturbable as Lizzy said, "He may be a sensible man; perhaps all you will need to do is drop him a hint, or tell him outright it would be better for him to stop flirting with Lydia."

"And if he is not so sensible?" Experience had taught Mary that Lydia's friends usually were not sensible people.

"Then you must draw his attention away—split it between you and Lydia. There will still be gossip, but it will mean less if the world is not sure who Mr Cole favours. Indeed, if they think she was only paying him attention for your sake, it will be very respectable indeed."

Mary's dry laugh hurt her chest, as though it scraped against an old wound. "Attract a gentleman myself? And worse, one who likes Lydia first? Lizzy, this is a poor joke."

"You can do it. We are a handsome family, every one of us. You think you are not pretty because you wear old clothes and compare yourself to Jane. None of us are anything compared to Jane." Lizzy's eyes crinkled in a rueful expression, showing she had had similar feelings.

"You think that because you have made a brilliant match, we are all capable of it. I assure you, I am not."

"You are pretty and intelligent, and you have a good heart. You can turn this Mr Cole about your finger if you so choose," Lizzy insisted.

"Nonsense! I could not, and I would not if I could." Mary's chin jerked down. "It is wrong to engage in idle flirtation."

"Is it idle when it saves Lydia's reputation?"

"The ends do not justify the means." Mary knew she sounded sententious, but she clung to her idea of virtue to avoid being swept away by Lizzy's intensity—and a secret gleam of interest of her own. Was it true? *Could* Mary be the sort of person Lizzy imagined, a wily, charming belle who snatched men from the grasp of her sister? It seemed a ridiculous dream, but one with a glamour that intrigued her despite herself.

"Are there not examples in the Bible of women laying out to attract men for the greater good?" Lizzy said.

Mary could not resist the opportunity to display her scriptural knowledge. "I am no Esther, nor am I Ruth."

"I am only saying that your morals need not cavil at such a project." When Mary hesitated, Lizzy made the most of it, bearing down with an entreaty Mary found hard to resist. "Please, Mary. It is for the good of the whole family, and Lydia's as well. Surely you do not wish to see her scorned and shunned?"

A sliver of guilt slid into Mary's gut. She *had* entertained thoughts of some disaster befalling the Wickhams, and readied herself to deal with it—was that not wishing ill on them? *Of course I do not really wish to see Lydia hurt.* But the thought meant little when she compared it to her self-righteous imaginings of the last few weeks, and she felt she had no real evidence of sisterly kindness to prove her heart pure. Doing what Lizzy asked of her would be proof, though. "I will speak to Mr Cole, then. I cannot promise more."

Lizzy's nose wrinkled in a way that suggested she thought Mary could promise much more, but she nodded. "Thank you, Mary. You have relieved Mr Darcy and me of a weighty burden of worry." Her acquiescence to the compromise was so sudden and complete that Mary suspected Lizzy harboured hopes Mary would be led on to do more if it were necessary. *But I simply cannot flirt with a man I do not even know.* She could not even flirt with the Lucas boys, and she had known them forever and was close friends with Harry Lucas. *At least, I was friends with him once.* She drove that particular memory from her mind.

Lizzy's coachman set them down at a bookshop, and Lizzy rewarded her sister with a gentle camaraderie that warmed Mary's heart despite her doubts. She and Lizzy had never been close before, but she felt her sister taking an interest in her, and she thought it not wholly a matter of winning Mary to her way of thinking about Mr Cole. *Perhaps I am more interesting now that I am the only one unmarried,* Mary thought, but she knew the cynicism was unjust. Lizzy was simply enjoying exploring the world—including the family members she might have passed over before—as a young wife yet without children. Though their tastes in reading were different, Lizzy selected one of the prosy sermon books Mary liked to read before bed, and Mary accepted a present of a light-hearted novel. *Perhaps this is what a flirtatious belle would read.* Mary traced the edges of the book with her fingertips, choosing to keep it in her lap in the carriage, rather than have it wrapped up in paper with the rest. She still could not picture herself charming any gentleman away from Lydia's frolics, but rather than appearing the sordid tale of fallen humankind, the novel now seemed the bearer of a bright new world—one she would probably never enter but might enjoy looking in upon.

When Lizzy dropped her off at the Wickhams', Mary found Lydia stretched back in an unladylike pose on the sofa, her arms thrust upward. "So you are back? What a day I have had! All highs and lows. The low was that my new gown will not be ready for the Crestwoods' ball next week."

"What was the high?"

Lydia winked, looking even less ladylike. "Why, I just happened to run into a certain gentleman in the jewellery shop today. It is a pity you would not come. You could have met him."

Mary gave an uncertain smile. "It was not Mr Cole, was it?" She had harboured a hope that Lizzy might be mistaken about everything, that Lydia's interest would drift away without any need for interference, and things would go back to normal. But Lizzy was not often wrong about such things.

"Of course it was Mr Cole! I thought he might be there, and I was right."

Lydia's glee disturbed Mary, despite her attempts to reassure herself. She plucked at a thread in her embroidery, wondering what this Mr Cole was like. "What time should I be ready for his lecture tomorrow?"

Lydia sat up straight. "You mean that you shall go? I was beginning to think I could never lure you out of that bedroom, Mouse! Be ready at two—no, be ready a little earlier, and you may help me choose my gown. I want to look the pink of perfection and thrust Lady Crestwood into the shade." She laughed. "You will just adore Mr Cole. He is such fun!"

"I am sure he is." *And that, no doubt, is the problem.*

Four

It was absurd to think of a building as being like a bird, but when Mary arrived at Maddox's Assembly Rooms, it reminded her of nothing so well as a fat raven. Theoretically, the building was grey and blue—dark grey stone with a light grey mortar and midnight blue shutters. In actuality, soot had saturated the top of the stone thickly enough to turn it black, and more soot and particles streaked down the sides in swaths that tapered, rather featherlike in shape. The midnight blue shutters had a sticky residue of ash that made them look rippled in darkness. Though the shops on either side had been well cleaned, Maddox's Assembly Rooms sat between them in a dismal squalor, perched like a surly raven in a row of gentle grey doves, to continue the metaphor.

The interior did nothing to dispel the illusion of a macabre bird. Maddox's main hall would have ill served a ballroom in all practical matters—it was too small and too square, and the floor bore too many chipped places. It would have served even worse in decor. The drapes were the same midnight blue as the shutters, and though there was no soot sticking to them, they were frayed enough to look feathery. The spindly walnut chairs could have been bird legs. The podium hauled out onto the makeshift stage was also walnut, but it had been draped with a black cloth for some unaccountable reason...Mary's first guesses included a witch's gathering, funeral rites, or an assembly room manager with secret proclivities to vampirism.

Lydia had declared that Maddox's rooms were the only ones any ladies' society of any note used. Apparently such groups weighed the *cost* of the meeting place heavily and the *beauty* of the place lightly, however willing they were to invest in their own beauty; and certainly Maddox's rooms performed their function. The main hall adjoined two side rooms, perfect for arranging displays related to the lecture, helpful books, or sustaining viands for the weary learner. There were smaller rooms suitable for offices for the lecturers as well.

The assembly hall where ladies gathered to be informed (as fashionably as possible) on scientific topics was crammed with ladies in their best afternoon finery. The cramming was desirable, not only for a show of popularity, but also for comfort; the assembly hall was not kept as warm as the Wickhams' house, and Mary found the January cold unpleasant enough to inspire feelings of great affection for the stranger swaddled in merino on the chair beside her and overlapping Mary's simple wool with swells of fabric. Lydia, on Mary's other side, squashed against her with a sisterly informality that braced them both against the bite in the air.

Placards placed at the entrance had revealed the relevant "-ology" to be geology and presented Mr Richard Cole as a member of the Geological Society of London, despite his only recently having completed his education at Oxford. Although the audience was mostly ladies, an elderly gentleman with a frost of white hair sat in the front row with his arms folded, and the young man who mounted the platform scoured the old man with a gaze of disdain before beginning his lecture.

Even knowing Lydia was attracted to Mr Cole, Mary had expected to see some sort of spindly, anaemic-looking young man, her image of a scientist. Mr Cole was nothing of the sort. His body would have better fitted a bluff squire or a blacksmith: broad shoulders, thighs too muscled for the fawn cloth covering them to fit genteelly, and a height far beyond six feet. His chestnut hair curled slightly at the ends and was left mildly tousled in the current fashion. Although his nose was too broad for a sculptor's preference, overall, his handsome face commanded the homage of the ladies before him. The deep bass booming out from his chest did likewise. Mr Cole was of good family, distantly related to the Darcys, though they shared more with the Darcys in hauteur and family pride than in wealth. Mr Cole had enough money to remain a gentleman of leisure, but not much more. From the reverent way he spoke of science, he prized his education at Oxford far more than gold, and preferred delving deep into the earth for knowledge rather than whatever treasure might lie there.

It was lucky for Mr Cole that his physical beauty was great, for his theories garnered little mental application from the ladies, and he might have been entirely ignored without something to attract their fancy. The huddled mass of bodies gradually warmed the hall to a comfortable state, and several ladies nodded off, propped up by the pressure of frilled shoulders. Even Mary, used to diligently following the driest sermons, found her attention wandering. *So schist is a form of granite—no, was it the other way round? And where does this feldspar come in? Oh, I do hope I do not have to talk to anyone afterwards. Lydia will do all the talking, I suppose. Not about geology, I am sure.*

Mr Cole shuffled his notes, making a cracking sound against the podium, and ladies sat up straighter as they recognised the end of the lecture. "Any questions?" Mr Cole's voice reverberated with a pleasant rumble Mary could feel in her own body.

The elderly gentleman shot to his feet. "You have not taken into account the *force* of the pressures creating these layers, not properly, anyhow, Cole."

"That is because my whole theory lies in the *direction* of those pressures." Mr Cole's tone had gone from powerfully sonorous to testy in an instant. "And that is not a question, Sir Reginald."

"I do not have a question because the theory is wrong, quite wrong." Sir Reginald wiped his white hair back with an impatient gesture. "You cannot—"

"Are there any *genuine* questions?" Mr Cole appealed to the audience. A matronly woman in pale blue silk waved one hand slightly. "Yes?"

"Mr Cole, of what stone are the pyramids made?"

"The pyramids?" Mr Cole looked blankly at her. "I have not mentioned the pyramids, Lady Crestwood. My whole theory is about the formation of rock along directed lines of pressure. The pyramids are quite irrelevant to me."

"But surely a geologist would know?" Lady Crestwood's voice showed every confidence that her question was an important one, and the elderly Sir Reginald immediately responded.

"The pyramids were made with mud brick and limestone, Lady Crestwood," he said with a bow that showed spryness belying his age.

"Very informative! And what about the white cliffs at Dover?"

"Chalk, madam. The very sort of thing your Lady Lucy might have used on her slate as a child." Sir Reginald beamed at her. "And slate is, of course—" He continued at length, while Mr Cole shifted from foot to foot on his platform, making his tall figure teeter like a tower about to fall. When Mr Cole's irritation grew too great for silence, he broke in.

"Sir Reginald, I am quite able to field the questions myself. Kindly sit down."

"I am only helping out, my boy." The frost in the older man's voice suited his hair now, but he sat. Apparently the ladies had run out of questions, however, and Mr Cole was forced to dismiss the group to the refreshments provided in a neighbouring room.

"How rude Lady Crestwood is, asking about pyramids," Lydia whispered to Mary. "Poor Mr Cole looked quite upset. Never mind, I shall cheer him up." As the other ladies swept into the other room, tugging their gloves tighter against the fresh chill there, Lydia approached Mr Cole. Mary trailed her, smoothing her skirts. She usually did not think much about her gowns, but somehow Mr Cole's welcoming smile made her wish she had had time to fit this one better to her figure. *Perhaps I should have spoken to Addleby about it after all.*

"Mrs Wickham!" The joy in Mr Cole's voice rang out like a deep cathedral bell. "You are the only thing to give me any solace in this whole ridiculous—" He broke off, probably not out of politeness to the guests still filtering out of the room, but rather because his own irritation swallowed up his power of speech. Mary found the little wrinkle of disturbance between his brows oddly fetching; there was something open and frank in his countenance that attracted her.

"I shall have to be solace enough to make the meeting worth while," Lydia said, sidling her figure in a way that suggested both coyness and an attempt to draw attention. It was the sort of manoeuvre Mary had only seen made successful by her sister.

"You alone could manage that," Mr Cole said. The irritated draw of his brows was relaxing, and a hint of a smile appeared on his lips. "I see you are wearing the gems we discussed at the jewellers."

"They are quite lovely, aren't they? But here is my sister, Mary Bennet. Mary, this is Mr Richard Cole."

Apparently he had been so little aware of Mary's presence that he blinked in surprise when Lydia finally laid her gloved hand on Mary's arm. Her heedless introduction matched the light of mischief in her eyes.

"My sister simply had to meet you, Mr Cole, after hearing so much about you."

"Is that an homage to my scientific reputation, or have you been telling her 'so much' about me yourself?"

The two continued to chat, but Mary did not feel awkward standing silently by. She was accustomed to men overlooking her when Lydia was near, and Lydia tended to forget her. This time, being forgotten had a distinct advantage: she was able to watch the two together and gauge the nature of their friendship. The flirtation was evident, but then, Lydia flirted a great deal without necessarily tendering much affection to the gentleman involved. As for Mr Cole—

I do wish he would pay a little *attention to me,* Mary thought, admiring his good looks but beginning to feel prickled by the indifference in his stance. *It would do him no harm!* Her irritation puzzled her; although she had always disapproved of Lydia's flirting, she had never paid much attention to it before, and so far as she could tell, Mr Cole's attentions were perhaps foolishly public, but otherwise harmless. The annoyance spurred her to address Mr Cole with a surprising want of tact. "Your scientific reputation is receiving a blow today, Mr Cole. All the ladies have filed out for punch and biscuits rather than lingering to speak with you."

Mr Cole's eyes narrowed. "All the ladies except two, of course." He paused, as if to reassert his good nature. "Perhaps your conversation is worth that of all the others put together."

Lydia tittered in appreciation, but Mary frowned. "I doubt it. But I daresay you are welcome to it. That gentlemen with the white hair—Sir Reginald, was it? He will assist the ladies with any geological discussion they may want to engage in, I am sure. You have left them all in good hands."

Now Mr Cole frowned. "I suppose we had better join them," he said, and the sour note in his voice betrayed his jealousy of the other scientist. He offered his arm to Lydia, and they all treaded into the room with the collation. Sir Reginald immediately bent a low bow to Mrs Wickham and whisked her away as if he considered exchanging the heap of ladies in the room for the fashionable Mrs Wickham a fair trade. Lydia parted from Mr Cole with a friendly wave.

The room was lined on one side with long tables bearing sweetmeats, biscuits, and bowls of ratafia and punch, and on the other with matching tables bearing a scattering of little white boxes with open tops. Each box contained a rock, and most had labels scratched on the side, often with terse, unhelpful descriptions, like 'Schist, Germany' or 'Feldspar mica misc.' Mary busied herself with straightening the boxes so that the labels faced the viewer and spaced them symmetrically.

"Was that bothering you?" The humour in Mr Cole's voice showed he had forgotten Sir Reginald for the moment.

"What?" Mary's hands stilled, and she looked down at them and the little white boxes. She flushed. "Oh, I am sorry." As a matter of course, she would have dropped into silence next, but something about Mr Cole's amused smirk loosened her tongue. "When I was growing up, I was always tidying things for my sisters. Now I forget I must not touch what does not belong to me."

"I daresay they could use some tidying," he said in a careless tone.

He thinks I am simply fussing. "They could," Mary said. "You put them on display here so that people could enjoy them, did you not? It is hard to enjoy these rocks when the labels are nearly illegible, and they are scattered about like broken toys."

He had been scanning the group of ladies, but now he turned his full attention on Mary. "They should be valued whatever the presentation."

"I rather think that is how you feel about the facts in your lectures."

"What is that supposed to mean?"

Mary could hardly believe her own audacity, but she found herself not only speaking up, but being too forthright. "You made no effort to make the presentation of your facts pleasing to your audience. You must have seen many of the ladies found it dreadfully dull."

"That is their own fault, if they cannot see how important geology is." He shifted, his height tilting over Mary. "I posed a solid theory and weighty evidence. What more do you ask?"

"Nothing, if you are satisfied," Mary said, backing down. *Heavens, why am I trying to provoke him? It is hardly polite.* She plucked at her sleeve, which still hung too wide of her arm. *Lydia is right. I do look a fright. I ought to keep my mouth shut and hope no one notices.* Had she not listened to a thousand dull sermons without bothering the speakers about it? Why should she care if Mr Cole's lectures were dull? She was supposed to warn him off Lydia, but bringing up that subject felt impossible. *Lizzy should have chosen a braver sister for the task.* Her stomach rumbled, reminding her she had eaten nothing but half a breakfast. "I believe I will try the punch."

It was a good excuse for leaving Mr Cole, too, but he did not allow it. He followed her to the punch bowl and served her himself, as if forcing her to accept a drink from his hands would humble her.

"You are Miss *Mary* Bennet, are you not?" he asked her as he passed her the cup. "The one who lives with Mrs Wickham? The sister she calls '*Mouse*'?"

"Of course." Mary studied him, wondering what he was getting at.

His puff of breath made a slight mist in the cold air. The collation room had not had nearly enough time to warm as the lecture hall, but Mr Cole's crooked smile made Mary feel oddly warm just the same. "I just never met a mouse with such sharp teeth," he said. He bowed quickly and then waded into the group of chattering ladies, greeting them with an enthusiasm that made up for his previous neglect. Mary watched him go with a puzzlement that both excited and disturbed her. *Perhaps he is more of a threat to the Wickhams' peace than I expected.* If she found it hard to ignore the man's handsome face, no doubt Lydia struggled more to do so.

As if to confirm her thoughts, Lydia swept up to her and spoke in a low tone, throwing occasional sultry glances at the scientist as she did so. "Well, what do you think of him? He is *perilously* handsome, as a novel would say. That is what I think." Lydia gave a throaty chuckle. "And so charming!"

"He is handsome, I grant you," Mary said. "As for his charm, I cannot say. None of it has been directed at me."

Lydia paused in filling a cup of punch, letting red droplets cascade from the ladle as she stared at Mary. "What a funny thing to say!"

"What?"

"Why, I have never heard you complain that a gentleman didn't try to charm you before. Usually I say how glorious some beau is, and you say nothing at all." She trilled a laugh and returned to filling her cup. "I think you must be smitten."

"Certainly not!" Now the room was not chilly at all. It was far, far too hot.

"Oh, have no fear. I shall not expose your weakness for him, especially since *his* weakness is all for *me.*"

"But surely Mr Cole must understand your interest as a married woman is wholesome?" Mary said, as much to remind her sister of that as to speak of Mr Cole.

"Of course," said Lydia carelessly. "But married women are still allowed to have fun, are they not? And I am only seventeen, you know, and therefore in need of fun more than most!"

Lydia's confidence made Mary glum, and not just because her sister seemed oblivious to the dangers of gossip. *It must be nice to feel one has a gentleman pining that way.* Not that Mary expected it for herself; she well knew she was too bony, too quiet, and too bland for a man to appreciate. *Well, usually I am bland.* She did not know what had gotten into her this evening. She had been downright rude to Mr Cole, and she still felt an uncanny impulse of impertinence. *Perhaps I had better make the most of it while it lasts.* She might lack the courage to warn off Mr Cole, but she had enough to speak to her sister.

"Lydia," she said, dropping her voice further, even though her soft one was unlikely to be heard more than a few feet away. "People seem to be spreading tales about you and Mr Cole a great deal. Had you not better leave him alone?"

"You mean *he* ought to leave *me* alone," her sister said with a smile.

"Whichever. I am sure you could discourage him, and that would give peace to so many minds. Mr Wickham's, and Lizzy's, and—" *Mine,* she might have added, but even in a moment of daring, Mary did not think her own opinion mattered much.

"I do not mind vexing my husband a little until the matter of the drawing room is settled. And it is not Lizzy's business." Lydia studied her, and whatever conclusion she drew did not please her. "I am sure *you* do not wish to interfere with me. You know it all means nothing. It is simply a bit of fun."

"But if that is all it is, then—"

"I can brook no interference, and it does not suit you, any way. Now, where is my fan? I should not have brought it at all; I knew I would only lose it, and I certainly do not need it. This room is like Sardinia."

"Siberia, I think you mean," Mary said, scanning the room for the wayward fan. "The fan probably dropped to the floor in the lecture room. I will fetch it for you." Keeping track of objects had been a vital skill for Mary in the chaos of Longbourn, and she was almost pleased to use it in London, to prove herself useful.

"Now where has Mr Cole disappeared to? I must tell him all the ridiculous things Sir Reginald has said to me today. He has really grown too forward in his speech, the old roué." Lydia pattered off to look for Mr Cole, and Mary returned to the lecture hall in her own search.

The empty chairs were huddled too close together to make the search easy, but by hunching and peering, Mary at length found the fan slid under one of them. Her ear caught the sound of voices in the hall: Sir Reginald's tremulous tenor and Mr Cole's booming bass.

"And who was the young lady accompanying our divine Mrs Wickham?" Sir Reginald was asking.

"No one of consequence. Her sister, I believe."

"I do not say she is pretty, but she has a prettiness about her—"

Mr Cole's tone was decisive. "She stood with Mrs Wickham and me, and barely spoke for ten minutes."

"Oh?" Sir Reginald's disappointment carried in his voice.

"I do not think she would interest you much. Now a woman like Lady Sarah Randall—she is all fire. Dashing. Compared to her, this Miss Bennet is practically spiritless." Mary could almost hear a wince in Mr Cole's voice, as if part of him were ashamed of the harsh comparison. *And yet he says it.* "Do you know Lady Sarah, Sir Reginald?"

"Oh, yes, now that is a woman more to my taste."

Mary straightened as she heard the voices die down. The two scientists were no doubt returning to the ladies, but Mary had no desire to follow. *How abominable! To discuss ladies like that, as if we were—pigs in a market!* Her face flushed, but for once it was not in embarrassment. She felt angry. *And Mr Cole, first saying I am a mouse with sharp teeth, and then turning around and calling me spiritless!* Her hands shook. *He is a man with two faces, and I do not like either of them.*

Mary sat down, hoping the unfamiliar wash of rage would pass quickly. First the irritation that pushed her to insult Mr Cole, and now this rage—was London changing her? She hated the rapid, unruly beating of her heart, the trembling in all her limbs, the weak, flimsy feeling in her muscles, as if nothing were safe, as if she had no way to protect herself. *Just calm down.* Sitting in silence, her body eventually returned to its usual peace, her heartbeat slowing, her arms and legs steadying. Mary breathed a sigh of relief. *I should forgive them both. Perhaps they meant no real harm.* All the sermon books said forgiving was the Christian thing to do, but, at the moment, Mary was more interested in it for keeping her equanimity. Her breathing eased further.

"There you are!" Lydia strode into the lecture room, her deft feet carrying her through the mass of chairs as if she were performing a high-stepping dance. "The carriage is waiting."

"I am sorry, Lydia." Calm had reasserted itself, and Mary clambered her way out of the chairs to join her sister. "I found your fan."

"Oh, I had forgotten. Thank you." Lydia accepted the fan and tucked it into her reticule, and Mary followed her out.

Lydia's movement towards the door summoned Mr Cole to her side, his chestnut hair stirred by the frosty gusts from the street. Mary walked to the head of the carriage, unwilling to look Mr Cole in the face. One of the horses stamped a foot, and Mary felt a twinge of satisfaction, as if the horse were expressing an indignant contempt for the scientist. *But I must forgive him. I have forgiven him, I mean.* Mary was able to ignore Mr Cole's good-bye in the bustle of accepting a footman's assistance into the carriage. When the footman turned to Lydia, Mr Cole insisted on helping her himself. Then he shut the carriage door with a masterful *thunk*, and only when it was well on its way did he turn to join his guests.

"Such a satisfactory evening!" Lydia said as the carriage jolted along. "You had a wonderful time, did you not?"

Mary turned her sour face to the window and stared at the ice-crested windowsills lining the buildings. "Yes, Lydia."

Five

Lady Crestwood, that powerful monarch of fashion, threw wide open the doors of her London home for a ball, and the Wickham household was invited. Lady Crestwood sometimes held the Wickhams at a distance, her long standing in the *ton* making her more cautious with newcomers whose source of wealth was unverified. Her daughter's elopement with a captain in Wickham's regiment made her doubly careful; though Lady Lucy had received the Crestwood dowry due her, Lady Crestwood still gnashed her teeth at her daughter's selection of a mere Captain Roarke when she ought to have had a viscount *at least*. Still worse, Mr Wickham and Captain Roarke had become fast friends, further tainting the Wickham name to Lady Crestwood. Nevertheless, she sent the proper invitation to the Wickhams to her first ball of the Season. "Not exactly out of kindliness," Lydia had said, scanning the cream-coloured paper, "more to crush me with her splendour."

Left to herself, Mary would likely have wished to stay home from the event—dancing was surely not her favourite activity —but Lizzy's charge to turn Mr Cole's eye towards herself was yet in her mind. Would he even be invited? He might have been.

"I have got Addleby taking in your gowns right now," Lydia had said, "so there is no excuse, Mouse. Even a mouse has got to go somewhere to find a nice fat rat to marry."

Mary's mouth twisted in disgust at the metaphor, but she had obeyed. Now she stood in the pillared ballroom of the Crestwood home, squashed between feathered ladies and well-heeled gentlemen, with mounted bouquets fluttering ribbons down the pillars to swipe at her coiffure. The January cold was pushed back by the heat of bodies and two fireplaces, and the scent of woodsmoke tainted the perfumes liberally dousing the dancers. Conversation hummed in every direction, almost drowning out the brass and strings marking a minuet. As strange as the setting was to Mary, the strangeness of the people was more disturbing. She really knew only Lydia and Mr Wickham; though she had seen Lady Crestwood and Sir Reginald Colton at the geology lecture, she had never spoken to them. The mass of figures hungrily shoving into the supper room or banishing the night chill with a vigorous dance were all unknown to her. Lydia introduced gentlemen to her, but the interaction was invariably the same.

"This is my sister, Miss Mary Bennet."

A curtsey from Mary, a bow from the gentleman.

"It is a fine ball, is it not?" the gentleman asked—or perhaps he mentioned the number of couples, or the bite to the winter air outside. Whatever the remark or question, Mary nodded mutely. Then the gentleman tried again on another subject and received another nod, while Mary prayed that he would go away soon. Then Lydia, taking pity on the potential suitor, swept in to include him in her conversation, and Mary sighed in relief.

So this is what a London ball is like, Mary thought, picking at a loose ribbon on her gown. *Not so very different from the assembly rooms at Meryton. I cannot say I like it.* There was only herself to blame, of course. Anyone else would have found a hundred things to chat about, or relished dancing and supping on dainties. Mary's dances had been silent proceedings, making use of Lydia's tutelage in the new figures, but satisfying only in that the gentleman did not expect her to talk much. It was no wonder that Lydia threw her looks in which mortification mingled with amusement, and Mr Wickham retreated to the card room to escape making fruitless introductions.

"Mind my gown, my dear." Lady Crestwood's voice was not a booming bass like Mr Cole's, but it had the same inflexion of power, and her height and solidity suggested she could join Mr Cole in an impersonation of a blacksmith, albeit a less muscular one. Her plum silk gown suited her, curving along her voluptuous figure but remaining stately enough for a woman approaching fifty. Her creamy, smooth skin belied her years, though Mary could not tell if that was the result of art or good fortune.

Mary stepped back in obedience, though she did not think she had trodden on the plum silk. Lady Crestwood rewarded her with a smile and then turned her attention on Lydia and the gentleman with whom she was conversing.

"Disputing about ices, no less? How very foolish. You must both acknowledge lemon ices are the best. We have very fine ones in the supper room." The commanding note Lady Crestwood used even in ordinary conversation made Mary's eyes widen, and the gentleman bowed and scuttled off, as if to partake of a lemon ice at once. Lydia looked disappointed at his abandonment of her, but she smoothed her features into a smile for Lady Crestwood nevertheless.

"Why, here is my daughter," Lady Crestwood said, beckoning Lady Lucy to join them, and Lydia introduced Mary to them both, prompting the usual round of curtseys. "Lucy, dear, I never see you these days. You must get out more." She turned back to Lydia. "I believe you go everywhere, Mrs Wickham. *Almost* everywhere, at least."

Whether it was an insult of Lydia for never having been presented at court, or a slight at the Wickhams' ambivalent place in society with great wealth but a shady background, Mary could not tell, but Lydia bristled. "We go everywhere we wish to, Lady Crestwood," she said, then pressed her mouth shut as if that were the only way to ensure her politeness.

"No doubt, no doubt." Lady Crestwood's bland smile told another story. "Have you seen Miss Poppit, dancing over there?" She directed their attention to a tall young woman in a white silk gown, her blonde hair swept high off a snowy neck, a demure cross pendant bouncing at her throat as she hopped from foot to foot. "She is something of a protégée of mine. You would be astounded at the interest my little friend has attracted already. She is quite the belle of the Season."

"The Season has only just begun," Lydia said, and Mary could hear the pique in her tone, although if Lady Crestwood did, she did not acknowledge it.

"Yes, it is, and that is why it is so *astounding*, how decided the preference for her is already. Sir Reginald Colton, the great geologist, seems quite taken with her." Lady Crestwood beamed down on Miss Poppit from afar, and Miss Poppit, alert to her patroness's attentions, flushed with happiness.

"Sir Reginald, indeed," said Lydia in a tone just short of scoffing. With a sweet smile, she added, "And I am sure that old scandal of his is quite forgotten, is it not?" She gave a nod at the dance floor, where Sir Reginald's white locks had become tousled with his extraordinary efforts to keep up with a woman wearing a saucy smile.

"Sir Reginald is a great man, no matter what minor indiscretions gossips may whisper about," Lady Crestwood said, the sternness in her voice making Mary shift her feet uneasily, even though she was not its target. "But there is also Mr Covington, who is already disposed to pool all his thousands at Miss Poppit's feet, so I hear."

"Mr Covington?" It seemed as though Lydia was well prepared to speak heedlessly, so Mary interceded.

"Mr Covington? Now that would be a great match," she said, although in truth she did not know the man.

Lady Crestwood's smiled in a satisfied way and nodded at Mary. "Yes, it would, Miss Bennet. It would indeed."

Mary's face grew hot as Lady Crestwood examined her, seeming to gauge her as a potential rival to her Miss Poppit. When her ladyship settled back, clearly dismissing her from her calculations, the breath caught in Mary's chest loosened.

She did not want any part of the competition, however much Lydia seemed to enjoy it.

"A very genteel young lady," Lady Crestwood said, as if a judge pronouncing Mary's fate: incapable of causing mischief in the great lady's plans, and therefore innocent. Mary curtseyed at the compliment while Lydia fumed at the faint praise. Before her sister could launch into any further discussion of Mary's attractions, Mary backed away, bumping into the lady she had forgotten was with them.

Why, she is as quiet as I usually am! Mary begged her pardon, and Lady Lucy murmured that it was nothing. Lady Crestwood's daughter was nothing like her; where Lady Crestwood was thick, authoritative, and attired in the latest fashion, Lady Lucy was reedy, meek, and adorned with a heavily ornamented gown of last Season's style. Her hair was the same washed-out brown colour as Mary's, and Lady Lucy's grey eyes shone like wide, round mirrors, betraying nothing but the passing reflections of others. But Mary liked her hesitant smile. As Lydia, Lady Crestwood, and passing guests chatted, Mary and Lady Lucy maintained their companionable silence, exchanging occasional smiles.

I like her. Lydia would never have understood making friends by silence rather than chatter, but Mary sensed Lady Lucy knew the way of it. Understanding that neither expected the other to talk, the two young ladies settled into a friendly repose. It was only when Lydia threw a glance of impatience at her that Mary decided she had better make an effort to converse, if not with the intimidating Lady Crestwood, with someone.

Lady Lucy had an embroidered handkerchief clutched in one hand, and the arabesques of green vines attracted Mary's attention. "What lovely embroidery!" she said. Her voice was too low to be caught by the other ladies, but Lady Lucy acknowledged her compliment with a nod.

"I did it myself," Lady Lucy said, the admission colouring her cheeks. Mary knew the sensation her new friend must be undergoing well—the flush of embarrassment, not because one had done anything wrong, but simply because any focus on one's own life made a 'mouse' feel awkward. Seeing Lady Lucy's timidity made Mary feel brave in comparison.

"I do a great deal of embroidery myself," she said, glad to have found something in common. Though their conversation progressed very slowly from the kinds of threads and silks preferred, to the designs each had created, both Lady Lucy and Mary grew comfortable enough with one another to forget the other ladies chattering beside them.

"It is so soothing to have an occupation one can pursue in quiet." Lady Lucy's hands folded over her torso. "My husband is often busy, and I have so many idle hours waiting for him." The minor confession drew one from Mary in turn.

"I passed many hours that way at home," Mary said. "It seemed to keep me out of the way. I did not have many friends, and the few I had—" She broke off, thinking of the long hours hunched over her sewing, trying to forget the loss of Harry Lucas's friendship. Kitty had declared her lovelorn, but their friendship had been something beyond her ken—a quiet sharing of religious ideas, passing tracts to one another, discussing sermons. There had been no flirtation in it, only the gentle pursuit of the same dignified ideals. Kitty had not understood it.

"I had sisters, but we did not always get along. Families can be difficult." Given Lydia's predicament, that was an understatement, but Mary blushed with consternation. *I should not talk this way to an acquaintance of mere minutes!*

"Yes, families are difficult," Lady Lucy said, casting a wistful look at Lady Crestwood. That remark seemed to prompt another. "Have you met my husband, Captain Roarke, Miss Bennet? He is just there, dancing."

The blond, dashing young captain was leaning over Lady Sarah Randall and whispering something that made her giggle. Even if he had not been so engaged, Mary would never have guessed he was married to Lady Lucy. He was a handsome man, outfitted in the very pink of fashion. The captain's grin showed a decided liking for his dance partner, and Mary could see why. The haughty line of Lady Sarah's cheekbones, the richness of her raven locks, and the arch expressions flitting across her face made her suitable for the heroine of a novel. *She and Lydia are women of spirit,* Mary thought. *Whereas I am—what Mr Cole said. Spiritless.*

"Lady Sarah is very beautiful, is she not?" Lady Lucy did not wait for an answer; she seemed to view the judgment as self-evident. "She is the daughter of an earl, you know. Her lineage is quite ancient." She sighed. "I hear even her riding and singing are without flaw."

But her reputation is not. Mary dared not voice the criticism. She had scarcely been in London a week before Lydia had told her all about the scandalous Lady Sarah; Mary knew not whether Lydia censured her or admired her for her shocking behaviour.

But she wondered if Lady Lucy knew the woman she so admired had a reputation for violent flirtations, and many of them—and more. "Indeed?"

"Yes, even Captain Roarke says she is a perfect horsewoman, and he is quite particular about such things. She and my husband are great friends."

From the way the captain casually adjusted one of the curls on Lady Sarah's head, the 'friendship' was not one Mary would like to see her own husband indulge in. Lady Lucy seemed to take no notice of the intimate gesture, but Lady Crestwood, who had appeared immersed in a debate with Lydia on sleeve length, suddenly set her mouth in a firm line as her gaze passed over the dancers, and Mary knew she had seen it. *If the daughter does not resent it, the mother certainly does.* As intimidating as Lady Crestwood was, Mary liked her the better for it.

"Are you fond of dogs, Miss Bennet?"

Mary drew her skirts together in unease, as if a mastiff might bolt through the ballroom at her. "Not—not so very much."

"I adore dogs," Lady Lucy said, with an apologetic air, as if even a disagreement about pets were threatening.

Mary made an effort at the conversation. "My sister Lydia has a pug. His name is Prince."

"Indeed? My mother has two pugs at home!" Lady Lucy's eyes shone with delight, and she seemed to forget her hesitation. "He must be so charming."

Mary thought of the shreds of silk hanging from Prince's mouth, and the gruff barks he saluted her with. "Not particularly." She released her skirts and forced a smile. "Do you have any dogs yourself?"

"Oh, no. Our landlady—" Lady Lucy was quick to alter her explanation. "I mean, it is not practical at our current home. And I do not think Captain Roarke cares for dogs."

"Perhaps you could come and visit Prince, then," Mary offered. She was not sure it was polite to invite people to her sister's home, but Lydia had known Lady Lucy some time.

"I do not go many places. Indeed, this is the first time I have been out this Season." Lady Lucy glanced over the ballroom, where ladies swung joyfully on the arms of gentlemen or sipped ratafia along the walls and chatted with their friends.

"But why?" Mary did not realise her question was impertinent until she saw Lady Lucy finger a thin, worn spot on the front of her gown. It had not frayed there yet, but no doubt it soon would. It made Mary realise the gown was not a new one, but likely some relic of Lady Lucy's more prosperous maiden days.

But Lady Lucy merely said, "My husband does not wish me to expose my health to too many draughts. My constitution is not strong."

It was an excuse the translucent pallor of her skin might have made believable, had Mary not already guessed the truth. She found a budding irritation build in her gut. *The captain gads about in the latest of fashions, flirting outrageously, all while keeping his wife sitting at home! In* lodgings, *no less!* She struggled to press down the anger bubbling up. Lady Lucy was making efforts to keep peace with her husband, it seemed. It would be wrong to stir things up. *I do not really know anything about it. Perhaps everything is innocent and in harmony.* The idea soothed her. *Yes, it is all probably fine. And if Lady Lucy needed any defender, I would be the last choice, for anyone. Lady Crestwood would be a better champion.* Feeling better, Mary resolved to accept Lady Lucy's fiction.

"I can see you are quite pale. It is no wonder your husband worries for you," Mary said.

Lady Lucy nodded. "But of course I can—that is, if you have any interest"—the noblewoman took a deep breath and let her words out in a rush. "You could come a pay me a visit, Miss Bennet." She gave the address in a hesitating manner that acknowledged the place was not fashionable. To Mary's amusement, it was quite near Gracechurch Street; she wondered how many of Lydia's new acquaintances knew that she had relations in that neighbourhood.

"I will come." Mary found herself pleased with the plan. She had never had a real female friend before; she had been so unwilling to leave Longbourn, and there was always compan-ionship with her sisters. The idea of Lady Lucy actually enjoying her company warmed Mary's heart. Perhaps London had more than annoyances and dangers in it. She could take the time to relax with a friend...

Mary caught a glimpse of a tall, sturdy figure moving through the crowds, and the warmth of her heart chilled. In all her plans for enjoyment, she had forgotten the man who had insulted her and who was provoking Lydia's downfall; the man who her elder sisters hoped would turn his eye to her: Mr Cole.

Six

Mr Cole must have just arrived; his cheeks were stung red from the winter wind, and a crust of snow clung to his gloves, though it was melting rapidly in the radiance of the ballroom. His sudden appearance made Mary think of a dark fairy intruding without invitation—*no, that is silly. He has as much right to be here as anyone else.* But her whole body tensed irrationally, fearing some explosion of gossip or wrath. His pace toward Mrs Wickham was resolute, but there were many clusters of guests to weave through before he could reach his object.

Lady Crestwood had seen him, too. "Mr Cole is your particular friend, Mrs Wickham, is he not?" she said, with a clear warning in her voice. The caution was a reasonable one. No doubt she knew of the time Lydia spent with said gentleman. "Now you must not take up any of his dances. A married lady must leave the bachelors to the maidens who have not yet been so fortunate to secure their husbands."

Lydia tossed her head enough to make her curls bounce, despite the gold pin binding them. "Well surely one or two would not hurt. After all, I am not so married that I do not enjoy—"

"I trust you will certainly not dance more than one. It would set tongues to talking." Lady Crestwood replied firmly with eyes narrowed.

Lydia rolled her eyes, scarcely bothering to hide the impertinent gesture for Lady Crestwood, and excused herself, moving from their group to approach Mr Cole. Mary sighed as Lady Crestwood drew back.

I could have told her that would not work, Mary thought, watching Lady Crestwood's disgruntlement. Even Mary's efforts to rein in her sister had only compelled Lydia to set propriety at naught, and Lady Crestwood's remonstrances were not half so gentle. In less than a minute, Lydia and Mr Cole were dancing. It was not unnoticed by the others in the room, and a buzz went about almost immediately.

All they are doing is dancing! It seemed unfair, but Mary supposed after all that had come before, simply seeing the two together made the *beau monde* talk. Asking Lydia to show more restraint had done nothing. Mary followed the movement of the pair with her eyes, lingering on Mr Cole's face. *I was supposed to ask* him *to show discretion, not Lydia.* She owed Lizzy a letter, and had put off writing it in guilt of not having fulfilled her promise. The idea of broaching such a subject with a gentleman still rankled in Mary, but it was clear things were not settling down on their own. *I should probably just do as Lizzy advised.* She took a deep breath. *I will ask Mr Cole to leave Lydia be.*

It was easier said than done, however. Lydia expended her energy in a dance with him, determined to show her independence of Lady Crestwood, and Mr Cole's face shone with sweat by the time the vigorous country dance ended. Miss Poppit had slipped back onto the dance floor with a new gentleman, and Captain Roarke had shown enough sense of his duties to lead Lady Lucy there as well, but Lady Crestwood and Mary were there to witness Lydia's supposed triumph.

"I am *so* tired," Lydia said, belying her words with a few steps of the last dance as she playfully re-joined the group. "Mr Cole, you are a fine dancer."

When he bowed at the compliment, Lady Crestwood shook her head solemnly. "You are unwise, Mrs Wickham," the noblewoman declared in her most authoritative tone, and then she swept off to the card room, throwing one cross look over her shoulder as she went.

"With whom have you danced, Mouse?" Lydia asked. "Oh, do bring me a drink, Mr Cole, or I shall perish."

"From thirst? Or from lack of opportunity to gossip with your sister?" His tone showed no rancour at the subterfuge.

"First from one and then the other. I shall die *twice*—how is that for peril?" They exchanged smiles, and as he sauntered off to obtain her ratafia, Lydia set her shoulders in mock seriousness. "Now, Mary, tell me all."

"I have not danced at all since you left."

"Not at *all*?"

"No one has asked me."

Lydia pouted. "Well, then, tell me which of the gentlemen I introduced to you caught your fancy."

Mary sighed. "I do not know, Lydia."

"That means none, only you do not wish to say so. Oh, you little *mouse!* How can you learn anything about men if you do not open your mouth? You must talk more, express your desires and let the gentleman serve you—that sort of thing."

Mary's hands fidgeted at her gown. "You would not want me to act a queen, like Lady Crestwood, would you?"

"No one is asking you to be a bully. Just speak up a little more. Show you have some spirit."

Spirit. The word nettled Mary, and she could not help looking into Mr Cole's eyes as he returned with the ratafia. He had brought a glass for Mary, as well. Whether it was the unexpected politeness from him or Lydia's implication she was spiritless, Mary resolved to take action. She sipped her drink and tried to muster her courage as Lydia talked.

"Just imagine, Mr Cole, my sister has barely spoken ten words to a gentleman tonight, and now I find she has not danced once since you and I began," Lydia said in irritation. "What a Season she is having! We shall have to dance twice as hard, you and I, to make up for her lack of contribution to the ball."

Mr Cole looked amused at the suggestion, but not tempted. "Dancing that hard is a task better fit for children who have been closeted in a schoolroom all day."

"Oh, I have just as much energy as any child, do I not, Mr Cole? If we dance another time—"

Does she not see how foolish that would be? Mary resolved to stop her, even at the expense of a lie. "I think Mr Wickham was looking for you, Lydia." Mary tried to steady her voice, but it had an unfortunately mouse-like squeak.

"But I intend to dance with Mr Cole again. Do you hear? They are just beginning the allemande." Lydia's brow wrinkled.

"I do so enjoy the allemande," Mary said, trying not to wince at the untruth, "and I seldom have a chance to dance it. Perhaps while you are seeking your husband..." She looked at Mr Cole. The hint was too forward to be polite, but he responded immediately just the same.

"Permit me, Miss Bennet." He bowed and offered his arm, and his smooth, relaxed brow showed no discomfiture at exchanging one sister for another. Lydia watched them move to their position with an expression mixing disappointment and amusement. Mary could not help feeling a sense of triumph. For the moment, she had Mr Cole's attention. Leading her to the dance floor, he inserted them into the line of dancers with an expertise that kept them from standing out. The grace of it reassured Mary and gave her a moment for her pounding heart to slow.

"I am not so spiritless after all, am I?" she said, more to herself than Mr Cole. She had not expected her soft voice to carry enough to bring the words to him, but from the perplexed look on his face, he had caught her remark. She hurried to broach the necessary subject before her courage ran out. "I wished to speak with you, Mr Cole."

"I gathered that, as you do not seem to be overfond of dancing." His wink disturbed her; it was not altogether a genteel thing to do, and yet she liked it.

"It is about my sister." She struggled to find the words, but he soon assisted her.

"Let me guess. You are about to ask me to banish her from my side, thrust her out into the world friendless and alone—"

"Oh, you know very well she has friends." She smoothed her cross expression into blankness as she passed a stranger in the figure. When her hands clasped Mr Cole's again, the crossness returned. "You are making mischief to no purpose."

"I disagree. It is not mischief; it is simple friendship. And I find purpose in it. I find it highly amusing."

"It is hurting her reputation."

"The only people who fuss about it are old crows. They peck at us because they have nothing better to peck at." He shook his head. "You know your sister well. Would you say her affections are in any real danger from me?"

Mary bit her lip, reluctant to acknowledge his point. "It is true that she is in no danger in *that* sense. She is simply playing." Before Mr Cole's satisfied smile could spread further, she hastened to quell it. "But that does not mean there is no danger altogether. How people perceive your friendship matters."

"Anyone can see we simply like to flirt. There is nothing in it, nothing serious."

"If that is so, then it should be all the easier to dispense with it." Mary thought her argument compelling, but Mr Cole simply lifted and dropped his shoulders.

"I cannot think it is all so serious as you say. I certainly pay little attention to the private friendships of others. Why think others are so interested in me?"

Mary bit her lip, thinking. Probably Mr Cole truly did not concern himself much with gossip of others; he was immersed in scientific works, examining samples, debating theories. It made him a master of his subject, but a bit befuddled by the social realm. "I do not think you realise how much such gossip matters to most people in the *ton*. It may not matter to you, but others weigh it more heavily."

"It is very foolish of them, if they do." He shook his head. "Perhaps a few ladies with little to do sometimes stir up a dramatic-sounding story, but you will find it all settles down as soon as they get busy with something." Though he probably did not intend it, she sensed condescension in his voice.

"It will *not* simply settle down, if you and Lydia continue behaving this way." She snapped the words out. "You are disturbing the peace of all of us."

"I am not doing anything of the kind." His arm pushed her into a turn with more force than she expected, and she lurched to keep from stumbling. "I beg your pardon. I am not a good partner when the lady of my choice is vexed."

"But I was not the lady of your choice." Mary's eyes sought his. She hoped he could not see the plea in them, the desire for reassurance. *Why should I care anything about his feelings? I scarcely know him, and he is trouble.* "I chose you, remember? I hinted until you had to dance."

"Of course I remember. I was entirely shocked. It was quite unladylike." His easy grin showed her it was all teasing, but she found her shoulders straightening and her chin lifting nonetheless.

"It may have been unladylike; I do not know. But you cannot call it *spiritless*."

His brow furrowed. "That is the second time you have used that word. Is there some meaning to it—beyond the usual?" Before she could answer, he suddenly gave a sharp nod. "Ah. I remember. I used that word once. Perhaps you overheard it."

The ire in her belly finally spat out of her mouth. "Indeed I did! You told me I had sharp teeth, and then you turned around and told Sir Reginald that I was spiritless. You shift like a weathercock; no one could know your true opinions."

"I wonder that you care about them, whatever they are." His good humour was unruffled, and he had no difficulty giving a polite greeting to a friend as they passed through another figure of the dance. When his eyes met Mary's again, he added, "If you truly *care* to hear my opinion of you, I could explain it." The lilt in his voice suggested the mischief of a trap.

"I do not care a thing about it," Mary said.

"No, you only rope me into a dance and upbraid me about it, when I *thought* you were going to plead for your sister's propriety." He laughed as Mary's face took fire. "Well, how is this for a suitable peace-making? I acknowledge to you that I will continue to see Mrs Wickham, just as I please, but," he held up an admonishing finger, "I will soothe your pride by admitting that I only called you spiritless to Sir Reginald to keep his hooks out of you."

His smile became rueful. "He is a very great scientist, but very foolish about women. He particularly loves a good debate, whether with me at a lecture or with an elegant female in her drawing room. I thought if he decided you were too meek for pursuit, it would keep you out of trouble."

"Keep *me* out of trouble!"

"I cannot prevent you from hounding gentlemen onto the dance floor, of course. That requires your own restraint."

Mary's indignation warred with the laughter bubbling up within her. She had never felt so at sixes and sevens with a person, and yet some feeling of freedom and glee threaded through it all. *I can almost see myself a woman of spirit when I am with him*, she thought. The idea made her giddy.

"There, shall we have peace, then?"

"I...suppose." *But what about Lydia? He has promised nothing about Lydia.* "For the moment."

"A truce, then."

"For tonight, a truce." Mary wondered how she had been so easily turned from her purpose. Though the exhilaration of the dance buoyed her up as Mr Cole escorted her back to her friends, a wave of guilt lapped at her when she saw Lydia's ready smile at their approach. *A mouse is no good at arranging people's lives or interfering in their struggles. Speaking up usually only makes things worse, and yet—*

Yet I do not see how I can safely stand aside. Mr Cole's charm had turned out to be far more formidable than she had guessed, and not just for Lydia. She had tried to persuade both Lydia and Mr Cole to abandon their flirtation with rational argument, and that had failed. If she could not reason them into a better situation, then she would have to influence them another way. *They both seem to want a distraction.* Lydia might respond to sisterly advances for activities together, but that would not be enough if Mr Cole was still eager to seek her out. *I must distract him, as well.* The thought heated her whole body with a strange confusion. *I must occupy his mind with... geology, or...Sir Reginald...or some woman besides Lydia.* She could ask Miss Poppit to try to dangle after Mr Cole, but Lydia would never tolerate losing him to her rival. *Lizzy's logic seems inescapable. Mr Cole must be coaxed away, and there is no one to do it but me.* The idea was enough to shock any mouse. But if there was any better option available, Mary could not see it. She still could not see herself the way Lizzy seemed to, as a hidden beauty with secret charms waiting to be poured out.

And she had no experience of flirting; her friendship with Harry Lucas had been solemn and platonic, and no other gentlemen had paid any attention to her when there was Jane's beauty, Lizzy's wit, and the pranks and gambols of Kitty and Lydia. But however ill-equipped she was to perform this task, Mary knew she must do it all the same.

I shall just have to learn to flirt.

Seven

Distracting Lydia turned out to be more difficult than Mary had hoped. Her first thought was to create an outing for them to visit Lady Lucy, whom Mary was eager to see again. But the next day, when Mary suggested it, Lydia objected with surprising pertinacity. "It is not that I care about my carriage being seen stopping at such a place. You know I have no pride about that."

Lydia dabbed rouge on her cheeks with a delicacy that made the glow look natural. Mary would not have guessed her sister used such things if she had not been privy to Lydia's dressing room. "But heavens! It would be *agony* to sit with Lady Lucy in her dingy little hole. She is the most insipid creature! Why, she never had anything interesting to say before she was married, and back then she was permitted to go to all the best places in Lady Crestwood's train. And now —where does she go? Whom does she see? You will find her mind completely vacant."

Lydia lifted her hands, as if to mollify Mary. "Oh, I will go, I will go. You have never asked to go anywhere yet. I could always drop you off at Lady Lucy's and see if Mr Cole—that is, see who is strolling about on Bond Street."

It was time to try a new approach. "Lydia, you say my gowns are a fright."

"Yes?" Lydia's violet eyes narrowed in puzzlement at the change of subject.

"If you will promise to set aside Mr Cole, I will let you buy me whatever gowns you like, and I shall wear them whenever you say. You can dress me like a doll."

"What—give him up forever? Certainly not. He is too much fun. Lord, Mouse! You must make a better bargain than that."

"Give him up for a year." Mary watched her face. "A month, then."

"A week," Lydia said, "and I get to dress you just as I choose —bonnets, gloves, jewellery—"

"A week, full dress, but you must take Lady Lucy with us when we go shopping."

Lydia's eyes widened. "Lady Lucy again! Horrors."

"She hardly ever goes out, and I am sure she would like it." Mary tried to make her tone firm. "Have I your word?"

And though they agreed on the terms, a second obstacle arose in the matter of choosing a day. Lydia's schedule was full, and by the time the two found an appropriate day, January had slid into February, and a clinging fog hung over the piles of snow scraped back from the sidewalks. The lamps outside the address Lady Lucy had given were ill-lit, leaving the street half-shrouded, and there seemed to be more refuse scattered between the buildings than in the Wickhams' neighbourhood. Mary climbed out of the carriage and hopped onto a drier portion of the stones. Lydia stared up at the grey mists choking the sky.

"I am sure it will snow more today," she said, fidgeting with her reticule. "And there is so much to be done while we can still get about!"

Mary could sense the indecision. "Lydia—"

"I will leave a card, and you can make my apologies to Lady Lucy. She knows how busy I am. She will be happy to entertain you for an hour while I—"

"An hour! It is not proper to make a first visit so long."

"But no one visits her, so she will not mind it. Indeed, she will be pleased. I am already bound to spend our shopping day with her, and I find I cannot bear to witness the vacancy of her mind when I have so many other things to do." She beckoned at a footman to leave a card, and Mary shook her head, sighing.

I suppose we cannot all have the same friends. She did not think Lady Lucy was insipid, exactly, only mild. "You will be gone only an hour? And no Mr Cole, of course."

"Of course. And when I come back, you can tell me all about your visit—the interesting parts, any way. If there are any." She giggled, and Mary could tell she was relieved at avoiding the tiresome task. Mary stayed long enough to watch the fog swallow up the carriage as it rolled away, and then she patted her bonnet to check its angle. Even only a few moments in the fog had moistened the merino covering it. *I had better get inside.* The skin laid bare between her gloves and her sleeves was already growing clammy.

Mary rapped at the light wooden door of the lodging house, her chilled fingers forming a fist that looked weak to her, but which shook the frame of the door until it rattled. The stout woman who opened it nearly tore the door off its hinges as she did so, and after Mary passed through, the woman twisted and pulled at the door to set it into its proper angle as if she were accustomed to the procedure. Upon inquiry, the woman wiped at the greasy hair poking out of a hole in her cap and muttered, "the Roarkes—third floor, right."

The stairs shifted under Mary's light weight, saluting her arrival with an eldritch music of squeaks and creaks. The grime coating the banister discouraged Mary from touching it, but she soon found she had to; the strange way the stairs settled under her feet made her clutch at the rail hard enough to smear her gloves with dirt. A faint odour of unemptied chamber pots filtered from some of the doors by the landings, and the sour smells of stewing meat emanated from others. *This cannot be right. Perhaps I have the wrong building.* But the stout woman at the door had said the Roarkes lived here.

A plump maid answered the door on the third floor and ushered Mary in. Lady Lucy rose with embarrassment when she saw it was Mary, but bid her welcome. Mary had expected to see a difference in quality in the Roarkes' rooms; surely Lady Lucy and her husband would have it in better repair, or furnish it in such a way as to hide the nails poking out of walls, the uneven floors, and the draughts whistling in the ill-fit windows.

But the lodgings were not much different from the rest of the building. Lady Lucy had a few rickety tables covered with soft cloths, and muslin curtains too thin to bar the February wind, but embroidered with taste. Beyond those efforts to lighten the gloom and Lady Lucy's plain gown, there was nothing genteel.

It is like a fairy story. The bad part, the part before the heroine escapes with a prince. Only this part of the story happened *after* Lady Lucy met her prince. Mary tried to keep her gaze from scouring the room. She was familiar with poverty in Meryton, where she had visited the sick. Country poverty had looked so different—sparse, bare, but clean. *Visiting the sick here would be dreadful. I would feel sure every sufferer was going to die.*

Forcing a smile, Mary seated herself. "My sister could not stay, but she left a card, Lady Lucy."

"Oh, I understand." Lady Lucy's motions were hurried as she brought out teacups and busied herself scooping tea while the maid disappeared to get hot water. Lady Lucy did not look at Mary, but Mary could sense relief in her tone. "It will be quite pleasant, just the three of us."

"Three?"

"The captain has gone out for some biscuits. He will be back shortly."

A sudden thumping began, and angry voices, sounding hollow through the walls, made Mary jump in her seat. *Neighbours.* The poor in Meryton did not live so squashed together. Mary began to feel sick. *It is too sad. How can the captain and his wife bear to live here? How can Lord Crestwood allow his daughter to stay in such a place?*

The door swung open, and Captain Roarke tossed a packet onto the table. "There. There are your biscuits." The gruffness in his voice melted away when he saw Mary. "Miss Bennet! How pleasant to see you. I am not usually in at this hour, but when I heard you and your sister might be making us a visit, I made sure to be on hand."

"My sister could not come," Mary said.

A flash of disappointment crossed the captain's face, but he hid it well. "We shall have you to ourselves, then. Is the tea ready, my dear?" He turned to Lady Lucy, who threw him a joyful look at the appellation.

"It is ready, my love," she said, her voice almost cooing as she arranged the biscuits on a plate. Captain Roarke sat down with them, but angled his chair as if to create a tête-à-tête with Mary while he accepted his cup. The tea was watery, but hot, and Mary sipped it gratefully, relishing the heat of the porcelain seeping through her gloves. As if awakened by the tea, Mary's stomach grumbled. She had missed half of breakfast again, due to Lydia's hasty desire to dress, and at last night's dinner out, she had been too intimidated by the stiff footmen to ask for the foods she liked. But after a surreptitious glance at the Roarkes' sordid rooms, she only took one biscuit from the plate. *Perhaps the rest of them will be their dinner.*

Or just Lady Lucy's dinner. It was not surprising that the captain kept his regimentals clean and his boots well-polished, but other signs suggested his manner of living boasted better care than his wife's. Consulting his watch, he displayed an elaborate watch chain, glittering with seals, fastened to the hefty gold timepiece. His waist was still trim and soldierly, but by his vigour, Mary doubted he missed meals or dined on biscuits alone. *He has his income in the regiment. And Lady Lucy no doubt has a settlement from her parents. It cannot all be spent on clothes and dining out.* Given that he was Mr Wickham's associate, she wondered if he had the same pursuits: gaming, and investments one might better term speculation. If he did, he did not have Wickham's luck. *Perhaps it is only that she has yet to come into her money,* Mary thought hopefully.

"It is not often we get such charming visitors in this wretched place," Captain Roarke said, selecting a biscuit. "Miss Bennet, you have come to bless the place with your beauty. Heaven knows it could use some beautifying. It is ghastly enough to make one long for the barracks!" He laughed, and his merriment partly crumbled the biscuit, scattering fragments that Lady Lucy's gaze followed to the bare floor.

"Could you not find a place you liked better?" Mary asked. Her tentative appeal increased the captain's amusement.

"In half a moment, if we had the ready. Lord Crestwood is a stingy fellow."

Mary expected some reaction from Lady Lucy at such direct criticism of her father, but she did not look alarmed. She simply refilled her husband's cup and smiled faintly at his liveliness.

"Now, Miss Bennet, pretty ladies like you and my wife ought never to have to think of money. I would think Lord Crestwood would understand that, and see that we were taken care of properly. A captain does not earn much, you know, though England pays him with praises enough." He chuckled. "Of course, tradesmen do not accept praises in exchange for goods. And if a man is as unlucky as I am in—well, never mind all that. How can any gentleman think of troubles with such solace nearby?" He threw a smile at Lady Lucy, but the way it deepened when he turned back to Mary suggested he intended her as the true subject of his gallantry. When Mary did not respond, he shifted in his seat and tried again. "What a lovely bonnet, Miss Bennet. I hope the wind and cold did not hurt it."

"N-no."

"It was very kind of you to come our way. Very obliging. You do not know how lonely an old soldier gets some afternoons!" His smile showed he knew no one would count him old. "You would not like me to be lonely, would you?"

Mary struggled to think of something to say. Not only was she unfamiliar with flirting, but she did not want to encourage the captain's familiarity. At length, she gave up, and supplied him with her usual conversational move: "I do not know."

The captain blinked, as if disconcerted by her inanity. "Well, I am sure I could not be lonely if you will come and see us. You will alter our way of life like—like a djinn from an Arabian tale." When again she did not answer, he pressed her. "Won't you? I am sure you have a great deal of magic at your disposal."

"I do not know," Mary murmured. Knowing the answer was inadequate, she averted her gaze from him to stare into her teacup.

"Shall I refill it, Miss Bennet?" Lady Lucy asked, and Mary passed her the cup, regretting the loss of her focal point. She kept her eyes on her lap instead.

"Well." Captain Roarke heaved a sigh and pushed back from the table. "I think you have found a companion that suits you, Lady Lucy." The irony in his voice stung Mary, thinking of Lydia decrying the woman as insipid. "Perhaps I will look in on Wickham. I will tell him what an angel his sister-in-law is before we go off to drill. Good day to you, Miss Bennet. Good-bye, my dear."

"Good-bye, my love." Lady Lucy's gaze followed the captain out, as if longing to bind him to her. The open neediness of her affections unsettled Mary.

She loves him, but there is something—unhealthy—in it. Mary did not understand it. All the couples she knew were either happily attached to one another or grown peacefully indifferent. She did not see how Lady Lucy could preserve such affection for someone who appeared entirely indifferent to her. *At least he is gone now. I suppose a lack of spirit has its advantages.*

Now that her husband was no longer of the party, Lady Lucy seemed to regain some of her aplomb. "Let me show you some of the embroidery I was speaking of," she said, pulling out a workbasket and displaying its contents. She and Mary discussed their merits, and then Mary took out the handkerchief she had been decorating and they both began to sew. The companionable silence of sewing side by side seemed to soothe them both. Lady Lucy occasionally broke it with a comment—"Oh, my thread has broken"—"This red is too bright, I think"—of a sort that Mary recognised as bearing the 'insipid' character Lydia warned her of.

But for Mary, who usually strained to find anything to say at all unless she repeated a sermon, the bland remarks supplied a conversation that required no wit or struggle. It was relaxing rather than tiresome. Lady Lucy seemed glad for the extra time with her visitor, and Mary found herself liking the woman more and more. *I am glad Lydia did not come. She would have tossed back and forth in her chair and looked impatient or else chattered so much I might not have known anything of Lady Lucy's thoughts.* It still embarrassed Mary to be thrown on Lady Lucy's hospitality for so long, especially as Lydia's appointed hour came and passed without her arrival, but, on the whole, she was pleased with how things had turned out.

"This is very pleasant, is it not, Miss Bennet? I wish you could come and sew every day." Lady Lucy knotted her thread and bent over her work.

"I think it nice to be quiet."

"Then you are just my sort of person. When I lived with my parents, I was very quiet indeed. Often I would come to visit my father a moment in his study, and he would get immersed in his Parliamentary papers and forget I was there entirely."

"It is lucky you had no desire for state secrets. What a spy you would have made!" They both laughed. After a hesitation, Mary said, "My family would often forget I was observing them, as well. I always knew where my sister Kitty hid the sweets she stole, and when Lizzy had a book she ought not, and that sort of thing."

"And did you tell?"

"Of course not!" Mary's head jerked up from her sewing. "I kept all secrets—almost all—" She pushed down the thought of Harry Lucas. "I find things are much more peaceful if you leave people to themselves."

"Mama would say that is just what one ought not to do." Lady Lucy added another row of stitches.

Before Mary could reply, a brisk knock at the door startled them both. Lady Lucy recovered quickly, and when the maid opened the door, she had her smile prepared.

The woman standing in the doorway in cheap muslin might have been a maid, but Lady Lucy's greeting was too effusive for that. "Mrs Burton! I had hoped we would see you today. Is Betsy—"

A little girl, no more than five years old, peeked past her mother's skirts. "Lady Lucy, Mama won't let me pet the ponies!" Her face bore the red streaks that showed she had been scrubbed clean for company, and although the little girl's dress was faded, it fit her better than Mary expected from a child of poverty. Her black, curly hair had been cropped short, and its tendrils looped in every direction.

Lady Lucy's smile became angelic, as if in spotting the little cherub, she had turned divine herself. "Why, Betsy, you know it is not safe to run about under the horses' hooves. Your mother is quite right."

Mrs Burton shifted her feet when she caught a glimpse of Mary. "I did not know you had visitors, ma'am. Forgive me for disturbing you. It's only that I've got a full gown to sew, with hardly any time for it, and as you said you'd be only too happy to look after Betsy—"

"Of course!" Lady Lucy's arms opened, and Betsy rushed into them, rubbing her washed face against Lady Lucy's skirts as if to prove it was clean. Lady Lucy's delight soon evaporated, however, as she glanced back at Mary, clearly unsure whether it was proper to introduce a seamstress. Mary rose from her embroidery.

"Will you not introduce us, Lady Lucy?" Mary watched the seamstress's face; it was too lined to appear young anymore, but she could not have been more than thirty. A hard life must have bent those shoulders, drawn down those brows, and thinned that figure, but Mrs Burton showed no sign of it in her gown. The cloth was of low quality, true, but its seams were tidy and the shape superb. Whatever her troubles, Mrs Burton certainly possessed a skill to boast of. As soon as the proper things were said, however, the seamstress drew back into the hallway, and her expression showed her unwilling-ness to put herself forward among Lady Lucy's friends.

Betsy had no such qualms. "Do you like ponies?" she asked Mary.

"She means horses, really." Lady Lucy cuddled the child to her as the maid shut the door on the mother. "She has never even seen a pony. But she and her mother live in this build-ing, and she likes to look at the old mares drawing pie carts outside." Betsy nodded, keeping her eyes on Mary.

"Horses are so beautiful, are they not?" Mary said, hedging the question. They were beautiful—and frightening. Mary had never even wished to learn to ride.

"Yes!" Betsy danced about the room as Lady Lucy went into the kitchen a moment. "Bee-yutiful!" She paused to gaze out the window. "Why are there so many people out there and so few ponies?" She did not wait for an answer but returned to her dance. "Lady Lucy is wrong—I *did* see a pony once. In a book. They are baby horses."

"Not exactly." Amusement curved Mary's lips, but she hardly knew what to say.

"There should be more ponies. It should be all ponies in the street." Betsy's dance devolved into vigorous stamping. "Don't you agree? No people, only ponies—"

"But then you could not go and pet them."

"Only ponies and me, then. And Mama. And Lady Lucy." Betsy stopped her stamping to stare at Mary, and Mary was sure she was revolving the question whether Mary should be allowed there as well. She must have decided caution suited the day, for she merely returned to her stomping.

Lady Lucy returned bearing a plate of jam tarts, scalloped in perfect symmetry and carefully dusted with sugar. "I have something nice for you, Betsy." Betsy eagerly climbed onto a chair and accepted a tart. Lady Lucy hesitated before asking Mary, "Would you care for one, as well?"

"No, thank you." Mary watched the child gobble the confection and accept another under Lady Lucy's beatific gaze. *No ordinary tarts, those. Expensive.* It puzzled Mary. Clearly Lady Lucy struggled to make ends meet, and yet she provided exquisite treats for a neighbour's child. Something of her wonder must have passed through her expression, for Lady Lucy hastened to explain.

"I am the child's benefactor," she said, her chin lifting. "Her mother is a good worker, but earns very little." She did not mention a father, and Mary did not ask. "Mama says that we should always regard the duties of rank. I am quite pleased to help my little object of charity." Lady Lucy caressed the child, and her tone became more natural. "I do so love children. I had hoped—" She flushed. "But Captain Roarke says we cannot afford any at present."

"I am sorry." Mary did not know what else to say. She had not expected such a confession on such short acquaintance, but she could not blame her new friend. Held aloft from her neighbours by her rank, separated from her old circle by her straightened circumstances, Lady Lucy probably had no one to confide in at all. *The captain certainly seems to deprive her of her due. Perhaps I should say something—assure her she deserves better, condole with her—*But no, that would be too officious. What if Lady Lucy was offended by such an intrusion? Mary did not want to lose the first friend she had made. "How long have you known Mrs Burton?" she asked, dismissing the desire to ask Lady Lucy to confide in her.

"Ever since we came here. Of course she is only a seamstress, nothing like you and me." Lady Lucy smiled, but Mary shifted in her seat. "Betsy, would you care for another tart?"

"Yes, please."

Lady Lucy busied herself with the little girl, and Betsy's chatter soon revealed that her bright new shoes were the gift of Lady Lucy, and that Lady Lucy had promised her the material for a new dress as well. Mary mused on this but remained unwilling to speak up. *It is not my business. Her relationship with her husband, the way she spends her money—none of it is my business.* The thoughts bolstered her, and the unease that had been stirring in her belly relaxed. She was able to respond to Betsy's animated questions better, revealing to the little girl that she did not have a pony but did have a doll, agreeing that ponies should become more numerous on the streets of London than people (so long as they were *very gentle* ponies, a reservation which Mary did not expect to be satisfied), and promising to bring her doll one day to show Betsy. The good cheer that Betsy's presence inspired livened up both Lady Lucy and Mary, and when Lydia finally sent a footman up to fetch her sister, Mary found herself bidding good-bye to her new friends with an optimism that kept her shoulders relaxed and her heartbeat steady. The physical ease matched her sense of internal peace.

It is better to stay out of things, if one can. I am sure Lady Lucy will manage very well with time. If only I could say the same for Lydia!

Eight

Lydia's promised week of avoiding Mr Cole ended much too soon for Mary. Although she had determined on fixing Mr Cole's attention on herself, Mary had no idea how to begin. When Lydia winked and said, "The fourth of February already! And just in time, for the London Ladies Information Society is helping Mr Cole prepare for a lecture this afternoon."

"He is giving another lecture today?" Mary had heard nothing of it.

"No, merely preparing one. Really it is an excuse for ladies to mill about the assembly rooms while pretending to label boxes or count chairs. You need not fear we will do anything useful." Lydia giggled. "Stay here and answer Lizzy's letter, if you like. Or play with Prince. He is looking dreadfully dull lately."

The fact that Lydia was encouraging her to stay home alerted Mary to trouble. "What if I went in your stead?"

Lydia's mouth dropped open. "Without me?" The consternation quickly shaped into a frown. "Let me guess—you simply want me out of Mr Cole's way again. How can you pay so much attention to meaningless tattle?"

Before Lydia could get far in her indignation, Mary hurried to give her another reason. "Not at all! Perhaps I am merely curious to know him myself," she said, unsure whether she was lying or not. "At any rate, will it not pique him to expect you and be disappointed?"

Lydia tilted her head in consideration. "I do not really *need* such tricks, but I daresay there is something in what you say. It will be fun to poke his pride a little. Very well, go with my good wishes. I will get Mrs Appleton to chaperon you." Her smile bore something feral in it. "But I do not bend to scandal, mind you. I shall remain good friends with Mr Cole, and I do not give two straws what anyone thinks of it."

"Of course."

Being a woman quite submissive to Lydia's will, Mrs Appleton took Mary in her carriage without protest. When they arrived, several ladies stood in the main hall, staring over a sea of chairs and benches, and discussing their arrangement with a calm abstraction that suggested no one actually expected anything to be moved in this century. Miss Poppit and Lady Crestwood had settled themselves in another room, scrutinising orders for refreshments. Lady Crestwood glanced up from the parchment. "Miss Bennet, how kind of you to add your assistance to ours. Is your sister—"

"She did not come." It was hard to bear Lady Crestwood's commanding gaze, but knowing that what Mary said would please her ladyship made it easier.

"I believe Mr Cole was expecting her." Lady Crestwood's tone started out bland, but a hint of satisfaction crept into it. "He is in the little room across the corridor."

"Then I shall go and convey my sister's regrets," Mary replied, feeling bold. Mary walked where Lady Crestwood had directed, her steps slow and uncertain. The beat of her heart became uncomfortably palpable. The door was ajar, revealing Mr Cole sitting at a table, petting a scrawny hound that wriggled with excitement.

"Good afternoon, Mr Cole." Mary eyed the hound and drew her skirts closer.

"Miss Bennet! Would you like to meet Hercules?" Mr Cole tousled the dog's ears.

Mary's inclinations went very much the other way, but she could not expect to charm the man by rejecting his dog. At least the creature looked nothing like a Hercules—his height was remarkably short, his energy appeared more frenetic than powerful, and his limbs were thin and gangly. "Good afternoon, Hercules."

The hound bounded to Mary, shouldering her legs in an attempt to gain her affections, and Mary instinctively shied away.

"He will not harm you," Mr Cole said. "I fear he is rather ill-behaved for a hunting dog—that is why he is here—but he has no malice in him."

Mary made an effort to touch the dog lightly. Instead of the grasping jaws she envisioned, the hound smothered her hand with licks. "Ill-behaved?"

"Oh, you know. He bayed far too early, and at the wrong things, or he got lost from the group. That sort of thing. He belonged to a friend of mine, and his keeper had given up on the poor creature and was going to drown him, but I persuaded him to let me have him instead."

Mary's heart softened at this example of kindness. "I am glad you did." She braced herself to pat the dog more firmly. Prince would have objected to any such touch from her, but Hercules merely burrowed closer in her skirts. She hesitated. "Is he—allowed to be in the building?"

Mr Cole smiled. "I cannot say the man in charge of the assembly room is pleased I brought him today, but Lady Crestwood is both indulgent to dogs, and exceedingly persuasive to managers." For the first time, his gaze swept around Mary. "I talked so much about him, Mrs Wickham made me promise to bring him. Where is she?"

At least Lydia had better sense than to go to a gentleman's home to meet his dog. Even Lydia knew such a visit would be too great an impropriety. "She did not come today."

Annoyance crossed his face, and Mr Cole stood up. "I see. Well, I had better check on the other ladies."

"Wait!" Mary knew the other ladies might gossip if he spent too much time alone with her, but she was sure he would not have cut short the tête-a-tête if it had been Lydia who had come. *Now is the time to start charming him away from her.* "I have had so little conversation with you." When he merely stared at her instead of responding, she said, "I enjoyed your lecture a few weeks ago."

His tone mingled puzzlement with resentment. "No, you did not. You made that quite clear."

"Well, not the subject matter...not entirely... Not that I dislike geology, I think, only that the theory was very..."

Mary realised she was not flattering to any effect. "When the speaker is so"—*So what?*—"so cunning and handsome"—*Oh, dear. That is just how Lydia describes Prince*—"one cannot help but enjoy any talk a little." Her efforts at flirting left much to be desired, but at least he was smiling now. Mary sensed it was not because he was flattered by her, but because he found her clumsy attempts to pay homage amusing.

"I am glad you enjoyed yourself." The dry politeness in his tone shamed her. "Now, I must go."

"Wait!" She resisted the impulse to grab his coat. "I am here to help. You have not given me a task."

He gestured at the table, where the little white boxes she had seen before were scattered. "Perhaps you could arrange these geological samples for me."

"You want me to line up your rocks." Her tone was flat, despite all her desire to please him.

"It is what you did the other time, is it not? I am sure you can have no objection." He strode out of the room before Mary could form one, in any case. So much for her attempts to ensorcell a man.

Sighing, she sat down and tucked her legs away from Hercules, who curled up on the floor. There was a stack of parchment alongside the boxes, and although the writing was garbled and the content leapt from one topic to another, she gathered that they were notes on the collection of rocks, describing when and where he obtained each sample, with a few comments or speculations thrown here and there. *At least I can make his labels more effective.* She took up a pen and dabbed it in an inkwell, and 'Schist, Germany' became 'Schist from the base of a mountain in Germany, collected after a landslide.' 'Gneiss slate misc.' became 'A mix of gneiss, slate, and other stones, collected by a friend in the East Indies, probably pressed together in the pressures related to the earthquake in 1797.' Her adaptations made the labels much longer and in tinier print, but that would only slow the ladies as they passed from box to box and give them more to discuss. Without glue, she could not affix the labels with any solidity, but she folded them over the edges of the boxes and let the rocks weigh down the inner portion.

The calm perusal of Mr Cole's notes and the methodical work of labelling soothed Mary, and by the time Mr Cole returned to see her work, she felt cheerful and energised. She had even forgotten Hercules's presence, though the pup snored at her feet. "Come see what I have done, Mr Cole."

He read some of the labels and frowned. "They are very lengthy. I believe I only asked you to arrange the boxes, not change the labels."

"True." Her smile faltered. "But I only wanted to—"

"I am sure it will not do any harm." No doubt he meant his words to console her, but she bristled instead.

"Of course they will not harm anything. The other ladies will find the rocks much more interesting now, I assure you." She could see his feet shifting, preparing to leave again, and she grew desperate. "Do not go. I find you—you are very…"

She struggled to find some compliment to bind him to her, or some flirtatious self-deprecation that Lydia would use, but nothing came to mind. Mr Cole's brows drew together in impatience, and she said in a rush, "I can help! I can make your lectures more interesting. I know that is what you want, to…to ensorcell…"

"Ensorcell?" He barked an incredulous laugh. "How ridiculous! My lectures are excellent as they are. I need not employ any such arts to make the subject more palatable to idle ladies of society." The blacksmith shoulders straightened with pride, but despite the man's impressive figure, Mary sensed a quailing weakness in his uneven breathing.

"You never dream of any other reaction from your audience?" Mary asked. "Would you not like sincere enthusiasm for a subject you clearly love?"

He cleared his throat, evidently disarmed by her statement. "Of course I have the odd daydream of enthusiastic applause for the brilliance of my theories. Or of ordinary men and women diving into scientific exploration as a result of my influence." He made a wry smile, but something vulnerable flickered in his eyes. "But the important thing is the science. So long as I get that right, nothing else matters."

"The science is important, but if the reaction of the audience matters to you, there is no reason we cannot modify the presentation of the science."

He took a chair next to her, and Mary felt encouraged. *He is rather like Maria Lucas, yearning for the wild approval of others, but too embarrassed to admit it.* Relating him to someone she knew increased her confidence. "We can make it intriguing to people new to geology."

"I am not sure about that. I do not want to be like Sir Reginald, diluting lectures with silly comments to pander to the audience." His anger took on momentum. "That man is infuriating! Oh, he is brilliant, of course—that is part of the problem. Do you know, when I first met Lady Crestwood, she praised me to the skies, saying she had heard my lectures were gloriously entertaining and instructive? But it turned out she had mixed us up: Sir Reginald Colton and Richard Cole. The names are too similar, and she thought I was him."

Mary tried to say something, but Mr Cole's frustration was in full force.

"And the wife of my friend—the fellow who had Hercules before—she set up a ladies' luncheon with a speaker, and even *she* chose Sir Reginald to lecture rather than me! She was supposed to be my friend, but these lectures do not seem to be about friendship, or science, or anything good." His shoulders slumped. "You know the Informed Ladies of London Association?"

"You mean the group here?"

"No, this is the London Ladies Information Society. The group meeting today is insignificant," he said, waving a hand, "but the Informed Ladies—why, that is run by Lady Crestwood, and it is the most prestigious ladies' group of the sort. Only the best scientists are invited to their annual celebration lecture. For three years running, she has chosen Sir Reginald as her geology speaker." He cringed. "Of course it is not really important. It is only a ladies' group, not a genuine scientific gathering. But they do have influence—"

"And you wish to be chosen this year."

Mr Cole averted his gaze, and Mary watched with interest as a flush crept up his neck. "I would not refuse the offer." He began shuffling the notes Mary had carefully organised. "But I will not reduce my lectures to frivolous demonstrations and examples, as Sir Reginald does. I refuse to become an object of ridicule."

"No doubt he is only trying to interest his audience." Mary gently took the notes from his hands and set them aside. "And there is a great deal that you can do without behaving ridiculously. Most of the ladies who come do not think much about geology. If you began your lecture by explaining why they should care—"

"If they do not care about the subject, why on earth do they come?"

Mary's stomach fluttered. She disliked the sense of confrontation, but she had to admit she was holding Mr Cole's attention. "Some appear for fashion's sake, or to see their friends, or show off a new gown, or because they are dull sitting at home—"

His magnificent shoulders sagged. "How flattering. Here because there is nothing better to do."

His dry tone stung her, but she persevered nevertheless. "The demonstrations you speak of are no doubt entertaining to watch. They keep the ladies lively and make things more memorable." At his snort of disgust, she said, "What is the point of teaching them if your manner of instruction does not help them learn? You are only opening a showroom for their gowns, otherwise."

"Yes, that is all." He shoved back his chair, and Hercules leapt up in eagerness at the supposed invitation. "I am much obliged to you, Miss Bennet, for pointing out all my faults." The sarcasm in his voice made Hercules flick his ears uncertainly. "But I do not think I want your help. I will gain success on my own, in my own way."

"But if your way is not working?" He frowned, but despite the thrill of fear that went through her, she forced herself to continue. "I truly can help you, Mr Cole. An intelligent, remarkable scientist like yourself—"

"Your flattery is unnecessary."

She flushed. *How does Lydia do this? The man is impossible.* "I can get you that invitation to the Informed Ladies—um, whatever it is. And I will do so, if you will promise to leave my sister alone."

He stared at her, and then suddenly his bass voice broke into a booming laugh that carried down the hallway, and he slouched back into the chair next to Mary and sprawled his limbs. The laughter seemed to billow up from his belly and slide through every arm and leg, making them tremble, and his handsome face relaxed and leaked tears.

Why is he laughing? I do not see anything funny. Mary's muscles tensed as she waited for a clearer response.

"You are not serious, Miss Bennet." The grin on his face was insufferable.

"I am perfectly serious. You have drawn opprobrium onto my sister's name, and I find neither you nor she respond to reason. So, I will make a bargain with you instead. Will you promise, Mr Cole?"

The crinkles at the sides of his eyes deepened in amusement. "What man can make promises regarding Mrs Lydia Wickham?"

Mary's lips pressed together. Before she could reply, Mary caught sight of Miss Poppit in the doorway, who strolled in with a smooth, elegant gait and flashed a smile at Mr Cole. "Am I interrupting something?" The innocence in her voice did not fool Mary. "You must not overtire yourselves. You have been closeted together so long, working."

More gossip to spread, but at least it will not involve Lydia. Mary rose and smoothed her skirts, but she could feel her confidence drain away as she saw herself through Miss Poppit's eyes. Thin, short, her hair simply dressed and wearing a gown best described as serviceable—she was a far cry from Miss Poppit's dark curls and sparkling eyes.

How did Mary ever think she could hold a man's attention? She had none of Miss Poppit's grace or beauty. She had only irritated Mr Cole, or made him laugh at something that was serious for her.

"Not at all." Mr Cole nodded at Miss Poppit's entry. If he felt any discomfiture at her insinuations, he did not show it. "I wonder if you could find us some glue, Miss Poppit? The workmen or the manager may know where there is some nearby. Miss Bennet has been so good as to design some new labels for my samples."

Miss Poppit hesitated—clearly she had not entered anticipating being given a task—but at length she nodded and turned away, leaving the couple alone again. Mary's eyebrows drew up in surprise. "Have you something more to say to me?" She braced herself for more laughter, still feeling the uncertainty and shyness Miss Poppit's presence had inspired. *But should I not feel shy around Mr Cole, any way? How is it that I did not feel that more before?*

"I will not promise anything about your sister, Miss Bennet. Trying to achieve fame as a lecturer is gruelling, and she moves in circles that I aspire to." He was sitting up straight now, his blacksmith arms spread wide on the table. "And I do enjoy her conversation. She keeps me from thinking too much."

"I can well believe that." Mary bit off her words, wondering where the flash of jealousy had come from. "You say you want to inspire ladies with an interest in science, but you cannot believe that Lydia is the least bit inspired that way. She—" Mary was tempted to report that Lydia had not even known what science he had devoted his life to, but perhaps that was a revelation too harsh.

"You think she lacks intelligence?"

"Not at all. She has some native intelligence, but she has never been much interested in education. She has never been pressed to learn anything she did not like. My mother would never push her, nor did my father."

"And your governess?"

"We never had one," Mary said, wondering at the ease with which these family revelations dropped from her lips. "Perhaps we should have, although I do not know if it would have helped. No one can make Lydia do what she does not wish. She is not stupid—"

"Only a little spoiled, it sounds like." The good humour in his eyes palliated the remark.

Mary's gaze dropped to her lap.

"Well, talking to a pretty woman without too much sense is quite relaxing. I cannot say I have found your conversation *relaxing*, Miss Bennet. Stimulating, perhaps, but certainly not the sort to put a man at his ease." He rose from his chair. "Good afternoon. I will permit you to affix the labels when Miss Poppit returns with the glue." Hercules nosed Mary in the knee as a good-bye, smearing her dress with moisture, then trotted after his master down the hall.

Permit me to affix the labels? Well I daresay that is as much thanks as he is capable of. Mary's hands tightened into fists. *It is as I thought; he wants Lydia as a distraction from his troubles.* She gritted her teeth, surprising herself with the intensity of her pique—and was it jealousy? 'I cannot say I have found your conversation relaxing'...*Relaxing or not, I shall just have to make myself more distracting than she is.*

Nine

Lydia's favourite shop on Bond Street boasted wide plate windows full of millinery, a squeaking sign that swung in the February wind, and shop assistants with wide, attentive eyes and gushing praises for every customer. The fog had blown off for once, leaving the sky a milky white, and although the mottled remains of a snow gathered in some of the alleyways, most of the streets were dry. The red, raw chapping of skin in the cold was enough to make the ladies hurry inside the millinery shop, though— Lady Lucy's translucent pallor was rouged by the wind, Mary's cheeks were roughened into a darker red, and even Lydia's beauty was crimsoned into something awkward and glaring in hue.

"My fingers are frozen through!" Lydia lifted her gloved hands with a theatrical gesture, but her voice was cheerful enough. "Come, Lady Lucy, we must nestle ourselves in all this finery until we are safe and warm again." She giggled and led Lady Lucy to a display of scarves, muffs, and gloves, amusing her with the plot of a melodrama she had seen. Mary could not dispute Lydia's willingness to see a bargain through. Not only had her sister invited Lady Lucy to join them, as Mary had wished, but she had also made a special effort to make Mary's friend feel welcome. No doubt Lydia was alive to the possibility of pleasing Lady Crestwood through attentions to her daughter; the Wickhams' quest for a patron in the *ton* meant Lydia was often willing to smile on those she found dull. Lady Lucy lacked the wit to respond with the flattery or jokes Lydia would have appreciated, but the noblewoman supplied her with all the insipid, polite commentary she could muster.

"It is a very pleasing shop," Lady Lucy said, smiling and nodding at everyone as she trailed in Lydia's wake. Excitement ruddied her cheeks almost as much as the wind had, and Mary felt a surge of satisfaction at her friend's pleasure. "I have not been to Bond Street in so long! I used to go with Mama, you know"—her gaze drifted off—"but she does not spend much time with me, now that I am married."

"I am sure she is very busy," Mary said, eager to smooth over any unpleasantness. "No doubt she imagines you are as well."

"She has that Miss Poppit to sponsor now," Lydia announced blithely as she examined a bolt of fabric. It was impossible to tell if Lydia was aware she was persisting in a delicate subject or not. "She is determined to bring her out with all *éclat*, and snag every eligible bachelor for miles around London. As if Lady Crestwood and Miss Poppit have half the taste I do! You shall reign over them all when I am finished with you, Mouse —um, Mary."

Lydia's plan required Mary to be as little mouselike as possible, and in the interests of consistency, Lydia had determined to drop the old nickname. Mary rather missed it. *Or perhaps I miss being free of the responsibilities of being 'Mary.' 'Mouse' was not expected to attract suitors, but Miss Mary Bennet is.*

Mary poked at a selection of gloves, wondering if so many shades of kid were really necessary. "You ought to be grateful to Lady Crestwood," Mary said to Lydia. Perhaps the reminder would help her avoid saying anything awkward in front of Lady Lucy. "She invited us to her ball and gave us tickets for that concert."

Lydia rooted through the display with a self-assured negligence. "Oh, of course I am full of gratitude and loving kindness and all that sort of thing for Lady Crestwood, for she has done me many a good turn. And I hope I can please her well enough for her to do something nice for Wickham." She turned from the gloves with a grin. "All the same, I shall cut her to shreds—and humiliate her—and make her gnash her teeth with envy when she sees how you conquer!"

Mary flushed and avoided Lady Lucy's gaze. "That does not make any sense."

"Oh, yes, it does. When you understand people a little better, you will see it makes perfect sense." Lydia winked at Mary.

Mary turned to Lady Lucy. "I am sure my sister does not really mean any harm," she said in an apologetic tone, but Lady Lucy merely looked blankly back at her.

"People are always trying to overcome my mother." Lady Lucy's grey eyes shone, but it was the gleam of an empty mirror. "Mama says not to pay them any mind. She says while they are talking, she is doing."

"Touché!" Lydia laughed. "I ought to be doing, especially here, Lady Lucy. You are quite right." She beckoned to a shop woman, who hurried to her with a look expectant of good things. "We need several pairs of long gloves for evening, morning gloves both trimmed and plain, indigo ribbons, pink ribbons, red ribbons—crimson red, not darker—aigrettes, some clips, combs, fans, bonnets—what sort do you have?— stockings, slippers, if you have them…" Lydia's head tilted in thought. "And something for me, as well. A new bonnet, perhaps, but I will choose that last. I shall wish to inspect everything there is a choice of."

The shop woman's face beamed with gratification, and she led Lydia from table to table. Mary's hands fidgeted, but she forced them to still. *You made it through the warehouses for the silk and muslin, and the dressmaker's. This is just a little more of the same.* She still could not believe all the things Lydia thought needful to prepare Mary for one Season, though. *What does all this cost? Will Mr Wickham be angry with her?* Mary was supposed to be smoothing the waters between them. *If it keeps Lydia's mind off Mr Cole for a while, it will be worth it,* she assured herself.

Lady Lucy was examining a pair of yellow kid gloves. Unlike her own pair, this one had no stains or tears. "How pretty!"

They looked rather plain to Mary, but she instantly agreed. "Oh, yes." Mary repositioned them to get a better look, then glanced up into Lady Lucy's vacant face. "I hope you were not upset at what my sister said, Lady Lucy. About your mother."

"No, not at all. Mrs Wickham has always said just what she thought about my mother—and around her. I rather think Mama admires her for it." She suppressed a sigh. "I never could do it, myself. Mama does not tolerate disagreement very well in the short term, however much she may admire it later."

"Was there a great deal of arguing in your home?"

"The opposite. No one dared to contradict her." Lady Lucy gave a wry smile. "It was very peaceful."

Mary thought of how Lady Crestwood's powerful self-assurance had crushed the squabbles of the ballroom, her own opinion reigning supreme as a result. She supposed it was a kind of peace, that brutal intolerance for dissent. *I suppose peace is not always pleasant.*

"It is very interesting to hear Mrs Wickham talk," Lady Lucy said, and Mary prepared herself to hear more of the chatter Lydia called insipid. Her expectations were soon upset. "I often wonder what it would be like to be like her, and if that would please my mother. I am afraid Mama does not know what to do with me. I sort of—disgraced her."

"You mean your marriage."

Lady Lucy turned over the gloves to inspect the other side. "She did not like my running away, and she does not approve of Captain Roarke. She does not understand how good he is." Her wide eyes appealed to Mary as if asking her to support her claim.

Uncomfortable, Mary forced herself to nod. "He is a wonderful husband, I am sure." A sick feeling of wrongness slid into her belly, but she ignored it. *She believes it, so it is true. Besides, it is not my business.*

"Exactly." Lady Lucy's voice thrummed with satisfaction. "He says my parents are too—too frugal, too old-fashioned. They do not understand what a young couple needs to live on in these times. I am sure if we but had some small addition to our income, everyone would get along much better."

Does that mean she and her husband too? Mary did not ask, but she wondered about Lady Lucy's desire for a child and the dismal lodgings. Surely there was enough fodder for marital discontent there. *Yet she idolises him.*

"Have you made your selection, ma'am?" A shopgirl appeared at Lady Lucy's side, but Lady Lucy backed away.

"No, I have not," she said, hauteur entering her tone. "Kindly wait until you are summoned." The girl gave an uncertain smile and curtseyed, then hurried back to the counter. Lady Lucy pushed the kid gloves back into the pile. "Tradespeople are so coarse. I find I can bear it less and less these days. Can you bear them, Miss Bennet?"

"I...have not had many difficulties," Mary said uncertainly.

"They say Mr Ingleston is to marry a chandler's daughter. A *chandler!* His family is nearly as old as ours, and he degrades himself with a tradesman's daughter." Lady Lucy huffed in indignation. "Mama says they will never hold their heads up again after that—or should not, any way."

"I did not know." Mary could not see that the difference in rank mattered very much, but she supposed Lady Lucy had to cling to something in the upheaval of her life. Perhaps her reverence for rank, and the idea of herself as belonging to an elevated class of society, was her only sense of esteem now. "Those gloves are very pretty indeed, now that I see them better," she said, diverting the woman's attention. "Allow me to gift you with them, Lady Lucy, as a token of friendship."

"Oh, no." Lady Lucy blushed, and the hauteur drained from her voice. "I could not accept."

"Of course you may!" Lydia said, hurrying up to them. "Snatch them up quick, Mouse—I mean to give you both presents, in honour of our day together, and Lady Lucy shall not protest."

Lady Lucy did, however. "I really do not need any gloves, Mrs Wickham." Her gaze wandered to the cards of lace stacked in tasteful array on another counter. "But what about some lace? I am embroidering a handkerchief for Betsy, a little charity girl I patronise. This lace would make it quite elegant."

"I think Betsy has had enough boons," Mary said. The memory of the shoes, gown, and tarts made her tone firm enough to surprise herself.

"Lace-trimmed handkerchiefs, for a little girl!" Lydia's breath caught in indignation. "Surely not!" She accepted the kid gloves Mary offered her for the noblewoman's gift and threw a glance of disgust at the lace table. "Not that I deny that little girls have plenty of running noses. I grant them that."

She moved on to another table, a shopgirl trailing after her. "I shall give you these gloves, instead, Lady Lucy. And a tippet." She bent in consultation with the shopgirl, but Lady Lucy thumbed through the cards of lace with a regretful sigh. Though Mary was too far from her to see closely, she thought Lady Lucy paused on examining a particular card of double-edged French lace. Mary passed on to another display, this one bearing bonnets of every shape and colour.

Why, this one looks just like my doll's! She pulled the bonnet down with glee, scrutinising the close-woven straw, the white satin trim, and the decorative cherries. The sight bubbled up happiness and warmth within her, reminding her of the day she had made the purchase, spreading her pennies on the counter with tiny fingers, eager to treat her doll and hasty to spend before her younger sisters could claim her pocket money for themselves. *What fun it would be to wear this! I still think it the prettiest bonnet I ever saw.* Mary suppressed a giggle, and she turned to beckon to Lady Lucy.

Mary's breath caught. Lady Lucy had been holding a card of lace—the same French lace she had been admiring—but quick as a flash, the card seemed to disappear, and a bulge swelled the woman's sleeve.

Did she just—take that? Mary turned back to the stand and replaced the bonnet with a slow, hesitant motion. Surely not. Lady Lucy was aristocracy. She was moral, upright, kind. *I must be imagining things.* That was it. It was a discombobulating place, a millinery shop full of fripperies and fun. It was natural to become a little confused. *She must have set it down next to her sleeve, and I was a goose and thought it went up it.* Relieved, Mary gave the bonnet a twist on the stand to reposition it. It was a very pretty bonnet, indeed. Mary could not remember asking for any item for herself, from anyone, except her doll all those years ago. Perhaps it was unwise, with Lydia already spending so much—*But I need to distract Mr Cole, don't I? Even if he does not care for the bonnet, I will, and that will make all the difference in my demeanour.* "Lydia, may I have this bonnet?"

"Heavens, what a question! Take it, and the one beside it, and any other that you see. We shall ransack the entire establishment!" Lydia's cheerful voice drifted from where she still consulted with the shopkeeper. Mary took down the bonnet she liked and carried it to her sister. When the shopkeeper gave a firm nod to Lydia's instructions and hurried to complete them, Mary dropped her voice.

"Are you sure it is all right?" Mary spun the bonnet in her hands, unable to keep from admiring it from every angle. "I thought Mr Wickham...I mean, we spent a great deal on cloth from the warehouses, and then the dressmaker..." Her fingers began to fumble, and the bonnet pitched askew in her hands.

Lydia's eyes flashed, the good humour of moments before turning instantly into peevishness. "What do you mean by that?"

Mary hesitated, but her conscience prodded her further. The allowance that Papa gave her would never cover what had been spent on Mary, even if she had saved it all. "I mean that I still do not understand how Mr Wickham even became so wealthy, and as he now complains that you spend a little too freely..."

Lydia put a stack of gloves down with more force than necessary, scattering a few from their careful arrangement. "Ladies do not need to know anything about all that, Mary. My husband says he is just lucky in things—cards, shares, commissions—but I know it is his cleverness. He is as clever as anything, so of course he became rich. And why should I not spend what we have? It is so dull at home!" She puffed out a breath, as if trying to calm herself. "Well, to set your anxious little mind at ease, I will tell you I asked Mr Wickham how much I might have to fit you out, and I have not gone beyond that yet. So *there!*"

"Please do not be angry, Lydia." Mary's eyes watered, and she pressed her chest with her hand, willing the pounding heart to slow. *It is nothing only a little spat, even if it feels monstrous and huge. What is wrong with me? Why do these things trouble me so? Others seem so unaffected by them.* She hated the anger that swept through people, destroying homes, upsetting her peace, and she hated even more when that anger was directed at her. Verses from the Bible pertaining to anger and temperance sprung to her lips, but she resisted them; they would only vex Lydia further.

Her plea mollified Lydia, and her sister dropped her tone and tidied the gloves she had disarranged. "However nettled Mr Wickham gets at my purchases, he is not at all averse to spending what is proper. Especially not for you. He thinks we cannot do too much for our little Mou—our Mary." She corrected herself with a smile, and relief flooded Mary. The pounding in her chest became less palpable, and she could breathe easier.

"I understand," Mary said, nodding with a bit too much enthusiasm in her eagerness to return to harmony.

"Now, which ribbons would you say suit the white silk gown we planned?" Lydia led her to another table and prodded the ribbons to put their loose curls in better light.

The white silk evening gown. 'We' certainly did not plan that one. The sharp decolletage, costly material, and distinctive shell-shaped sleeves were all Lydia's idea. "The crimson is very bright," Mary said, meaning to disparage it.

"I think so, too. It will set off your brown hair very well, and attract just enough attention in a ballroom without appearing gauche." Lydia sighed in satisfaction and tucked the roll with her other choices. Mary eyed the crimson loops with distaste, but she could not deny her plan was working. Her sister was immersed in the project of bringing her out with *éclat. And that is the point. So long as she is happy and busy with this, she is not trailing after Mr Cole. It is worth a few red ribbons.*

And perhaps there was another point—Mary found herself wondering, again and again, just how Mr Cole would respond to the new gowns and bonnets. Would he notice? What if Lydia was right—that a few fripperies and well-made costumes could turn a mouse into a belle? *Perhaps all this will serve to distract Mr Cole as well.* The thought slid through her whole body like molten metal, and she had difficulty justifying the response. *It is not that I care to attract him for my own sake. It is for the Wickhams. Lizzy said it was the best plan.*

She realised she had wandered over to the pile of boxes and packets containing Lydia's purchases and had restacked them in neater piles, the heaviest on bottom, so that the footman could carry them more easily. One of the shop girls was staring at her, no doubt puzzled with her preoccupation when there was gleeful shopping to be done. Mary flushed and retreated, but now that she had found her bonnet, she seemed to have exhausted her stock of opinions. Lydia appealed to her for preferences in colours, sizes, and decorations in vain.

"We have worn her out for today, Lady Lucy," Lydia said, patting Mary's shoulder. "And I could go another ten hours! La, you have no stamina for shopping, Mary. And here I was, thinking we could go on to the jewellers. Emeralds would be perfect with your new green gown."

"Mama says emeralds are only appropriate for those with green eyes," Lady Lucy said. "Our family has a lovely emerald necklace that has been passed down for generations, but she never wears it because she says the emeralds would look ill on her. She said she would give it to me someday, but I do not see how that would help, for I have grey eyes like hers." Lady Lucy dropped her chin, musing on the dilemma, but Lydia had no patience for it.

"Well, I think emeralds would be beautiful on Mary. And Lady Crestwood's grey eyes can pop right out of her head when she sees them on her, if she likes. Then she can wear as many emeralds as she chooses." Lydia beckoned to a footman to begin carting out their haul to the carriage. "I wish we could go and buy them tomorrow, but I promised to go and read to Mrs Holt. She has been abed all week." She turned to Mary, and her coral lips pursed in thought. "Perhaps you could go in my stead. You are so quiet, I dare say you are just right for a sickroom. Mrs Holt likes Bible reading and that sort of thing."

Mary averted her gaze, suddenly seeing Sir William Lucas's drawing room and Harry Lucas's head bent towards her, reading a psalm. The Bennets had often visited there, Lizzy closeting herself with Charlotte, Kitty and Lydia romping with Maria, and Mary engaging in calm, earnest debates with Harry about religion. His voice had been like embers softly glowing in the grate, quiet and soothing, until some ideal was touched, and then it sparked into passionate defence like flames leaping in reckless abandon.

"Well, Mary? It would be a great favour." Lydia tapped her fingers on her reticule impatiently, as if she resented having to ask twice.

Mary knew her reluctance would not hold out, but she made a paltry effort. "I do not even know Mrs Holt."

"She will not mind that. It is settled; you shall go and read to her tomorrow, and I will plan a few more things for your gowns." Lydia did not see Lady Lucy's look of sympathy cast at her sister, but Mary acknowledged it with a rueful smile.

"Yes, Lydia."

"A few more days of shopping, and a week or two of fittings with the dressmaker, and you shall be queen of the *ton*! Then Lady Crestwood and Miss Poppit will swoon with envy, and we shall all be content." Lydia led the way to the carriage, where the boxes and packets had been strapped onto the back, stuffed into the seats, and piled onto the carriage floor.

A few more days? A week or two? It was not enough. Keeping Lydia busy with bringing her out would only go so far, and Mary could already see the day approaching where her sister would return to her flirtations. She climbed into the carriage, propping a bandbox on her lap. Perhaps it was the one containing the bonnet she had chosen. The thought made her wriggle in her seat, as if she were a child. *At least I have that to show for my efforts.* She realised she had never even tried it on, and endeavoured to picture herself in it, but her doll's face kept popping into her mind. *Oh, well, I am sure it is fine. I wonder if Mr Cole will notice it.* She glanced at Lydia's face, searching it for some sign of discontent or ennui, but her sister merely looked satisfied with the day's efforts.

It will not last long, however. I must hope I have better luck distracting Mr Cole.

Ten

Lizzy's face showed exactly the disappointment Mary had feared for weeks. There was kindness in her smile, but also a tension that was plain evidence that she had hoped for more. "It sounds like a very good beginning," Lizzy said encouragingly. "But I think you ought to put yourself forward a little more."

"Forward?" Mary frowned. Forward was everything she was not. "I cannot do so without becoming unladylike."

"Not so! I wish you had spent more time with Miss Bingley; she would strike the right note of ladylike impudence admirably." Lizzy chuckled to herself, and Mr Darcy took her hand with a small smile. Mary did not like discussing such things in front of a gentleman, even if he was her brother. But Lizzy seemed to take him into the conference as a matter of course, not merely because they were all packed into the Darcy carriage and could not help sharing conversation, but also because sharing her plans with her husband—as she shared every other part of her heart and life with him—came naturally to Lizzy. Looking at the pair of them, one could never imagine there was a time when Lizzy had disliked him.

Mr Darcy had noticed her study and spoke up. "From what I have seen of you, Miss Bennet, your decorum will never be bent to an unwise degree," he said, and his vote of confidence gave Mary an unreasonable amount of reassurance. Blushing at the compliment, she stared at the doll in her lap. The Darcys had agreed to drop Mary off at Lady Lucy's, and Mary was bringing her doll to show Betsy, as promised. She did regret the air of childishness carrying it gave her, though, especially in front of the impressive Mr Darcy of Derbyshire.

"I just do not think I can do it. I am not charming, Lizzy." Mary's tone was still plaintive, but it held a new note of desiring to be persuaded now. *Does Mr Darcy really think I can do this? Or is he merely seconding Lizzy's wishes?* Mr Darcy's gaze, so solemn generally, warmed into a fervour that dazzled when he looked at his young wife, and it was easy to believe he would go to a great many lengths to please her. *But he is also scrupulously honest.* The thought, touching on a thousand sermons she had read, consoled Mary. She could rely on his principles.

"You are quite pretty enough, I assure you," Lizzy said, apparently sensing Mary's need for cajoling. "Your new things suit you very well." She gestured at Mary's pelisse, fresh from the millinery, and the pearl comb pulling tresses from Mary's neck. With Mary's usual sombre colours exchanged for ones that better suited her, her mouse-brown hair now looked more like ripened wheat, a blend of light browns and richer shades melded together. "And even Lydia says your conversation has improved."

"She means that I do not preach at her so often." Mary had not intended it as a joke, but Mr Darcy barked a laugh and Lizzy tried to hide a smile.

"Well, at any rate, you have everything required for drawing off this Mr Cole," Lizzy said.

"Could not you speak to him yourself, Lizzy? Or you, Mr Darcy?" Mary turned from one to the other, but both shook their heads.

"I do not even know him." Lizzy's tone was calm, but Mary sensed an undercurrent of amusement, as if Lizzy had other reasons she was unwilling to display.

"And a warning from me would appear too serious, too offensive. I will do it if I must, but things are not at such a pass yet." The light in Mr Darcy's eyes suggested he was in on the secret, whatever it was.

Perhaps they like the changes in me. Mary was not sure she liked them herself yet. They were too new, and she felt too different. She made one last effort to avoid her task. "Could not Kitty tempt him away then? Her husband is getting leave soon, and they are to stay with us at the Wickhams' next month."

"We cannot wait a month," Lizzy said firmly, but then she caught sight of the buildings out the window and gasped. "Good heavens, where is the coachman taking us? I thought we were going to the Roarkes'."

"This is the correct neighbourhood." Mary could not say she had grown used to the dingy lodging houses, rickety meat carts, and swarms of beggars, but now that she had been visiting Lady Lucy regularly, her shock had decreased. "They are very poor, Lizzy."

She hesitated, wondering how much would be proper to say. "I wondered if you could think of some way to help them. I thought of giving Lady Lucy my allowance," her words began rushing out as her sister's incredulous expression turned to indignation, "but that did not seem quite the thing, even if she would accept it."

"I should say not." Lizzy shook her head, giving a quick glance at her husband.

Mr Darcy's cool composure mastered the occasion. "I believe the Crestwoods gave her a substantial settlement, paid to Lady Lucy every quarter. And Captain Roarke receives pay from his regiment, of course." His brow furrowed. "If they are living here, it is not due to restricted income, but to excessive outlay. What does Lady Lucy say becomes of the money?" Though he probably did not intend to sound imposing, Mary shrunk back. She felt a sudden desire to protect her friend.

"She has not said anything, but I know she struggles. She may not even know where it all goes. Certainly she does not spend it."

"She does not know where it goes?" Lizzy sounded incredulous, and Mary flushed.

"Well, why should she? It is gentlemen's business to make sure she is comfortable. Her father and husband should take care of it all." Mary's defence took stride as she became more personal. "Why, Lydia has no idea how Mr Wickham obtained *his* wealth. She guesses cards, or investments, or buying and selling commissions, but it is clear she knows nothing about it."

"She does not—" Mr Darcy bit his lip, clearly holding himself back from some cutting remark. "Mr Wickham informed me of an inheritance he received, before he came to London. I doubt that is the full explanation, but he would not give me another." The long look he shared with Lizzy suggested it was a topic often discussed between them.

"I think we are straying from the matter at hand," Lizzy said, her tone sensible. "We cannot sit in the carriage outside these lodgings all day. The question is, are we going to call on Lady Lucy?"

"Of course we are!" Mary's back stiffened, and she laid a hand on the carriage door as if to leap out if they tried to drive away. "Judge not, that ye not be judged—" Mary had not even realised she had slipped back into sententious quoting until Lizzy's eyebrow lifted. She swallowed. *It is so hard, declaring my own opinion.* It made her feel weak and vulnerable, but Mary tried. "She is my friend, Lizzy, my only friend. I do not care if she is poor."

Lizzy exchanged another look with Mr Darcy, then she patted Mary's hand, which clutched her doll as if someone were going to try to snatch that away as well. "Then we shall call. But I do not advise giving her any of your pin money, Mary, until Lady Lucy is ready to confront her husband with a little more steadiness."

Mary thought of Lady Lucy's helpless adoration of the captain, and finally she felt a twinge of guilt on her friend's behalf. "Very well."

"And if her parents have not removed her from these lodgings, there must be a reason. The Crestwoods are not heartless people. They have probably offered to help her in some way, and for some reason, she refused." Lizzy's good sense made the issue seem clear and settled, but Mary's heart swarmed with chaos.

Gripping her doll, she clambered out of the carriage, and when the Darcys followed, Mary saw the lodgings with their eyes—the dilapidation, the grime, the ineffective attempts at gentility. *It is truly awful that a woman of the aristocracy lives in such a place.* But Lord and Lady Crestwood had not rescued their daughter from it. Perhaps they knew where the money went, when others did not.

Lizzy made no further remarks as they trudged up the stairway, but her glance paused on each smear of mud on the floor and every gap in the balusters. No doubt the odours of unwashed clothing and spilled gin were equally noticeable. At least this time, the maid answering the Roarkes' door looked in better humour, and they entered a room better tidied than Mary had last seen it. Both the captain and Lady Lucy were there, as well, and their welcome was warm enough to soothe Lizzy's tight-lipped expression into one of ease.

"We are so pleased to see you," Lady Lucy said. "Mama says having guests is the best part of having one's own home."

"Not that we have had many." The captain shook his head. "Such a hole as this is! You are a brave vanguard, Mrs Darcy, Mr Darcy."

Mr Darcy gave a polite bow, stiff enough to show he was not conciliated by the man's address, however smooth. Captain Roarke endeavoured to put Lizzy at her ease, and Mary finally saw him at his best: witty, deferential, and downright kind in seating her sister at the fireside to warm her hands. Lady Lucy had fluttered uneasily at Mr Darcy's sternness, but now she sat peaceably like a hen smoothing down her feathers after a startle. Listening to Lizzy and the captain make pleasant conversation, Mary mused on their comfortable banter. Captain Roarke had always been a favourite with ladies, despite his profligate ways—or perhaps even because of them. After all, a man could repair any insufficiency of income with exertion and wits, while women in such circumstances were generally condemned to sink in the mire of poverty. And in the meantime, a man could be praised for generosity or a fashionable recklessness. Mary doubted that Lizzy had lost sight of the Roarkes' inconsistencies, but clearly Lizzy could make the most of a moment and enjoy their company despite her reservations.

No amount of charm could make Mary forget her friend's troubles, however. The captain's flair for conversation entertained Lizzy until he had to take his leave to attend to his military duties, but Mary watched him with increasing dissatisfaction. Lady Lucy's eyes glowed with approval of his wit and seemed to find nothing amiss, but the moment he departed, her mouth drooped with disappointment. That made Mary uneasier still, but she resisted the sensation. *You are too judgmental,* she scolded herself. *The captain was quite kind to Lizzy, and Lady Lucy is very well pleased with him too. The fact that she idolises him is a good thing, not a bad one, especially in a marriage with so few other comforts. It makes her happy. Wrangling with him would serve no purpose; it would only disturb her peace. I daresay that is why Mr Darcy does not tax him on the subject of their money.*

"Lady Lucy, have you been enjoying this turn in the weather?" Lizzy's inquiry was merely polite, but Lady Lucy looked delighted.

"Why, it has been almost warm. We have been quite snug in our little home. Mama says the daffodils may be fooled into blooming early; it is so warm."

"And have you taken walks to any of the shops nearby? My uncle Gardiner has a warehouse not far from here."

"Oh, no." Lady Lucy's vacant smile conveyed nothing, and her conversation little more. "We have been quite busy. Mama always says it is important to stay busy."

Lizzy shifted in her chair. "Well...how is your embroidery coming along? I see it there."

"It is coming along quite nicely. Mama says I have a neat hand."

Seeing her sister's increasing amusement, Mary roused herself. "We often sit and sew together, Lizzy. Lady Lucy has taught me a new way to make roses. It makes them look more like buds, half open."

Lady Lucy nodded. "Mama says roses are the sweetest flower—"

"Your mother seems a veritable fount of knowledge," Lizzy said, with a gentle smile, "but I believe I have been seeking your opinions, not hers." She might have gone on, but Mr Darcy, who had been staring out the window for much of the visit, broke in.

"Forgive me, I must hasten downstairs. There is a little girl in the street, nearly under the horses—" He was already making for the door, and Lizzy hurried to follow him, pausing only long enough to explain.

"A strange man accosting the child might frighten her, and others." Perhaps it was a motherly impulse, or perhaps Lizzy was grateful for a moment to escape the Roarkes'.

"It is probably Betsy," Mary called after her. "You can bring her here, Lizzy." She only heard Lizzy's steps thumping down the stairs, but hopefully her sister heard.

"I am glad Mr Darcy spotted her. Naughty Betsy!" Lady Lucy spoke with an absent air, as if she were thinking of something else. Mary supposed she was used to Betsy's antics. As Mary passed to the window, her gaze was arrested by a card of lace half-hidden in the workbasket. It was a full card, not the lengths one might have severed at a milliner's, and it was the same French pattern they had seen while shopping.

Perhaps Lady Lucy went back and bought it later, Mary thought, but a sinking feeling dragged her down nonetheless. *I should just ask her about it; that would clear everything up. There must be a good reason for her having it.* But her throat felt thick and tight, and she could not bring herself to speak the words. *No, I will not mention it. It is probably nothing.*

She looked out the window, shifting the curtain to get a better view of Mr Darcy sweeping Betsy up into his arms, the little girl's pudgy hands still stretching to try to pet a horse's muzzle. "It *is* Betsy," she said, but when she turned to Lady Lucy, she spied a tear trickling down her face. Lady Lucy quickly wiped it away, and Mary turned back to the window. They both pretended Mary had not seen.

Was she crying about Betsy? Mary doubted it. *Is she sad about her husband? Or did she steal the lace that day?* Questions pressed at her from every direction, but all Mary could do was clench her fists and insist that it was not her business. Even if Lady Lucy felt distress sometimes, her life was peaceful. Nosing out her troubles would only stir things up and make things worse, surely.

Mr Darcy threw open the door, still towing Betsy, his wife on his heels. "Apparently this child's mother has run off without her." The declaration did not produce the results he expected; Mary tilted her head, and Lady Lucy rose and gave Betsy a smile.

"She did not run off, Mr Darcy. Her mother probably had to bring the gown she was sewing somewhere. Betsy, did not your mother say to stay inside?" Lady Lucy spoke in an admonishing tone, but Betsy jerked her arm free of Mr Darcy and rushed into her arms.

"Lady Lucy, I was *so* good, almost the whole time, but then the man stopped his pony right in front! I couldn't stay inside, then, could I?" Betsy's rosy lips parted as she waited for the answer.

"You could, and you should have. It is dangerous to wander outside. You must promise not to do it anymore." Lady Lucy drew out a handkerchief. The edges bore two thick layers of French lace, the very kind Lady Lucy had admired at the millinery—the very kind she now had a card of in her basket.

"I promise!" Betsy said, her gaze glued to the handkerchief. "Is that for me?"

"Yes, since you promised. I finished it early." Lady Lucy surrendered the gift, and Betsy held it up to the lamp to admire it.

"Two rows of lace on a child's hanky!" Lizzy seemed at a loss for wit.

"*Noblesse oblige*, Mrs Darcy." Lady Lucy lifted her chin and folded her hands, making herself the picture of prim nobility. "I am this child's benefactor. The Crestwoods have always tended to the those of the lower classes in need."

"The *Crestwoods* may have," Mr Darcy began, and though he did not finish his thought, Mary could almost hear it. *But the Roarkes cannot afford it.*

Mary was not sure Lady Lucy understood, but the threat of conflict rose up in Mary's gut, crushing her chest. *No arguing, please!* She ought to have guessed that Mr Darcy would not spar with a poor noblewoman, but even the possibility of it unsettled her. She flailed for a distraction. "Betsy, I have brought the doll I told you about. Would you like to see her?"

"Oh, yes!"

Mary made a fuss about demonstrating the doll's possible positions, the gowns she had made for her at Longbourn, and the superior silk scraps she had obtained at the Wickhams'. "Now her attire is practically Parisian," she said, glancing at Lady Lucy and Mr Darcy to check for tears or frowns. They seemed to have recovered their aplomb, and Mary's chest relaxed. "You may hold her, if you like, Betsy."

Betsy took the doll gingerly, showing just the amount of respect and care Mary would have hoped. "She is so pretty!"

"I am glad you think so." Mary could feel lines of tension easing around her eyelids.

"What is wrong with her shoulder?" Betsy poked her finger into the open seam and peered into it.

Mary's muscles tightened and her lips thinned. "That is the way my mother made her; that is all." She took the doll back, despite Betsy's squeal of protest. "You should not ask impertinent questions."

"I am sure Betsy is just becoming tired," Lady Lucy said, her soft voice reassuring them both. She rose and pulled Betsy into a hug. "I will have her lie down for a nap."

"We must be leaving, any way," Lizzy said. Their good-byes were crisp, as if everyone had had enough of each other. But when Mary stumbled down the steps and into the broad sunlight glazing the street, she could not get the vision of

Lady Lucy's teardrop out of her mind. *Her marriage is peaceful, yet—she is unhappy. Did I do right? Should I have said something?* Surely it could not be right to tarnish Lady Lucy's idea of her husband, nor to make silly remarks about lace.

But somehow Mr Darcy's half-criticism seemed to have more heart than all Mary's cautious kindness.

Eleven

"**A**nd though red sandstone may differ in colour from the other prominent sandstones, it is essentially the same, as you will no doubt see when you examine the striations in the samples."

It seemed unfair that such a melodious bass voice could ever drone, but somehow Mr Cole managed it in his next lecture for the London Ladies Information Society. The lecture was opened to the general public, and the assembly hall was filled with ladies and gentlemen who loved the sciences—or at least were prepared to feign an interest. Both the lovers and the pretenders struggled to show appreciation for the tedium they had been exposed to. A fresh March breeze had swept away London's haze, and the afternoon sunlight filtering in the windows warmed the assembly rooms enough for ladies to loosen pelisses and spencers. Mary's shoulder ached from Lydia's head resting against it, and her stomach growled in protest at missing most of breakfast due to Lydia's hurry to dress for the occasion.

This time, Mr Wickham had joined them. Whether he felt it a husbandly duty to discourage needless gossip or he had genuine concern for Lydia's affections, he had insisted on attending them, and Lydia took it in stride. She probably considered her flirting harmless enough that her husband's presence need not deter it. Certainly she had flashed enough knowing looks and simpers at Mr Cole during the early part of the lecture, before her eyes grew heavy and her head slumped on her sister's shoulder. Mr Wickham sat bolt upright beside Lydia, but he shuffled his feet and sighed periodically, and though Mary knew he was an intelligent man, Mr Cole's long-winded explanations in technical language did not appear to enlighten him much.

Mr Cole stood with an expectant expression at the podium, and Mary realised he had meant his last remark as a conclusion for the lecture. *What was it? Something about sandstone being red...* She did not like to draw attention to herself, but on seeing Mr Cole's polished smile begin to droop, she began clapping. Others soon joined, and in a moment the whole roomful of people expanded into stretches, yawns, stamping numb feet, and light chatter laced with relief that they could move about and enjoy themselves again.

Lydia, stirred into wakefulness with Mary's clapping, went directly to congratulate Mr Cole as he stepped down from the makeshift stage. Her hips shifted, gently stirring her flounces and giving her a coquettish air, and she listened to Mr Cole with a wide-eyed concentration that had been missing during his lecture. Mary glanced at Mr Wickham, who watched the proceedings with surprising indifference. *I do not think he really believes her heart is in any danger.* The revelation flooded Mary with relief. *He is just here for appearance's sake. He knows flirtation is just part of Lydia's nature.*

The reassurance did not satisfy her long, however. Mary could overhear the murmurs of the ladies around her, and most had something to say about "Mrs Wickham's scandalous behaviour" or "Mr Cole's shameless adoration." Miss Poppit even said in an aside to Lady Crestwood, "She was always like that, was she not? No man is safe with her." She threw a glance back at Mr Wickham's expression of indifference, "except perhaps her husband."

Mary forced herself to rise, and walked slowly towards Lydia and Mr Cole. Though Lizzy had pressed her to make more of an effort, now that the Darcys had departed London for their travels, Mary felt the loss of their backing with pain. Her resolutions to distract Mr Cole seemed weak and silly now. When they were alone, she had somehow been able to speak up, even if only out of irritation at the man's clumsy intellectualism. But now, with Lydia twitching her skirts and beaming at him, she felt far in the background, even when she stood at Lydia's side.

"And I told her that Mrs Holt was probably shamming—she is a great one for shamming—but she said that was not the case at all." Lydia's cheerful chatter bounced from topic to topic, but all of them were light and amusing, and the darkened expression of Mr Cole's face gradually cleared into a satisfied smile. Mary could not find the right moment to intervene; somehow her sister's talk was so fast, and Mary's reluctance to speak up so strong, that she never felt a break in the conversation wide enough to insert her own comment.

Perhaps he will notice my gown. She was wearing one of Lydia's choosing, and although her figure was too thin to do it justice, the pale yellow India muslin draped with a fashion-able air and made Mary's cheeks look more pink and her hair less like a mouse and more like golden-hued wheat. The amber cross dangling below her throat and the yellow nankeen half-boots peeking below her gown showed similar elegance. But if Mr Cole noticed, he said nothing about it.

Mary fidgeted and cast her gaze helplessly around the room, hoping for inspiration to compel her to speak. At the tables of punch, Miss Poppit received compliments from gentlemen and acknowledged their homage with a self-possession Mary envied. Miss Poppit looked cool and in control, swayed neither by praise nor criticism, serenely holding her own in the midst of competing belles and eager suitors. It looked like Lady Crestwood's protégée was the clear choice for the belle of the Season.

I ought to be more like her. But the sense of competition discour-aged her rather than inspiring her, and Mary drew back a little from Lydia's side. *I cannot, though. I will never be as elegant and beautiful as Miss Poppit.* Indeed, if it meant having so many people trying to talk to her at once, she did not even want to be in Miss Poppit's place.

From the corner of her eye, Mary spotted Mr Wickham sipping a cup of punch with a weary patience as he watched Lydia from afar. *At least Mr Wickham is making an effort. He dares not reproach Lydia too much, or she will rebel, and yet he dare not leave it all alone either.* A surge of energy passed through her, and she pushed herself a little in front of her sister, catching the end of her speech.

"But, of course, I have no inclination to read some dull good book to Mrs Holt, however ill she may be. I sent Mary to do it instead, although they had not been introduced. I do not think she liked it, but you would never hear her complain. Not these days, any way." Lydia smiled at her sister with an affection that seemed almost maternal.

"I believe I have heard her complain," Mr Cole said, his lips twitching with amusement.

"No, you must be mistaken. I tow her about here and there and make her do all manner of unpleasant things—well, unpleasant for her, anybody else would love them—and all she says is, 'Yes, Lydia.'" She laughed and tapped Mary with her fan. "Patient as an angel!"

"She sounds like my brother, Thomas." Mr Cole's eyes unfocused, as if he were seeing something the others could not. "He was angelically good like that. The staff our father could lean on, our mother's comfort. I always said not even a demon could hate him, because Thomas always did the right thing, and yet he never made anyone feel bad for doing less. With all my mischief, he could have snubbed me, but he did not."

"Were you that mischievous?" Mary asked, willing herself to speak up normally rather than in her usual soft tone.

"Oh, yes. I can remember one day when we were boys—I was seven, I think, and he only a few years older. I was pitching rocks at a dog."

"That is horrible!" Lydia said.

"Thomas thought so too, but he did not say that. I had been interested in the physics of the matter: how the arc of the stone differed with different speeds as the target moved, that sort of thing. I was not really thinking of the dog. Thomas simply reminded me, in a quiet, stern voice, that the dog was a living creature. He did not try to make me feel like I was awful. He said it was natural that I was curious, but that I should throw rocks at targets that were not alive." He shook his head. "Of course, being a little boy scientist at heart, I said I could not find out what I wanted to know without moving targets. So Thomas tied some old pamphlets and fans to a tree so they would swing in the wind, and we threw rocks at them. He made it a sort of brotherly project." Mr Cole sighed. "He made me feel like a good person who had got turned the wrong way round for a moment, not someone evil or rotten inside."

"That is a fine thing." Mary smiled at him, and when he returned it, warmth flooded her.

"So where is this angel now?" Lydia asked. "Helping your father on the estate, I suppose."

"No." Mr Cole's expression went blank. "He died of an illness last year. There is no one helping my father now." He turned from them, casting his gaze over the room. "Perhaps some of the other guests have questions about my lecture." The energy entering his voice sounded forced, as if he expected failure. "I should move about the room. Mrs Wickham, your husband looks as though he must be wishing for your company." The remark was clearly a dismissal, but Lydia took it with a social ease that Mary envied.

"Oh, poor Wickham. I shall liven him up a bit, do not worry, Mr Cole." Lydia strolled off to join Mr Wickham. Mary dogged Mr Cole's steps as he walked about the room. She feared no one had any particular questions about geology—at least, not the sort Mr Cole would approve of—and she hoped to remain near him when he discovered that. They made a circuit of the room, and although several guests expressed a polite satisfaction with the lecture, and a few offered irrelevant questions about gemstones, none appeared to appreciate Mr Cole's ideas with any depth.

"You have been my silent shadow all afternoon." Mr Cole finally addressed Mary as she hung back behind him.

She flushed. "I am sorry. Have I bothered you?" She remembered too late she was supposed to be flirtatious and witty, and bit her lip.

"No, you are no trouble." His gaze wandered over the assembly room, and his tone sounded absent.

"I know I ought to speak up more," Mary said, hoping the confession would draw him to her, but he still studied the guests. "I do try. It is just hard to think of something to say."

"You are saying something now."

"It is easier when there are only two people." She dug her toe into the floor. "I am sorry about your brother."

Now his eyes met hers, but his lips drew down with annoyance. "It was no one's fault. There is nothing to be sorry about." He must have realised his irritation was misplaced, for he continued in a gentler tone. "He was a great man. All the servants adored him. My parents relied on him. Everyone was looking forward to the day he would be the active squire of the estate. He would have been the perfect master, the perfect landholder, the perfect country gentleman." He hesitated. "The perfect son."

"And now it falls to you to be all that?"

Mr Cole coughed, looking away. "I could never match my brother's skill. Or character." His words became rapid. "Besides, I have a life here in London. I wish to become a great orator for science, and my theories will not only advance geology, but will also inspire the gentry with a passion for knowledge. I cannot leave all that to play country gentleman."

"I see." Mary did not know what else to say, and she drifted behind him as he began another circuit around the room. Miss Poppit still reigned over several young men, her thin smile approving them, while her heart appeared untouched. Lady Crestwood chatted with the Wickhams in a surprising degree of harmony. *She must be glad to see Lydia staying by her husband for once. And Lydia must be on her best behaviour, hoping to win some patronage for Mr Wickham.*

Mary's stomach gurgled with an embarrassing insistence and volume, and her cheeks heated when Mr Cole turned around.

"Are you hungry?" he said, leading her toward the plates of biscuits and pastries.

It was useless to deny it. "I did not eat much this morning. We have been very busy." He filled a plate for her, and Mary nibbled while trying to look ladylike and unconcerned with the needs of the flesh.

"That is a very pretty gown," Mr Cole said, examining her. Mary became all too conscious of her body, a sudden heat passing through her, along with the usual urge to be suddenly invisible. How she wished she had more of Lydia's plump curves! *But Lydia is not afraid to ask a footman to bring round the food she likes, nor too timid to ask for another helping if she is still hungry.* Mary could not break herself of the habit of careful restraint at meals. She had spent too many years declining dishes so she could look abstemious and pious, or watching her mother's face as she decried Lizzy's more robust appetite compared to Jane's. But somehow, Mr Cole's attention made those self-denials seem silly and unnecessary. She took a bigger bite of biscuit and quietly finished it.

"Thank you," she said with a stateliness that made her feel calm, despite the warmth rushing through her.

They stood in silence for a few minutes. Mr Cole's feet shifted and he pushed a stack of plates on the refreshment table back farther from the edge. Then he plucked at his waistcoat until exasperation overcame him. "Well? Have you anything more to say, Miss Bennet?"

"I am sorry. I was trying to think of something." Oddly enough, his irritation made her feel even calmer.

"And what is the difficulty?" His brows furrowed. "Anyone could think of twenty things to say in that amount of time."

"I am sorry." She placed her empty plate on the table. "It is just that I do not assume what I think of to say is interesting, so it takes a while."

"That is tweaking my nose, is it not? You are going back to our earlier debate—you mean that I assume what I say in my lectures will interest people."

"I did not say that."

"Well..." He threw back his shoulders, as if determining something. "Perhaps it is true, whether you said it today or not. I cannot deny people do not seem as fascinated as I hoped. If you are still willing to help me, Miss Bennet, I am willing to hear your ideas."

"Truly?" Her eyes shone.

"It is clear I need help from someone, and you seem sure you can aid me. I must admit your labels were a success. People spent twice the amount of time looking at my samples, and the ladies talked about *them* almost as much as their gowns this time." He gave her a rueful smile.

"And what about—the bargain?" At his blank look, she added, "About my sister?"

"Oh, that. Miss Bennet, you need not fear my attentions to your sister. I merely find her diverting." His head tilted, and Mary had the feeling he was looking her through and through. "By the by, I find you amusing too."

Mary did not know what to say to that. Her period of indecision prevented her from saying anything, for Lydia abandoned her post by Mr Wickham and swept up to them. "Heavens! I simply must have a drink. Alleviate your disciple's suffering, Mr Cole, and draw me a cup of punch." Her carefully tousled curls slid back from her temples as she accepted a cup and drank.

"If you are my disciple, Mrs Wickham, you are a very poor one," Mr Cole said, his smile broadening. "Do you remember anything from my lecture?"

"Of course! It was all about rocks. But I will tell you what I find *more* educational, my friend, and that is that you had my sister trailing you ever since you finished it. I have never seen her behave so! If she is a disciple, she is a very faithful one." Her dark eyes sparkled. "You had better be a good master to her, for she has not had any such since Sir William Lucas's sons grew up."

"They taught you geology, did they?" Mr Cole turned to Mary, who flushed with irritation at Lydia's vulgar wit.

Lydia answered for her. "No, but Harry Lucas taught her religious things. Pamphlets and sermons, that sort of thing. They are good friends."

Mary's back stiffened as memories creeped in, as if a slow poison was paralysing each muscle, one by one. "My sister is mistaken." Her throat threatened to close on her, but she forced her words through. "Perhaps we used to be friends, but he has not spoken to me in above a year."

"My, how dramatic you sound, Mouse! He has not spoken to anybody in that long—anybody we know, I mean." She leant in to Mr Cole and whispered, "He turned Methodist, and now his family will have nothing to do with him."

Mary averted her face, willing the tears standing in her eyes not to fall. Mr Cole must have seen it, for he took Lydia's arm and guided Lydia a few steps away to chat with her, giving Mary space to recover. *Poor Harry. It is all my fault. I should never have tried to interfere.* She turned to see Lydia hanging on Mr Cole and joking with him, and her feelings mixed further. *Am I doing the right thing? Perhaps I should let Lydia and Mr Wickham sort things out for themselves.* A few deep breaths restored some of her calm, and she stepped unseen towards the couple, only to pause at the sudden undertone Lydia used.

"You will meet me at the gallery on Thursday, then? It will be such fun!"

"I think you want to meet me just to tweak the noses of your friends." Mr Cole's voice was full of good humour.

"Oh, does that matter?" Only a true coquette could have given such an airy seductiveness to her tone. Lydia's long lashes fluttered. "You did not think you had won my heart, did you? Hearts are not so easily stolen, even by handsome young men." Her tone grew determined. "Besides, I am tired of everyone telling me what to do. Even the little mouse is always watching me."

"I am not sure the world really pays so much attention as you seem to think." Mr Cole's tone was bemused, as if he thought Lydia were exaggerating the importance of their friendship. "But of course I will see the portraits with you, if you wish."

Mary's stomach lurched. *An assignation? How can Lydia be so foolish?* Surely it was only a prank, with no serious intent of wrongdoing, but it would pollute the Wickhams' reputation further if Lydia was caught making a rendezvous. *Any other two people in the world could run into each other in a gallery and plead it was happenstance,* Mary thought. *But no one will believe it in this case, even if Lydia and Mr Cole call it coincidence. Everyone will know they were trying to spend time together, and nearly everyone will decide the reason why is illicit love. Oh, Lydia, how can you?*

Clearly Mary's efforts at gentle reproaches were counterproductive. She could reveal what she had overheard to Mr Wickham, but she did not see what more he could do without spurring Lydia into greater rebellion. She could try to persuade Lydia not to go, but that, too, seemed likely to prick her pride into revolt. Mary sank back into the background, struggling to find a solution. No one had noticed her movements forward or backward. *A mouse is made privy to everybody's secrets,* she thought sourly, *but at least no one realises it. What to do?*

She hated to interfere, but she could not think of any other course of action. She knew where and when they were planning to meet—and that made it possible to disrupt the rendezvous, one way or another. It might require a bold move, but as Mary watched Mr Cole respond with spellbound devotion to her sister's frolics, she felt resentment well up. She had been making progress with intriguing Mr

Cole, and Lydia had undone it all within minutes. He seemed to relish her company as much as ever. The sight of his adoration sent a strange pang through Mary, and the resentment grew. *For his sake and hers,* she thought, *perhaps I can risk a little boldness.*

Twelve

T he weather at the beginning of March had promised sweet, soft spring, but bitter winds and a snowy sky broke the vow the following week, dropping layer after layer of ice and snow on the rooftops and streets. The keening of the wind in the chimneys and between buildings was shrill enough to make Mary shiver with fear as well as cold; it sounded too much like some ghostly figure trying to tear down the walls and rend the people within. Though she had planned to visit the ailing Mrs Holt that day, the ice lining the window panes made Mary decide to remain at home beside the Wickhams' fireplace instead.

It is not as though I am fit for a visit any way. Her eyes blinked with weariness from lack of sleep; she had spent too much of the night trying (and failing) to devise a way to stop Lydia's rendezvous with Mr Cole. Feigning illness, breaking a carriage wheel, sending false news of a visitor—all her solutions seemed both dramatic and ineffectual. She wrapped herself in a shawl and pulled a chair close to the fire, determined to ruminate and doze.

"That is just right," Mr Wickham said, settling a screen near her. His trim figure bore a waistcoat in mint green—a favourite colour of Lydia's. Probably Lydia had had as much fun dressing her husband as she had Mary. "Stay here and tend your health."

"I am not ill, only a little tired." She could not help but brighten a little under his care. She still did not trust him in matters of money, but he did know how to make a lady feel important.

"Mrs Wickham will run you ragged if you let her," he said. The fire in the grate lit his classic features, and he lifted his hands and turned them back and forth in front of it to banish the chill from them. "She does keep things lively, though." The thought made him smile in appreciation.

"Yes..." Mary wondered if she ought to say something about Mr Cole. Mr Wickham might have poor morals, but he seemed to have good sense. Perhaps he could think of a way to stop the rendezvous without causing scandal. *Would telling be betraying Lydia?* She watched Mr Wickham hunch closer to the fire. His eyes were half-closed with the satisfaction of warming, and the lazy, pleased expression reminded her of a cat sunning peacefully. She hated the thought of disturbing him. *Probably everything will turn out all right. There is no need to trouble him.* A twist in her gut warned her she was only trying to convince herself, but the aversion to bringing up a distasteful subject was strong. She could remember Harry's sunny smile, his head tilting as he made his plea.

"You will not tell anyone where I have gone, will you?"

"No, of course not." She had been only too glad to promise.

*Harry had always been gentle with her, understanding her
quietness and ensuring she got what she needed despite it.*

*"My father would never understand these meetings. He sees
religion only one way."*

"I know. I will not tell."

But she had told. The memory drove a shudder through her,
and her brother-in-law adjusted the screen, thinking she was
shaking with cold. "Allow me, Miss Bennet. We are very
pleased you are here, you know," Mr Wickham said. "Your
sister Kitty and her husband are to come for a visit, too. Did
my wife tell you?"

"She said Lieutenant Stubbs received a minor wound and
was due for leave any way." Mary tugged the shawl tighter
around her. She could see the attraction of Mr Wickham,
despite his faults, but she could never see it in Lieutenant
Stubbs. Kitty's soldier had a prickly nature, eager to suspect
an affront, and in the army, he had earned a reputation for
duelling. Mary could not understand anyone wanting to be in
the army at all; it seemed the antithesis of the peace she
craved.

"Well, it shall be livelier still with them here." Mr Wickham's
eyes closed all the way as he basked in the fire's warmth for a
moment longer. He looked so relaxed and vulnerable that
Mary felt glad—if a little guilty—that she had not dredged up
problems to him. He spent a few more minutes warming
himself in companionable silence, and then shuffled back to
his study.

I dared not tell. People are not reasonable when they discover secrets. Sir William Lucas certainly had not been. Mary had known him to be a cheerful, courtly sort of person—almost a second father, given how much time the Bennets and Lucases spent together—but that amiable demeanour shifted violently the day she told Harry's secret. Mary had only been trying to reassure Sir William, but it had made no difference. Stretching her feet towards the fire, she tried to push the memory back down, but it flooded her nonetheless.

Sir William had been so worried, wondering where Harry was all day. He suspected Harry was out drinking, when really he was attending the meetings of those Methodists, the ones who ranted and raved and made Mary tremble at the outpouring of emotion as she passed by. She had thought if she broke it to Sir William, then he would be more likely to listen, and would go to Harry and plead with him to stop, appeal to his sense of family love and decency. And holding the secret made her uncomfortable, like she was lying to the Lucases.

That should have been a clue—what did it matter what my own comfort was? When you start thinking of yourself, you make trouble. Yet she spilled it all, thinking maybe it would make things right.

It was the worst decision she ever made.

> *Sir William's face grew redder and redder with Mary's revela-tion, while Lady Lucas's paled, as if the colour were being drained from her into her husband. Though Mary begged Sir William to wait, the man stormed out, too eager to confront his son to keep the matter private.*

"Do not leave me, Mary." Lady Lucas had clung to Mary's hand as her husband strode out, the older woman's fingers trembling as she sought comfort. Though her belly roiled, Mary stayed. She held Lady Lucas's hand and tried to recite a passage from the Old Testament, but her voice faltered on the descriptions of forgiveness, and she soon dropped into silence. They waited in misery together. Mary's hands were still within the grasp of Lady Lucas when she heard Sir William and Harry's voices coming up the drive. Their conflict became clear as they entered.

"You are betraying me, betraying God, betraying all of us!" Sir William yelled, and Mary shuddered as she looked at his livid face, all red blotches and purple smears.

"I never wanted to be a damn curate!" Harry yelled back. *"You pumped it into me and pushed me out into the world with it. Now it's twisted in a way you didn't expect. You can't take it back. If you have taught me to pay attention to God, now you must live with the consequences. I won't stand in a surplice and bow and smile. I'll tell people what I really think, and they'll listen, and cringe, and then change for the better. Change!"* He threw his fist into the air, and Mary shrank back unthinkingly. She knew he would never hit his father—at least, she thought she knew. Who could tell?

"After all I've done, after all your mother has done—"

"I never asked you to do any of it! I just wanted to be left alone. Nobody in this town leaves anything alone." Harry threw a glance at Mary, and she ducked her head, unable to

justify herself. She had been clearly wrong to have mentioned anything. She was only trying to help—but helping meant insisting you knew best, while she never knew anything at all.

"Do not be angry with Miss Mary. She knew her duty—"

"You bullied it from her, probably."

"She volunteered where you were. She knew what a risk to your soul it was."

Mary slipped her hands from Lady Lucas's grasp and covered her ears like a child. "Stop, Sir William! It wasn't like that at all."

They continued to argue, not listening to anything Mary said, probably forgetting she was there entirely. The raging sounds grew in volume, then in tempo. The unsafe feeling in her gut churned and churned. Thoughts circled mercilessly in her head: What's going to happen? Oh, why did I ever speak up? This is all my fault. If I had stayed quiet, Harry might have reconsidered. He would have re-joined the faith. Or Sir William would have loosened up, let Harry do his own thing for a while. I have forced them together at exactly the wrong moment.

"I hate you!"

Mary did not know which one had said it to the other, but it did not matter. Tears blurring her vision, she dashed outside, still covering her ears, though it did little to block out the shouts. When she hurtled into Longbourn, she nearly knocked over Kitty. Ignoring her, Mary threw herself onto the sofa and shook, weeping helplessly.

"Why, Mary, what is wrong?" Kitty gave her an awkward pat. Though Mary could not see her face through her tears, she could hear the puzzlement in her voice. "Is it the row at the Lucases? I could hear it from the garden. They are awfully angry, aren't they?"

"It's all my fault," Mary whispered between sobs.

"No, it's not. They're shouting about Harry being a Methodist." Kitty smoothed her hair, almost maternal for all her sixteen years. Mary must have appeared quite a wreck to inspire any motherliness for Kitty's least favourite sister. "Sir William's not angry with you, Mary."

"I know."

"Neither is Harry, I'm sure."

Mary was less sure, but it did not matter. How could Kitty not sense the conflict rushing over the house like a vast wave? Whether they were angry with Mary or not, they were angry. They were fighting. No one was safe.

I am so sorry, Harry. I should never have interfered. I should have stayed quiet.

She pleaded with him mentally as she dared not aloud and

continued the silent litany while he packed up his belongings and gave silent hugs good-bye to his brothers and sisters.

I am so sorry, Harry. I should have left things alone.

Mary's eyes were shut tight as she relived the memory and endured the cascade of emotion that went with it. She forced them open and abandoned her cosy spot at the fireside. Perhaps there was some mending to do or something to tidy —anything to distract herself. She padded upstairs to her room, but everything was in place as it always was, and she could find nothing that needed mending. The Wickhams' household ran much more smoothly than Longbourn did.

"Shall I have a fire lit in here for you, miss?" Hannah's head ducked in the doorway. The maid's form had thickened, and her young face had sprouted additional creases of worry. She held Prince's basket, and with Prince's bulk swaddled in the blankets, it was heavy. The way she held it signalled to Mary something more than weight, though. She had noticed Hannah's figure changing slightly, but a greater clue had been the woman's motions—oddly off-balance, sometimes jerky or hesitant. When Hannah put down the basket, the maid bent over in an unnatural angle, and Mary hurried to help her.

"You should not carry such heavy things in your condition," she said without thinking, taking the basket handle. Prince whined within the mass of blankets.

"My...condition?" The colour drained away from Hannah's face, and her hands began twisting together. "I...that is, miss..."

Mary dragged the basket inside, loath as she was to welcome Prince into her room, and beckoned Hannah in before shutting the door. Her cheeks heated when she tried to speak, but she managed it. "You are going to have a baby, are you not, Hannah?"

"Oh, miss!" Tears welled up in Hannah's eyes and slid down her face. "I'm a good girl, miss, I am!" She hitched a sob.

Prince gave a sharp bark, and Mary shoved the heavy basket farther from them with her foot. "I am sure you are a good girl, Hannah, but there is going to be a baby, is there not?"

Hannah sobbed louder, but she nodded through her tears.

"And the—young man?"

Hannah shook her head with vigour, though something about her insistence struck Mary as insincere. "He's long gone, miss. I don't wish to speak ill of him. We were just...I was only..." Her shoulders lifted with another sob, and Mary patted the girl's hand. "He cannot help me."

Mary sighed. Finding the father and forcing some sort of help from him sounded impossible. *What if he is not so long gone?* There were a dozen rumours in Meryton of tradesmen's daughters being meddled with by Mr Wickham. *That is unfair. I have no reason to suspect him in this case.* But Mary still felt uneasy and disturbed. For a moment, she wished she had pretended not to notice Hannah's burgeoning motherhood. *But then she might be dealing with it all alone.*

"Have you told anyone?"

"No. I didn't think anyone could tell yet. But if you guessed—"

Mary scanned the woman's body, gauging the size of the thickness in her middle. "I do not talk much, and it gives me more leisure to look about me. I do not think anyone else will be able to tell for a while yet."

"I can bind myself tighter as I go along," Hannah said.

"That is not good for the baby."

"What else can I do?" A note of panic entered Hannah's voice. "If Mrs Forrest finds out, I'll lose my place; and no one would hire me—as I am. I must work here as long as I can, until I can save a little more, or find someone..." She did not seem very clear about a solution, and Mary could not blame her. She could think of none herself. "I know I can't hide it forever, but I need time. You won't tell anyone, will you, miss?" Hannah's trembling hands clutched at Mary's.

Mary squeezed back, but a sinking feeling enveloped her. Hannah's condition not only threatened the maid's livelihood, but also complicated matters for the Wickhams. The morality of the servants was thought to reflect the morality of the mistress. The *ton* would expect the Wickhams to repudiate any servant the moment she showed such...weakness. If others discovered the Wickhams had harboured a pregnant servant, however inadvertently, they would think it further evidence Lydia was a loose woman. *Why does this have to happen, just when I am trying to redeem Lydia's reputation?* She could report Hannah to the housekeeper, and the girl would be turned out of the house, left to wander the streets and unlikely to find a new employer—at least, no employer for respectable work. Or she could help Hannah stay, hiding the truth for as long as possible. If she kept it from Lydia's knowledge, at least the Wickhams could deny having any part of it, though Mary doubted anyone would believe them. *It would make too juicy a piece of gossip to say Mrs Wickham encouraged her maids in illicit love.*

Indecision wracked her, but after a moment, Mary's shoulders slumped in submission. *Am I doing this because it is right, or because I am too cowardly to speak up?*

"I will not tell, Hannah." Mary could almost feel the weight of the secret pulling her down, dragging her in some dark undertow, but the hope awakening in Hannah's eyes almost made it worth it.

Thirteen

Mary had hoped the drifts of snow would persist long enough to discourage Lydia from her rendezvous, but by Thursday, the weather had turned again, and the white barriers that had piled throughout London were melted into soggy mush too high for pattens but no hardship for a carriage. The snow did last long enough to give Mary much time for deep thought over her sister's situation. She realised that most of her more imaginative schemes were simply too unrealistic. Breaking a carriage wheel required either stealth and skill—or bribery of a servant who possessed such—and the latter posed other risks. Feigning illness might slow Lydia's exit, but Lydia had no flair for medicines or sickrooms, and very likely she would simply send for a doctor, express her sympathy, and then march off to her rendezvous—late, perhaps, but Lydia never minded lateness. She could insist that she go with Lydia to the gallery, despite all discouragement, but since Mary never insisted on anything, it would no doubt raise Lydia's suspicions—and then her hackles!

Ideally, she should not even know that I did anything to prevent the meeting. Then there would be no spur for rebellion. As Thursday approached and Mary had no clear solution, dread began to well up within her and drag down her thoughts. She wished she had Lizzy to confer with, but she was not sure which stage the Darcys were at in their journey, and there was not time for a letter to pass back and forth. Mary floundered to come up with anything practicable herself. *I could tell some lie to drive them apart. Maybe I could say Mr Cole had done something horrible, something bad enough Lydia would lose interest in him.* Given Lydia's careless acceptance of Mr Wickham's scandalous past, it would have to be something very dire to discourage her, and Mary could not make murder or mayhem believable of Mr Cole. *Or I could tell Mr Cole that Lydia is going to have a baby, and he was interfering at a time when husband and wife should be calm and close.* But Mary doubted her ability to lie successfully. It was one thing to keep a secret; that usually meant just not saying anything, which was Mary's natural inclination any way. But lying required a degree of composure that was beyond her.

In the end, she wound up committing to an uninspiring plan: go off to Mrs Holt's for the day, thereby lulling Lydia into a false sense of security, and then take a hack from there to the gallery by herself. An unmarried young lady ought not to go unchaperoned, but there was no way to persuade an invalid like Mrs Holt to go anywhere, and at least Mrs Holt's lazy indifference would keep her from questioning Mary's actions. If Mary got to Mr Cole early enough—likely, given Lydia's habitual lateness—she could try again to persuade him to leave Lydia alone. If she got there later, she could at least stick close to the couple and avert any gossip from declaring they were alone. Lydia would fume, but it was better than the alternative.

When Mary arrived at Mrs Holt's house, a warm breeze gusted down the slushy streets and tugged at her new bonnet, the one that matched her doll's. Mary had put it on that morning with an air that mingled reverence and determination. *Today, I need all the help I can get.* A favourite bonnet was not much of an ally, but tightening the ribbons gave Mary a sense of reassurance any way. After she plodded into the house, made the proper greetings, and finally opened the Holt Bible to read, Mary's nerves settled a little. The warm smile on Mrs Holt's face soothed her further.

The invalid had enmeshed herself in a pile of wrappings, determined to block out every draught, and her scrawny neck emerging from it gave her the air of a baby bird stretching for a meal in her nest. Despite her doctor's reassurances, Mrs Holt deemed herself too sick to speak in a natural tone, and breathily whispered more often than not. "My dear Miss Bennet. How good of you to come. I hope you can stay longer than you did last time."

"Yes, a few hours." Mary's breath came in and out more easily, and she felt more relaxed already. Mrs Holt was so gentle, and very little happened in her home during the day —it was a haven of peace, compared to Longbourn. Even the Wickhams' home often burst with guests or rang with Lydia's eager voice as she hastened from one activity to another. Mrs Holt pleased herself with books and tisanes until her barrister husband had time to gossip with her. Mr Holt took his wife's self-indulgent ideas of illness with good humour, and he chatted about the news of the day while patting his wife's hand before hurrying back to his offices.

I wish I could find that sort of happiness. The thought surprised Mary; she had been so focused on Hannah's troubles and the Wickhams that she had largely forgotten about her own future. But the affection the Holts had for each other touched her heart, and the life of peace felt doubly seductive after the push and pull of rescuing others. It would be nice to find a doting husband like Mr Holt, and to settle in some quiet place and amuse herself.

Mary read for an hour, Mrs Holt's birdlike head sometimes nodding into a doze, other times lifting with interest. Occasionally Mrs Holt stopped her to discuss a passage, and Mary felt it was almost like old times, she and Harry Lucas poring over a text and dissecting it. The old occupation cheered her, and she found herself slipping into more casual conversation as well, though Mrs Holt leaned heavily on topics of health.

"I suppose I have found a *few* foods that disagree with me," Mary said, after Mrs Holt delineated precisely which foods did or did not alter her condition. "But of course I eat them just the same." She felt comfortable enough with the invalid to admit more. "I do not like to bother the footmen to bring something different, or to offend my sister by asking her to have other dishes."

"And sacrifice your health?" Mrs Holt's eyes widened.

"I do not think it is as bad as all that."

Mrs Holt shook her head with just the sententious air Mary used to have. "You should speak to your sister and order the footmen about just as you please. If you do not ensure you obtain what you need for your own body, how will you ensure that you get enough for your other needs? Or anyone else's, for that matter."

I just do not need as much as other people, that is all. Mary had always felt a glow of pride at how little she could live on, how much less attention and resources she took up compared to her sisters. It felt like Mrs Holt was trying to take that away. Mrs Holt made Mary's polite unease at causing the trouble required to get more food sound like —cowardice.

Mrs Holt must have taken Mary's silence as permission to press. "It may be woman's lot to bear and forbear, as the preacher says, but we can bear and forbear nothing if we do not have the basic sustenance for health and life."

"I am not starving, Mrs Holt."

"But you are harming your own health, and for such foolish reasons!"

Mary had to admit she had been feeling the wear on her body more and more in London. At Longbourn, she ate little and slept little, but there were few active demands made on her. She mostly stayed in the house, mending and reading and keeping out of people's way. But here, she had been draining her energies with balls, formal visits, time with Lady Lucy, doing errands for Lydia, and trying to repair the Wickhams' marriage. *But that does not mean I have done anything wrong.* She still felt a stubborn, hard place inside her, like a fist that refused to relax. *Everyone wants me to be different than I am. Lizzy wants me to be clever enough to distract Mr Cole. Mrs Holt wants me to pamper my body. Lydia wants me to charm suitors and speak up.*

*And now I have to save my sister's marriage from shipwreck, and keep Hannah's secret...*In the mirror over Mrs Holt, Mary caught sight of her own reflection. The young woman in the mirror glared with defiance, and Mary felt shocked at the intensity of the rage within. But the shock did not decrease it.

"I am perfectly well," she told Mrs Holt in clipped tones. "I am sorry you feel I have not the grasp on my constitution that you have on yours. At any rate, I cannot discuss it any longer, because I am due elsewhere."

"Elsewhere? I thought Mrs Wickham was sending the carriage—"

"If it comes, you can send it back. I will find my own way home. I have an errand to do before I return to the Wickhams'." The heat of anger sustained Mary in gathering her things with an aplomb that dissuaded Mrs Holt from objecting. Mary perched her bonnet on her head and tied the ribbons, feeling strengthened by the silkiness going under her chin. "Thank you for a lovely day, Mrs Holt."

"Of—of course." Mrs Holt settled back with a limpness that showed her confusion. Before the woman could recover her wits enough to ask any questions, Mary strode out of the drawing room and out the front door, giving a nod to the footman who opened the door for her.

It was only when she was out in the street, awkwardly clinging to a pillar and waving half-heartedly for a hack, that the anger ebbed and the anxiety underneath it swelled to drown her.

THE RIDE TO THE ROYAL ACADEMY AT SOMERSET House went by all too quickly, and Mary felt almost dumped onto the sidewalk by the hackney coach. Her trembling fingers pressed coins into the driver's hand. A few months ago, she would have had no idea how much such a trip should have cost, nor how much to tip, and very likely would have been swindled dreadfully. *I suppose life in London does make one less naive.* The thought did nothing to reassure her; in fact, it soured her mood further, and she glanced up at the palatial entrance to the gallery with distrust. *Wait—what if this is not the right gallery?* She had assumed Lydia and Mr Cole had been speaking of the most popular one in London, but there were others. Panic leapt up her throat, and her breath wheezed. *No, I am second-guessing myself. At any rate, whether it is correct or not, I am here. I might as well look inside.*

The entryway teemed with people, and the air that had been brisk and fresh outdoors sweltered into a thick, musty odour of dust, oil, and sweat. Mary dodged between art lovers eager to squint at landscapes and squeezed against walls to avoid chattering ladies gesturing with excitement. There were only a few rooms that displayed portraits, but Mary did not know which one Mr Cole would lurk at. She chose one at random and hurried in.

"Why, Miss Bennet!" Miss Poppit caught sight of Mary, and before Mary could work out a plan the woman joined her. "I did not know you were fond of art. I suppose you came with your sister?"

"Lydia is not here." Mary wished she had more presence of mind; the words slipped out without thought. "I mean, she may be here…"

"You do not know?" Miss Poppit's eyes narrowed, and her sudden interest reminded Mary of a cat who had scented a mouse.

No wonder Lydia does not like her. Mary felt she had fallen into a trap, running into such a person at such a moment. She had to find Mr Cole quickly, before Lydia arrived. "I…cannot say." Feeling helpless, Mary lifted her hands and threw caution to the winds. "Miss Poppit, may I ask you a very great favour?"

"Of course you may ask." Her subtle wording warned she might not grant it.

"I am looking for Mr Cole. I must speak with him. Please do not mention to anyone—" Mary struggled to plan. Quick thinking was not one of her talents. "Please just do not say anything to anyone, about me, or Lydia, or Mr Cole. Nothing at all."

Miss Poppit licked her lips, and Mary could almost see the deliberation going on in the woman's mind: a delightful piece of gossip, or a show of solidarity for an acquaintance? Perhaps Mary's meekness worked in her favour, for Miss Poppit eventually gave a slow nod. "Very well. I will say nothing."

"Thank you." Mary lurched in the direction of the room adjacent, but Miss Poppit grabbed her arm.

"Do not go in that room. Mr Cole is not there, and Lady Crestwood *is*."

"Thank you again." Relieved at the narrow escape, Mary gave her a weak smile and hurried in another direction. Lady Crestwood would never have kept it secret. She thought she could probably count on Miss Poppit to delay her mentor in that room for a short time, and the gift of aid was very welcome. *Miss Poppit is not so bad as Lydia says.*

The next room held one group of gentlemen and ladies goggling at a portrait of a heavy, thick-browed judge who stared back at the viewer with a sternness that seemed to both titillate and disturb the patrons. "By Jove! Is that really old Harcourt?" one of the gentlemen said. "He looks cruel enough, but why is one lip such an odd colour?"

"Perhaps he has been eating blueberries," a lady said.

"I assure you, the colour is perfectly correct," another man said. "I painted it with a minute attention to detail."

"My dear husband, no one doubts that, but one cannot deny that his left hand only has four fingers." A fleshy woman, so heavily doused with powder that Mary could smell it across the room, patted the artist's arm. "Mr Cole, what do you think?"

The group parted enough to reveal Mr Cole, whose eyes met Mary's across the room. Mary's heart did a wayward flop, but she forced herself to approach.

"Any praise human lips could offer would be unworthy of it," Mr Cole said, giving an ironic bow to the artist.

The artist's face lit up. "Why, thank you! My love, do you hear what Mr Cole says? He said only angels could praise my work properly." His group began ambling toward the door, and the crinkles of amusement around Mr Cole's eyes revealed another meaning to his words. Mary stifled a giggle as she joined him.

Even at such a moment, he can make me laugh. The thought unsettled her, but she tried to push it from her mind. "Mr Cole, it does not seem worth your effort to devise hidden insults for poor painters."

"Oh, he is not poor by any means." His gaze swept the room, and Mary realised he must be thinking Lydia brought her.

"She is not here. Not yet, any way."

His gaze returned to Mary, and his brows drew up in perplexity. "No? But you are here."

"I took a hack."

He blinked, but soon smoothed his features. "By yourself?"

"I had to speak to you." All the way—all day long, really—she had dreaded this moment, the moment where she would have to face Mr Cole and yet again plead with him to have better sense. And yet, now that it was here and she was standing in front of his strong, broad shoulders and quirky grin, she felt almost happy. *Do not be cajoled by his charm, Mary. Keep to your business*, she chided herself. "This meeting is beyond foolish. Anyone who sees you together will assume it was planned."

"It *was* planned. But how did you come to know it?"

"I overheard you speaking of it." Mary brushed back the strands of hair from her temples. "Sir, you must comprehend the problem? If you are seen together here, it will feed the gossip tarnishing her name."

"Surely not."

"Indeed," Mary insisted, much against her nature. "There has already been talk—"

"I care nothing about that."

"But a woman's reputation is always more fragile than a man's. Lydia is married, but her youth at times promotes incautious behaviour."

His stance relaxed as he studied her, though she still knew not if her words had penetrated his understanding. "If anyone realises you came all this way in a hackney coach just to try to stop us, it will create much worse gossip."

"No one will know that unless you tell them," Mary replied. "And you will not do that I am sure."

"No, I shall not. However, am I just supposed to abandon my afternoon's plans on your whim?" He tilted his head and paused, and Mary braced herself for an argument. But to her shock, none came. "Very well. I shall go on home. Hercules will be overjoyed."

"You—you will?"

"You are a very interfering sister, Miss Bennet. I only hope it is the kind of interfering that does more good than harm."

Interfering? No one—no one—had ever called her interfering before. Preachy, perhaps, but not actively interfering. She was the mouse of Longbourn. What had Lydia—no, what had Mr Cole—made of her?

She knew Lydia might turn up at any moment. She knew Miss Poppit might not be able to keep Lady Crestwood away for long. She knew time was of the essence, and yet she could not help but detain the man a moment. His acquiescence had unsettled her. "Why are you so willing to help now, all of a sudden?"

He shrugged. "I told you that I wanted a distraction. However entertaining it would have been to chuckle with your sister in a corner, I think her sister rampaging across London to try and stop idle gossip is *at least* as amusing."

"Rampaging?"

He ignored her indignation. "You know, if Mrs Wickham guesses someone actively prevented our meeting, she will only be the more eager to accomplish it."

"You understand her well. She is contrary like that."

"You do *not* understand her. As one of the most fashionable ladies in London, she is under constant scrutiny. Whatever she does is exaggerated, amplified by the awe of the crowds. She tells a joke, and the world finds it far funnier than they ought. She makes an error of judgment, and the world condemns her as the greatest villain imaginable. She senses the injustice when it works against her, but not at other times. That is why she rebels."

"You are saying that all the attention corrupts her?" Mary clutched her reticule tighter, unsure whether to defend her sister or pity her. "But you relish all the attention you get, as the gentleman associated with her. You are not so careful of yourself."

"Frankly, I think I have better sense than Mrs Wickham."

"Yet you pursue glory in the form of your lectures, even though the whole endeavour seems to disgust you. Perhaps you are not so incorruptible as you think."

His lips pursed with annoyance, but he made a polite bow. "Perhaps not. Good-bye, Miss Bennet. Try to get home without causing too much scandal." The amused smile creeped back over his face as he watched her indignant reaction. "Fear not, I will come up with some excuse for Mrs Wickham." He strode off.

Perhaps he does not mean to keep his word. Though it was a risk, Mary followed him at a distance, hanging by the edges of the rooms, and paused at a window to watch him get into a hackney cab. The wheels scraped with the sudden motion of the carriage, and the cab hurtled down the street. Relief tingled down Mary's neck, relaxing her shoulders. Whatever his faults, apparently Mr Cole was a man of his word. He had repeatedly refused to make idle promises to stay away from Lydia, and he left today, just as he had said. As Mary hurried into a coach, she caught sight of Miss Poppit and Lady Crestwood strolling out of the gallery with languid elegance. Miss Poppit turned the noblewoman to admire the pillars as Mary's carriage rolled away.

Perhaps people are not so bad as they seem. She felt confused by the sudden aid of Miss Poppit and Mr Cole, as if she had charged forward to break through a gate, only to find it open and abandoned. The day's trials pressed down on her, sinking her body into the cushion of the carriage seat, and Mary sighed with exhaustion. *I wonder if Mr Wickham has any books on geology in his library.* If Mr Cole was indeed going to be more helpful, the least Mary could do was contribute to his lectures as best she could. But the weight of loss of sleep bore down on her, and she knew her mind would be too muddled to accomplish much today. *Tomorrow, then. I shall have to make more of an effort to sleep tonight. I wonder if the cook would warm some milk for me.* For once, the embarrassment of asking for something did not seem to bother her. She slumped against the wall of the carriage and watched Mr Cole's smile flicker in her mind's eye. *He is not so bad as he seems.*

Fourteen

"Now, Lieutenant Stubbs, you must sit and tell us all your dreadful war stories. Do make them thrilling! Put in some helpless foreign women that you rescued, and a brave subordinate dedicated to your safety—"

"As I am only a lieutenant, I cannot expect much in the way of devoted subordinates and protection," Kitty's husband said, his mouth twisting as if he had bitten down on a lemon. He had little patience for Lydia's frolics, and when the couple had arrived at the Wickhams' earlier that afternoon, he had responded with indifference to most of her teasing, compliments, and silly talk. He had seemed duly impressed with the magnificence of the house, however, and had appeared downright pleased with Mr Wickham, whose amiable but soldierly demeanour reassured him. While Kitty had embraced her sisters with enthusiasm, Lieutenant Stubbs had given Mary a perfunctory bow, a little awkward due to the wound in his arm, but otherwise had not much to do with her.

Mary felt relieved rather than miffed. She had never felt close to Lieutenant Stubbs, and presently she felt especially unsuited for the social demands of the day. The warm milk she had obtained from the cook last night had soothed her, and though worried thoughts had popped into her mind, Mary had focused on relaxing enough to drift off into a deep slumber. The morning had been refreshing as well: she had curled up with a geology book and only stopped reading to pen a few notes. But as the day went on, Mary found herself getting more and more nervous at the advent of her sister, worrying that Kitty's playfulness would encourage Lydia to be wilder still. When the Stubbses had arrived and they had all dined together, the sight of Lydia and Kitty at the table brought up a hundred memories of Longbourn dinners—the squabbles, the hurt feelings, and most of all, Mary's retreat from it all by making herself as little noticed as possible, careful not to speak nor eat much, and quoting something religious when she felt it important to speak. With the flood of memory, Mary found she could hardly touch her plate, and now her stomach grumbled at the negligence. No one had said anything unpleasant, but the air felt stifling and full of suspended doom. It did not help matters that they were in Lydia's accursed drawing room, the one with aging yellow curtains and stolid, ill-carved furniture. It had been a point of contention so long in the household that Mary felt it an unlucky omen that they had wound up there for their after-dinner tea.

"Surely you can tell us some sort of story or other," Lydia said, brushing her curls back with an impatience that showed she was near to losing her temper. Mary was not surprised to see it; Lydia had been on her best behaviour all day, full of pretty tricks and a warmth that would have engaged most people. No doubt she was tiring quickly.

Nothing dampened Lydia's spirits more than having her charm go unappreciated.

The lieutenant certainly did not appreciate it. Though in his presence, Kitty showed a salutary shift to sense and calm, Lydia remained in their childish habits of gambols and frivolity. Kitty and Lydia still shared their tall, pleasingly-curvaceous figures and dark hair, but either marriage or her constant perusal of war news had altered Kitty's character to some degree, making her more serious, though not as sullen and prickly as her husband. Both husband and wife were handsome, Kitty's lips coral-bright and her hair swept up in simple elegance, Lieutenant Stubbs with heavy eyebrows, a strong chin, and a moody Byronic beauty. The soldier's composed, yet haughty smile both created the sense of distance and attracted one to collapse it.

At least, if one were not his sister-in-law. Mary could acknowledge the man's beauty and military prowess, but neither appealed to her. She would much rather have Harry Lucas in the family, with all his ugliness and gentleness, than Lieutenant Stubbs. *But I will probably never see Harry again.* She turned her gaze to Lieutenant Stubbs again, resigned to try to love him.

"Perhaps there is a story I can tell," Lieutenant Stubbs said. His brows narrowed as if he were willing himself to charge up a hill at the enemy, and Mary realised Kitty's husband was indeed making an effort to make himself agreeable to them all. "There was a day when my captain…"

The story was not long, but it included enough blood and death to make Lydia's eyes widen and to make Mary hunch up in her seat. Mr Wickham coughed in a way that suggested he thought the subject inappropriate for a drawing room, but he listened politely nonetheless. Lieutenant Stubbs must have felt the failure of his story, for when he completed it, he folded his arms and lifted his chin, and made only curt replies to questions after that.

Lydia, too, made an effort. Finding that her usual chatter had failed to produce the usual success, she sat in prim stateliness and made the kind of dull, proper conversation she must have supposed palatable to a man of Lieutenant Stubbs's nature. She played the part of obedient, submissive wife, echoing Mr Wickham's statements and attending to his comforts rather than summoning him to carry her tea or to hail a maid for a forgotten object as she commonly did. Mr Wickham yawned and drooped at his wife's change, and Mary almost giggled to see how unsatisfying the 'proper wife' was for both of them. *I suppose Mr Wickham really does like Lydia's sauciness.* Lieutenant Stubbs viewed the transformation with a pleased but suspicious expression.

But it was not until the next day that the source of his suspicion was made known. With Kitty trailing behind him nervously, he entered the drawing room where Mary and Lydia sat, every inch the man of purpose, and requested a conference. Lydia snorted and pronounced him droll but agreed to hear him.

"You seem to have grown comfortable in your marriage, Mrs Wickham. I am glad to see you are not so restless as Kitty feared you might be." There was something repellent in the self-important manner of his congratulation, and Mary winced, remembering her own errors of that kind.

Lydia's eyes narrowed. "Mr Wickham and I are quite content."

"I must confess, I had heard some reports of an alarming nature..." Lieutenant Stubbs's dark brows drew down. "Appalling things, things I really could not leave alone, as your brother-in-law. I am relieved to find them untrue."

To this, Lydia only stared, the expression on her face reminding Mary of the time that one of the neighbourhood boys had refused to let her win at lottery tickets. It was a mixture of confusion, mortification, and pique, and it did not sit well on her.

When she refused to comment, the lieutenant added, "The rumours involved a gentleman—if I can call him that—by the name of Mr Cole. I suppose you do not actually know any such person?"

Seeing Lydia's eyes light with scorn, and sensing a scathing retort or fit might ensue, Mary hurried to intervene. Lieutenant Stubbs seemed to startle, and Mary wondered if he had not realised she was even in the room. "We both know Mr Cole," she said, hoping to provide the truth, and yet downplay it. "He is a geologist, and sometimes we attend his lectures—along with Mr Wickham, of course."

It was not strictly true—Wickham had only attended them the one time—but the last thing she wanted was an argument. But perhaps Lieutenant Stubbs could be an ally—he could help persuade Lydia and Mr Cole to leave one another alone. The thought quickly died. Lydia would never stand for Lieutenant Stubbs's interference. He would only make things worse.

Lydia's face heightened with colour, and she spoke warmly. "He is a very dear friend, perhaps the dearest I have, aside from my beloved husband."

Kitty's mouth dropped open, and she gasped loudly. "Then it is true! You do go gadding about and flirting with him, meeting with him clandestinely—"

"I have never!" Thanks to Mary, the latter was true, at least. "He is my friend, and what people call flirting—why, that is just fun. Mr Wickham knows it."

Lieutenant Stubbs said, leaning forward, "Mrs Wickham, your name has been coupled with Mr Cole's in a way that demands correction. If you will not alter your reckless behaviour, the rest of the family will have to suffer your loss of respectability with you. I cannot imagine why the other gentlemen of your family have not already corrected you." His mouth drew down into a real grief. "Do not stir needless trouble, Mrs Wickham. No friendship is worth the loss of your good name."

"My good name is in no danger at all. The only people who threaten it are busybodies with no sense."

"Those busybodies can ruin you, whether they have sense or not."

Although Mary agreed, she wished the lieutenant had not taken such a bullying tone. *But then, my pleading did not do much either.*

"Please, Lydia!" Kitty folded her hands, and for a moment she looked almost prim. "We are not children anymore. There are rules that govern society, and you must learn to follow them." Though she only glanced at her husband, her pride in his regal demeanour was clear. "Sam only wishes to help. He is part of the family now, and he knows about such things."

"Mr Bingley and Mr Darcy do not think I am doing anything wrong," Lydia retorted petulantly.

Now Mary had to speak up, though she fumbled over her words. "Mr Darcy has expressed his concern already, Lydia, and I know Mr Bingley would as well, were he not so concerned for Jane's confinement at present."

Lydia shifted tactics as easily as a child. "'Tis nobody's business but my own!" She curled her lip with enough hauteur to match her brother-in-law's.

"If your good name is ruined, then Miss Bennet's chance of marriage is harmed. Your other sisters would be forced to put you aside to save their own honour." The Byronic handsomeness seemed to deepen as his voice recited the aspects of potential doom. "Your parents' hearts would break at such a scandal. All of us would be shut out from good society. These are the consequences of your folly. Do you still say it is none of my business?"

"I do!"

"My dear—" Mr Wickham appeared in the doorway, his hair ruffled as if he had been running his hands through it in perplexity. "My dear, I have unfortunate news. Will you come with me to my study?"

"Sir." Lieutenant Stubbs stood. "I fear we have been, already, speaking of most unfortunate matters which also demand your attention."

"I thank you, good sir, but I must beg my wife to accompany me—"

"Oh, just say it, Wicky," Lydia interrupted irritably. "This man thinks he can solve any problem with his high-handedness, I am sure whatever it is can be dealt with summarily by him."

Wickham glanced back and forth between his wife and his brother-in-law. "I am not sure—"

"Mr Wickham, we are family, are we not?" The lieutenant said. "It would be a great honour to me to be of service to you in advising you in any way I know how."

"Very well." Wickham licked his lips then plunged right in. "Markham and Mrs Forrest inform me that there is a house-maid who is...with child. I fear we must have her removed at once."

"With child?" Lydia looked at him in bewilderment. Mary found herself scrutinising Mr Wickham's face, searching for any sign of guilt in Hannah's predicament. She could find nothing, but then, the man was an accomplished liar.

"Her name is Hannah Cupp, apparently." Mr Wickham's cheeks showed no sign of flush, no indication he knew Hannah in any personal way, but Mary still distrusted him. "I told Mrs Forrest she must be displaced, of course, though perhaps we can give her a few days to—"

"One of your maids has ruined herself, and you want to let her stay in your house?" Lieutenant Stubbs pounded on the back of a nearby chair. "This is exactly the sort of fodder the gossipmongers are hungering for! Do you not see? Everyone will take this as evidence that Mrs Wickham is a fallen woman herself. You must show you harbour no weakness for such things and turn her out immediately."

Mary dared to speak up. "It would be hard for Hannah to find employment in her condition, and she has no family to help her."

Lieutenant Stubbs rounded on her. "What do you know about it, Miss Bennet? How do you know she has no family to help?"

She flushed. "I have spoken to her…a little." Her embarrassment revealed the rest.

"You *knew!*" Kitty sounded as outraged as her husband. "How long did you know this scandal and say nothing?"

Even Mr Wickham looked disappointed in her. "It is a serious matter, Miss Bennet."

Mary swallowed hard, simultaneously wishing to cry and yell at them. Had they forgotten their own elopement? And that

Kitty had known and hidden the truth? How quickly two years had turned their own youthful folly into nothing!

She had hoped to keep Hannah's secret for weeks longer, but so it was. With a little lift of her chin, she said, "She is in great difficulty, Mr Wickham. I was afraid she might be thrown into the street." Resentment entered her tone. "Clearly that is what Lieutenant Stubbs wishes, any way."

Lieutenant Stubbs's shoulders straightened and pulled against his military uniform. "You must know I do not wish anyone harm. But she cannot remain here, and she cannot be supported by the Wickhams—that would lend the same immoral appearance, only slightly mitigated. No one likes to send her away, but this girl has brought this on herself."

"At least give her a few weeks to try and find somewhere to go. If Mrs Forrest and Markham are discreet, no one need know yet." Mary turned away from Lieutenant Stubbs and appealed to Mr Wickham instead. "It would be cruel to send her away tonight. I promise I will find a place for her to go, if you only grant us time."

Mr Wickham fidgeted with his waistcoat, thumbing the buttons until he grew calm. "I will give you three weeks, Mary. Until then, Hannah can stay. I daresay she can be given lighter duties upstairs for that time."

"Three weeks! You cannot expect servants to keep a secret like that so long." Lieutenant Stubbs paced back and forth, scuffing the carpet with his boots. "It will ruin you all." His wife made noises of agreement.

"We cannot be cruel, Lieutenant Stubbs," Lydia said.

He levelled a glare at her. "God help you if your maid's laxness is due in any part to your example."

Lydia gasped at his effrontery. "Now see here, Stubbs," Wickham began.

Lieutenant Stubbs shook his head. "I do not think you guilty in the worst sense, Mrs Wickham, but you are guilty of making light of a woman's honour. We have been speaking of your wife's friendship with Mr Cole, Mr Wickham."

"Wicky, you know it is all nothing," Lydia said, a wheedling tone in her voice.

"It must end now," the lieutenant declared. "If you refuse to restrain yourself with this Mr Cole, I will be forced to defend your honour and call him out." He rubbed at the wound in his arm in an absent manner. "Whether he is a scoundrel or a fool, I have no wish to spill his blood. Do as I say, Mrs Wickham." He strode out of the room, his footsteps thumping over the carpet of the drawing room and then echoing as he ascended the stairs beyond.

"He does not trust my judgment at *all*," Lydia said, but she waited until Lieutenant Stubbs was well out of hearing.

"Your brother makes some good points." The stiffness of Mr Wickham's tone chastised her. "I could wish you were more discreet, my dear." He then turned to Mary. "I hope you can indeed find a place for Hannah, Miss Bennet. I regret that I cannot simply pay for her to live somewhere else, but your brother is right. People would misinterpret the action as condoning her loss of virtue—or worse, as an expression of guilt for it."

Of course, Mary had wondered if... but no, there was no sense casting stones when efforts of a charitable nature would be better received. "I understand." Mary tried to tally up how much money she had herself, but the distress of the moment disordered her thinking. *I do not think it would last her long, whatever the total is. And perhaps if the money came from me, it would carry the same false impression.* "I will help her, somehow." Perhaps Lady Lucy would have some ideas. If Mary invited her for a visit, they would have a chance to discuss it—and better yet, there would be a stranger in the house to defuse the family tension. Lieutenant Stubbs would hardly yell in front of Lady Lucy.

Mary's head dropped, feeling the weight of her worries. She could spy a series of loose threads where Lieutenant Stubbs's boots had caught the carpet in his pacing, and they curled over in a dejection she sympathised with. "Lydia, I think I hate your drawing room too."

Fifteen

It was two days before Lady Lucy could come and stay with Mary for the day, and Lieutenant Stubbs passed his time at the Wickhams' in silent condemnation of his sister-in-law. Mary had broached the subject of Mr Cole with him only once, and that to invite him to attend her next week when she was to assist him in planning his lectures.

"You are still going to see him?" The incredulity in his voice made Mary hesitate, but she pressed on.

"Breaking off interaction with him too sharply would cause more gossip," she said. "We must let things die down slowly—if anything, we ought to let them think it was all for me that Lydia spent time with him. Besides, I promised I would help him."

"I do not see why you would promise anything to such a man."

"He did me a favour about Lydia." She hoped the idea that Mr Cole was a reasonable man might percolate through Lieutenant Stubbs's mind.

He considered. "I give you leave to go, Mary. I am busy on

Wednesdays myself, but I will trust you to manage the matter. But keep things distant and polite."

She could not like his assumption of authority over her, but Mary was too desirous of avoiding an argument with him to protest. Still, the idea of behaving with indifference to Mr Cole felt wrong and strangely disappointing. Though the man's flirtation infuriated her, she could not help wanting to see more of him.

It is only that I have become interested in the subject of geology, she told herself. The books she had borrowed from Mr Wickham's dusty shelves and the library had been surprisingly engrossing. Somehow the idea of ancient landforms, pushed by pressures and pummelled by sea, rain, and wind, satisfied a need in her. The rocks remained stoic, despite all the slow weathering of years, largely untouched despite centuries of history. She found herself oddly envious of them. *What are men to rocks and mountains, after all?*

While waiting for Lady Lucy's visit, Mary passed the time in consoling Hannah, who between bouts of weeping informed Mary that Mrs Forrest had guessed the truth with an eye as observant as Mary's. Mary wrote to her parents and the Bingleys for assistance, but neither group was of much help. "These things happen," Mama had written, bestowing compassion but nothing practical. Jane's letter went unanswered, perhaps set aside unread in the hubbub of the approaching birth. If the Darcys had not been travelling, Mary would have relied on them, but she did not know where to address a letter, and the weeks of waiting for a letter to be forwarded about from Pemberley were weeks too long to help Hannah materially.

Mary had best hoped for Lady Lucy's intervention, and when the day of her visit arrived, Mary tried to make things as comfortable as possible for her guest. March had swelled far enough into spring to furnish a warm breeze, and Mary opened the window of her bedroom and placed a chair near it so that Lady Lucy could have lots of light for her embroidery. She positioned a shawl nearby, in case the pleasant breeze turned to a nasty draught, and she attired her doll in her best clothes. When she greeted Lady Lucy downstairs and brought her up for a companionable chat, Lady Lucy exclaimed over the doll's gown.

"So pretty! Mama says white gowns are the most genteel, and I think she is right." She giggled. "Even for dolls."

Mary smiled. "I have a bracelet now that is large enough to serve as a necklace for her. I will show you." She rummaged through the jewellery from her box, strewing it over the dressing table. "Perhaps Lydia borrowed it. It may be in her bedroom."

"Where is Mrs Wickham?"

"Oh, she went to some sort of charity function. She will be back later." Lydia had been uncommonly well-behaved since Lieutenant Stubbs's arrival; Mary could not tell if it was an attack of conscience or fear of her brother-in-law's temper that motivated her. It could not be fear of Kitty's disapproval; though Kitty sided vehemently with her husband, Lydia only scoffed at her. After several mornings of listless lying on sofas and sporadic attempts to read, Lydia had finally gone out for a day.

Mary led the way into her sister's dressing room, where silken gowns lay spread out or hung from hooks, and a veritable treasure of jewellery was heaped on tables or in boxes fresh from the jeweller. It took a few minutes for Mary to sort through combs, necklaces, rings, and bracelets to find what she wanted, but at last she retrieved the thin gold bracelet she sought. "Here it is! You will admire my doll so much when you see this, Lady Lucy."

But Lady Lucy's attention had been drawn elsewhere. "Oh! It is Prince!" Lady Lucy's exclamation of reverence was better suited to a real prince, but she swept the pug in her arms with a delight that Mary could not help but admire. Prince always snapped at Mary, and barely tolerated Lydia, but he nestled in Lady Lucy's arms as if he honoured her. "How fat you are, Prince!"

"He is spoiled, I think," Mary said.

"I cannot blame Mrs Wickham for that. Such a sweet thing!" She carried him into Mary's bedroom, and when he grew restless in her hug, she swirled a blanket into a comfortable shape and deposited him inside, and he promptly began snoring. Mary ornamented the doll with the bracelet and showed her friend.

"You can wear it out, and she shall wear it in," Lady Lucy said, tracing the gold curve with her finger. For once, Mary did not mind someone touching her doll. Lady Lucy used the same decorous gesture she would herself, as if the doll were alive and worthy of respect. Lady Lucy's smile encouraged Mary to bring up the subject of Hannah. She told Hannah's story as briefly as possible, emphasising the girl's lack of means and family.

"I know that you love children," Mary said. "I thought perhaps Hannah could come and work for you. Lydia and I could give you the money for her wages—I know *you* would keep the secret where others would not, so no one would think the Wickhams are supporting her."

But the congruity Mary had seen with regard to her doll was not to be seen in the matter of Hannah. "It does not seem... practical." Lady Lucy's mouth had cinched up, as if she had tasted a persimmon. "I do not think I want any maid like that."

"But when you know that she will be on the street, alone, otherwise?"

"I am very sorry for her, but I do not see what I can do. My husband would wonder where I got the money for a maid. Would you wish me to tell him?"

Mary had not thought about that. "I suppose you could not hide it, nor her situation."

"Indeed not. She would be a corruptive influence in our marriage." Lady Lucy's voice was full of indignation, but Mary misread it.

"I see. You think that because he has a—fondness—for Lady Sarah Randall and her sort, that a maid who had been indulgent to a man before might..."

Lady Lucy fired up. "Certainly not! Captain Roarke would never mix with a woman of that class." She took a deep breath, as if trying to calm herself. "He has a weakness for ladies, I admit. But you do not know his pride." Her voice became more confident. "He has quite a proper sense of what is due his birth. I am not afraid of any *maid* diverting his affections from me."

Mary was nonplussed, thinking any sort of adultery no bright proof of the captain's honour, but she did not argue. "I am sorry."

"You should be." Lady Lucy picked up Mary's doll, cradling it in her arms. As Mary watched, she saw indignation fade, to be replaced by sorrow before her friend continued to speak.

"Of course, it would be lovely to have a baby around, even if it were not my own… You do not know how lonely it gets, being home all day while the captain is away. He is very good to me, in his way, but it is not enough."

She began to cry, and not in the picturesque way a heroine might. These were sick, swollen, drooping, weepy tears, not the gentle ones one might see in a play nor the hot, fresh, vigorous tears one might see in a strong young woman. They were tears like a crumbling defence; a show of weakness that made the spark of compassion hesitate. Mary shifted her feet, unsure whether she ought to acknowledge the grief or pretend not to notice it.

When the tears turned into ragged sobs, Mary finally pulled out a handkerchief and offered it to the noblewoman. Lady Lucy buried her face in it. Mary wanted to tell her that it was not her fault, that the captain was to blame for all of it—their straitened circumstances, their childlessness, and his own faithlessness—but she feared to touch the sore pride of her friend. *I told myself remaining silent about these things respected their peace.* Mary averted her gaze from the woman. *Now I think I am just a coward.* She could not push through the fear, however unjustified it felt. *What can I possibly say?*

In the end, she merely patted her friend's back and murmured, "I am sorry." Lady Lucy wiped her tears and pressed the handkerchief back into Mary's hands. "Would you like to go home?" Mary asked, uncertain how to please her.

"Oh, no. It is so dull there." Lady Lucy sniffled. "Let us go to my parents' home. It is their visiting day, and I am seldom able to see them."

"Of course."

They moved towards the door, but Lady Lucy hesitated. "Might we bring Prince? He must get very dull here. And my mother has pugs, you know. He could visit them."

Mary viewed the snoring pug with a dubious expression. "I suppose, if you look after him. He does not care for me."

Lady Lucy, her red-rimmed eyes looking more cheerful, scooped up the dog and carried him while Mary sought out Addleby. The ladies' maid received the news of Prince's day trip with a smile that mingled glee and relief. "I shall try to bear his absence, miss." Dry humour tinged her voice as she turned to the noblewoman. "Do not let him run riot with your mother's gowns, Lady Lucy. It is all he lives for here."

Downstairs, Mary ordered the carriage while Lady Lucy held the dog. Lieutenant Stubbs met them at the door, and when he heard their destination, surprisingly, he volunteered to attend them. "Kitty and I could do with an outing," he said, riffling his thick, dark hair.

Mary did not welcome their presence, but she had no reason to deny it, and they all piled into the carriage. Kitty was feeling petulant after a quarrel with Lydia, so she sat tight-lipped in the corner. None of the other three were great talkers to begin with, and aside from a polite question from Lieutenant Stubbs and an inane answer from Lady Lucy, the ride to Lady Crestwood's was conducted in silence.

The house of the Crestwoods was on the same lane as the Wickhams', and it featured a similar white stone facade and elegant entryway. Unlike their home, this one boasted a full ballroom in the back and several more bedrooms. Lady Crestwood gave them a tour, accompanied by her protégée, Miss Poppit, who was staying with the Crestwoods this week. Lady Crestwood took Miss Poppit's adoration as a matter of course, but laid herself out to impress the other visitors with her home. "You have never seen it, Miss Bennet, Lieutenant Stubbs." Her eyes dropped for a moment. "And Lucy, dear, you have been so long from us, you may have forgotten where things are!" Lady Crestwood's laugh did not hold the same power and forcefulness as usual. It sounded almost wistful.

"It is truly an enviable home," Miss Poppit said as she accompanied them, "not only for the rarity of its decor, but for the friendly quality Lady Crestwood has given it." Her eyes crinkled with a light of affection, even as her tone remained fluid and polite. Mary puzzled over the woman's expression. Sometimes she felt sure Miss Poppit was an ambitious fortune hunter, anxious to acquire rank and whatever else she could get. At other times, the gentlewoman appeared almost...sentimental.

"I have never seen such an estimable place." Lieutenant Stubbs had doffed his cockaded hat when he had entered, but his every movement declared him a soldier. His lean, straight shoulders bore his epaulettes well, and his stride had the confidence of a man who had faced the horrors of a battlefield. But his voice held a tone Mary had seldom heard from him: deference. *That must be how he sounds to a commanding officer.* It made sense that he might respond that way to Lady Crestwood—nearly everyone found themselves an obedient subaltern to *her* commands.

"I am very lucky to be here." Sincerity rang in Miss Poppit's voice, and Mary wondered where Miss Poppit *would* be without her patron. Perhaps Miss Poppit's own home was not so pleasant. "Will you not tell me about some of your war experiences, Lieutenant?"

"I have found they are too grim for ladies, Miss Poppit." Lieutenant Stubbs's smile was wry, and it suited the dark, moody handsomeness of his face well.

Miss Poppit looked intrigued. "You may find me of stouter heart than most."

Kitty's vigorous nod seconded her. "My sisters cannot bear it, Miss Poppit, but some of us are not so squeamish, are we?"

She threw a look of superiority at Mary, who moved closer to Lady Lucy as a result. *Thank goodness I have a real friend now and need not rely on the approval of my sisters all the time.*

As they chatted, Lady Lucy spilled forth a voluble stream of talk to her mother, and Mary followed behind them all in her customary silence. She considered asking Lady Crestwood for help with Hannah, but she doubted the noblewoman would know of anything more to do than the London charity Lydia's vicar had suggested (after discreet enquiries), and she feared Lady Crestwood might indulge in gossip about a fallen maid in the Wickham household.

So Mary merely trailed behind, lost in her ruminations. When they returned to the drawing room for tea, Miss Poppit, Kitty, and Lieutenant Stubbs settled in a corner together—carefully apart from the rest, so as not to disturb them with ghastly war tales—and Lady Crestwood tugged on Prince's ears with a liberty that made Mary cringe and fear he might bite her.

"I shall just run up to Papa and see how he is," Lady Lucy said. Her eyes had lost their red rims, earned in her earlier bout of tears, and her skin had regained its usual pallor. All flush of prior emotion had been shed.

"He is doing something Parliamentary and confidential in his study, my dear, and likely will not have time for you." Lady Crestwood gave another exuberant pull at Prince's ear, but he only growled and snorted before rolling over for a rub.

"I will just see." Lady Lucy disappeared. Prince sat up to see where she went, but then rolled over to enjoy Lady Crestwood's pats again.

"Here is tea at last." Lady Crestwood straightened as the teacart was rolled in and gestured at Mary to prepare it. As Mary worked, Lady Crestwood glanced at her protégée, whose eyes were lit up as she listened to Lieutenant Stubbs's tales. "What are you speaking of, Miss Poppit?"

"Lieutenant Stubbs was telling me about his last campaign." Miss Poppit's back regained its rigidity, and she no longer leaned towards the young man, though a splotch of redness heated her cheeks. "I rather think he must have been very brave." Her words were cool, but there was an insistence to them Mary did not understand.

Lady Crestwood's eyes narrowed. "I am sure he was. No doubt almost as brave as Sir Reginald was, travelling to the Holy Land to obtain rock samples. Or Mr Covington, in the latest hunt."

"That is hardly the same thing, madam." Miss Poppit's tone was surprisingly chilly, given she spoke to her benefactor, but with a graceful lift of one arm, she dismissed the topic as if it meant nothing to her. "Mrs Stubbs, shall you be going to Almack's this week?"

"We do not have vouchers." Kitty accepted the teacup Mary offered her with a grim smile. Miss Poppit received hers with gentle fingertips, as if the cup were a bird alighting on a trembling limb.

"That is hard," Lady Crestwood said, with a hint of compassion that subtly edged into something else as her eyes rested on Miss Poppit. "A voucher to Almack's is a dearer prize than any spoil of war, is it not?" She gave a light laugh, as if to suggest it was merely a joke, but there was an undergirding of iron in it.

"Are you coming, Miss Bennet?" The eager light of competition in Miss Poppit's eyes was intended for Lydia, not Mary, no doubt. "I cannot believe that Mrs Wickham was denied tickets...was she? I believed her to be friends of the lady patronesses." Her eyelids lowered demurely as she asked, but her gaze remained fixed on the source of the answer.

"Lydia has vouchers," Mary said, "and of course we shall attend. But from what I hear, we shall both enjoy our time at the London Ladies Information Society more than Almack's."

"Do not be ridiculous." Lady Crestwood had been tipping her teacup to watch the cream swirl in it, but now she set it down with a clack. "The London Ladies is all very well, but when one has the duty of bringing out a young lady, Almack's is the obvious choice, and very pleasing it is too. Miss Poppit and I will attend every Wednesday."

"I do not think it is the attraction of the *ladies'* information *or* society that lures Mrs Wickham." Miss Poppit raised her cup almost as if it were a weapon, and in the glint in her eye, Mary saw a ferocity that disturbed her. *Thank goodness I am too much of a mouse to have a rival. Miss Poppit seems so pleasant...until Lydia is brought up.*

"What do you mean?" Lieutenant Stubbs's voice was carefully controlled, but his limbs had tensed, and his fists were clenched at his sides.

With a light lift of her shoulders, Miss Poppit said, "Oh, nothing. Pray, where has Lady Lucy got to? Lord Crestwood must be more talkative than usual to keep her this long."

"I am here." With a guilty blush, Lady Lucy entered, stepping over one of her parents' dogs and taking a seat close enough to permit her to scratch his ears. Mary served her tea and biscuits and, after a moment of hesitation, served herself another two biscuits. Usually she would take one and nibble it in ladylike fashion the entire time, fearing to appear voracious. But the grumble in her stomach seemed to matter more to her now. *Perhaps Mrs Holt is right. I cannot help Hannah and Lydia if I am famished, can I?* She chewed on a biscuit, letting the sweetness crumble over her tongue and mingle with the bitterness of the tea.

"Lord Crestwood must have had a great deal to say," Miss Poppit said.

Lady Lucy's blush deepened. "Oh, Papa was very busy arranging papers for his safe. I spoke to him, but he did not mind me much." She reached back down to the pug and rubbed his nose, cooing at him and abandoning the conversation.

Prince apparently took offence at Lady Lucy's petting a new dog, for he trotted over and pushed his head into the young woman's hands, snarling a little at the Crestwood pugs. They snarled back, and the resulting *contretemps* took enough of

Lady Lucy's attention that her mother felt safe enough to speak of her.

"Poor Lucy!" Lady Crestwood's smooth bulk could not lean with any grace, but she cast her voice low enough not to be overheard. "Her father and I guarded her like hawks—" Her voice broke. "Actually, perhaps we did not lay on such a guard as we ought. I did not think we had any need. Lucy never seemed to care very much for anything."

"I do not think she had much space to care, Lady Crestwood." Mary was shocked at her own daring, but she clamped her mouth shut to prevent herself from taking it back. For better or worse, Lady Crestwood did not seem to think of her comment.

"Our home was so peaceful, all in harmony." The dogs snapped at each other, and Miss Poppit and Kitty delayed their chat enough to throw disconcerted stares at the pugs.

"I do not think that Lady Lucy—" Mary wanted to make the mother understand, but Lady Crestwood was accustomed to ruling on every matter.

"She picked up every notion from me, and we were all content. Then this accursed Captain Roarke came along! He quite cut up our peace."

You thought it was peaceful, but that is because you had no idea what Lady Lucy was thinking or feeling. Mary had enough courage to *think* the thought, but not to speak it aloud. Her hands balled up in frustration, crumbling one biscuit, which she set down hastily. "Lady Crestwood—"

"I cannot help her much now, poor girl."

"You could invite her here more often."

Lady Crestwood's eyes widened. "But she is always welcome! We always wish her to come. But she knows we disapprove of her husband's behaviour, and in some misguided loyalty, she stays away from us unless there is a special reason." She studied her daughter, who was now hugging a Crestwood dog. "I do not know why she came to us today."

Mary's gaze followed Lady Crestwood's. Her revelations shed new light on Lady Lucy's sudden interest in visiting her parents. *She must have felt very sad indeed, or very angry with the captain.* Mary wished again she had asked Lady Lucy to confide in her.

"There is little I can do for my Lucy." Lady Crestwood sighed again. "But I *have* learned something, and I will do better by Miss Poppit." Lady Crestwood's brow furrowed as she watched Miss Poppit laugh at something Lieutenant Stubbs said. Miss Poppit's usual hauteur had thawed, and she craned towards the lieutenant and Kitty. "She fancies herself in love with a poor soldier, a lieutenant like your Stubbs there. Lieutenant Babbingford, he calls himself. I did not keep a keen enough watch on my Lucy, but I will not make the same mistake again. No spendthrift adventurer will make off with *this* young lady."

The undertone changed to a more usual, drawing-room tone of voice, and Lady Crestwood said, rising, "Lieutenant and Mrs Stubbs, we must not keep you and your sister any longer. Mr Covington is so good as to take Miss Poppit riding with his sister in Hyde Park, and she must not be late."

Miss Poppit's eyes had been crinkled in amusement in talking with Lieutenant Stubbs, but her face smoothed. "Good-bye, Lieutenant. Good-bye, Mrs Stubbs."

Lady Crestwood had not finished her commands. "Lucy, I will take you home myself."

"Yes, Mama."

As Mary joined the Stubbses and sought out the carriage, she cast a glance back at the mother and daughter. Perhaps her talk with Lady Crestwood had produced some small good, and the two would have a meaningful talk on their ride home. *I daresay Lady Crestwood is not too cowardly to have unpleasant conversations.*

"A very pleasant visit, was it not?" Kitty said, her good cheer restored by the visit. Her husband made a sound of assent and helped Kitty and Mary into the carriage. A footman presented Prince, holding him at arm's length and waiting.

"Oh, I forgot him." Mary almost cursed when she realised they would have to take the pug home without Lady Lucy to charm him. "Just, um, place him here." She waved a hand at the carriage floor and scooted back in her seat when the footman deposited him. Prince's spirits must have been lifted by his own visit, for he did not growl even once, and Lieutenant Stubbs hummed and slapped his knee, gazing out the carriage window.

"Lieutenant Stubbs, I do not suppose that you have any ideas about what to do about Hannah?"

Irritation creased lines in his face. "Certainly I have an idea. Shove her out into the street and be done with it."

"Oh, Lieutenant Stubbs! Surely you can think of something else. What are we to do with her?"

"How should I know what is to be done with such a person?" His chin lifted. "You cannot think that *I* have ever—"

Mary's cheeks heated. "No, of course not."

His chin came down, and Lieutenant Stubbs was mollified enough to offer a suggestion. "Well, perhaps there is some charity in London that will take her."

"That is what the vicar said, but Hannah does not want to stay in London."

"Who on earth cares what the girl wants?" Kitty said, her good humour ebbing at the subject. "She has had enough of what she wants already. She will simply have to make do." She studied Mary's face as they bounced along and swung with the motion of the carriage. "I do not understand you, Mary. You always preached a great deal, but you never took things further than that. Now you cannot seem to stop interfering in things."

"Interfering!" It was the second time she had been called that, and it stung from Kitty even more than it had from Mr Cole. After all, she could say that Mr Cole did not truly know her, but her sister surely did.

"Well, whatever you do, at least have the decency to keep us informed. I hate it when people go creeping round my back." The lieutenant's humming did not resume, and the sullen look had returned to Kitty's face. Mary regretted ruining their mood, but she found herself floundering deeper and deeper with the obligations she had bound herself to.

There must be someone who can help. Perhaps Mr Cole would have an idea. Surely he would have more compassion for Hannah than Lieutenant Stubbs or Kitty did. Though his careless flirting enraged her, he also treated her with more respect than Lieutenant Stubbs ever did. And he had a ready laugh and intelligence. He would have some ideas, she was sure. And he would listen to her, and teach her geology, and together they would craft a lecture sure to make Lady Crestwood choose him for the Informed Ladies of London Association. Even his dog was benign, perhaps enough that Mary could learn to love him...

Amid her musing, she reached down to pet a dog, and Prince's indignant bite wounded both her daydreams and her hand.

Sixteen

The London Ladies Information Society had had enough of the general squalor of Maddox's Assembly Rooms, and with donations from the Informed Ladies of London Association and a host of other groups, they had gathered enough money and volunteers for a thorough cleaning and refinishing of the assembly hall. Lydia, still keeping her head down to please Lieutenant Stubbs, did not come to assist, but Kitty agreed to go with Mary and aid in the transformation.

Mary was all too glad to enter the dark assembly hall and escape Kitty's company. The whole ride there, Kitty had been repeating her husband's denunciations of Lydia's conduct, and though Mary had tried to mollify her by agreeing, the rant had continued. It was a relief to slip into the mass of ladies and know Kitty could not speak of such things therein. *Did my preaching ever sound like that?* Mary supposed it must have. She must have alienated the very people she intended to persuade, again and again, all because of her self-righteousness and insulting tone.

Mary hoped that after evading her sister, she would find Mr Cole at once so that she could help him with his lecture preparations, but Mrs Appleton found her first. "Miss

Bennet, I am sure you will not mind scrubbing the hallway floor." For most people, Mrs Appleton was a nonentity. She barely spoke, was inattentive at lectures, and wore the demure sort of matronly clothing that allowed a woman to fade into the background.

"Scrubbing?" Even with such an unimpressive person as Mrs Appleton, Mary hesitated to displease. "I thought there would be servants who did that sort of thing...?" It was true that Mary had been told the ladies would be cleaning and restoring the building, but as a gentleman's daughter, she had supposed they would be supervising a horde of maids, not taking an active part. And since she had hoped herself to slip away with Mr Cole, she had worn her best afternoon frock to allure him.

"You must come along here." Mrs Appleton led her into the hallway, pointed out the relevant parts of the floor, and provided Mary with a scrubbing brush and a bucket. Mary looked down at her new white muslin and bit her lip.

"Could I dust, like Miss Poppit?"

But Mrs Appleton had already walked away, and Mary lacked the courage to refuse the task altogether. She bent down, tucking up her skirts as best she could, and attempted to scrub. A few minutes of awkward struggles to preserve her gown and yet remove swirls of grime from the floor soured her mood. *I am supposed to be helping Mr Cole. I am supposed to be distracting him from Lydia!* Her annoyance with the task grew, but she wiped her face and persisted.

"Miss Bennet, what on earth are you doing?"

Mr Cole's amused voice startled Mary out of a grim reverie involving Mrs Appleton and a witch's cauldron in the macabre assembly hall. She pressed her scrubbing brush into the floor with vehemence. "I am cleaning this floor, obvious-ly." The bitterness in her voice was for Mrs Appleton, not Mr Cole, and he seemed to sense it was not personal.

"It looks like dirty work."

"Does it?" This time her acid tone bit at him in particular.

"I cannot think you were intended to do that." Mr Cole squatted next to her. "Who set you to this?"

"Mrs Appleton. She thinks that I ought to scrub, while Miss Poppit waltzes about and preens and dusts." She stopped scouring long enough to look him in the eye. "Why is that? Why do ladies set people like me to scrubbing floors and set people like Miss Poppit to light dusting?"

His lips pulled into a smile. "The Lord tempers the wind to the shorn lamb, perhaps."

Mary gave a disgusted look at the bucket, which now bore a thin film of oil over its soapy water. "I do not see why Miss Poppit is a tender lamb, and I am always some great woolly thing."

A laugh erupted from Mr Cole, and he hauled Mary to her feet. "I do not see why, either. Let us go into the office, and you can help me as you promised. You have not forgotten?"

"Of course not. Only, I should finish this—" She grimaced at the half-cleaned floor.

His grin broadened. "Might as well be hung for a sheep as for a lamb, hmm? Just come along. Wait a moment—you have a smear of something—"

His thumb rubbed against her cheek, and Mary's breath caught. The pressure of his thumb warmed her face with an unnatural heat, and her eyes widened and stared into his, rapt into a feeling unknown to her, but dazzling. His dark eyes bore into hers, and some flicker of emotion passed through him as well, something that made him cough and turn away. The spell was broken.

I should have done something to tantalise him just then. But oddly enough, Mary felt sure no deliberate flirting from her would have affected him so much as her gaze rapt in his. The thought caused an upwelling of delight.

She could not speak as she allowed him to lead her into the office, but the palpable heartbeats that usually disturbed her now felt friendly and exciting. *I did not think a heart pounding could ever feel so...nice.* She suddenly realised she had spent several minutes in anger—downright anger—at Mrs Appleton, where usually she would have made excuses for anyone who put her in an awkward position. *Have I changed? I never used to get angry so easily. Nor feel this other feeling...*

The other feeling was jolted away when Mr Cole threw himself into a chair and said, "I cannot believe you obeyed Mrs Appleton. What nonsense! I would have told her to stick her head in the bucket." Hercules was sprawled in the same spot as on their previous visit, and the hound gave a cheerful bark as if to applaud the suggestion. He nosed Mary's hand as she sat down. "You are so obedient to Mrs Wickham, as well."

"The meek shall inherit the earth." Mary did not like defending herself, yet she could not let disapproval on Mr Cole's part rest.

"Yes, after the bold have roamed all over it and picked up all the choice bits. The meek will get the scraps left over." Mr Cole's joking might have amused him, judging by the sparkle in his eye, but Mary's brows drew down.

"Whatever you say, Mr Cole, the world could not function without quiet, well-behaved followers."

"No doubt, no doubt." The agreement sounded more polite than sincere.

"And so much disputation is on trivial matters. It wastes time."

"I suppose that means you thought it would waste time to tell Mrs Appleton you are a lady, not a scullery maid." He winked, and as Mary bristled, he shoved forward a box of parchment sheets, each annotated. "Well, we shall not waste our time, shall we, Miss Bennet? Here are my notes for the lecture. If you really can work some magic on them, now is your chance to turn straw into gold."

Part of her wanted to continue to argue, but she could hardly press the merits of meekness by doing that. Biting her lip, Mary sifted through the pages, skimming the words. Some of the topics were unfathomable, but most she could connect with the reading she had done, and she began sorting them.

Then she took up the pen and began drawing out a rough plan. Mr Cole watched with a sceptical arch to his brows.

As she worked, Mary soothed herself into a state of bemused calm. The sound of voices discussing candelabras and lamps drifted down the hallway, and the skritch of the pen on the parchment added a restful quality to the ambiance.

I was angry, really angry, with Mrs Appleton. And with Kitty, she realised, though she had not dared to think such a thought before. *Why can they not be friendly and quiet, like Lady Lucy? Or Mr Cole.* Though Mr Cole was not always respectfully quiet, he was now. He took a moment now and then to lean over her and read her work, but for the most part, he rummaged through notes of his own. He might be sceptical of her skill, but he was willing to give it a chance. *It is pointless for Kitty to tell me how awful Lydia's behaviour is. We all already know that. I should tell Kitty and Lieutenant Stubbs to stop preaching at me.* The thought shocked her. Standing up to the lieutenant, even in such a small way, felt dangerous, and Mary's heart began to pound again. *I would be terrified, but perhaps it would be worth it...*

Mr Cole, sensing she was finished, seized the page she had been writing on. "I do not see how this is supposed to work." His gaze danced over the page, and his nose wrinkled with distaste. "Why do you wish me to begin with talking about the Blarney stone? And the old Roman ruins? You are as bad as Lady Crestwood asking what the pyramids are made of."

"People have heard of those things and can picture them. It helps to begin with something less abstract. Begin with what is familiar and concrete, and then move into your theories."

He skimmed further down. "And here, where I begin my theory on igneous rocks, you have me discussing Pompeii! An old city engulfed by ash from a volcano has nothing to do with my theory."

"But people find Pompeii fascinating." Mary struggled to keep her patient tone. "By including a small discussion of the matter, you attract their interest again—"

"Again? That assumes I lost it with my theory."

Mary's voice hardened. "Not an assumption. A conclusion based upon evidence from previous lectures. Pompeii is a little aside from your main topic, I agree, but it will pay dividends in generating engagement in your audience." She gave him a wry smile. "No one doubts that in an ideal world, everyone would be *fascinated* by your rocks with no help."

"You are teasing me."

Mary blinked. *I am!* The idea displeased her. She hated being teased, herself; it felt so aggressive. Was that what she was becoming—an aggressive young woman, rather than a modest young lady? Or was it simply Mr Cole that brought out the fire in her? "I am sorry."

Mr Cole leaned back in his chair, throwing his arms wide over the desk. "Why should you be? You are rather appealing when you are vexed and vexing." When she flushed, he grinned. "You *are* still trying to distract me, are you not? So that I do not bother your sister?" He folded his arms behind his head. "You know, I think you are the most—distracting—when you forget what you are supposed to be doing. When you forget about Mrs Wickham entirely."

She realised she *had* forgotten Lydia. She had not even noticed that Mr Cole had not asked where Mrs Wickham was. "You distracted me yourself." It was hard to admit, but there was something freeing in the confession. She sighed, but it was an exhalation of relief. "All week, there has been such tension. I admit I was looking forward to your banter." She blotted the sheet in front of her, avoiding his gaze. "All your silly talk makes me feel like things are not as serious as they seem." *As if life is something I can handle, weak as I am.* "It is not logical, but somehow I feel better when you are facetious and unruly. I cannot rebel myself, but I can cheer for a rebel." She gave him a lopsided smile, finally daring to meet his eyes.

"And before, you wanted me to be nice. Really you were just repressing my natural exuberance." The light in his eyes danced with hers.

"Miss Bennet!" Mrs Appleton appeared in the open doorway, her thick eyebrows lifting with surprise and disdain. "I thought you were cleaning the floor, not sitting alone with…" Her lips pressed together.

"I needed Miss Bennet's help with my lecture." Mr Cole stood up and gave Mrs Appleton a courtly bow. "I quite forgot she was a young lady who might need a chaperon. You could join us, Mrs Appleton. Miss Bennet was just working on distinguishing the kinds of sedimentary rocks formed by light pressures. As a regular attendee of my lectures, I am sure you can explain to her which kinds to focus on. Shall you give us your assistance?"

Mrs Appleton's eyebrows drew up and down in consternation. The vigour of the movement made Mary stifle a giggle.
They look like wriggling caterpillars.

"Well, Mrs Appleton?"

"I fear other matters require my attention." The woman
drooped, resigned to her usual status as a nonentity, and
Mary felt a stab of guilt for removing one of the lady's few
chances to exert power.

But she ought not to have abused it. Mary watched her go. Mr
Cole sat down again, tapping his fingers on the desk. "We
shall not be bothered again, I think," he said.

Does he really want to be alone with me? Of course, even if he did,
it might mean only that he valued her help with his lectures,
however much he disputed her ideas. But if he did have any
feeling of friendship...Mary's mind wandered to peaceful,
cosy talks, laughter and fun, before remembering she still
had duties weighing on her. *I have not even brought up Hannah.*
Another stab of guilt drove into her, and she cleared her
throat.

"Mr Cole, I wonder if you could help me with a delicate
matter." She outlined Hannah's situation as briefly as she
could, hoping the gentleman would understand the need for
discretion. "I thought perhaps you could find a place for her
on your father's estate. That would be far enough from
London for her."

As Mr Cole listened, lines popped up on his brow. "That
would not be advisable, Miss Bennet." At her look of
entreaty, he said, "I do not know how to state this for a

lady's ears. If I were to beg a place for this maid on my father's estate, everyone would assume—you understand—"

"Oh."

Mr Cole shrugged. "It would hurt both her reputation and mine. Can you imagine how the servants would feel, working for such a squire as me, when they might have had my saintly brother Thomas?"

Mary could not give up hope so easily. "But that would be a long time from now. They will all have forgotten, or realised you had nothing to do with Hannah's trouble, or gotten used to the idea if they *did* believe it, by then."

"It will not be so long as all that." His brows drew down, and his tone was grim.

"What do you mean?"

His broad chest produced a heftier sigh than Mary's could. "My father is very ill. It is difficult for him to handle the estate as it is, and we do not know how much time he has left."

Puzzled, Mary stared at him. "But then surely you will return home at once, and these lectures will not be needed—"

"Not at all." His tone was cold. "I have no wish to turn up on the estate with Thomas gone only a year. The last time I was there, all I heard from the servants was 'If your brother were here, such and such would be done' and 'We will never have so fine a master as Mr Thomas would have been'. And it was worse with my parents." His lips compressed into a brief line.

Mary hesitated, sensing he wished to tell more, but she did not know how to encourage him. "I...am not sure what you mean."

"There is no point competing with a dead man, especially not such a good man as my brother was." He shifted in his chair. "We all knew where we stood, before. My father was as keen on Thomas being the squire as Thomas himself was. And I was the younger brother, just a scamp crawling over the hills to find interesting rocks, spending my money on enjoyments in London—"

"You never thought you would have to be the responsible one."

"And I am not suited to it. Not like Thomas was." His breath gusted out. "I know how I must look to you—shamefully callous to my family. But you do not know how it is." His chin lifted, as if he had summoned some courage for vulnerability. "When Thomas died, my father was full of rage and grief. He told me he wished it had been me instead, lying there in that grave, and I said something in bitterness—" He broke off. "In the end, he said he never wanted to see me again. My mother writes to ask me to return, but even she says I ought to do it because it is what Thomas would do. Not because it is right, or practical, or in my own character. Only because it was what Thomas would have done. No doubt she, too, wishes I was the one who died."

Mary's gaze met his. "You cannot know that. And what your father said, he said in anger. Perhaps he regrets it now."

"Then all he must do is say so." Mr Cole shook his head. "No, until they forget Thomas enough to accept me, how can I ever go back?" His tone turned more pleading, as if convincing Mary would convince himself. "If I make a name for myself in London—if my mother hears of my success with the kind of people she values, ladies' societies and such —if my science is impressive enough to men my father respects, they will see me as a significant person in my own right. I will be more than the poor substitute for Thomas. I will be someone in London, and no one will expect me to leave it all to play squire."

"But when your father dies, you will have to leave it all the same."

"Eventually. But perhaps by then it will be tolerable, forever being contrasted with my saintly brother. I will have proven myself in London as a geologist."

Mary shook her head. "It is not a good plan for the long term. And what if your father needs you now? He is ill."

"He can manage for now." Mary could not tell if the determination in Mr Cole's face meant that claim was certain, or if he merely wished it were so. "Oh, I know that you despise me. You are Thomas's sort. You would do your duty, no matter the cost to yourself. But I cannot resign myself to trying to substitute for a man everyone loved and honoured. I never wanted to be squire." That last was said with a touch of petulance.

Mary could not imagine making Mr Cole's choice, delaying the inevitable in the hopes of seizing a few moments of acclaim and self-esteem. *I would have gone the moment my parents said they needed me—no, they never would have even had to say it. I would have guessed it and sacrificed my desires already.* But the realisation did not make her proud. She felt like both Mr Cole and she were twisted trees, grown up in convolutions necessary to the circumstances but unhealthy and degraded nonetheless.

"Well? Shall you refuse to help me now?" Mr Cole brushed back his chestnut hair with an impatient gesture.

"Of course not." Mary's voice was meek, but she tried to make it stronger. "We will go on as before. Nothing need change—"

"What does not need to change?" Where Mrs Appleton had appeared in stodgy ire, Lydia now shone forth like an angelic apparition, her silken hair pinned to perfection, yellow satin moulding her curves, and a white bonnet ringed with silk bright enough for a halo.

Oh, heavens, Mary thought.

Seventeen

"I cannot tell you how dreadfully dull it was, staying at home for ages and ages," Lydia said, stepping into the office and laying her reticule on the desk. "Lord! The tedium was so relentless that I actually wrote my sister Jane a letter! Now that is saying something."

"Lydia, you are not supposed to be here." Mary dropped her voice to a throaty hum. She had meant it to be a whisper, but her anger and distress added an intensity to the words she could not suppress. "If Lieutenant Stubbs finds out—"

"Well, I will not tell him." Her pert assurance annoyed Mary, and Lydia turned in appeal to Mr Cole. "Will *you* tell, Mr Cole?"

"My lips are forever at your service, Mrs Wickham. Seal them —or do whatever else you like with them. I await your command." He rose and bowed with a flourish, and Lydia tittered in appreciation.

"Then I command you to make no mention of my visit to my dour brother-in-law Lieutenant Stubbs." Lydia rewarded him with a smile.

"But Kitty will tell him all the same—" Mary said.

A shot of fire went through Lydia's tone. "Kitty would not dare." Just as suddenly, she relaxed and trailed her hand over the stack of papers. "What is all this? You are not actually working, are you?" She threw a wry glance at Mary. "Trust you, Mary, to actually help a man when you promised you would! Why, Mr Cole, was I ever any help when I came before?"

"Not in the way of geology." Mr Cole's easy good humour must have satisfied Lydia, but Mary found something within her drying up at the sight of him warming to her sister.

"No, we just laughed and laughed, and every once in a while some impertinent woman would come and look at us. Has anyone come today?"

"Only Mrs Appleton, and she did not catch us laughing." Mr Cole's eyes were sparkling with amusement.

"How unfortunate! We will give her something better to look at now, if she comes back." Lydia clapped her hands with mischief, and Hercules leapt up. As Mr Cole made introductions between them and Lydia patted the dog's head, Mary felt herself receding from the situation more and more.

It was not supposed to be like this. Why could she not stay away? She felt cheated, but some part of her warned it was not merely worry for Lydia's reputation that tore at her. She felt cheated of something else, some closeness to Mr Cole that she was beginning to count on. Mr Cole would certainly not confide in Lydia the way he had with Mary, but the fact seemed like poor consolation when she saw the ease in their camaraderie and knew herself forgotten. Fading into the background had always felt safe to Mary, the proper placement for her...until now. Suddenly being in the background felt positively perilous.

He is forgetting me already. He will never think of me now. "Mr Cole, I have not been able to tell you my idea," Mary said, with a loudness that sounded brazen to her ears.

"What idea?" The two paused in their conversation long enough to look at Mary.

"An expedition." She had meant to bring out the idea in a proud, stately way, but now she hurried so that she could keep their attention. "I suggest you lead the Informed Ladies of London Association on an expedition to a nearby site, where we can see striations in person. I understand Moseley Gorge is not far from London, and it would make a good place for a picnic."

"Hmm." Mr Cole rubbed his chin. "The land shifts a good deal there after the rain. If we went soon after a rainfall, we might see some layers that had been previously covered."

"Not *too* soon after," Mary said, her chest warming as she saw he took the idea with favour. "If it is muddy, the ladies will not thank you for taking them there. A few days after, when the land has had a little time to dry out. If you give them a delightful picnic and an excuse to feel scientific, they will adore it, and the annual lecture will be yours."

"What a clever idea!" Lydia clapped her hands together, but for once, Mary found her sister's approbation of no account. Her eyes glued to Mr Cole's face.

"It is a good idea," he said, nodding. "It will take a great deal of planning, though. Can you commit to that, Miss Bennet?"

"Of course." Now her heart was throbbing with excitement and relief, and the warmth in her chest swelled to suffuse her whole body.

"A picnic! It will be perfectly charming," Lydia said, hugging Hercules. "You must bring your dog, and I shall bring mine. They will be great friends." She stroked Hercules's ears, and the scruffy hound licked her hands. "Did you know Mary is afraid of dogs, Mr Cole?"

"Not afraid, exactly." Mary's hands twisted together. Everything Lydia said seemed to pull Mr Cole closer to her and farther from Mary. *Is it intentional?* Probably Lydia was flirting her hardest as an internal revenge against Lieutenant Stubbs. She wished Mr Cole did not respond to it so readily.

"Now a cuddly puppy is my idea of heaven. What's your idea of heaven, Mr Cole?" The lilt in Lydia's voice made it seem like a leading question.

Mr Cole answered without hesitation, and darted a sly, almost conspiratorial look in Mary's direction. "Why, being with intelligent, beautiful ladies of course."

Lydia gave a sultry smile, quick to take it as a compliment to herself, but beside her, Mary felt a jolt. Had he really looked at her? Of course not. But...he was not likely to describe Lydia as intelligent, was he? Confusion made her clumsy, and she began speaking with no idea what she meant to say. "I will tell you what my idea of heaven was, when I was a little girl," she said. The matter was not directly related, but Mary was having difficulty keeping up with their ready flow of talk. "I have a doll that my mother made for me, and my dream was to take my doll to a faraway castle, where just she and I would live. And we would play together on the ramparts and dress in lovely gowns and walk in the woods and throw rocks into a stream." She blushed. "I do not know why I always thought of throwing rocks into a stream. I did not really do that as a child, because it would get my hands grubby and because the Lucas boys were always throwing rocks and getting in trouble."

"What a wicked thing to tell a geologist! Throwing rocks!" Lydia giggled. "I never knew you had such a strange idea of heaven. But then, you have always been such a quiet little thing, Mouse."

"I thought you did not want me to be called 'Mouse' anymore." For weeks, Mary had missed the name, but now its resurrection seemed ill-timed.

"That is right. Not while we are getting you to be a jolly debutante brave enough to talk to gentlemen. But Mr Cole is different."

Different how? Different because Lydia considered him part of *her* train? Different because he was a real friend to Mary? Mary could not tell.

Mr Cole gave Mary a sidelong glance. "Miss Bennet has been of great help to me today. You should see the outline of the lecture she has designed. If I did not know better, I would say she has been studying on her own."

"Oh, she has," Lydia said, her fingers trailing over the desktop in a light, fanciful swoop. "She ransacked Mr Wickham's library, and when that was not enough, she got more -ological books at the library. Geological, I mean." She corrected herself with a moue that showed she thought the mistake charming, and Mr Cole laughed in appreciation.

"Then I thank you, Miss Bennet, for your hard work." His gaze was steady, and his words were uttered with solemnity that flattered Mary. An expression flitted over his face—concern? unease?—and he turned to Lydia with a heartiness that confused and dismayed Mary.

I could almost say he is distracting himself from me...with Lydia. That was nonsense, of course. Looking into Mary's face must have reminded him of their discussion about his father, and he must have sought distraction from that. Whatever the reason, Lydia was happy to oblige him, capering with words and pretty gestures, making light of the world and everything in it. *She is flirting harder than ever. Oh, Lieutenant Stubbs, why did you have to be so stern? Trying to suppress her never works for long.*

Mary's mood sank further when she remembered Mr Cole had not furnished any ideas for Hannah's predicament. By the time Kitty discovered them and scolded Lydia into going home, Mary felt dismal enough to argue with Lydia in the carriage.

"You are disgracing yourself, Lydia. Mr Wickham will never understand this if he finds out about it." Mary shoved back as far as she could from her sister in the carriage and glared out the window.

"Mr Wickham knows I am a flirt. He accepts me for who I am. When you first got so testy about Mr Cole, I explained everything to Mr Wickham—how I have always had gentlemen admire me, and I like it, and it does not mean anything. Why, I even told him about Captain Roarke."

"What about Captain Roarke?" Mary drew her gaze from the lamps glowing in the fog to Lydia's dark eyes.

"Just that before we got rich, I let Captain Roarke take me about and pay for things. Sweets, little presents, that sort of gentlemanly thing. I had so little coin back then! I even asked the captain to sell a little jewellery for me, to pay a milliner's debt I did not want Mr Wickham to know about. But I braved it all and confessed, weeks ago. So you see Mr Wickham knows my sordid past—I need not fear anything."

"Accepting presents from a gentleman is—" Kitty began.

"Oh, I know, it was very foolish. La! I thought I would never tell Mr Wickham, but you see I did, as a wifely confidence, and it served very well. He trusts me."

"For now, perhaps." Mary chewed on her lip and hugged her arms around herself.

"Why, Mary, you are in a dudgeon! I have not seen that in ages." Lydia laid a hand atop her sister's, and when Mary only looked at it with resentment, she removed it. "Are you really angry because I did something foolish long ago? Or is it because…I interrupted your tête-à-tête with Mr Cole?"

Mary could not answer Lydia's question, nor her wicked smile.

Eighteen

Lydia's teasing continued the next day, and she pestered Mary with enough arch references to maidens in love at the breakfast table to make even Lieutenant Stubbs lift his head in wonderment. He did not understand the reference, but he assumed Lydia was vexing their sister about a suitor. "Do stop, Lydia," he said, cutting his ham with a briskness that showed breakfast was more a physical need than a social affair for him.

Kitty toyed with a piece of toast. "Such jokes are in poor taste, any way."

"I do not care a fig for what you think is in poor taste, Kitty."

The argument spiralled into a morass of bitterness. Though Kitty had agreed to keep Lydia's visit to the assembly rooms secret from Lieutenant Stubbs—perhaps fearing his wrath on the matter as much as Lydia—the two found plenty to dispute any way, and Mary was sorry to be the excuse for this one. The more Kitty and Lydia defended their views, the more they seemed to cling to them—Kitty, who was never particularly scrupulous until meeting her husband, now deepening her reverence for decorum, and Lydia, intensifying her value for independence. *I can see how a soldier must love his country more* after *fighting for it,* Mary mused as she watched them. It was a dynamic she had not considered before, that arguing or war might bond a person to their values more strongly, and she was not sure how she felt about it. Certainly in the present case, it did not seem to be doing much good.

"Come along, Mary, and help me choose my bonnet. If you will go to Mrs Holt's for me again, I can spend the day at the shops and try to forget Kitty's absurdities." She glared at Kitty, whose return glower matched her ferocity.

Mary's hands trembled, and she kept her head down. "I have not finished my breakfast, Lydia." Her voice shook almost as much as her hands, but her annoyance steadied her resolve. "And I do not wish to pay your visits for you." *I need time to think. I still have to figure out what to do with Hannah.* The reasons sounded like excuses in her head, and the impulse to obey nagged at her, a wriggling guilt in her belly. "If you made any promises to Mrs Holt, you may satisfy them yourself."

"Brava, Mary!" Kitty's applause only made things worse.

"You keep your nose out of this!" Lydia tossed a napkin at Kitty, but Kitty plucked it out of the air like a conjurer and set it aside. "Mary, I cannot bear a sickroom. You know I am no good in them."

"Then you ought not to have promised her you would go." Mary dared not look up, but she delivered her words as if she were driving in nails. "I. Will. Not. Go."

"Selfish thing!" Lydia whirled and left the table. The sound of her footsteps pounding up the stairs reverberated through the house. Lieutenant Stubbs munched on a roll with indifference, but Mary's whole body felt like lightning was shooting through it, shaking her limbs and producing uncomfortable sensations in her head and gut.

How do people bear it? She hated the sensations; they felt overwhelming and unruly, as if no place in the universe was safe. *I hate being angry. I hate disagreements. I just want there to be peace.* And yet, she had refused to do what Lydia asked. *Perhaps I was wrong. Is it really so bad to sit with Mrs Holt again? It would make Lydia so happy.* Second thoughts spun in her mind, sticking like cobwebs to every corner of it, but in the end she stayed where she was. Though she felt unsure she had been right, it was still a sort of victory to have denied Lydia's will.

"We must be off," Lieutenant Stubbs said, swallowing the last of his coffee and hurrying with Kitty away on an errand.

Lydia soon left, too, tossing a hopeful glance at Mary to see if she had relented, but then sallying forth with a sway to her hips that made the skirt of her silk dress snap and rustle. It was Lydia's way of reaffirming and demonstrating her power. With Mr Wickham drilling with the regiment, Mary was now left alone in the household to try and contrive a plan for Hannah.

When the maid's secret had first been discovered, Mary had visited her upstairs every day, but soon the sight of Hannah's tear-streaked face grew more and more intolerable as Mary realised she was failing in providing any help. Curling up on a chair in the drawing room, Mary struggled to think of something. *Mama's letter said Papa knew of no place for her in Meryton. Jane still has not written.* Should she dare asking Lady Crestwood for aid after all? Or Miss Poppit? The young lady had helped Mary once, but such a piece of gossip would be hard to resist. Mary's mind felt as though it was turning end over end and getting nowhere. *It seems I cannot think clearly.* And after she had gone to such lengths to defy Lydia and stay at home! *Well, after all, I do need a break, even if I cannot think of anything for Hannah.*

Mary was about to reach for a book when the butler's appearance made her lift her head.

"Mr Richard Cole, miss." The butler disappeared in an instant, and Mary realised he must have been bribed to allow Mr Cole inside. *And the Stubbses left in such a rush, he probably does not realise they are not here anymore...*

Which meant that she and Mr Cole were...alone.

She swallowed hard and rose to curtsey, watching Mr Cole's polite bow. His fawn breeches were well-tailored, and the cut of his apple green morning coat showed his broad shoulders to good effect. Though his chestnut hair had been trimmed short, the March gales outside had managed to tousle it, poking a few locks in wayward directions. His gaze flew over the drawing room as he smoothed his hair. "I gave the man a good tip, but I did not expect to be nestled away with a lady alone."

He grinned and reached down, and Mary realised Hercules had followed him in. Mr Cole rubbed the dog's back with one hand and flourished a bouquet in the other.

"Mrs Wickham is not here."

"I know—I asked the butler. It is doubtful whether he would have let me in otherwise, even with a bribe." When he finished petting Hercules, the dog pattered over to Mary, and she put her hand out without thinking and stroked him. "I did not come to see Mrs Wickham. I came to see you."

He placed the bouquet on a table and winked. "And to leave this for Mrs Wickham."

Mary's stormy look ought to have made the man run. "I will not give it to her." She eyed the hothouse flowers. "I will not tell anyone you brought such a thing for her. If necessary, I will say they were for me."

He shrugged. "As you like. Perhaps she will guess, even if you do."

The anger that had been building all day seemed to surge into one frothy wave in Mary, and she drew a deep breath, ready to unleash a torrent of scorn upon Mr Cole. Before she could break forth, he tilted his head and said, "I thought I should come and thank you for your help with my lecture and for organising my notes. I used to think that because I remembered where things were on reflection, that was organised enough. But I see now that a little physical tidiness to things makes them more efficient."

The appreciation put Mary off-balance, and she hesitated.

"You have set me on a good path for attaining the Informed Ladies' lecture," he said. His dark eyes were warm and cheerful.

"And yet you bring flowers for my sister?" Her tone held acid but not so much as she had originally intended.

"I wanted to see you. Surely you cannot object to that?"

Mary's hands tightened into fists at her side. "No, uh…no, I do not object."

His wide, slow-blinking eyes made him the epitome of the muddled scientist as he studied her, trying to glean what she did not say. "Oh, because if your brother-in-law were to come in, he might bluster a little. Well, what of that? I daresay a bit of a wrangle might do us some good." He glanced around as if expecting him at any moment, and Mary realised he must have assumed Lieutenant Stubbs was in the house.

"You do not know Lieutenant Stubbs," she said, shaking her head. "He will not just wrangle—"

"Do you know, I think *I* might have some objection to your behaviour here."

Mary was so surprised she lost her thread of argument. "My behaviour?"

"Yes, you. You feel better when things are peaceful, and so you try and impose your idea of peace upon all of us. Never mind that some of us like to spar a little and others would prefer to be free to pursue our own interests whether they clash or not. You insist that everyone get along, just so that you can feel good."

Mary's face heated. "You know nothing about me!"

"I only know that you bend over backwards trying to please your sister, and seem terrified of your brother-in-law's displeasure, and stay meek as a mouse anytime anyone wants you to do something for them, like that Mrs Appleton—"

"That was one time!"

"Mrs Wickham tells me of others, and I can guess the rest. Peace at any price, no matter the cost to yourself. Or anybody else." His breath panted, and he wiped back his hair, disarranging the smoothness he had just created.

Mary folded her arms. "Then you would be very pleased with my day today, for I have had no peace whatsoever. Lydia is angry with me for not going in her place to Mrs Holt. Kitty is annoyed because I do not listen to her complaints anymore, and Lieutenant Stubbs—Lieutenant Stubbs is not angry with me yet, but he will be when he finds out Lydia came to see you last night and I said nothing. This is not peace. This is chaos."

She had expected an apology, or some other show of humility, but instead Mr Cole began to laugh. Hercules scampered about, sensing the mood of his master had shifted, but Mary nearly stamped her foot in frustration.

"What on earth is the matter with you now, Mr Cole?"

"Why, I—"

Whatever explanation he could have given, Mary was sure it was inadequate, but she never found out what it was. Lieutenant Stubbs's appearance in the doorway was too far from the window to cast a shadow, but it felt as though the drawing room was suddenly immersed in an eclipse. Her brother-in-law's uniform lacked the gentility and polish of Mr Cole's attire, but the stern solemnity of Lieutenant Stubbs's countenance made him look almost kingly. *How did he get back so quickly?* Mary wondered if the butler had sent someone to fetch him once he admitted Mr Cole or if it was simply bad luck—a forgotten glove, a dropped purse. The fact that Kitty did not appear suggested it was only ill timing; she would not miss such a *contretemps* waiting in the carriage even if her husband bade her to.

"Mr Richard Cole," Lieutenant Stubbs said, each word a pronouncement and a declaration of war, "I know not what you are, gentleman or otherwise, but you have been harassing my sister-in-law." He placed his hands on his hips, his gloved fingers tensing on his belt.

Mr Cole blinked in surprise. "Nonsense, it is merely a rational disagreement."

"Not *that* sister-in-law." The testiness in Lieutenant Stubbs's voice sounded petulant for a moment, but he soon reined it in to controlled ire. "Mrs Lydia Wickham."

"Oh, her." Mr Cole seemed surprised the subject had been reintroduced, as if he still did not fully gauge its importance. Mary found herself repressing a sigh at his inability to appreciate the degree of scandal involved.

Lieutenant Stubbs gave him no quarter. "Do not pretend or play games, Mr Cole. Your presence here is an insult to our family. I must insist you leave at once and have nothing to do with any of us in the future."

"I have no difficulty dispensing with your company," Mr Cole said, his lips twisting in a wry smile, "but I fear my happiness might be impinged by the loss of the company of others in your family."

"I have no concern for your happiness." Lieutenant Stubbs's tone heated further.

"Mr Cole made a simple error in judgment," Mary said, throwing a worried glance at one and then the other. "He was just leaving. There is no reason to make a scene, Lieutenant Stubbs." She raised her hands in a placating gesture. "None of us wants to make gossip for the servants, right? Let us put this behind us."

"Certainly. Once he gives his word as a gentleman to leave Mrs Wickham alone." Lieutenant Stubbs's hands were tensed hard enough for iron. Mary's heart began to pound, and her stomach soured with fear. Hercules paced back and forth, nosing at his master from time to time, as if trying to sense the shift in the situation.

"I am not harassing Mrs Wickham. So far as I can tell, she is free to make friendships where she chooses," Mr Cole said. His brows had drawn together in a troubled expression, but there was a hint of impatience to it, as if Lieutenant Stubbs's rage were sparking an ire of his own. "What right do you have, sir, to interfere in another's business? If Mrs Wickham finds my friendship problematic, she is free to discontinue it at any time."

"I have the right of a *brother*, who protects a foolish sister from herself."

"Stop, both of you." The words came out as whisper, the air barely able to push through Mary's constricted throat. She could feel tears leaking at the corners of her eyes, as if they, too, were being squeezed out of her. "Stop fighting." She could hear distant shouting, the breaking of Lucas Lodge furniture, Harry's curses, his father's accusations. She could smell the sweat of her own fear from that day long ago, the day she had broken a family. *It is all my fault.* "We can all be friends, I know."

"Friends? With him?" Lieutenant Stubbs's disdain was clear, but Mr Cole leaned towards Mary with a face full of concern.

"Miss Bennet?" His eyes searched her own, but she squeezed them shut.

"Do not fight." Her voice held an unnatural strain, a wild lilt, and she took a step back.

"You know nothing about such matters, Miss Mary," Lieutenant Stubbs said. "If we must settle this the way gentlemen do—"

"Do not speak to her that way." Mr Cole's voice held more heat than she had ever heard in it, and Mary backed away again, opening her eyes only to have her sight blurred with tears. The thundering in her chest felt explosive. She knew she should stay and try to make peace between them. She should try to smooth things over, for Lydia's sake, for Lieutenant Stubbs's sake, for Mr Cole's sake, for the good of the family. Mary forced her feet to still, but her voice tore out of her, like some chained imp finally shrieking its way up from the depths.

"Just stop it! STOP IT!"

The moment was a release, but it horrified her to hear her own anger joining the fray, abandoning her to the chaos. She turned on her heel and dashed out of the room, running all the way to her bedroom. *I am as bad as they. I have lost all control.* That was what anger did; it made a kindly father disown his son, it made a loving son spit curses at his father, it made a dutiful sister scream in hate. Mary grabbed her doll and threw herself into her bed, dragging the silk coverlet over her as if she were a child hiding from a monster. *I failed. They will argue more now, and then they will have a duel. One of them will die, and it will be all my fault.* The chain of reasoning was not logical, but she suffered while thinking such thoughts any way. Her tears turned into ragged sobs, an ache that raked across her chest.

Why did Mr Cole talk nonsense about peace being control? Peace was safety, pure and simple. Peace meant everyone survived and stayed together. *Maybe my need for peace is unusually strong, compared to most. But what is the alternative? Let everyone feud and separate, or worse? That is no alternative at all.* That was what Mr Cole did not seem to understand.

But in the darkness under the coverlet, her reasoning sounded empty, like a mindless recitation supposed to exorcise a ghost but lacking the power to dispel it. And as Mary reassured herself that peace was the obvious solution, and disputes were the evil to avoid, all the while a word haunted her thoughts, hovering beyond each one like a persistent spirit howling with misery.

Coward.

Nineteen

M ary spent the rest of the day in bed, sending down the excuse of a headache to avoid dinner with the Wickhams. At first, remaining in her room soothed her, and she sewed a new garment for her doll with a growing calm. "It is all too much for me," she told the button eyes, feeling almost proud of her distance above the chaos until she remembered the phrase was one her mother used again and again. Mama would take a pile of mending upstairs and leave her children to fend for themselves, insisting she could not handle their squabbles, their pleadings, and their needs. *And I was overlooked by everyone, and Kitty and Lydia grew wild, and—why, all of it could have been mitigated, if Mama had deigned to come downstairs and help.* The flash of anger jolting through her made her drop her doll. She could not remember ever feeling such rage at her mother before.

This is what anger does. It is poisonous. If you let yourself feel it a little, it taints everything. Mary swallowed hard and picked up her doll again, smoothing the puffed sleeve of the dress where it layered over the gaping shoulder. *Poor Mama! Anyone would get tired with five girls and a house to take care of. I ought not judge her.* She shoved the anger back down again, but the rest of her time in her room was spoiled by it any way.

Though it did not lift her spirits much, her time upstairs did seem to magically erase much of the chaos of Mr Cole's visit. When Mary came downstairs the next day, the bouquet was gone—whether taken away by Mr Cole or disposed of by Lieutenant Stubbs, she dared not ask—and Lieutenant Stubbs's mood showed a reassuring irritation. She was sure if Lieutenant Stubbs and Mr Cole had agreed to a duel, Lieutenant Stubbs would be solemn and polite to everyone to fit the grandeur of his commitment. The fact that he scolded Mary for not sending Mr Cole away at once and glowered at Lydia across the breakfast table sent a wave of relief through her.

They spent a full week in a state of civil tension. Lydia took Mary to Almack's rather than to a biology lecture with the Informed Ladies of London Association. After hearing so much of how ladies of higher society greedily sparred for vouchers, Mary expected Almack's to resemble a palace, but in truth it was simply another set of elegant supper rooms, card rooms, and a ballroom. Gilt curled over the edges of looking glasses and covered parts of the pilasters, and the sofas weathered their visitors with good stuffing and smooth fabric, but beyond those things, Mary did not discover any notable attraction. No doubt the lure was supposed to be the company, but Mary found that wanting as well. Every young lady was on her best behaviour, prim and correct, and every gentleman prattled the dull talk of weather. Mary and Lydia milled at one side of the room and endured the tedium. Lydia refrained from dancing to better attract men to her sister, and Mary's lack of conversation discouraged most gentlemen from asking her to dance, so the two stood and sipped ratafia while Miss Poppit fended off suitors and Lady Crestwood preened at her protégée's success.

By the end of March, the strong winds whipping at bonnets had softened into playful breezes, and the steady warmth of the spring sun made gentlemen shed their greatcoats and loosen their cravats. The nights still breathed a chill outdoors, but when Lady Crestwood gave a rout at her home on the first of April, the indoors were stifling enough to inspire hundreds of ladies to wave their fans and complain of the swelter.

The frenzy of Lady Crestwood's rout put Almack's to shame, as far as the enjoyment of the guests went. The mad crush pummelled Mary's ears with the hum of conversation, shouts attempting to carry to an ear a few feet away, and raucous laughter from gentlemen who had partaken of Lord Crestwood's vintages with too great a liberality. The tangy scent of freshly opened wine bottles melded with the puffs of perfumed air emanating from well-coiffed ladies. The repeated shoves of guests around her drove Mary into a corner, and it was not until she spied an opening at a whist table and secured it that she felt safe from stomping feet and friendly buffeting. The noise in the card room was less obtrusive, though still great—the hiss of distant ocean, rather than the emphatic crash of waves upon rocks. The others at the table nodded a greeting at her, saying little as they divided the cards and studied their hands.

Clutching her cards in one hand, Mary dabbed at her neck with a handkerchief, hoping to remove the sheen of sweat on her skin and keeping her gaze uplifted. Every time she glanced down, the expanse of bosom displayed by her gown shocked her. Lydia's tastes had shifted from those of a country maiden, and she had ensured Mary's gowns would be *à la mode*.

More than that, Mary's curves had filled out since she had grown daring enough to ask for more of the foods she liked, and Addleby had spent two days letting out all her gowns. The idea of having curves where she was accustomed to bones and skin disconcerted Mary, but she had to admit her figure had improved. Perhaps she still had a long way to go, but now she was recognisable as Lydia's sister, despite the difference in hair colour.

Mary nodded in appreciation to something her whist partner said. The clatter of dishes in the supper room and the hum of talk here made it hard to make out her partner's words, but as Mary was more accustomed to nodding than adding any substantial remark to the conversation, she found little hardship in the noise. She simply played her cards, smiled at the players, and tried to keep her gaze from seeking out Mr Cole.

Even if he were here, I ought not speak to him. She immersed herself in the game again, but all too soon, her head popped up to check the crowd another time. She did not find Mr Cole, only Lydia, who chattered at the other players as she drew Mary away.

"So sorry! If I had not seen you had just finished a rubber, I would not dare to claim her," Lydia said, flashing her pearly teeth in way that could be taken as a smile or a warning, just as her audience chose. "A gentleman is *very* pressing, and he will not be satisfied until he has seen my Mary."

At that, Mary's heartbeat became palpable, thrumming with an unsteady pace in her chest. "Who is it?" she asked in a casual tone, as Lydia led her from the card room.

"Do not faint when I tell you." Mischief lit Lydia's blue eyes, and she squeezed Mary's arm. "Mr Covington! He usually escorts Miss Poppit all around the room while everybody stares, but tonight, he desires to walk with *you*. What a *coup*!"

The image did not appeal. "Must I, Lydia?"

"Of course you must. Now say, 'Yes, Lydia,' and I will make all your dreams come true." She did not wait for Mary's answer, though, and tugged her sister to Mr Covington's side. Admittedly, the tugging was appropriate in such a pushing crowd; there seemed little other method for proceeding. Mary wondered how anyone could stroll about the rout in such a mash. *At least it will be impossible for everyone to stare at us.*

Lydia kept up a stream of chatter as they went. "La, you look ten times better these days, Mary. Why, you actually have a figure! And your gown suits your colouring quite nicely. But it needs a little something. I meant to lend you a brooch—a little wreath of gold, whose red stones match the colour of your sash exactly—only I could not find it. I shall have to scold Addleby for losing it, for it would have completed your *ensemble* to a nicety."

"Oh." Mary could not peel her mind away from the upcoming '*coup*' enough to make more of an answer, but

Lydia was used to that. She pranced to a throng of gentlemen, tossing a few flirtatious smiles here and there as if she
were throwing flowers.

"Here she is, Mr Covington! Do take care of her." Lydia
patted Mary's arm before wriggling into the mass of people,
leaving Mary to turn wistful eyes on Mr Covington. *I hope he
will not expect me to say much.*

The dark blue of Mr Covington's coat drew taut across the
man's shoulders and rippled slightly over his chest, making
Mary think of a fast-running stream. The loose curls of his
dark hair were slicked with sweat, adding to the illusion.
"Miss Bennet, how pleasant to see you. Shall we walk?"

Mary nodded, grateful she did not have to say anything, and
wondering how Lydia had finagled the gentleman into
singling her out. For better or for worse, their progress
through the guests was erratic and halting, requiring them to
pull up short again and again, or even study their feet to
avoid stepping on those of other guests. The concentration
needed for simple movement prevented much conversation.

"Let us pause there for a moment," Mr Covington said,
tilting his head towards a series of pillars at one end of the
room. It was an out-of-the-way enough place to catch one's
breath, but a few other couples had already discovered that—
most notably Captain Roarke and Lady Sarah Randall.

Lady Sarah's gloved hand rested on the captain's arm in an
innocent way, but she leaned over it to whisper in his ear
with an intensity that disturbed Mary. Lady Sarah's lowered
lids barely hid the sultriness of her gaze.

"Good evening, Captain," Mary said, able to find her voice at last. "Where is Lady Lucy?" Her glance at Lady Sarah was sharp, but the noblewoman paid her no heed.

"She is ill. Nothing serious, but she could not come." The captain bobbed a bow and began leading Lady Sarah away.

"I will come and visit her tomorrow, then," Mary called to him as he disappeared into the mass of bodies.

"Lady Lucy is Lord Crestwood's daughter, is she not?" Mr Covington's voice held no interest, only politeness.

"She is." Mary could not think of anything to add to that, so she pretended to be intrigued with a nearby wall hanging.

"Would you like a glass of ratafia, Miss Bennet?"

"Oh, yes." Fetching a glass and pressing through the guests would take a great deal of time, and Mary sighed with relief as Mr Covington waded in on his errand. For a moment, she watched the London elite in peace. Captain Roarke still flirted with Lady Sarah, but at a more discreet distance. Lydia and Mr Wickham passed by, squabbling with an air of contentment that made Mary wonder if her efforts at smoothing vexations between them had deprived them of a comfortable closeness. *I think they almost* like *teasing one another.* Mary averted her gaze, unwilling to consider the idea further, and spotted Miss Poppit stepping through the milling groups with a practised grace.

"What a delightful evening!" Miss Poppit's cheeks were bright with colour, something more than rouge. "Lieutenant Babbingford and I have been quizzing the guests. He has such wit." Miss Poppit leaned in towards her, though no one was likely to hear her over the hum of the rout any way. "Though I fear Lady Crestwood does not care for him."

"I think she is looking higher for you, Miss Poppit."

Miss Poppit acknowledged the comment with a frown. "I am much indebted to her ladyship, of course, but…" Shaking her head, she dove into an altered line of thought. "Lieutenant Babbingford knows your brother-in-law very well. I told him all about that day at the gallery with Mr Cole, and the favour I did you, and he thinks Lieutenant Stubbs ought to be told."

"You told him all that!" Mary flushed in indignation. She had never even met this gentleman, and Miss Poppit's *tendre* for him had apparently drawn him into their secrets.

"It was on my mind, Miss Bennet." The sententious air Miss Poppit gave her declaration reminded Mary of herself, in an earlier, pious mood. "Lieutenant Babbingford is the height of discretion, however. So you have no need to worry he will bandy it about."

"I hope *he* has better discretion than you have had." Mary could not help but show her irritation, though she knew she needed to conciliate Miss Poppit to prevent further divulging of her secret meeting with Mr Cole.

"I only did what was right." Sure of her ground, Miss Poppit lifted her chin.

"Well, you have committed me to telling Lieutenant Stubbs, lest his friend tell him before me. And my brother-in-law is so prickly! You do not know what you have done."

"Truth is best, Miss Bennet."

Though Mary generally agreed with the sentiment, and even with the self-righteous air Miss Poppit gave it, she found it only vexing now. "I hope that comforts you, if Lieutenant Stubbs decides to call out Mr Cole." Perhaps it would not be as bad as all that—really, Mary had averted the worst of the trouble by preventing Lydia's meeting Mr Cole. But Kitty and her husband might focus on the scandal risked rather than the actual consequences.

"Duelling is a part of a soldier's life."

"It is not supposed to be." Mary's voice sounded sour. "They are supposed to save their bloodlust for the battlefield."

"Miss Bennet!" Miss Poppit's wide eyes showed Mary she had gone too far.

Further proof anger cannot be contained, Mary thought, regretting her outburst, but she still felt nothing kindly for Lady Crestwood's protégée. "I fear I am out of temper. You may inform Lieutenant Babbingford that I will make my brother-in-law aware of what happened, and that I trust both he and you will not mention it again." It was awkward enough discussing it at all in the middle of a rout. Mary wished Miss Poppit had been more circumspect in where she introduced the topic.

"Of course we will not!" The heat in Miss Poppit's voice surprised Mary, but the young woman soon got hold of her feelings and smoothed them down the same way she smoothed the front of her gown. "I only wanted to make sure justice was served. As your sister's husband, Lieutenant

Stubbs has a right to defend his family." The colour began seeping from her cheeks, leaving them their usual light pink. "Your secret is safe with my friend and me."

Mary believed her, not because she thought Miss Poppit had truly repented, but rather because she trusted Miss Poppit's enjoyment of sharing secretive conversations with her beau. Miss Poppit would not give that up lightly.

"Thank you." Mary forced the words out. She turned to face the crowd, where the riverlike current of Mr Covington, bearing aloft a glass of ratafia, battled the eddies of guests. His lips, tensed with the concentration of navigating the masses of guests, relaxed into a smile when he saw Miss Poppit, and even as he presented the glass to Mary, he spoke with animation to her friend.

"How pleasant to come upon you again, Miss Poppit! Might we have another dance?"

"We have had two already, Mr Covington." Miss Poppit's tone was firm, and the man relented and submerged them in chat instead. Mary listened with half an ear.

Kitty and her husband will be so angry at Lydia. Not that Mary was well-pleased with the dashing Mrs Wickham herself, but she hated to spur on the arguments with more information. Her muscles tingled with exhaustion, as if she could feel the sensations of terror and angst rattling her already. *Mr Cole must be right that some people enjoy wrangling with one another. What else can explain all the foolery this Season?* She felt tired of rescuing Lydia, tired of preventing quarrels and mending fences for other people. She wished she had a ruthless side like Miss Poppit, who could hear war stories with a gleam in her eye and was proud of her beau's penchant for duelling. *But I am not like that.* The memory of her rage spilling out when Lieutenant Stubbs and Mr Cole had argued rose up unbidden.

Am I?

Twenty

Now that Miss Poppit was with them, conversation with Mr Covington proceeded with more ease. Miss Poppit supplied any deficiencies in Mary's answers and offered new subjects, shaping the talk with an adroitness that made Mary envy her polish. Mr Covington relaxed into the exchange, and his smiles and nods signalled a greater comfort. Although he paid compliments to Mary, his eyes remained on Miss Poppit as he did so.

I suppose he only singled me out to make her jealous. Try to, any way. Miss Poppit did not look perturbed in the least, not even when Mr Covington compared Mary's beauty to an orchid. *He has not touched her heart. But somehow Lieutenant Babbingford has.* It was unfortunate for everyone. As a suitor, Lieutenant Babbingford did not have the *éclat* fitting for the protégée of Lady Crestwood and the belle of the Season.

Suddenly Mary spied a chestnut-haired head above the grouped gentlemen and ladies, and thick, wide shoulders pushing them apart. Mr Cole moved as directly as he could towards her, jostling and being jostled as he went. Mary's stomach fluttered, and she could feel ratafia slosh within. Though pressed against her elbow, Miss Poppit felt very far away from Mary now, and Mr Covington even farther.

"Miss Bennet." Mr Cole only had room for a tiny bow, but he performed it with dexterity.

Mary knew it was wiser to make excuses and avoid him, but her heart sang too wild a song when he smiled. She curtseyed, unable to speak.

"I had thought I might see you at the biology lecture on Wednesday."

Did he really mean to pretend he and Lieutenant Stubbs had not argued? Did he not see it with the severity she did? "My sister took me to Almack's that night. I fear it took so long to prepare, we did not go anywhere in the afternoon."

"Ah, I suppose that is *de rigueur* for a young lady's Season."

Somehow Mary could not leave him with a false impression. "It may be, but it was very dull. I had much rather have been at the lecture. I know so little of biology. Will you tell me about it?"

Pleased, he entered into a recapitulation of the subject matter. Mary discovered that when he was not trying to impress anyone, Mr Cole could deliver a scientific explanation with clarity and succinctness. "That is the gist of it," he said, finishing.

"You have explained it well. I wish you made all your lectures so clear and simple." A wry smile played upon her lips.

"Well, I am working on it. No doubt your suggestions will help with next week's. You will not desert me for dressing all day for Almack's then, I hope?"

"I do wish to be there, but I do not know…" Mary hesitated, thinking Miss Poppit might overhear, but when she turned slightly, she realised Miss Poppit and Mr Covington had wandered off. In Mary's focus on the geologist, she had never noticed their going. "It is awkward, with Lieutenant Stubbs and Lydia and all."

"Oh. Of course." His nose wrinkled with irritation.

"Do you know, Miss Poppit thinks I should tell Lieutenant Stubbs about that day in the gallery, the day I met you to persuade you not to meet Lydia."

"Whatever for?"

"She says his friend in the army will tell him, otherwise." Though the topic still pained her, she found humour in it now that Mr Cole was near. "Perhaps he is feeling excluded."

Mr Cole broke into a loud laugh, slapping his thigh. "Excluded? What do you say, Miss Bennet—shall we bring him to our next clandestine meeting?"

"There are not going to be any more such meetings," Mary said, but she was amused and flattered nonetheless by the idea.

"Poor fellow! By all means, tell him, if it will bring him any comfort." Mr Cole's laughter had ended, but his whole being was suffused with a cheerful jocularity that made Mary feel safe.

I suppose it is rather droll. Her chest felt lighter, and she ventured to take Mr Cole's arm. "Apparently Lieutenant Stubbs hates secrets almost as much as scandal."

"Well, if I cannot appease him about the scandal, the least I can do is reveal some secrets." Mr Cole's fingers tucked around Mary's, securing her grasp on his arm. "Your brother-in-law is proving nearly as great a distraction as you are, Miss Bennet."

"But not as great as my sister?" It was an awkward question, but clinging to his arm as she was, Mary felt brave enough to ask it.

He studied her face, the humour draining out of his own. When he spoke, his tone was wooden. "Of course, Mrs Wickham is very distracting." He averted his gaze, and Mary cursed herself for bringing up the subject of Lydia.

Why does he sound so strange? He was always flippant about her before. Could it be that his feelings have become something deeper for her? The idea swept through her like cold water dousing her entire body.

"Are you trembling, Miss Bennet? Are you unwell?" Mr Cole had paused their stroll, and his gaze was again fixed on her.

"I am well." She forced herself to take a deep breath. Luckily, Sir Reginald passed by at that moment, and his hearty greeting distracted Mr Cole. The two indulged in a cheerful review of the rout, the biology lecture, and Lady Sarah's new tiara. The camaraderie between the two puzzled Mary.

They seemed to spit venom at each other earlier, and here they are, chatting like friends. The thought reminded her of the Wickhams and their playful squabbles as they passed through Lady Crestwood's rout. The smaller Lucas brothers had been like that, too: bitter one moment, chums the next. Mary had never understood it. How could they let go of hurtful words so easily? How could they forget the past without effort? Or was it that they *enjoyed* the sparring?

The way I enjoy sparring with Mr Cole. It was not the first time she had acknowledged that banter with Mr Cole was strangely satisfying, but now she saw it in a new perspective. Perhaps the world was not full of angry people, as she had always imagined. Perhaps most of them were just relishing a competition of words and postures. The notion drove a sour, sickly feeling into her belly, one that hinted Mary might have been dangerously, painfully wrong for more of her life than she had ever realised.

As Sir Reginald moved off, Mr Cole returned his attention to Mary. "How is your...um...friend?"

She could tell he meant Hannah. "I have not found a solution for her. But her situation is not obvious yet, so Mr Wickham agreed she could stay a few weeks longer. It was generous on his part."

"He seems a patient man." Mr Cole looked thoughtful, rubbing his chin with his hand.

"He is." *And you have reason to know it.* Mary did not want to bring up Lydia again, though. "Have you heard anything more about your father?"

Mr Cole winced. "He is still ill, if that is what you mean. He is not likely to get any better."

"If you delay going back to the estate, he may not have a chance to teach you how to run it," Mary said, her words inching out in caution, feeling her way.

"Believe me, I have thought of that."

"It would make you feel like an even less worthy squire than—"

"I know." His abrupt tone held no animosity, only hurt. "It must seem foolish to you. I cannot stand to be counted as the second-best brother and the second-best squire, so I hold off and stay away and will no doubt make an even worse squire than I might have been."

"Then why do it?"

"You do not know what it is like, having a hundred tenants and servants stare at you and mutter that you will never be the man Thomas was. You do not know what it is like to have your father and mother sigh at your arrival, wishing a different son had lived." His arm tensed under Mary's finger-tips. "No one should have to bear that." His dark eyes bore into hers. "And anything that draws me towards that, anything that pushes me to settle down on a country estate and suffer ignominy—anyone who cajoles me into doing that, is my enemy."

She was too surprised to take offence. "Is that a threat?"

He shook his head, his intense expression dissolving into a glum one. "I did not think you would understand. You are too much like Thomas. You angelic types cannot understand how hard it is for we mere mortals to perform a duty. You may be able to sacrifice yourself to make your sister's life easier, but I cannot sacrifice myself for Thomas. Or for my father."

"I did not think you really believed me to be angelic. I have certainly given enough evidence of my faults." Mary gave him a tentative smile, but he turned away.

"Yes, you have faults enough." His voice was listless as they moved through the thinning crowd. Lady Crestwood's rout would continue for hours yet, but the more fashionable guests were moving on to other gatherings, unwilling to stay in any one place too long. Mary's feet had room to step farther, and she kept pace with Mr Cole's slow walk easily.

"You mentioned my need for peace. You said it was a form of control," she said. "Did you really believe that?"

"Of course."

Her brows drew together. "I do not understand that. I only want peace because that is what is best for everyone." But already she had begun to doubt that, noticing the little quarrels that bothered her did not seem to bother others. "At least, that is what I thought."

"And now?"

She could not hide the discomfort she was feeling. "Now I am not so sure." She dropped her gaze to the floor. Spying Lieutenant Stubbs across the room, she dropped Mr Cole's arm and took a step away.

Mr Cole did not protest her motion. "Thank you."

"For what?" She risked looking into his eyes, and the warm tenderness in them made her catch her breath.

"For showing a little vulnerability. I always wondered what sorts of things Thomas thought about, what worried him. He never said. But when I talk with you, I feel as though I understand him better." He had a wistful tilt to his head, as if he were remembering something long ago.

"I am glad. Good-bye, Mr Cole."

"Good-bye."

She ambled across the room, stepping between couples without thought and meandering to the doorway. Lieutenant Stubbs and Kitty were too engrossed in talk to notice Mary at first, but she took Kitty's arm and herded them to the carriage.

"Must we go, already?" Lieutenant Stubbs's voice was not sullen for once. "What about the Wickhams?"

"We will send the carriage back for them," Mary said. "Let us go alone, for now. I wish to speak with you." It would not be easy to tell the Stubbses about going to the gallery, but Miss Poppit had not given her much choice. *I hope they will take it better than I fear.* She did not feel saintly or angelic, only tired and resigned. She wondered if Thomas Cole had felt like that as well.

Whatever he was like, he is nothing to Richard Cole. However moral and full of integrity, he could not have had Mr Cole's boisterous laugh, nor his muddled disregard of foolish propriety, nor his sharp intellect and instinct for science, nor his provoking smile. The more she knew of him, the more Mary liked him. *Others might have idolised Thomas, but had I met him, I am sure I would still have preferred my Mr Cole.* She blushed at her own thoughts. *Well, he is not* mine, *of course. I mean only that he is the one I know.* He had a charm and a value no other possessed, not even his doughty brother.

But Mary did not know how to make him see that.

MARY CLIMBED THE STAIRS OF THE ROARKES' lodging house, avoiding the weak boards in the stairs with a dancing adroitness as she ascended. The maid-of-all-work gave a familiar nod at Mary as she let her inside, and soon Mary was beaming at her friend as they nestled by the window and embroidered. The April breeze looped through the window and tugged at their embroidery silks, but it was a welcome relief to the stifling warmth of the lodgings. London had not grown that hot yet, but somehow the lodging house soaked up all the stale air and made the rooms feel hotter than they ought.

"I feel as though I have just braved two dragons," Mary said, giggling. "Lydia wanted me to stay home to receive callers, and Kitty wanted me to go with her to Lady Crestwood's, but I denied them both." The memory of their disappointed faces still stung, but Mary could feel something underneath the guilt, a feeling of strength that had slept too long and was now beginning to stir. "Captain Roarke said you were too ill to come to the rout last night, and I was determined to see if you were all right."

Lady Lucy dropped her gaze to the neat arabesques she was sewing around the edges of a neckline. "I was not very ill." She pushed her needle through the fabric with a slow, hesitating motion. "Did you enjoy the rout?"

"It was hot and crowded, but I was able to play cards for a long while, and people do not expect you to talk much when you are playing, you know." Mary smiled in remembrance. "And Mr Cole was rather kind. He told me more about his brother."

"Was Lady Sarah Randall there?" Lady Lucy kept her eyes fixed on her stitches.

"Y-yes."

"And my husband—he spent a great deal of time by her side?"

Mary's lips drew down. Part of her suggested smoothing things over, lying or making light of the captain's behaviour, but the sleeping strength stirred again, as if it were turning over in bed. "He did. Lady Lucy, I do not mean to make trouble, but he seems overfond of Lady Sarah."

Lady Lucy's hands stilled. "I know he is. You are not revealing anything I did not know, really." She sighed. "It is understandable. She is so lovely and witty. Her father was an earl, you know."

Before Mary could reply, the front door was thrown open and Betsy came prancing in, stomping her feet and making whimpering noises that Mary suspected were intended to be whinnies.

"Betsy, you must knock first." Mrs Burton hurried in after her child, clutching a half-sewn gown to her chest and looking anxiously at Lady Lucy. "I am so sorry, Lady Lucy. Betsy ran out again, and some days the only way I can keep her indoors is to tell her she may visit you. She will be a good girl, if you but let her stay a few minutes."

Lady Lucy's tired face broke into a broad smile. "Why, of course she may visit, any time she likes. Betsy, would you like a tart? I bought one especially for you."

"Ponies don't eat tarts!" Betsy said, swinging about as if she had a long horse body rather than that of a tiny girl.

"We will call it an oatcake, then, my dear. Ponies like oats, do they not?"

Betsy nodded, and Mrs Burton threw a grateful look at her benefactor before returning to her own rooms to work. As Lady Lucy set the table and displayed the tart, Mary noticed a gleaming brooch on Betsy's dress. It was small, but of good quality: a gold wreath with red stones studding it. Just like the one Lydia lost. Mary's stomach soured. Or did she lose it? She could not help but review the trip to the shops with Lady Lucy, and the furtive gesture Lady Lucy seemed to make with the lace. As Betsy ate, Lady Lucy prepared tea for herself and Mary. Mary watched her friend's deft, ladylike movements and bit her lip. *I must be mistaken. She is the daughter of Lord Crestwood, not a thief.* But she could feel a slow resolve begin to build as Betsy finished her treat and pranced out the door, led by the maid to ensure she did not make a detour outside. *I will ask her, any way.*

"Betsy is a sweet child," Mary said, feeling her way. "You must like her very much. It seems as though you give her many gifts."

Lady Lucy sat down next to Mary and picked up her embroidery. *"Noblesse oblige,* Miss Bennet. And little girls like presents, pretty things and treats their mothers cannot buy them."

"You gave her that brooch, did you not?"

"Yes." Lady Lucy's lower lip trembled a moment, but she soon pressed on. "Betsy's mother almost refused to accept it, but I made her see sense."

I doubt it. She had sense on her side. Betsy's mother had probably seen the foolishness of giving a small child such a gift in such a neighbourhood, but had backed down when threatened with losing Lady Lucy's favour. Mary phrased her next words with care.

"My sister had a brooch very like it, but now she cannot find it. Did you happen to see it, the day you visited me? We went to Lydia's room to find the bracelet for my doll. You remember." When Lady Lucy did not answer, Mary pressed her, though a pang of sympathy went through her at the necessity of it. "And the day we went shopping together—there was a card of lace you seemed quite interested in." Mary paused as her friend lowered her head into her hands. "Will you not confide in me, Lady Lucy?"

"I—I took them. Both. And other things." The words began to flood out. "You do not know what it is like. We have so little compared to what I am accustomed to. I used to be able to buy any little pretty things I liked. Papa and Mama did not care. But now—" She suddenly shifted topics, as if her mind struggled to convey it all at once. "It gets so lonely here, with the captain away so much. No one visits but you. But Betsy is so lively and pleasing. She would not want to come very often, perhaps, if I did not give her nice things. And I owe it to her—she is far below my rank, and I must do something for those beneath me."

"Keeping an eye on Betsy while her mother is working is generous enough."

Lady Lucy shook her head with impatience. "That is the sort of thing a commoner would do. A friend of Mrs Burton's rank could offer that alone, but the daughter of Lord Crestwood has a distinction to maintain." Her eyes watered. "The captain says our finances are quite straitened and he cannot give me much money for the household. So sometimes I—take things—just to ensure I have something special for Betsy, or something I can sell." Her cheeks reddened as tears began to slip down them. "I know other ladies bear their decline in position with resignation, but I refused to let it all go. I turned into...a thief."

Mary stretched out to take the noblewoman's hand. "It is not entirely your fault, Lady Lucy. The captain is partly to blame as well."

"He courts other ladies, and gambles a great deal, and speculates, and spends our money on himself. I know it. I tried to pretend I did not know it, but I did. Oh, Miss Bennet! If you had known him while he was courting me, you would have seen how devoted he was, how kind. They were the happiest days of my life. He has gone a little astray, but I love him still." Her shoulders straightened in defiance. "Now that I have stolen, I am no better than he is." She rose and walked to the table, shifting the plate with the remains of Betsy's tart. "We are quite a pair. I can never reproach him now." There was an odd note of triumph in her voice, as if some small part of her was relieved.

"It is not much of a solution, to stoop to his level." The words sounded cruel to Mary, but she uttered them nonetheless.

Lady Lucy fished out a handkerchief and wiped at her tears. "Maybe we are fit for each other. Maybe all this is as it is meant to be." She drew a deep breath. "I can bear his fondness for Lady Sarah, but what are we to do for money? I said nothing when he took the pearls from my jewellery box and gambled them away. I did not reproach him when he wanted to exchange my wedding ring for a less expensive one—to pay our debts, he said. But we must have something to live on and some sort of comforts, and he gives me so little to spend." Her chest hitched. "Perhaps I am not supposed to have a baby because I would be even more tempted to—take things—if I had one."

"Do not say that." The sight of Lady Lucy's despondency drove Mary's thoughts into a mire of regret. *All this time, I told myself I was protecting her peace of mind by keeping silent. And now it seems she was suffering all the while. If I had pressed her to confide sooner, perhaps she would not have taken the brooch. Perhaps we could have done something to mend matters sooner.* She rose and stroked Lady Lucy's shoulder. "Things can yet turn out right.

If you stand up to your husband and insist on keeping more of the money your parents settled on you in your hands—"

"I could never do that. He would be so disappointed and angry!"

"Let him be angry." Mary could hardly believe the words coming out of her mouth. "It will make your life better, Lady Lucy." The image of Captain Roarke's self-assured, handsome face passed through her mind, and she found herself sharing Lady Lucy's doubts. *I do not know that I could stand up to him, either. And I am not in love with him.* "If you have not the courage, let us ask your parents for help. They will take measures to secure your comfort if you tell them what has been happening."

"Oh, no." Lady Lucy shook her head again, this time with an emphasis that showed determination within her distress. "I will get the brooch from Betsy and return it to you, and I will find some way to pay for the lace if I must, but I will not tell Mama what I have done. Nor Papa. They would be so ashamed, and my husband would feel so insulted at my relying on them!" She grasped Mary's hands. "Promise me you will not tell anyone, Miss Bennet. It would kill me to have my...bad behaviour...known."

Mary drew back. "I think nothing will change until you do something, and the best way is to let your parents know—"

"I cannot! Please, are my troubles not grievous enough already? Do not let me fear the betrayal of a confidence on top of everything." Lady Lucy's grip on her hands squeezed tighter. "I did think we were friends, Miss Bennet."

Mary avoided her gaze, but that meant glancing over the stained tablecloth, the thin curtains, the grimy floors, and the last-Season gown her friend had been trying to embroider into a semblance of newness. She remembered, too, the pang of Miss Poppit's betrayal of a confidence. The strength in her drowsed and then fell deep asleep. "I promise, then."

Lady Lucy forgot her pride enough to throw her arms around Mary and give her a fervent hug. "Thank you! I will get the brooch back the next time I see Betsy, and I will give it to you on your next visit. And I will put right the other things I took, somehow." She gave Mary a little push, as if eager to put distance between them before Mary could ask any more awkward questions. "Come and visit again in a few days, and you will see, things will be better."

What will be better? Annoyance stabbed through Mary, but she packed up her embroidery and retrieved her reticule. *The underlying problem yet remains.* She allowed Lady Lucy to usher her out the door, however, and tread downstairs with a thoughtful air. *What I thought was Lady Lucy's peace appears to have been—stagnation, or resignation, or something. She has sacrificed so much to keep a show of peace, but it did not secure her happiness. I feel sure nothing will change for the better until she speaks up.* But Mary could not deny her friend a promise of silence, even when she knew speaking up for Lady Lucy was vital. It was understandable that Lady Lucy would fear standing up to her husband and revealing a painful secret to her parents. But what excuse did Mary have?

Who is the real coward here?

Twenty-One

"It would be exactly the sort of particular attention that I would expect from a gracious wife," Mr Wickham was saying to Lydia as Mary entered the breakfast parlour. Several days had passed since her visit to Lady Lucy, and Mary had spent them mostly at home, trying to entertain a sister full of ennui. Lydia had stayed away from her usual haunts of society meetings and shops, and the change paled her face and gave a petulant pout to her mouth.

"And I would do it with all my heart if I but had it, Mr Wickham!" Lydia tossed her head, and Lieutenant Stubbs watched her with a solemn disdain.

"Do what? Had what?" Mary asked, lingering in the doorway. She was not sure she wanted to sit down to breakfast if there was going to be a row.

Lydia turned to her, her expression full of consternation and misery. "The Forsters are in London and are coming to dine tonight. Wickham says they have been very kind to us, given the unusual way we married. General Forster was quite put out when I left them in Brighton, but he got over that." Lydia never seemed to feel shame about their elopement; the most she would do was describe it as 'unusual,' however many lectures she was given. "They welcomed us back into their circle—after we became rich, any way. Wickham wants me to wear the brooch Mrs Forster gave me, but I cannot find it anywhere."

Mary's heart stilled. "The gold wreath? The one you told me about at Lady Crestwood's rout?"

"Yes, that one." Lydia turned back to her husband. "Surely Mrs Forster will understand that it is lost."

"*Is* it lost?" Mr Wickham question was pointed, and Mary winced.

But Lydia merely blinked uncertainly. "Do you mean one of the servants might have taken it? I am sure Addleby did not. She is quite loyal, and the brooch really very paltry compared to my other things."

"Paltry!" Mr Wickham compressed his lips and shoved back from his seat at the table. He paced back and forth one full length before he spoke. "You never will understand the value of things." He paced again. "Their means are not as great as ours, Mrs Wickham. I assure you, coming from the Forsters, that was a significant gift."

"You must not be rude, Lydia," Kitty said, her brow furrowing.

"Oh, I did not mean that. La!" Lydia pulled her hands to her lap, abandoning her toast. For once she looked chagrined. "Addleby will look again. Perhaps it dropped behind something. We will search the whole house, if you like. If any of the servants took it, I daresay we shall find it again."

"If the person who took it carried it off to sell or pawn, you will not find it." Mr Wickham's eyes narrowed, and though Lydia seemed unable to understand his suggestion, Mary caught it. A sinking feeling went through her core.

"Well, perhaps they have not taken it there yet," Lydia said. "They would not get much for it, any way."

The careless remark stung Mr Wickham, making his handsome face redden and his tongue loosen. "It would not pay for your trinkets and gowns, certainly. If you took it to the captain to sell for some bills you ran up—"

"Why, what an idea!" Lydia's eyes widened.

"You did it before."

"She did what?" Lieutenant Stubbs leapt up from the table, knocking over his cup. "Which captain?"

"Captain Roarke." Mr Wickham folded his arms over his chest.

"Yes, I did that, but it was long ago—ages ago. And you accuse me of this, Mr Wickham, after I told you about it and everything!" Lydia rose from the table as well, but her ordinary grace had turned into a wobble.

"Who would believe you, Lydia?" Lieutenant Stubbs asked, shaking his head. "You do everything you can to create scandal and secrets."

"Addleby and I will search everywhere, and we will find it, and you will be sorry for what you have said!" She rushed from the room, but Lieutenant Stubbs followed her with a grim set to his jaw.

Mr Wickham turned to go, but Mary stepped forward. "Mr Wickham, I can explain about the brooch."

"Can you?" His grimace did not encourage her.

"A person took it." She flushed, realising how ineffective her explanation sounded. "I cannot say who, or why, but I can get it back again if you let me have the carriage."

"You cannot say who? How convenient." Mr Wickham was normally the soul of politeness to Mary, and she blanched at his mocking tone. He said, "No doubt your loyalty to your sister prompts you—"

"No! No, Mr Wickham, it was not Lydia. Truly. It was someone else who took it, but she wants to return it. I will just go and fetch it from her." Mary had to hope he would not ask the carriage driver where Mary went; if he learned she had gone to the Roarkes, it would either reveal Lady Lucy's secret, or convince him Lydia had sold it to Captain Roarke.

"I need the carriage myself, but you can go in a hack." His expression still held suspicion. "Take Addleby with you, if you like."

"I will bring Hannah instead." She was sure Hannah would not reveal where they went.

"The maid with child?" Mr Wickham's frown was monstrous, as if the fires of jealousy and distrust had finally lit within him, only to explode into a bonfire. "She goes, this very day. I will not allow my reputation to be jeopardised by her presence any longer. At this stage, I need respectability to keep hold of that which others invest—" He broke off in confusion, and suddenly smoothed his face. "Not that I hold much, of course. I really care for respectability because it is the moral thing, is it not, Mary?"

Mary tried to ground herself, but she found his shifts in the conversation perplexing. "It is very moral, of course. But so is compassion. I had hoped for more time to help Hannah—"

"You have had weeks upon weeks. I cannot help it if you are not competent in dealing with such matters. No lady would be." He passed by, and Mary watched him go with a building distress. Hannah would be devastated; she had been counting on Mary to find a solution. *And now the best I can do is the London charity the vicar mentioned.* The maid would be humiliated, but at least she would not be out on the street.

After breaking the news to Hannah, taking Addleby to Lady Lucy's, retrieving the brooch, and restoring it to Mr Wickham, Mary felt herself drained and hopeless. Mr Wickham seemed somewhat mollified by the reappearance of the jewellery, though he still held his body taut, as if on guard. *Let us hope Addleby keeps her mouth shut. If he discovers I went to the Roarkes' to get it, I do not know what would happen. I should have insisted on getting the brooch from Betsy at once. I should have confronted Lady Lucy about the lace long ago. Perhaps none of this would have happened.* Passing by Lydia's room did nothing to cheer her; she could hear Lydia crying through the shut door. Mary had seen her sister cry before, of course. Often it happened when a gentleman was near and Lydia had not gotten her way, and her tears made her brown eyes round and lustrous. From the way sobs hitched beyond the door, Lydia's eyes were not likely round and lustrous now. *Probably squished and red, like mine are when I cry.* She felt sympathy for Lydia, but her sister refused her admittance, and Mary had to go to her own room in dejection.

Her doll waited on the vanity, posed for a cheerful outing. Mary picked her up and hugged her. "I just need to make things peaceful again," she told the doll, but doubts slid around the perimeter of her mind. She had feared having a conflict with her best friend, and the result was refusing to ask Lady Lucy about problems and then keeping a promise of silence that caused the Wickhams unrest. Her attempts at keeping peace had only made things worse.

"Perhaps it is not working quite the way I wanted," she said, propping the doll back up again. The tufts of stuffing were hanging further out of the gap in the shoulder, and Mary pushed them back in. "But I must keep trying. What else is there to do?"

The doll had no answers for her.

Twenty-Two

A grumble of thunder shook the windows of Lydia's drawing room, but Mary ignored it. Normally April thunderstorms would make her shake with fear, but no feat of wind or torrent seemed formidable next to Lieutenant Stubbs. He was grumbling into his teacup, his long, uniformed legs stretched out as if he were resting on a rampart rather than in a drawing room. He only looked up long enough to throw glares at Mary.

It is a disagreeable plan, but it is the best plan we have. While the Wickhams were out, Mary had been explaining Lizzy's idea that Mary should capture Mr Cole's attention to the Stubbses. Kitty took the idea in with wide eyes and giggles, while the lieutenant's brows drew lower and lower. "Pressing Lydia does not help anything. It only makes her upset, and then she acts more foolishly," Mary said, hoping the reminder would serve to deter Lieutenant Stubbs from making *her* upset as well.

"Fighting scandal with scandal? It cannot work any better than putting a fire out with fresh tinder." Kitty's husband moved his legs in restless agitation. It was clear he wished the solution could be something active on his part—an embankment to dash up, an enemy to skewer with a bayonet.

Mary stirred in her seat, catching a little of his restlessness. "Lizzy thinks this will work. She has more cleverness than all of us."

"You ought to let *me* do it," Kitty said, fielding her husband's annoyed look with a swift turn. "I would be more interesting for him. It is not as though you are accustomed to charming men, Mary."

Mary felt a stab of jealousy at Kitty's suggestion. It was unreasonable, given how much she had dreaded trying to flirt with Mr Cole. *It is just that once I have begun a task, I intend to finish it. That is all.* "No, Kitty. You do not know him, and Lydia has been competing with you all her life. If she saw you take an interest in him, she would pursue him all the more. She finds my efforts to attract him—amusing. Not threatening." Mary realised she was using Lizzy's arguments, posed against her all those months ago. Kitty was only phrasing the doubts and suggestions Mary herself had had.

"It seems a fool idea." Lieutenant Stubbs was far from convinced, but he agreed that Mary might as well try. Though he did not have the distaste for a duel that Mary had, he had no desire to take life needlessly, either. "I suppose Kitty had better chaperon you to Maddox's, and then disappear at a convenient moment." His brows furrowed further. "If you are sure you are safe with him." The iron in his voice warned he would not stay his hand if Mary were harmed.

"I will be fine." As far as Mary was concerned, the matter was settled, but hours later she found Kitty had other ideas. With little to do in the Wickhams' household, Kitty had lounged about and mulled over the puzzle. Even as one thunderstorm dwindled and left London to soak in its puddles in silence, and then another storm stirred into life afterward, Kitty's brow furrowed in thought. By the time the two ladies were ready to go to the assembly rooms, a wry smile teased Kitty's lips.

Oh, dear. Mary viewed the sight with a shiver of annoyance. Kitty had played the role of a serious matron for too long, apparently; she positively jumped at the chance for a little scheming.

"Be careful, Kitty," Lieutenant Stubbs said as they left him, as if Mr Cole might torch the assembly rooms with her in them, or drag her to pistols at dawn.

"Do not worry!" Kitty's smile enveloped the man as she touched his arm in reassurance, and then she hurried after Mary, her figure backlit by a flash of lightning. She and Mary had to dart into the carriage as it rolled up, clasping their bonnets to their heads as rain gushed over them. When the carriage door slammed shut, the roar of the rain faded to a hiss, but the musty smell of stirred dust and electricity in the air remained.

"I think it will all be great fun, outmanoeuvring Lydia," Kitty said, "but do we really need to go in a downpour? The assembly rooms will be half empty, no matter what the ladies promised."

Mary felt her heart leap at the sudden crack of thunder, but for once, the sensation felt giddy and pleasurable. "So much the better. I will have more of a chance to beguile Mr Cole."

"Beguile!" Though the velvet clouds outside dimmed the daylight, Kitty's expression was clear enough: amusement crinkled her eyes and nose. "I have never heard you talk like that before, Mary. You used to give sermons about how demure ladies ought to be."

Mary cringed at the thought. Not that she did not still agree ladies should be demure—at least, a little demure here and there—but she did not like thinking of how stuffy and knowing she had tried to appear, year after year. *And really I knew nothing at all.* "I used to talk like that, Kitty, but I have grown a little since then."

"I would say you got younger, not more grown up." Kitty chuckled. Mary stared out the window, smelling the stale air of the carriage mix with the clean scent of the rain outside. The gush of pleasure welling up within felt strange to her, but welcome. "So, what exactly are you going to do at the assembly rooms?"

"I promised Mr Cole I would help him plan the expedition to Moseley Gorge." The wheels of the carriage sprayed water in every direction as it rolled forward, and Mary watched the splashes with a glee unusual to her. *The drops are like diamonds. No, better, they are twinkling stars, and we are riding through the heavens.* She suppressed a giggle.

"So you and he will sit there and plan a party—"

"An expedition, not a party. We are all to go collect geological samples and take refreshment near a landslide."

"A party with rocks, then." Kitty was unimpressed. "And I am to sit there beside you and watch you plan? It sounds dull for all three of us."

"You are right, Kitty, it *would* be dull for all three of us. That is why you should help the other ladies supervise repairs while I help Mr Cole."

Kitty's mouth drew down in disappointment, although she knew her role was to disappear. "There must be more I can do. I was thinking I could help you allure him." She slouched back in her seat, thinking, and Mary tried to think faster, to give Kitty something to do before her boredom prodded her to change the plan.

"Perhaps you can distract Mrs Appleton."

Kitty looked up, curious.

"Most of the ladies will not be there today, because of the rain, and the few who will, likely will be too busy to notice I am alone with Mr Cole." Mary smoothed her pelisse, scattering raindrops that had lain atop it like beads adorning a gown. "But Mrs Appleton will interfere."

"Mrs Appleton?" Kitty could not hide her disbelief.

"She likes to take charge of me."

"You are mad! Mrs Appleton could not say boo to a goose, not even if it were sitting on her head and honking. I have never heard her speak more than a few words to anyone."

"Then she must think me less than a goose, because she certainly orders me about." Mary's eyes narrowed. "Probably she is too scared of you, and most people, to turn dictatorial. But with me, she is almost…a despot."

Kitty wore a bemused smile. "So Mrs Appleton has a taste for power, does she? Interesting." Her hand flexed on her reticule. "I suppose I can keep her crushed underfoot for the evening, if it will serve any purpose. She is no despot to *me*." Mary's quick agreement mollified her further. "But why is this man so fixated on Lydia? She cannot share any real interests with him." She gave Mary a narrow look. "Do *you*?"

"Lydia may not be as interested in geology as I am, but her beauty and charm distract him. I distract him too, he says."

Kitty tapped her lips with her fingers in thoughtfulness. "What does he need distracting from?"

"He has—family difficulties." She did not feel comfortable revealing Mr Cole's confidences, but she was not sure if that was because they truly were a secret, or if she simply wanted to keep more of him to herself.

Kitty puffed a breath, as if dismissing the subject. "Probably his parents want him to marry, and he does not wish it."

Mary turned back to the window in irritation, trying to catch more gleams of splashing raindrops. "Why would you say that?"

"Because he was chasing a married woman. No man who wants to wed does such a thing. It is a way to keep suitable young ladies at bay." The increasing patter of rain on the carriage roof muted her words, but somehow they stood out like rolling thunder to Mary.

"That is ridiculous!" For some reason, the idea of Mr Cole marrying disturbed Mary, even if only a hypothesis.

"You think he is seeking a partner, then? Miss Poppit is quite a lady. I daresay any family would be pleased to welcome her as his wife." Kitty's statements felt more and more like prodding, and Mary shifted in her seat. "I suppose your theory is that he has a *tendre* for her, or someone like her, and he is putting everyone off the scent by chasing Lydia."

"He is not doing anything of the kind." Mary could imagine Mr Cole settling down on his father's estate, marrying some decorous young woman of his town for her money or rank, and living in a kind of dull contentment. The image was uncomfortable, but it was nothing to the idea of Mr Cole loving such a person. *I can understand marrying for tranquillity at home, for rank, for wealth. But if he truly loved someone—if he teased her, and kissed her, and worshipped the ground she walked on...* The thought was intolerable. *No, he must stay in London, and we shall see each other again and again. I do not wish to lose him.* The stream of water rippling down the London streets still caught flashes of lamplight and glinted, but Mary could not find the joy in it anymore. *I was so happy a moment ago, and then Kitty had to be cross.* She had not been cross, though, not exactly. She had simply said Mr Cole might marry someone else.

A crushing feeling squeezed Mary's heart, and she felt her head spin. Why should such things so disturb her? Why should she feel so light-hearted knowing she was going to see Mr Cole, and then so upset at the thought of his marriage? *It is so obvious. How have I fooled myself for so long?* It was too cruel a fate, to fall in love with the man who lived to flirt with her sister.

The carriage heaved to at the doors of Maddox's, and Mary and Kitty dipped into the water and hurried inside, leaving the carriage to launch itself back down the swirling puddles and currents. Mary left her sister as soon as she could, unwilling to see how much Kitty had guessed from their conversation. *Does she suspect that I am the one with a* tendre? *Did she mean to warn me?* In her rush to get away from her, Mary stumbled over a wet dog lying at the door of the office where she worked with Mr Cole.

"I am sorry, Hercules." She reached down to pat the dog, who leaped up and licked her hand with canine forgiveness. Mr Cole sat back in his chair, his legs stretching out in a casual pose. He did not even rise to greet her with a bow.

He does not act like a suitor, but like a friend. She told herself she had no reason to expect otherwise, but some secret part of herself was disappointed.

"This rain is perfect for our purposes," Mr Cole said, beckoning her to a chair. "If we plan the expedition for later this week, the disjoining in the land will be quite fresh."

"We cannot do it as quickly as all that," Mary said. She buckled down to work, explaining the arrangements she had planned for refreshments, carriages, servants, and an itinerary.

Mr Cole listened with an impressed air. "And here I thought I had been quite practical, gathering enough tools for the ladies to use in scraping samples." He leaned forward, tucking his legs under his chair. "Do you really think this will please Lady Crestwood?"

"I am sure. It will be exciting for the ladies, and it will make them feel important. You cannot do better." A crack of thunder made her start, and she pressed a trembling hand to her head. *I hope something will please Lady Crestwood, for she has some painful revelations to come.*

"What is it? Are you ill? Is it the storm?" Mr Cole drew his anxious face to hers.

"I am not ill. I just had some unpleasant surprises recently." When he gave her a sympathetic look, her heart melted. "Among other things, Hannah has been sent to a London charity."

"I am sorry. I know she did not want that."

"I still hope to think of something, but it appears she will be stuck being pointed at by all her former friends." Mary sighed. "And Mr Wickham and Lydia had a disagreement."

"Not about me this time."

The certainty in his voice irritated Mary. "How do you know that?"

"Because I have been so obedient to your will." The mocking lilt to his tone infuriated her further, but he took no notice. "You wished me to distance myself from her, and I have."

"You came to her house and asked for her!"

"But I knew she would not be there. I made sure."

"And then you argued with Lieutenant Stubbs, as if you were determined—"

"Well, I was not going to let that sneering pup think he could order me about. Of course I had no real intention of pursuing his sis—Mrs Wickham." He flushed, the redness mottling his skin. "And I stayed away from her all during Lady Crestwood's rout. And since you and she have been going to Almack's on Wednesdays, I have not seen you at lectures. Not even my own." The genuine disappointment in his face shamed Mary.

"I wanted to come. But after Mr Wickham and Lydia argued —I dared not do anything to disrupt things further." She had sacrificed something Mr Cole valued to keep the peace, and now she felt the wrongness of it. "How was it?" she asked in a tentative voice.

He shook his head with chagrin. "It actually went very well. No one fell asleep this time. And several people asked questions—foolish ones, for the most part, but at least it showed they were interested." The lines around his eyes softened. "I suppose I must admit some of your advice was good."

"I am glad." She cast her gaze down. "I have been thinking… about some of your advice, as well."

"My advice?" His eyebrows lifted. "I do not remember giving any."

Her voice faltered. "It was about needing peace too much. Trying to control people, just so that I could feel safe. I think you meant that I should let people go their own way a little more, even if it means they argue with one another. Or with me." Her fingers pressed against her palms, squeezing as she gained confidence. "I cannot say I agree with you completely, of course. I have seen how destructive conflict is in a family."

Without intending it, Mary found herself spilling out the story of Harry Lucas's estrangement, admitting it was her revelation of his secret to his father that began the feud. "It may be true that people like you and Sir Reginald can argue openly and still be friends because you both share underlying values, like scientific truth. But Harry and Sir William talking just hurt everyone. If I had kept silent, as I usually did, Harry would still be a part of their family."

Mr Cole's legs shifted, pushing his chair back. "Perhaps. If he were, he would likely be miserable."

"Miserable! As one of the Lucases!"

Mr Cole's expression turned wry. "As the scamp in a family, I can testify to the need to break free and pursue one's own way. Harry is probably happier as he is, strange as it might seem to you." He gave a bark of a laugh. "If it got him away from fellows like that sullen brother-in-law of yours, I can understand his satisfaction very well."

Mary folded her hands, trying to keep them from showing her distress. "Lieutenant Stubbs may be a nuisance, but he is one of us." Watching Mr Cole's knowing look, something shifted in Mary, and she found a giggle bubbling up to the surface. "Well, I always did prefer the Lucas boys. I would much rather Lieutenant Stubbs had feuded with us all."

"It would have provided a great relief to many," he said in a dry tone, and she giggled again. Hercules's tail wagged, sensing the happiness of his friends, and he nuzzled Mary's hand on her lap. When she petted the hound, Mr Cole surveyed her with amusement. "I rather think you were terrified of him at one time."

"I was a little nervous. But he has grown on me." She gave the dog one last pat, and then turned back to the stack of notes for the expedition. "Shall we get back to work? We do not have that much time to secure your triumph in London." This time, the teasing note in her voice did not trouble her.

"Ah, yes, my triumph." He drew closer to her, pulling his chair next to hers. Though his thigh was not touching hers, it was near enough that she could feel the heat from his body. "I ought to repay you somehow, if this works."

"Staying away from Lydia is payment enough."

Her response made him frown, though she did not know why. He bent over the pages of notes, running a finger down the list, but his mind did not seem to be on the task. "I suppose if I have rousing success with the Informed Ladies, my mother will not dare to ask me to visit for months and months."

"And you can play the scamp a while longer."

Again, her answer seemed to dissatisfy him, though he only furrowed his brow and avoided her eyes. He bent yet closer to the pages, and incidentally, nearer Mary's head. "It is a pity I am not brave enough to return home. You might encourage me, Miss Bennet."

"Encourage you?" She was surprised enough to lift her head and gaze straight into his dark brown eyes. "But it is not my place to determine for you. It is true that I think you ought to go back and be the acting squire, but—"

He made a vexed sound. "Miss Bennet, you have an uncanny way of disarming every attempt I make to—" He blew his breath out and reached out a hand to stroke the line of her chin, settling his palm against the side of her face and cupping it.

Mary's eyes widened, and her breath caught as she stared into his eyes. *He is going to kiss me.* The thought heated her cheeks, and she could feel her warmth melding with the warmth of the hand that cupped her face. *But what does it mean? He cannot love me. He is not a real suitor. It is only flirting.*

Flirting, like Lydia. She hoped her sister had never kissed him, but there was no telling. Her aspiration to be more like Lydia now felt like a travesty, if it meant the man she had grown fond of only thought of her as a playmate, a foolish way to pass time. *And someone might come in at any moment. Mrs Appleton even!* Terror shuddered through her, and she fumbled to her feet, making the wooden chair screech against the floor. "I...um...should check on Kitty."

Mr Cole's eyelids had lowered too much for her to read his expression. "If you wish."

"I will take care of my part of things for the expedition, you may be sure," Mary said in a hurry, her words tumbling over one another in a dizzy fashion that mirrored the slow swoop in her mind. "If I do not see you before then, do not worry. I will meet you at Maddox's before we all travel to Moseley Gorge."

"No doubt." His tone gave away nothing.

Mary backed out of the room, dipping an awkward curtsey and then hastening down the hallway. Kitty was in the main hall, watching Mrs Appleton hoist a fabric against the window and raking a disdainful glance over the draping folds.

"This is what they chose for the curtains? They may not be tattered, but this colour is better fit for a pall." Kitty's sharp tongue might have intended to reproach the chooser of the fabric, but from Mrs Appleton's weary expression, she had borne many reproaches from her herself. "Mary, have you seen this? I thought this was supposed to be a house of mirth, not a house of mourning. Or must scientific ladies prove their wisdom with sombre decor?"

"Let us go home, Kitty." The note of authority in Mary's voice surprised them both, and after a moment, Kitty nodded.

"Just as you please." Kitty left Mrs Appleton sagging against the wall, whether from relief or exhaustion from lifting draperies, Mary could not tell. She almost pitied the woman, pressed back to her position of downtrodden insignificance.

But there are worse things. Things like struggling to attract while competing with her sister. Things like enduring the lieutenant's pouts and Mr Wickham's agitation. Things like failing to rescue a fallen maid or failing to prevent a friend's sinking into larceny.

Things like playing the fool to ward a gentleman away from her family, and then realising she had fallen head over heels in love with him.

Casting one glance back at Mrs Appleton, who wiped the sweat from her brow with a limp handkerchief and looked murderously at Kitty's back, Mary pressed her lips together. *You do not know how easy you have it.*

Twenty-Three

Two days later, the rain had ceased, leaving the spring air uncommonly fresh and luring Mary into strolling outside the Roarkes' lodging house for a moment. Fewer coal-fires belched smoke into the air now that the sun's heat was simmering the city, and a wild breeze tangled the ropes of dray-carts and flapped the laundry slung out of windows. Though the Roarkes' neighbourhood was rough and seedy, the clarity of the air tempted many to dawdle, and Mary felt a flash of rebellion at bidding the Wickhams' carriage to go, then leave it lingering in the mash of passersby.

Besides, it is not as if I know what to say to Lady Lucy. The noblewoman's confession had put their friendship out of kilter. Mary still thought Lady Lucy ought to tell her parents, but she felt constrained by her promise not to tell anyone herself. *Which means I either harp upon the subject with Lady Lucy and pressure her or let the matter drop.* Neither alternative felt right, and Mary stepped around a pile of refuse and wandered a few more feet away from the lodging house. It felt like ages since she had been alone—well, unaccompanied. She could hardly call herself alone with a meat-pie seller hollering in her ear and workers in close-fitting caps shouldering by her to run errands or carry goods. Lydia was still vegetating within the Wickhams' home; instead of going out to her usual flutter of social commitments, the belle now pined and pouted and remained indoors. Mr Wickham looked unhappy with the change. Probably he wished he could take back his strictness, but with Lieutenant Stubbs's certainty that the scandal with Mr Cole had really grown too much, he continued pressuring Lydia to play the quiet wife. The constant company of her sister had eventually wearied Mary, and she was pleased no one seemed to mind her visiting Lady Lucy unchaperoned.

Mary's steps roamed farther, and her ear caught the sound of a child chattering. That was not surprising in a busy neighbourhood, but the voice was recognisable, and Mary walked far enough to see Betsy, hand in hand with a woman in a soiled black dress. The woman in black nodded absently at the little girl's words and glanced back and forth with a furtive air.

That is not Mrs Burton. It must be some sort of nursemaid hired to watch the errant child. Betsy looked confident enough with the woman, trotting at her side and smoothing the pristine apron Lady Lucy had given her. The ruffles of lace on it matched those on the little girl's dress, and her new shoes danced over the leftover puddles of rain and sprayed drops everywhere.

"Stop that!" The woman in black jerked Betsy's arm, and the girl looked up at her in wonderment, as if too unaccustomed to such harshness to take offence.

Mary chewed on her lip as she watched. The cuffs of the black dress were frayed, and the woman's gown had a torn spot on one side. Mary was surprised Mrs Burton would allow even a nursemaid to look so untidy when Mrs Burton could patch things up in a trice. *Perhaps the nurse does not care to mend it herself and would not accept help.* People often did have a strange pride about such things.

The woman hurried Betsy along, angling her farther and farther from the lodging house. Mary supposed they must be on a walk. It would be good for Betsy to stretch her legs and tire herself out; she had sat inside too often for far too long. *Yes, it is a good thing.* Still, something tugged at Mary's thoughts, and she found herself following the pair. *It will not hurt anything to watch a little longer. Not that anything is wrong.*

The mere idea that something might be amiss made Mary's heart palpitate and her stomach drop. *Nothing is wrong. Just a new nurse taking Betsy for a walk.* Mary could not bear trying to speak up to the woman, insinuating she was some sort of child-snatcher or thief. What would she think? It would be beyond rude, and Mary had no proof of anything. Mrs Burton had a right to hire anyone. There was no reason for Mary to be informed. *This is probably all as it seems to be, just an ordinary walk.*

The thought soothed her, and the reassurance that there was no need to confront a stranger in public made Mary's knees almost weak with relief. *I would have made a fool of myself to no purpose, and probably that woman would have scolded me into tears.* Mary paused, ready to turn back towards the lodging house, but Betsy had spied a toy in a shop window and pulled the woman to it so Betsy could press her face against the pane.

"A toy pony!" Betsy's shout of delight rang even over the clatter of hooves in the street and the squeal of the cart's wheels. "I want to go in and see!"

"Not now." The woman's black dress gusted in the wind, and her grip tightened on the little girl's arm. "Come along."

"No, no! I want to see!" Betsy struggled against her, the desire for the toy gluing her to the spot. "I want the pony!"

"Come *along*." The woman yanked hard on Betsy, making her stumble, but the woman in the black dress did not even glance down at her. Her gaze searched the crowd with anxiety, her face draining of colour. "Hurry up."

Mary moved towards them with reluctance, still uncertain of herself, but sensing a growing dread within her. As she approached the two, the woman began dragging Betsy along.

"Wait a moment," Mary said. The throbbing in her chest warned she was making something out of nothing. The trembling in her hands told her she was about to cause a needless scene.

"Ain't got a moment," the woman said, walking faster, despite Betsy's pull.

"Miss Bennet, I want to see the pony!" Betsy's eyes lit up at the prospect of another adult to further her wishes, and she struggled harder.

"Who are you? A new nurse?" Mary's voice ought to have sounded stern and authoritative, but instead it came out as a squeak.

The woman in black glared. "That's right. I haven't time for you, miss."

"What is your name?"

The eyelids of the woman flickered. "Mrs Thomas, miss. Ain't got time. Must go." A hard set to her mouth showed what she thought of Mary's interference.

"Betsy, who is this? Is this your new nurse?"

Betsy stared at Mary in confusion, either because she did not understand the question or did not know the answer. A barrette Lady Lucy had given her had gone awry in her black hair, poking some of her curly locks straight up. "Can I see the toy pony?" she asked, her expression clearing and becoming suffused with hope.

"I just said I was her nurse," the woman said, but instead of sounding irritated, she sounded scared. "Come along, Betsy."

"What is Betsy's mother's name?" Mary asked, taking hold of Betsy's other arm. *What am I doing? I am making a scene for nothing. I should just go back to the lodging house and ask. Lady Lucy will tell me all about the new nurse and I will avoid this stranger's anger.* But too much seemed wrong, and she repeated the question. "What is her name?"

"Why, don't you know?"

"*I* know. If you are truly her nurse, you will know as well."

"I don't have to prove anything to you or anybody." The woman threw her shoulders back, and her voice rose in a shrill castigation worthy of the greatest shrew in London.

"Imagine! Stopping honest folk and arguing with 'em, as if I haven't better things to do for my mistress. Go and bother her with your questions, not me. Learn to mind your own business. Witch!"

The pounding in her chest felt as though it would shake Mary apart. "If you do not tell me at once, I am going to scream for help." Passersby were already slowing as they passed, glancing at the scene with increasing interest, and though Mary did not spy any watchmen, she had no doubt her screams would attract assistance. The woman in black must have thought so, too, for she suddenly released Betsy and darted into the crowd.

Mary's legs wobbled, and she fell to her knees, hugging Betsy. "Betsy, does anyone know you are out?"

"N-no." Betsy's black eyes were mystified at Mary's emotion.

That woman was going to take her—probably to sell her clothes. They are too nice for this neighbourhood. And what would have become of Betsy when she had them? Mary shuddered. If Betsy was lucky, she might have been released in an alley and found her way home. If not...*And I almost let it happen. I would* have, *if Betsy had not been so set on that toy.* Mary staggered to her feet, keeping her hand clenched around Betsy's arm. "Let me take you home."

"And the toy pony?" The desire was apparently irrepressible, despite Betsy's near adventure, and Mary shook her head in resignation.

"I will buy it for you later." She supposed it was fitting; without the presence of that toy, Betsy and the woman would have continued on their way, and Mary would have returned to the Roarkes', only eventually to learn there was no new nurse and Betsy had disappeared on the streets of London.

I almost let it happen, all because of fear. All because I did not want to speak up. Sickened, Mary shaded her eyes, trying to focus on getting the little girl back to the lodgings. She did not want to look at anyone. Shame was engulfing her, tearing at her inside and out. Her desire to keep things smooth and peaceful had nearly meant the loss of a child.

Even when Betsy was back in her mother's arms, chatting with energy about the toy she had seen, even when Lady Lucy and Mrs Burton exclaimed over Mary's rescue and praised her, even when she rode back alone to the Wickhams' and should have had a moment to forget, shame bore down on her. *I cannot stay like this.* Before, she had considered speaking up more as an idle pursuit, a possibility she might play with. Now her cowardice bit at her, and made her character feel intolerable. However often she reassured herself that Betsy was okay, Mary could not erase the horror she had felt when she realised her fear had somehow become more important than the life of a child.

I talked myself into believing everything was fine—because I wanted to believe it. It was the same as convincing herself Lady Lucy had not stolen the lace, clinging to a pretence in order to avoid a scene. *But I cannot live like that anymore. Better chaos and conflict, than peace that costs so much.* She drew her breath in sharply. *The mouse must die. I must be something else now.*

The resolution felt, oddly enough, like relief.

Twenty-Four

Facing her own cowardice pushed Mary into action, and though she second-guessed her own decisions, she resolved to deal with Lady Lucy and Lydia more directly. She had assumed for so long that if only everyone around her would be in harmony, Mary would feel safe and cared for. But now, it seemed that even if she succeeded in producing peace, Mary might wind up paying a price too high —either sacrificing too many of her own needs, or suppressing some more important value to convince herself everything was okay.

I have to remember what almost happened to Betsy. And now that her figure had filled out more, and Mary experienced the surprising satisfaction of being well-fed, well-rested, and well-dressed, she realised how much she had lost in her martyrdom. The image of Mr Cole's smiling face and broad shoulders made her heart beat hard in her chest, and day by day she felt less and less inclined to let go of his friendship. *If Lydia ever does leave him alone, everyone will expect me to stop seeing him. No one in our family wants him as a friend after that…except me.* But unlike times before, the fact that she desired something felt meaningful—vital, even. *I will remain his friend, no matter what.* It felt like a daring choice, and her confidence in it made other, lesser choices easier.

THE NEXT DAY, MARY HAD INTENDED TO BROACH the topic of Lady Lucy's thefts the moment she arrived at the Roarkes', but Lady Lucy gushed forth before Mary could even sit down. "We are all still so indebted to you, Miss Bennet, for your brave rescue of Betsy. Mrs Burton talks of nothing else."

"Oh." Mary wished they could drop the topic; even a passing mention made her sick with regret.

"We have agreed, she and I, that Betsy need not have so many fripperies, at least not while she is too young to look after herself." Lady Lucy sat down on a thin-cushioned chair and beckoned Mary to do the same. Though the noble-woman's shoulders were weak and bony, she straightened them as if she were a soldier like her husband. "Instead, I intend to sponsor Betsy's education."

Mary could see the change pained Lady Lucy. "That is very good of you. Without the treats, Betsy may be less enthusi-astic towards you in the short term, but I believe she will acknowledge a greater debt of gratitude in the long term."

Lady Lucy's brow wrinkled, but she nodded.

Mary's hands balled into fists in her lap. "Now I am afraid I must embark on a more difficult topic. About your—taking things."

"Oh?" Lady Lucy's hauteur appeared, erasing the friendly rapport they had established.

"If you will not tell the captain and your parents about taking things, I will," Mary said in a rush. The idea of deliberately revealing Lady Lucy's secret to her parents scared Mary, because it was so like what she had done to Harry Lucas. *And that ruined everything.* But she no longer had the patience to watch her friend suffer in silence. Mary had to grit her teeth to bolster her resolve, but she succeeded in looking authoritative.

"But you promised!" Lady Lucy's translucent face grew even paler as she took in Mary's meaning.

"I will break my promise." The firmness in her voice sounded unnatural to Mary, but she pressed on. "Nothing is getting better, Lady Lucy. I know you have tried to make amends to the milliner, and you returned the brooch, but you cannot remain sequestered here, unhappy, lonely, impoverished, longing—"

"That is my business, not yours." The fire of pride lit the woman's eyes, giving a bright contrast to the pallor of her face.

"Perhaps it is. I do not know if what I do is wise or not. I only know that I have information that can make a difference, and I cannot stand to watch you suffer any more. Besides, how long will it be before you are tempted to take things again? A sturdy intention to do right will only last so long, and your circumstances look as though they will last much longer than that, if I do not intervene."

"Interfere, you mean." Lady Lucy glared at her. "Friends do not betray one another."

The comment stung. "It is a betrayal, I admit. But it is what I intend to do. I suggest you tell them yourself, for it will come better from you." Mary's hands felt clammy with sweat as she took her leave, Lady Lucy's icy nod her only acknowledgement of the visit's end. Her legs wobbled as she descended the battered staircase, and this time, the cause was not mere weak wood and flimsy banisters. *I may have lost a friend just now. My first real female friend.* But she climbed into the carriage without a tear. She still did not know if she was doing the right thing. Very likely, in her desire to free herself from the need for external peace, she would make a great many mistakes on the wrong side, diving into conflict too often or too cruelly in her haste to correct her imbalance. She hoped this was not one of those mistakes.

LADY LUCY SOON SENT A LETTER, VENOM sarcastically shrouded in polite language, affirming that she had indeed informed her husband and her parents of her 'slight difficulties,' and describing the *contretemps* that had resulted. As one might expect, the Crestwoods blamed the captain, and the captain blamed the Crestwoods. As the Crestwoods had the pecuniary upper hand, they pressured the captain to go abroad—or else they would reveal the extent of his debts and likely he would be jailed for them. Though the Crestwoods expected Lady Lucy to return to their fold, she clung to her husband instead, bewailing their cruelty to him and insisting she would stay by his side wherever he went.

Can she not see how indifferent he is to her? Is she willing to endure so much for the pleasure of being presented as his wife? Or is it some moral strength in her, determining her to be with him for better or for worse? Or is it that she will do anything in the hopes of having a child? Mary could not sift the woman's motives. Lady Lucy's relationship with her husband had always puzzled her, and she felt as though she understood it now less than ever. She could only turn her mind to the next conflict: facing Lydia.

After weeks of remaining mostly at home, Lydia had wilted like a surly, disgruntled flower. At first, Mary had thought it simple *ennui* that had thinned her sister's cheeks and paled her face, but now she realised it was something more. Once Mr Wickham had spoken outright of suspecting his wife, Lydia had crumpled inside. The face she turned to Mary as she entered Lydia's elegant boudoir was positively haggard. "Oh, Mary," she gusted a sigh.

"You must talk to him, Lydia."

"I did that. It only made things worse." The tears spilling down Lydia's face were different from her usual ones. Her general method of weeping produced silky droplets that swept down her face like rolling pearls, barely tinging her eyes with pink. These tears flooded and poured, and Lydia's eyes were squeezed half-shut with redness. "I never thought he would really suspect me, but he did after that. Why does he not understand? Flirting—I flirt all the time. I always have. It is only for sport." She blew her nose. "What sort of person does he think I am? I love him! And even if I did not,

I made a bargain. Does he think I would go back on it and disgrace him? I keep my word!" She mopped at her face with her handkerchief, the linen billowing at another sigh.

"Can you not tell him all this?"

"I *have*. At least, mostly. He is hard to talk to about serious things."

"He must talk to you all the same, Lydia." Mary paused, watching her sister's eyebrows lift in confusion. "I think you are afraid to be open with him."

"What have I hidden?" Lydia's forehead creased with indignation, and the impulse to cave in and reassure her jolted Mary. The idea of displeasing anyone still made her heart pound, but Mary had realised the discomfort in her body did not mean deaths or feuds were imminent. They were mere sensations, however uncomfortable, to be felt and then let go. *I thought the alarm in my body meant something terrible was going to happen, and I should back away. But when Betsy was taken, trying to soothe away those sensations made me foolish and passive.* She clenched her fists. *I cannot be that way any more.* Her sister deserved her truth.

"I mean you are not open…in a feeling way." Mary struggled to explain. "You do not show your true feelings—at least, when they are soft or make you vulnerable—you usually do not seem real—"

"Real? But I am real every which way!"

"Oh, I cannot make myself clear. You talk in a breezy way about things, and it makes people believe whatever you think and feel is on the surface. Why, most people assume you are a dunce, and I know that is not true. You simply talk as though you do not care about most things, and you pretend to be sillier than you are."

Lydia's shoulders shrugged under her lace wrapper. "I truly do *not* care about a lot of things."

"But not everything." Mary pressed her point. "You have a cleverness of your own—why have you not shown it to Mr Wickham? Find something in common with him, or have a child—"

"Oh, everyone thinks that is a solution. I do not know if I ever want a child, Mary, and I know I do not want one *now*. Not now, when I am supposed to be a queen of fashion in all of London!" She blew out her breath. "Though it has not added up to as much as I thought. Lord, Mary, I get so dull sometimes! All I have is shopping and flirting, and it is not enough." Her dark hair had become too stringy to bounce as she shook her head. "Somehow I thought it would be much more fun to be a rich wife."

Mary patted her hand and listened.

"Mr Cole is such good fun. He took my mind off my tedious life, and I took his off his failures as a lecturer. It was such a pleasant bargain! I do not see why people did not leave us alone."

"Because it had gone too far—at least, in people's minds."

"It is not fair. If those gossipmongers had half a brain, they would see I flirted with him so much because I could tell his heart was never at risk. And he scarcely ever knew what any of it was about! For such a smart man, he mostly seemed rather insensible to my teasing. It was safe for both of us." The brown of her eyes had softened into black with her tears, making her gaze feel even more poignant to Mary when she said, "It is different with you."

"What do you mean?"

"Why, when he is with you, Mary—he is different. His heart is in it, whether he likes it or not." Seeing Mary's poleaxed expression, a bit of the old Lydia resurrected. "La, Mouse! Why do you think I left you alone together so often, or flirted with him so hard? It was just fun at first, but when I saw you liked him and he liked you...Well, I knew you would never have the spunk to speak up to him without some sort of prodding, and as I liked poking ill-natured gossips in the eye any way—"

"Lydia, you are not saying that you flirted so much with him because of *me*." Mary's breath caught.

"No, not completely. As I say, it was good fun. And good revenge." A mischievous smile hinted at the corners of her lips. "But I did like to play matchmaker, a little." She leaned forward, the lace of her wrapper dangling as she moved, making Mary think of a spider's web draping closer. "Did it work?"

"Lydia!"

"Only say that it worked, and that you love him and he loves you, and I will feel as though not everything is vanity and vexation. There, that is Mr Collins's sermonising coming through. I must be more sorrowful than I thought." Despite her words, Lydia sounded more cheerful than before, and Mary felt a tension in her chest begin to ease.

"Well, speak to Mr Wickham before you feel too much better. Be *honest* with him, Lydia, and insist he be honest with you." Mary still wondered what sort of enterprises Mr Wickham was mixed up in. Perhaps Lydia's vulnerability would encourage his own.

"I still do not know what you mean." Lydia tugged at her wrapper, seeming intent on rectifying its position—too intent. Mary had to hope that meant her sister did understand, at least a little, and was embarrassed by the idea.

"Just try. If you speak to him with your whole heart, he will not care a fig what nonsense Lieutenant Stubbs spews."

Lydia's eyelids were carefully lowered. "Of course, it would *help* if I could tell him that Mr Cole was soon to be married…"

Mary's cheeks heated, and she pushed up from the chair by her sister's bedside. "Do not talk nonsense. I must be going."

"It is as bad as all that, Mouse?"

Mary paused at the door. "I do not think I am a mouse anymore, Lydia. I am sure I will always be on the quiet side, but—" She fumbled with the door handle as her thoughts churned. "I want to be able to speak up for myself and to fight for what I need." Mr Cole's smile warmed in her memory and she added, "And for what I want."

"La! A change, indeed. What shall I call you, then?"

"Oh, nothing, I suppose. I do not need a nickname." Mary hurried from the room, feeling inadequate and questioning just how much she had left her mouselike qualities behind. *Lydia understands gentlemen. Lydia knows Mr Cole well. If she thinks he is in love with me…* Perhaps his attempt to kiss Mary had not been mere flirtation. Perhaps he really did have feelings for her of an honourable nature. *If I had had the courage to kiss him, I might know by now what it all meant.* Her heart squeezed and turned in a giddy flip-flop. *At the very least, I would have a pleasant memory and proof I am no mouse.* Settling into her room and ruminating on her talks with Lady Lucy and Lydia, however, reassured her.

Perhaps I did wrong with Lady Lucy. And perhaps I did not do much with Lydia. But they are steps—small steps. She found herself picking up her doll and stroking the puff of stuffing at her side. In a few minutes she had needle and thread prepared, and she poked her fingers into the shoulder, smoothing out the stuffing underneath. Her long, expert stitches bound up the shoulder, completing the work begun long ago. *I cannot wait for you to finish her anymore, Mama.* She posed the doll before her, admiring the new symmetry of the two shoulders. *I can do it myself.*

Twenty-Five

"**I** am so pleased to have some time with you, Miss Bennet." Miss Poppit's white muslin gown was lit by a ray of hot May sunlight slanting into the phaeton and grazing over the folds of material, as if the sun were gesturing at the perfect, ladylike attire and recommending it to Mary. The chip straw bonnet that cupped Miss Poppit's face fluttered with silk ribbons, their crimson stretching under her chin and around the back of the bonnet. Here in the countryside outside London, the air smelled musty with shoots of grass, floating pollen, and the moist soil after another bout of thunderstorms. Mary hoped Moseley Gorge was not too muddy; she might have advised putting off the expedition again, but too many of the arrangements for food and travelling were fixed. Even now, a long line of carriages trundled behind them, a caravan of amateur geologists eager to experience something novel.

Mr Cole's phaeton led the way. The scientist drove the horses himself, sitting alone on the wooden front bench heated by the sun, while Mary and Miss Poppit gossiped in the seat behind, Hercules curled at their feet. The open air breathed new life into Mary. Playful breezes swished the hair at the back of her neck, despite the pins supposed to hold her tresses. The yellow glaze of sunlight saturated the farms and fields they passed, making everything appear angelic. The bounce and sway of the phaeton kept the ladies shifting into new positions, turning their heads to catch new sights, bumping one another's elbows with a patient friendliness.

And Miss Poppit did seem friendlier than ever. Though Lydia complained of the woman's pride and stiffness, Miss Poppit showed little of it to Mary, and none today. Mary supposed she did not rank as requiring the rivalry and set-downs that a belle like Lydia would, but there seemed to be more to it today. From the way Miss Poppit kept glancing behind them at a curricle bearing Lieutenant Babbingford with another gentleman driving, Mary could guess at the sudden elation of spirits.

Though Mary had not answered, Miss Poppit took her assent as given and continued. "Though I cannot bear the country-side in general, I believe we will have a very fine outing. Lieutenant Babbingford tells me we may expect great samples of pumice at the site."

Mary was annoyed enough to respond. "Lieutenant Babbing-ford knows nothing about it. There will be no pumice, Miss Poppit. I am afraid your friend is no expert in geology." Despite his disinterest, she was not surprised he had insisted on joining them. Whole crowds of people who had showed little interest in the shiftings of the earth beforehand now clamoured for the right to be of the party to Moseley Gorge. It was not surprising that the Stubbses were rolling in the caravan, making use of the Wickham carriage, since business had confined Mr Wickham to London and Lydia remained with him. Lady Crestwood, Mrs Appleton, and the other steadfast members of the Informed Ladies of course came, but more surprising were the league of brothers, sisters, friends, and acquaintances that rallied to the expedition when it became clear it would make a lovely holiday. Even the Darcys, who had finally completed their travels and were on their way back to Pemberley, joined them. Lieutenant Babbingford was an unimportant addition compared to the Darcys of Derbyshire, especially since Lizzy and Mr Darcy showed genuine interest in the knowledge to be gained, while Miss Poppit's beau mainly shot smiles from the curricle behind them like Cupid's arrows.

The arrows certainly did not go astray of Miss Poppit. "Well, Lieutenant Babbingford has other talents," she said, giving a demure nod back at him. "I so admire a strong gentleman, one of courage and honour. Soldiers are so often unruly and degenerate, but this one has preserved all his dignity in the profession."

"Um, yes." Mary turned her head towards a tumbled-down fence to hide her smile. The phaeton wheels scratched up dried mud, flicking it in several directions, but even that looked festive this morning. A sense of celebration throbbed within Mary. It was not just that she was confident she and Mr Cole would persuade Lady Crestwood to give the annual Informed Ladies' lecture to him. It was not just that Miss Poppit seemed uncommonly amiable and happy.

It was her placement, riding in Mr Cole's own phaeton. *I got what I wanted.* The recognition still buzzed within her, a dawning awareness of possibilities she had hitherto dismissed. Lieutenant Stubbs had looked scandalised at the mere suggestion of Mary riding there, however well accompanied by Miss Poppit, and Mr Wickham had shaken his head with discomfort when he heard Mary's intention. But Mary had insisted, and the two men had dropped their objections surprisingly quickly. *I always thought Lydia got her own way so often because she was beautiful.* Mary examined her fingers, curling them into a fist. *But perhaps a great deal of it was simple firmness.* Whatever the exact reason, Mary found her resolutions carried more weight than she thought possible. The idea delighted her.

Miss Poppit regaled Mary with elegant conversation—emphasising books, music, and art—but whether the young lady thought such matters would please Mary or whether she was more interested in proving her degree of culture, Mary could not tell. She found herself wishing for Lady Lucy's inane, yet peaceful, chatter or a solid discussion of science with Mr Cole. Still, she could not help but appreciate Miss Poppit's efforts, and she divided her attention between nodding at her companion, enjoying the pastoral scenes around them, and straightening her pale blue muslin when the wind tugged at her gown.

The caravan proceeded through the little village of Evans, which bordered Moseley Gorge and from which some of their supplies had been acquired. As the phaeton creaked its way down the main street, Mary caught sight of an itinerant preacher waving his arms in front of a crowd, his drab, battered coat blown half-open by the breeze, his words carrying on the wind. Her heart stilled.

It is Harry Lucas. No one knew exactly where Harry had wound up; his rambles from one Methodist community to another seemed almost designed to elude pursuit, though Sir William certainly had no interest in finding him. But there he was and only a few minutes' walk from the site of the expedition. The raucous exhortation emanating from the man made Mary think more of rooks cawing than a sermon, but from the way the bodies pressed around him shifted and leaned, the lower class of Evans found it intriguing. *What shall I do?*

She could pretend she had not seen him and let the matter drop. Mary doubted Harry had paid any attention to the caravan passing by in the middle of his sermon, and even if he had, it was doubtful he recognised Mary in such a brief glimpse. If she had not known his voice so well, she might have doubted it was her old friend in the crowd. But though she pondered the idea of avoiding him, deep down, Mary knew she had already chosen. She owed him an apology, and this might be her only chance to deliver it.

The phaeton rolled on to Moseley Gorge, which proved to be more of a shallow trench than the stately alpine vista Mary had envisioned. When they came to a stop, Mary clambered down, barely aware of Mr Cole's offer of assistance and Hercules's exploratory barks as he roamed the trench. She kept glancing in the direction of Evans, wondering how to slip away unnoticed. If Kitty knew Harry was there, she would forbid Mary to have anything to do with him, worried that it might offend Sir William. *And I need to see him.*

"I have a surprise for you later, Miss Bennet." Mr Cole's solidity threw a shadow over Mary, blocking out the spring sun, and Mary could not read his face. In his expedition gear, he looked more like a blacksmith than ever. Instead of his usual superfine coat and fawn breeches, he wore a loose, shabby coat with pockets for tools and plain trousers. His boots were not his usual shining black ones, but a pair of dirty topboots. Though he did not look elegant, he moved with a casual strength that showed his comfort with scrabbling in the rocks. "You are fond of surprises, I hope."

"Of course." She realised her tone was absent as she mulled over how to see Harry, and she struggled to refocus. Mr Cole still needed her help. "Here is Lady Crestwood's carriage. Shall we give her a proper welcome?" She led the way, Mr Cole hanging back, Hercules darting around her legs. The hound jostled into Lady Crestwood's two pugs as they descended from the carriage, and the three dogs began an introduction of sniffing and spinning.

"I cannot say your dog has any breeding, Mr Cole, but I like a man who is not afraid to bring one to a suitable occasion." Lady Crestwood beamed at him, though Mary suppressed a giggle at her 'suitable occasion'. From what she could tell, every occasion was suitable for canine accompaniment, according to Lady Crestwood.

"Hercules is the rejected member of a pack. I fear he has no earthly notion how to hunt, nor guard, nor do anything, really. But I love him just the same for all that." Mr Cole's cheerful rejoinder was offered at the same time as his arm, and he helped Lady Crestwood manoeuvre her thick, voluptuous form down from the carriage.

"Not all dogs are gifted." Lady Crestwood's proud smile showered appreciation on her own dogs as they waddled in Hercules's wake.

Mr Cole peered into the carriage. "Are not the Roarkes here? I thought they were coming."

The smile vanished. "My daughter and her husband are preparing to relocate to the Continent." Lady Crestwood's lips drew tight, almost as if she were bracing herself, and Mary cringed.

"What a pity! I hope they will be able to visit often." Mr Cole noticed the lady's discomfort, but as he could assign no reason for it, he stumbled on. "I know you will miss them."

"Not as much as you might believe." The harshness in her voice seemed intended to forbid the subject, and Mr Cole gave a quick bow and left them, moving to a table set up near the shallow gorge and fumbling with the tools on it. Other carriages were arriving, dispensing their passengers in a flurry of twisted gowns and excited voices, but for the moment, Mary and Lady Crestwood were alone.

"I hope you will try to make things up with Lady Lucy, Lady Crestwood," Mary said. She could not look the noblewoman in the face, but she pushed herself to speak plainly. "It was my fault things came to a head as they did. I pressed her to tell you about her—difficulties—and though she hated me for it, she did so. I have tried to make things up with her myself, before she goes, and although she is still angry, she forgave me." Mary smoothed down the front of her gown. "She loves you dearly. It would hurt her a great deal, to leave without—"

"She need not leave at all." Lady Crestwood's tone was cold, but wrinkles gathering at the corners of her eyes suggested suppressed tears. "I do not see why she clings to such an abominable gentleman."

"I do not understand it myself." Mary sighed. "It is hard to let a daughter do as she pleases, I am sure, especially when it seems she is doing something...unwise." She ducked her head. "I should probably never have pushed her to speak."

"Why, no, Miss Bennet! That was quite proper. As her parents, we had a right to know." Lady Crestwood gave the comment the full weight of her authority, which had always been considerable. "As it happens, my Lucy is choosing to make a fool of herself. And now—" Lady Crestwood's gaze swept over Miss Poppit, who was selecting a trowel and a digging knife with Lieutenant Babbingford.

"Lieutenant Babbingford has his faults, Lady Crestwood, but he is not like the captain," Mary said. "He will never ignore or mistreat Miss Poppit. And if I may say so, Miss Poppit is not like Lady Lucy. She will always have a vigorous sense of her rights, and will defend them." Mary could not help a crooked smile at the thought. "It is not the same."

Lady Crestwood only sighed instead of answering, but that more than anything signalled hope for Lieutenant Babbing-ford's marriage. Mary began ambling toward the table, leading Lady Crestwood and recommending particular tools with an officious sweetness well-designed to soothe an offended lady. And when Lady Crestwood recovered her spirits and launched into an extremely decisive—and extremely incorrect—recitation of what events formed

Moseley Gorge and its striations, Mary listened and nodded with her best mouselike air. In less time than she would have expected, Lady Crestwood was immersed in activity and lauding Mr Cole's genius in organising such an event.

I suppose my time being a mouse served more purpose than I thought. Mary could not deny some of the skills she had acquired in a life of self-denial were useful. So long as she applied them wisely, they might do her a great deal of good still. *But I must never slip altogether into that old role.* Even as she flattered Lady Crestwood and disarmed a dispute between two other ladies by offering one of them her own trowel, Mary kept in mind her own goal for the day.

"Where are the Darcys?" she asked Kitty, who frowned down on the scattering of rocks at her feet. Though most of the Bennets felt obliged to honour Sir William's wishes, Mary felt sure Lizzy would help her see Harry Lucas.

"Their horse threw a shoe, so they fell behind. I daresay they will get here sometime." Kitty did not seem troubled by the Darcys missing any of the entertainment. She kicked at a rock with her half-boot and gave up her efforts at geology. "Let us find something to eat, dear," she said to her husband, who obediently rose and escorted her. Mary watched them go. Kitty was too great a friend of Maria Lucas to wish to upset her family, and her husband did not like anything indecorous. If they knew the exiled Harry Lucas was nearby, at best they would shake their heads and avoid him. At worst, they might scorn him and press Mary to do the same.

If Lizzy is not here, then I shall have to go alone. The thought unnerved Mary for a moment, but the remembrance of

Harry's wild, pained expression and the bitterness of the feud steadied her in her resolve. As soon as everyone seemed preoccupied with collecting samples and selecting refreshments, Mary strode to the road and made for Evans, bracing herself to dare encountering a cluster of agitated Methodists —and the friend she had wronged.

Twenty-Six

Stumbling her way through the chunks of dirt in the road, Mary made her way towards the village. Her face flushed from both the heat and the concern of walking so far from the group, alone. She could have asked Miss Poppit to accompany her, but there was no telling what low place Harry Lucas might get to after his sermon, and Miss Poppit might feel she had to tell Lieutenant Stubbs. Mary would have preferred the company of Mr Cole, but so long a walk together alone would stir up yet more gossip, and perhaps make Lieutenant Stubbs come running.

Thus it was that Mary trudged into the village alone. The throng of Methodists—or potential Methodists—had already dispersed, leaving only overturned rocks and a swirl of dust where Harry had been preaching. *If I know Harry, his throat is parched from talking and he wants a drink. Though probably he asks for water, now.* A tavern stood nearby, its crooked walls angling in a way that suggested danger not merely from drink and gambling. Looking askance at the warped wood of the walls, Mary drew a deep breath and hurried inside.

The contrast of the dark interior blinded Mary for a moment, and she stood in awkward hesitation near the door, waiting for her vision to adjust. The sour smell of spilled gin and the biting scent of cheap tobacco hung in the air, clinging in her throat. She coughed and moved forward as the spindly chairs and tables became visible. She could spy Harry in the corner, huddled up with a mug of lemonade and speaking earnestly to a listless barmaid.

"Mr Lucas." Mary stood in front of him, twisting her hands together as guilt swam in her belly. The barmaid took in Mary's appearance and gave a low whistle as she sidled away. Harry pushed back his mug and jumped to his feet.

"Miss Mary? Is that you?" He ruffled his blond hair, the curls longer than Mary remembered. The drab coat he wore fit him ill, and the linen shirt underneath would have suited a workman with little interest in laundering. A tobacco stain mottled one leg of his trousers. He looked less like a gentleman than Mary had ever seen him. *But he is no less a worthy man.*

"Yes. I was in the neighbourhood with some friends, and I saw you preaching." She swallowed, uncertain how to frame the apology she had spent over a year agonising about. No words had ever seemed adequate. "I have missed you, Harry."

"And I, you." His brows were drawn together in consternation, but he shook Mary's hand in spite of the audience of barmaids and drinkers. "You look so different. You used to be thin as a rail. And now you are—" He gestured at her help-lessly. "And you look quite the height of fashion."

"I am living with Lydia now, and she helps me." She hesitated. "You know that she is married?"

"I had heard." He leaned on the table, his hand smearing loose tobacco dusting the top. "But you should really not be here. It is no place for a lady." His lopsided grin suggested he considered it good enough for himself.

"I know that, but I had to see you. To apologise." She decided rushing through it was the only way she would be able to say it. "It was my fault. Everything was my fault. I told you I would not tell Sir William about the Methodist meetings, but then that day he was worried about where you were, and I thought I was reassuring him—I see it was foolish, now—I think deep down I was more afraid of keeping the secret, of being disloyal to your parents." Her whole body trembled. "I should not have interfered, Harry. It is my fault the whole feud began. I do not blame you if you hate me."

"Oh, Mary." Harry's sigh shook the cheap fabric of his coat, and he adjusted the position of the mug on the table, avoiding Mary's eyes. "Do not be foolish. Certainly, I do not hate you."

Tears stung at the corners of Mary's eyes, but she did not let them fall. "I broke your family apart."

Finally, he lifted his gaze to hers, shaking his head. "It was an awkward time for the secret to get out, I admit, but you merely sparked what was inevitable. Did you really think my father and I would have lived happily ever after together, if you had not spoken out? It was only a matter of time. He never understood me. I could not live his way, and he could not let me live mine." The anger rumbling in his chest warned that Harry's sermons of forgiveness had not had full effect yet. "We are better off apart, both of us. Of course, I am sorry if some of my brothers and sisters feel they cannot speak to me."

"I am sure most of them do not care a fig about your"—years of her vicar's preaching made even the word unpleasant to her, but she persisted—"Methodism."

"I hear from Charlotte now and again. She sends her letters to a friend of mine, so her husband does not know, and I call for them there."

"She does?" Mary never knew, but she could see why Charlotte had not mentioned it. Determination seized her. "Well, then, I am sure Lizzy will, too, and I through her. Give me the name and address of this friend." She blushed. "If you are willing, I mean."

"Of course." Bemused, he repeated it to her, and she memorised it until she could write it down.

"You truly do not hate me, then?" Mary dared to smile, though the smile wobbled on her lips in uncertainty.

"I was very angry for a while, especially when I saw you expected me to knuckle under and beg pardon and go back to how things were, just like the others. You ought to have known I couldn't do that, with my calling. But it has all worked out for the best. I am far happier doing the Lord's work in this way than in any other." He shifted his threadbare coat, and his shoulders stiffened with pride. "I would not change my life for anything. You can tell my father that, if you would like."

"I had better not." Now Mary was the one to give a gentle push to the mug, her fingers sticking to some unidentifiable stain on its exterior. She drew her hand back and forced herself not to wipe it on her gown. Disappointment seeped through her. As much as she had feared Harry would revile her, there had been another imagined outcome hiding in the back of her mind, one where he repented his ways and raced to embrace his father. Only now did she see how foolish that vision had been. *They are not going to reconcile. There is not going to be peace, and the Lucases will not live in perfect harmony. Neither will we Bennets, for that matter.* She accepted that now. As much as she would have liked Harry reuniting with the rest, she could find contentment in what he had chosen. "I am happy you are free, Harry," she said, a surge of shyness obscuring her voice, but he understood any way.

"I am free. And happy."

A slant of light glared into the room as the tavern door opened and shut. Mr Cole blinked uncertainly for a moment, and then strode to Mary, his gaze raking over Harry with distrust. "Who is this, Miss Bennet?"

Mary's gaze took in Harry's coarse shirt, the grime on his boots, and the relaxed manner in which he leant against the gritty table. She felt ashamed of him, and ashamed of being ashamed. "This is my friend Mr Lucas, Mr Cole."

"The wild one?" Mr Cole grinned and offered his hand to Harry. Harry studied Mr Cole's unkempt clothing, curiosity pushing his eyebrows up as Mr Cole continued. "I was the wild one in my family, too. My brother was positively saintly."

To Mary's surprise, Harry grinned back as he shook Mr Cole's hand. "None of my brothers are saintly, but the eldest one's prudish enough. Really, as a minister, I'm supposed to be one of the saintly ones." He winked, and Mr Cole laughed.

"Saintly as you may be, I cannot say this is a proper place for Mary—er, Miss Bennet."

"It is not. I told her that."

Mary tried to interject. "Yes, but—"

"I will take her on back to our party, then, if you have finished."

"Certainly."

"*I* am not finished," Mary said, finally able to get a word in. She turned to the clergyman, ignoring Mr Cole for the moment. "Harry, would you do a favour for me?"

"I shall not write my father any letter, nor shall I go and visit—"

"I mean something else."

"What?"

"I have a friend who is going to have a baby, and she is not married. She is worried that the people she knows will all judge her—" Somehow, as she had been speaking, Harry's eyes had grown bigger and bigger and rounder and rounder, and Mary halted, disconcerted.

"She means a maid, in Mrs Wickham's house," Mr Cole said dryly.

"But she *is* a friend." Puzzled, Mary watched as the two exchanged unreadable looks. Surely Harry, of all people, did not begrudge her a maid as a friend? "I thought one of your Methodist societies would have a charity that would get her out of London. She wants to go someplace she is unknown."

"I see." Harry's smile showed too much amusement. "For you, Mary, I will see what can be done for this girl. I will write to that friend I told you about, and you do the same. He and his wife will escort her to a place in the country, if I ask them." He gave her a wry look. "You have asked the right person. I have run into too many young women with that trouble."

"Thank you!" A rush of pleasure went through Mary at the thought of Hannah's relief.

"I have never heard you ask for anything like this. Nor have I ever heard of you braving a tavern...You have changed." Harry's curious gaze swept over Mr Cole, perhaps showing he thought Mr Cole could explain it, or perhaps seeing him as the explanation.

"If that is all, Miss Bennet, we had best head back." Mr Cole tilted his head, narrowing his eyes as he studied Mary. She squeezed her friend's hand one last time and then took Mr Cole's arm. He guided her out of the tavern and into the blaze of light on the dirt road. Mary took a deep breath, letting the spring breeze cleanse the tavern air from her lungs. Though things had not turned out perfectly, she felt proud of herself for speaking to Harry. *He does not blame me after all.* The reassurance buoyed her spirits, but oddly enough, she felt even if Harry had fumed at her, she still would have felt better for speaking up about her guilt.

Mr Cole and Mary strolled down the road, and Mary took in the sweeping green vistas of trees nodding in the wind, butterflies half-blown by the wind in curling eddies, and the palpable sun's ray heating her bare forearms.

"I was worried when you disappeared." Mr Cole's saunter showed indifference, but the creases at the corners of his eyes showed he spoke the truth. "I ducked my head into every building in Evans, almost, looking for you. I thought you might have noticed we were running low on supplies for the expedition."

"I suppose I ought to have told someone where I was going—"

"And requested accompaniment. Especially if you intended to go into a tavern."

Mary averted her gaze from him. The swaying stalks of wild-flowers charmed her eye, and the feel of Mr Cole's arm pressed by her fingers made the walk idyllic, no matter how much he scolded. *I was brave today. Harry is not angry with me. And I have more time with Mr Cole.* There was too much to rejoice over to worry. "I did not intend to go into a tavern when I left. I was simply seeking Harry. If Lieutenant Stubbs had found out, he would have forbidden my going, so I did not risk telling anyone."

"Did you think I would tell him?"

She turned her eyes to his. "No, but you could not have come. We two should not be off walking alone."

"Which we are, any way." Mr Cole adjusted her hand on his bicep, incidentally squeezing her hand as he did so. *Or perhaps not incidentally.* "Well, it gives us a chance for the surprise on the way back." He redirected their steps, cutting across a field where fragrant herbs melded with the breeze and purple petals dotted the landscape. At first, Mary thought he meant her to pick flowers or admire a view, but he led them farther afield and then down the banks of a stream, whose waters tossed restlessly, filled to the brim with spring rain. A neat pile of rocks formed a pyramid near a fallen log, and other trees held the sun at bay, keeping the grass beneath moist and cool. "Behold your heaven, Miss Bennet."

"What?"

"I have prepared your own sort of heaven for you. There is no castle for you and your doll like you told me about, but there is a stream you can throw rocks in." He grinned. "Not important rocks, of course."

Mary laughed, releasing his hand and stepping carefully through the long grass. She picked up one of the rocks, delight surging in her as she hefted its weight, and then she threw it into the stream in one smooth motion. The rock plopped into the water with a satisfying sound, as if the current had gulped it down.

Mr Cole eased his way down the bank with more speed and grace, and his toss made a round stone bounce over the surface of the water again and again, finally disappearing in depths unseen. Giggling, Mary chose another rock and threw it more vigorously than the first, creating a blast of ripples that scattered over the churning water.

"That is not skipping at all," Mr Cole said. "I can teach you—"

"I never said I wanted to skip them. I just want to throw them." Mary heaved another into the water, watching the cascade of ripples overset a leaf riding on the stream. She threw again and again, something in her chest loosening as she did so, and soon Mr Cole ceased throwing himself and merely stepped back to watch her. The plash of droplets blown into the air revived some deep feeling in Mary, some forgotten sense of her own power and individuality. She forgot all about the expedition, about Lady Crestwood, about reputations, about everything but the joyous moment of making splashes.

When the pyramid was used up, Mary turned to her friend, a new light sparkling in her eyes. "That was wonderful."

"It looked like you enjoyed it." His voice sounded pleased. "When I came here a few days ago to scout for the expedition, I thought this would make a good spot for your heaven and gathered a few rocks for it."

She gazed into his dark eyes, losing herself momentarily. "It has been heaven, indeed."

"Then I consider the endeavour a victory. Shall we go back?"

She took his arm again, and this time, their pace quickened, as if each had remembered the duties abandoned. Mr Cole pushed back the hat on his head, rubbing his forehead. "You will be pleased to know that Lady Crestwood has offered me the annual lecture for the Informed Ladies of London Association."

"Then we have succeeded?"

"Had succeeded, perhaps we should say. She will not be pleased I left the expedition for so long, nor that I have endangered another young lady's reputation." He gave her a sidelong glance.

"Perhaps we can talk her 'round." Mary walked faster, her legs feeling uncommonly strong. When they arrived at Moseley Gorge, Lady Crestwood accosted them at once.

"There you are, Mr Cole! So many ladies have had questions, and you were not here. Where on earth did you go?" The matron dusted her hands on the front of her gown, and by the smudges, Mary could see that unlike many of the others, Lady Crestwood had been willing to climb down into the gorge and take samples.

"Nowhere on Earth," Mr Cole said, sharing a look with Mary. "Well, one place perhaps. Miss Bennet's friend was in Evans, and we went to see him."

It was still hard to talk to Lady Crestwood when the note of outraged authority was in her voice, but Mary hoped with practice she would be more accustomed to it. "It was my old friend Harry Lucas, the son of Sir William Lucas. I will just tell Kitty he is here." It was a pointless excuse—Kitty would not want to see Harry at all—but Lady Crestwood did not know that.

"You can tell her in a moment. Are you saying you were scampering over the countryside with a gentleman alone, Miss Bennet? With *this* gentleman?" Lady Crestwood's eyes narrowed on Mr Cole.

"I did," Mary said. "But it did no harm, Lady Crestwood."

"I should think it did! I am not sure I desire any *distinguished lecturer* who abandons his own expedition and winds a lovers' path while he is supposed to be assisting ladies of science." The offence in her tone seemed to be as much for her own importance being ignored as for concern over Mary. "Miss Bennet, you had better go inform your sister"—her mouth twisted in distaste as she turned back to the lecturer—"and Mr Cole, you will accompany me and explain this red striation in the gorge to the other ladies."

Mary dipped a curtsey in response. As Lady Crestwood turned to go, confident Mr Cole would follow, Mary whispered to him, "Let her command awhile. Do not try to justify yourself yet." He gave her a rueful smile back, and Mary passed over to Kitty, her stomach grumbling over the sight of the roast chicken dangling in Kitty's hand. If she was going to have time to get a plate before returning to render humble homage to Lady Crestwood, she would have to make short work of Lieutenant Stubbs and Kitty.

"Kitty, Harry Lucas is in Evans, the little village down the road. You can speak to him if you like." Her tone was bald, but she made no apology for her hurry.

"Harry Lucas?" Kitty paused, still holding her chicken aloft. "Maria's brother? I mean, the gentleman who chose to…"

"Oh, do not get on a high horse, Kitty. Speak to him or not, just as you will. I did, and I feel better for it." She wondered if she was letting slip a secret, but she continued any way. "Apparently Charlotte writes to him."

Kitty grimaced and threw down her chicken. "Well, that is foolish. I shall not speak to him, to be sure." Her husband nodded his approval, apparently familiar with the story of Harry's disgrace, and they sauntered off to join Miss Poppit, who hung on Lieutenant Babbingford's arm with an unmistakable air of ownership and prattled of wedding plans.

Miss Poppit must have finally chosen heart over pride. Mary was happy for her. She could not be sure Lady Crestwood would grant her approval gracefully, but she believed the noblewoman would finally accept Lieutenant Babbingford as a suitor for her debutante. It seemed she had little choice in the matter now. *Poor Lady Crestwood! It will humble her to have her daughter shipping off to the Continent and her protégée choosing a man of no special éclat in her grand Season.* Perhaps there would be some bitter hours of recrimination between Miss Poppit and her mentor, but Mary faced the possibility with a surprising degree of indifference. *I will probably always hope that everyone gets along,* Mary thought, *but now, I do not* need *it.*

So many changes in so short a time bewildered her, and she took a moment with a plate of dainties to sit on a stump and watch the people milling in the gorge. Mr Cole attended Lady Crestwood with patient persistence, and only resigned his place placating her when Lieutenant Babbingford approached them, presumably to ask Lady Crestwood's blessing on a union with Miss Poppit. No doubt Lieutenant Babbingford would have to endure a similar talk with Mr and Mrs Poppit at some future period. *He will be a busy man, even if they put off the wedding until his next leave.*

"Have you even been into the gorge yet, Miss Bennet?" Mr Cole came to a stop before her, replacing a tool in his gaping pockets.

She finished the last of her lemonade. "Not yet." Rising, she set her dishes aside and followed Mr Cole down to the tumbled sides of the gorge. Where the rain had softened and slid off a slice of the cliff face, delicate layers of rock showed. Mr Cole began pointing out the significant ones, remarking on their history. Mary listened and asked questions.

"I cannot tell you how satisfying it is to have proper questions for once." Mr Cole sighed in contentment. "You are a born geologist, Miss Bennet. Perhaps it is no coincidence that your idea of heaven includes rocks?" He winked.

"I never knew anything about them before I met you."

"And now you could almost give the Informed Ladies' lecture yourself. Pray do not, however—my mother will be ecstatic that I did anything so fashionable." The amused tone he used showed a greater comfort with speaking of his mother. It surprised Mary.

"Does that mean Lady Crestwood forgives your errant stroll?" she asked, her tone wry.

"Oh, I let her order me about until it was clear I was entirely subjugated, and then I told her something that made her look more kindly on my attending you." His gaze into Mary's eyes was so steady that she felt unnerved, as if he were peering into her soul.

And if he sees what is there, he will know I love him. The thought frightened her, but it intrigued her as well.

Finally he broke his gaze, turning to watch servants hauling stacks of plates and baskets to a delivery vehicle. "It looks as though our expedition is ending, Miss Bennet. Lieutenant Babbingford has begged a seat in my phaeton, in the back with Miss Poppit. I am afraid that means you will have to sit with me."

"That is no hardship." And while other ladies complained to each other of gowns sodden with dirt or lauded the lemonade, Mary climbed up onto the phaeton's box with a light heart. A few carriages were already rolling away, transporting ladies with a greater collection of facts about geology—or at the very least, with a greater collection of memories of pleasant outings. Lieutenant Babbingford and Miss Poppit paid scant attention to anyone, huddled close together in the carriage seat in a way that suggested Lady Crestwood had been as merciful as she was great. Mary took one last look at Moseley Gorge as the phaeton lurched forward, and the crumbling stone and streaks of colour made her think of distant ruins, ancient cities, history coming to life and then being swallowed up by time. All things changed, all things passed, but for the kernels of joy a soul made of its life.

And I do think now I have more joy than ever.

Twenty-Seven

Mary cast a glance back at Lieutenant Babbingford, Miss Poppit, and Hercules grouped behind her as the phaeton jolted its way down the road past Evans. Though Lieutenant Babbingford and Miss Poppit seemed too immersed in conversation to pay attention, Mary spoke in an undertone. "Lieutenant Stubbs never reproached me for walking with you, and now he does not seem to care that I am at your side. And he said he was only coming on the expedition to look after me!"

Mr Cole's lips twitched with amusement. "I think we made the expedition enjoyable enough to attract a great many visitors." He let the reins loosen as his brow furrowed. "Perhaps I owe him an apology, though. I did make a tangle of his family."

"We were tangled before that." The admission was freeing. "But by all means, apologise for chasing my sister. It will please him immensely." She gave him a sidelong look. "So long as you truly *are* sorry, at least."

"In a way, I am, and in a way, I am not." For a moment, Mary thought he would leave the subject with that enigmatic reply, but after a moment, Mr Cole continued. "You know she was just a distraction for me, Miss Bennet?"

"You have said so, many times."

"And you believe it?" His eyes were earnest now, boring into hers with a need she was beginning to understand.

"I believe it."

The simple answer seemed enough for him; his shoulders relaxed, and the tension in his brow dissipated. "Flirting with women like Mrs Wickham is safe, or at least I thought so. They are married—unable to sue for breach of promise. Their hearts are engaged already. And they have not the allurements necessary for a long partnership." He coughed as dust stirred on a drier portion of the road. "Had I flirted with a woman of a certain character—that is, if I found a lady I considered truly marriageable—" He seemed unsure how to continue.

A gnawing sensation of discomfort grew in Mary. "You might have been tempted to marry."

He nodded. "And that would have ruined everything, I thought. If I wed, I would have to return home, face my parents' disapproval and my own grief, settle down and be a squire with geological leanings."

Mary pressed her lips together tightly, feeling disappointment hum through her, but she forced herself to relax. "But as it is, you do not. It must have felt good to hear Lady Crestwood offer you the annual lecture. It will persuade your parents that what you are doing is worthwhile."

"In truth, it did not feel as good as you suggest." He guided the phaeton around a turn, watching the horses toss their heads at the gnats that thronged a puddle. "Have you ever been to a dentist, Miss Bennet?"

Mary shuddered. "Thankfully, no."

"Well, hearing that I was to have the place of prominence, giving the annual lecture, was rather like needing a tooth pulled, tramping over to the dentist's office, and then discovering the dentist is out and cannot pull it today." He shook his head. "It felt like a reprieve, but one that would not do me any good."

"I do not understand."

"Miss Bennet, your sense of honour warned me that I ought to go back to the estate and relieve my father. I knew it was the right thing to do, but for a long time, I simply resented it so much I refused to consider it." Adjusting the reins, his tone changed, becoming hesitant and almost pleading. "But I saw how you faced your fears again and again to help your family. You tried where I rebelled. I was inspired by your diplomacy, your wisdom, your kindness, your courage—"

Mary shook her head at his list, but the disappointment was draining away, leaving a giddy churn of hope.

"I will try to face their favouritism of Thomas and do the right thing, whatever happens. But—" One hand snaked from the reins to take Mary's. "I must admit, with you beside me as my wife, what might be a grudging duty will change to a joy. Will you marry me, Mary?"

Happiness gurgled in her throat, garbling her words. "Yes!" Her hand squeezed his, and she was only faintly aware of the broad blue sky rolling overhead, the soft murmur of Lieutenant Babbingford's voice behind her, the tilt and jarring of the phaeton beneath. It was a ridiculous place for a proposal, but she felt none of that sort of strangeness, only an ecstasy that wound tight around her heart and lifted her up. A giggle escaped her. "So *that* is what you told Lady Crestwood to set things right."

He smiled. "She does not mind our walk so much now. Of course, had you refused me, I would have been in a pickle."

Mary dropped her gaze in shyness. "You ought to have known I would not do that. Have I not pursued you left and right?"

"In defence of your sister. How was I to know how you really felt? When I tried to kiss you—"

Shame made the back of Mary's neck burn. "I was a coward."

A light began to dance in his eyes, and he leaned closer. "And how brave are you feeling, now?"

Mary knew Lieutenant Babbingford and Miss Poppit were ensconced only a few feet away—hopefully preoccupied, but the moment was far from private. *Yet I want to kiss him.* The desire felt keen and true, a solid shining in her heart. She leaned towards Mr Cole, and they kissed.

She never knew if Lieutenant Babbingford and Miss Poppit saw. If they did, they treated the matter with discretion, perhaps hoping for a similar lenience for themselves. Mary settled closer to Mr Cole's body, feeling the line of his thigh against hers. "It is all so hard to believe." Suddenly she frowned. "Oh, heavens, Lydia was right!"

"She guessed I cared for you?"

"And that I cared for you. She even said that was part of why she flirted so much, to give us an excuse to see one another and for me to speak up." Mary sighed. "I shall never hear the end of this."

"I, for one, will thank her. Meeting her in a way to make society talk was its own fun, creating a secret together, meeting in places with no one knowing. But making *you* a part of the secret was more fun than the secret itself." The corners of his eyes crinkled with happiness as he glanced at Mary. "When I realised I liked your trying to *stop* me from seeing her more than seeing her, I knew I was in trouble. And when I realised I would rather argue with you than harmonise with anyone else, I knew I was lost."

Mary chuckled. "Of course, you do like a bit of a debate."

"I do enjoy a bit of a fracas now and then, with society or with a pretty lady." His smile showed he meant Mary.

"I know. I think that is one of the things that drew me to you, actually. I was so accustomed to trying to get along with everyone, and there you were—wilfully stirring up trouble just to enjoy yourself. It was infuriating, but also liberating to see." Her eyelashes lowered. "Not that I wish for squabbles day and night…"

"But a little banter might not come amiss?"

She smiled. "Just a little. Or more, so long as I get the better of it."

He laughed, twitching the reins to speed the horses along.

Mary watched his graceful motions with appreciation, and then fell to musing. "I did not even know there was a rebellious part of me until I came to London. You helped me find it."

"And I suppose you helped me find the part that is willing to do unpleasant things for others. Water down my lectures, drag myself to the estate—"

"Now I know you are teasing me."

His grin admitted it, but he atoned with another kiss.

Twenty-Eight

"Did I not tell you just how it would be? Did I not say he only flirted with me as a distraction?" Lydia trumpeted her victory with enough rhetorical questions to satisfy a Roman orator. "Did I not say he was madly in love with you, Mou—I mean, Mary?" The momentary stumble made Lydia's brow wrinkle, and she grasped the side of the carriage as it banged over a bump in the London streets. The May evening sky would have still harboured light in the countryside, but here the clouds of coal dust snuffed the sunset, and the only stars out were the orange-tinged lamps dotting the sidewalks.

"Yes, Lydia." The meekness seeped away as Mary remembered Mr Cole's kiss. In the darkness, she doubted her sister could see the flush shading her cheeks, but she felt brave enough to show her love for the gentleman even if she could. "Mr Cole has gone to see Papa, but I am sure Papa will say we must not announce any engagement yet. He will say we have not yet known each other long enough to wed."

"Oh, do wait a little. As much as I love a wedding and your eternal happiness and all that, it would be dreadful to have to find a new companion so soon! La! You must stay a while longer with us, at any rate."

"I will." Mary felt pleasure in Lydia's satisfaction with her, however moderated. "But if you and Mr Wickham squabble, I warn you, I shall not play peacemaker any longer." Mary shifted as the carriage turned, her silver silk gown rustling with the movement and sliding its sleekness over one hand. The evening gown was cut low for the opera, and Mary had borrowed a set of pearls from Lydia to adorn the decolletage —or at least cover it up a little.

"Oh, that is all over. We are the best of friends now." Lydia saw her sister's sceptical look and amended her statement. "Well, we have reconciled, and everything looks bright as sunshine for the future. While you were out traipsing over stones and batting your eyelashes at Mr Cole, I went to Lady Sarah Randall's 'at home.'" Indignation crept into her tone. "You must know what Lady Sarah is like—why, she is a vixen and a meddlesome—and *her* morals, I shudder to—"

"You are not being very coherent."

"If you had been through what I went through that day, you would not be any more so. She had me practically rushed from her drawing room, as if I would contaminate her with my licentiousness. And she had her butler intimate that I need not come back!"

"It is certainly very hypocritical, if half of what I hear is true." A slant of lamplight lit Lydia's hair as they passed it, making Mary think of a thunderbolt, given Lydia's present ire.

"I went right home, cried myself silly, and then chased Mr Wickham down and made him talk to me. I told him all about Lady Sarah, but he was not nearly as indignant as I."

Lydia tugged at her opera glove. "He said we must put up with people's silly English prejudices for a while longer, but that soon we shall have a much better time." Lydia's eyes lit up with gleeful expectation.

"What does that mean?" Mary asked.

"Dear Wickham says England is too constraining for his business interests, and that he shall have a much better field abroad. And he says the people in Baden-Baden, or wherever we choose to go, will not be so prudish and silly to take offence at a little flirting." Her expression suddenly opened up, revealing the vulnerability Mary cherished in her. "I suppose he really was worried about how my playing about looked—it made it harder for him to settle his affairs. He was *so* affectionate, and he begged me most prettily to hold back a little until we get abroad, and then I may do just as I like." Her face gleamed with satisfaction. "Any way, I think he was pleased I was turned out from Lady Sarah's, which was cruel of him, but it did do something to mend matters." Her brows drew together. "Horrid woman! I am glad she was good for *something.*"

Mary tried to keep sternness from her voice. "But I do not understand. How can Mr Wickham perform his duties in the regiment if he is abroad? Do you mean he is granted leave?"

"Oh, no, he intends to sell out. He can do much better than the regiment." Lydia's confidence in her husband's cleverness was supreme, but Mary thought she was piecing together another story. *What business could he have abroad, besides gambling and questionable investments? And why would Mr Wickham leave the London lifestyle he and Lydia adore unless he had to?* Probably he had been up to his old vices, and London was too hot to hold him. Lydia's breezy talk showed she thought her husband's 'troubles' no more than flyspecks. "We will stay a few months longer, probably, and then we shall head to the Continent. Wickham's friend Captain Roarke is going there, did you know?" Lydia did not wait for an answer. "So we shall not be lonely."

I doubt Captain Roarke and Lady Lucy will benefit from the Wickhams' company. How much of Mr Wickham's income had been won from Captain Roarke's foolish gambling, ultimately siphoning from Lady Lucy's settlement? *Captain Roarke would be a fool to stick to his old friend—but then, people so often are fools.* The bitterness in Mary's thoughts surprised her.

"Everything is working out for the best, just as Wickham said." Lydia smiled from ear to ear. "Just think, I will not have to look on that ugly old drawing room anymore. I am sure we shall have much better rooms when we are abroad. And we can change whenever we like, go from city and city. I shall be so well travelled!"

No doubt Mr Wickham's activities require frequent changes of scene. Again, Mary swallowed her bitterness. It was hard to see her sister so overjoyed with what she ought to condemn, but then, Lydia had always been that way. *And none of my preaching ever helped.* Perhaps a different tack would, though. "Lydia, life on the Continent is so uncertain. It might be wise to—" Mary could tell Lydia's attention was drifting from the moral strain already. "Would it not be lovely to hold a surprise for Mr Wickham?"

Lydia's dark eyes fixed on her. "A surprise?"

"Yes. As I said, things are so uncertain. Perhaps you could keep some money by you, and say nothing about it, and then one day if Mr Wickham is in trouble—"

Lydia clapped her hands. "A fine joke! I could rescue him. But I do not think he will ever need that, and how could I keep money in my pocket so long without spending it?" Lydia shook her head.

"Perhaps if you had a trustworthy friend you could give it to —or a reliable maid—" Mary floundered, trying to find a solution, but in the end she shrugged. "I do not know." Though she disliked giving up, she did not see how she could help Lydia. *Or Lady Lucy. They will be so far away, and each devoted to a husband who will not guide her very wisely.*

"Oh! Look at that fellow in the street." Lydia peered out the carriage window. "I do believe it's Mr Covington. I will have to get him to dance with me now that Mr Cole is gone to Longbourn." She saw the disapproval flicker across Mary's face. "Oh, I shall be respectable enough, Mary; don't look at me so." She giggled. "Wickham does not expect me a saint, you know."

"I suppose not." Mr Wickham's jealousy had seemed only to flare when Mr Cole's name had been paired with his wife's for a perilously long time, and it had affected his respectability enough to mar his financial concerns. Now that Lydia's husband could be sure Mr Cole was no longer a threat, it was likely he would return to an amused appreciation of her lesser frolics.

"Life is the most lovely thing, is it not, Mary? You shall marry Mr Cole—and Lieutenant Babbingford shall marry Miss Poppit. What a *coup*! She will be ground into the dust, socially speaking, and all for love."

"I do not think it will be as bad as all that."

"No, indeed, she is probably already crowing about the Crestwood family's influence in military circles. No doubt she intends Lord Crestwood to prop him up into something better than a lieutenant. That is probably why she is not coming to the opera tonight; she is off writing to somebody influential. But even if she does not, Lieutenant Babbingford shall be very well off. The husband of Emily Poppit will always be important. She will make him so, if he is not impressive enough himself." Lydia arranged the rubies at her throat with a delicate touch, which the jolting of the carriage soon made useless. "Horrid carriage! Horrid roads! Will we ever arrive at the opera? All the characters will be corpses by the time we arrive, and I like to hear them sing *before* they get to their death scenes. It is much more cheerful than walking in to a lot of greasy men bewailing their fates on the floor."

Her wish was granted; the carriage pulled up to the front of the opera house, allowing Mary and Lydia to emerge into the musty spring air. Mr Wickham, who had come in a hack from the City, met them on the steps with an unusually affectionate smile for Lydia that made Mary wish Mr Cole could greet her in the same fashion. *But he is miles and miles away.* Indeed, perhaps it was better as it was—Lady Crestwood's estimation of him seemed to vacillate, and they were to join her in her box this evening, along with Lord Crestwood and Lady Lucy.

Lady Lucy's pallor grew red roses when she saw Mary, but she greeted Mary with politeness enough to show she intended to make things up with everyone before she sailed to the Continent with Captain Roarke. The fact that she was appearing in her parents' box was a surprise to those who had heard of the captain's sudden need to leave the country. Mary was glad to see her, though. *I am sure she would regret not reconciling with them if she moved to the Continent without doing so.*

The opera's music swelled with a surge of violins and harp, and a ruddy young man with a solid build burst into a song of love. Lydia sighed with relief as she settled into her seat, tucking her emerald silk safely away from the legs of the other chairs. "No one dead yet," she whispered to Mary. The clinging scent of bodies distracted Mary from answering, and she sat down next to Lady Lucy in silence. Though Lady Crestwood chatted with her husband over the music, Lady Lucy said nothing, and Mary was reminded of the first day they met, long ago at Lady Crestwood's ball.

Have I destroyed our friendship forever? It seemed likely. Mary was not intending to go to the Continent anytime soon, nor would Captain Roarke be free to return to England until he could somehow pay his debts. Mary still did not know if she had done right to threaten Lady Lucy with breaking her confidence. Lady Lucy was convinced it was a blackguardly act, while Lady Crestwood thought it the heights of pure-mindedness. *Perhaps, for once, the point was not to do the saintly thing, but rather to do what I felt I needed for myself.* Whether right or wrong from a moral point of view, Mary felt sure it had done her good as a person.

The love song soared into a finale, and the act ended with a dramatic fall of curtain, giving the audience a moment to stir from their seats if they chose. Several gentlemen and ladies shifted in their seats, lifting lorgnettes to survey the crowd for acquaintances. Lady Crestwood's enamelled lorgnette showed her something that made her start with surprise.

"What is it, Mama?" Lady Lucy asked, her curiosity prompting her to peer over the wall of the box to the woman her mother was watching. Mary leaned forward as well. The woman was a stranger, a blowsy brunette wearing a green gown that looked like a cheaper homage to Lydia's. A glitter of gold and emerald hung about her neck.

"Impossible!" Lady Crestwood rose from her seat, snapping down her lorgnette on her husband's arm to get his attention. "My lord! My emeralds—the Crestwood emeralds—are on the neck of that trollop!"

"You must be mistaken." Lord Crestwood took a look, and his brow furrowed. "It cannot be..."

"What woman?" Lady Lucy's voice escaped in a gasp, breathy and weak. "That awful woman? That common strumpet?" Her tone held some emotion unidentifiable by Mary, as if she were moved in some way.

"I shall have her dragged out for the Bow Street Runners!" Lady Crestwood's air of authority dashed any hope of restraint. She swam out of the box, her skirts rustling as if they bristled with her rage, and Lord Crestwood hurried after her, whether to second her or merely to watch, Mary did not know.

"That is Captain Roarke next to her!" Lydia said, glancing at Lady Lucy. "I believe she is Mrs White—the, um..." She did not finish, but Lady Lucy supplied a term.

"The harlot." The young noblewoman's face was suffused with red, as if blood were trying to pour out of her. The resentment that tormented her unbridled her tongue. "Apparently *that* is the sort of woman my husband favours these days." Her hands clenched on her lap. "That is no lady. That is no gem of nobility like Lady Sarah."

"But I do not understand. Does she really have Lady Crestwood's emeralds? And why?" Lydia tilted her head.

Mary felt dread roiling in her belly. From the light of fear and rage in Lady Lucy's eyes, Mary suspected her friend was pushed to a new state of distress. Lady Crestwood's voice thundered from below the opera box, condemning Mrs White as a thief for all to hear. The captain's tenor defended the woman, but half-heartedly. He kept throwing glances up at the Crestwood box, where Lady Lucy sat tight-lipped and, to his view, impassive.

"He is no thief, is he, Lady Lucy? At least, not the way your mother thinks." Mary stretched out to touch her hand, but Lady Lucy jerked it away.

"I took them that day we went to my parents' house," she said, curtness slicing the words, as if she could not bear to give a full explanation. The drama of her parents confronting the paramour of her husband unfolded beneath them, attracting more and more of the audience's attention.

"When you visited your father in his study," Mary said.

"Yes. He had the safe open for some papers he was organising, and he barely knew I was there. They all barely know I am there." Her resentment stung Mary even though it was not directed at her.

"But I thought you gave everything you stole back!"

"I did not steal them! They are mine. Mama always said they would be mine." Lady Lucy swallowed hard, fear overwhelming her anger for a moment. The rage soon reasserted pre-eminence, however. "What does it matter when I use them, if they are to be mine in the end? I need them now. I intended to sell them, to pay some of our debts before we go and leave a little besides for Betsy."

Lydia hung over Lady Lucy's shoulder while Mr Wickham coughed and drew back, uncertain what the proper response would be. "But then how did Mrs White get them?" Lydia asked.

"Is it not obvious?" The bitterness in Lady Lucy's tone shamed them all. "My husband took them from my jewellery box and gave them to his sweetheart."

Mary could hear the captain's voice carrying over the increasing murmur of the crowd. "I cannot explain how these emeralds came to be here, but Mrs White is not at fault. She is innocent of any theft," he said. Casting another glance at Lady Lucy, his resolve seemed to strengthen. "I am not at liberty to explain, but I assure you that it is all a misunder-standing."

He is shielding Lady Lucy. Mary was almost disappointed at his valiant effort; she wanted to believe the man was entirely a villain, entirely wrong. No doubt it would have been shameful to him to admit in public that he had given what he thought were his wife's jewels to his mistress, but Mary did not think that was his sole motivation. Even though he knew his wife must have taken the emeralds, he would not defame her in public. *I rather think he would confess to taking the emeralds himself rather than expose her. There is more of a gentleman in him than I thought.*

Mrs White's strident voice joined the fray, appealing to the crowds thickening around them in a way that showed she did not dislike all the attention, however much she might dislike being taken up for theft. "I am innocent! These emeralds were given me by a—friend," she simpered.

"The setting is quite distinct! It is the Crestwood family emeralds, which has been passed from parent to child for decades and now is wrapped about the neck of a"—Lady Crestwood drew a deep breath—"whatever you are, madam."

In the opera box, Mary and Lady Lucy stared at the scene. "The Bow Street Runners will be here soon, Lady Lucy. You must speak up," Mary said. Though Lady Lucy moved her hand again, Mary succeeded in grasping it. "They will arrest that woman or your husband if you do not. Tell your parents what has happened. Or simply tell them you borrowed the jewels and then loaned them to Mrs White. You can end this."

"Why should I?" Lady Lucy breathed hard. For once, her shoulders were straight, her chest full with inhalation, the muscles of her arms contracted, her chin lifted with authority. For once, she was the image of her mother, power incarnate. "Let them put him in prison. Let them put *her* there. What do I care?"

"Oh, Lady Lucy!" Lydia was scandalised.

"I would have stood for anything, so long as he remembered his place. But a woman like that! She is not even a *lady*." The scorn suffocating her words reddened her face further, and Lady Lucy folded her arms over her chest. "I will have nothing to do with it."

"Then I must." Mary stood, her motions slow as she walked to the door, wishing for some better alternative to arise. *But I was part of this from the beginning. If I had spoken to Lady Lucy the moment I saw the lace, perhaps none of this would have happened.* As she passed out of the box and down the hallways, seeking the entry to the lower part of the opera house, her pace quickened. *Lady Crestwood knows that I already know about her daughter's...problem. She will listen to me.* Much as she did not like the look of Mrs White and much as she despised the captain, they did not deserve to be arrested for Lady Lucy's fault. She sighed. *I suppose 'Family Fracas at the Opera' is a more bearable headline than 'Family Fracas Puts Son-in-Law and Mistress in Jail.' That is the best we can hope for, now.*

Approaching Lady Crestwood through the crowd of jeering, yet entertained, opera-goers took more courage than Mary had expected, but she elbowed her way to the matron and seized her arm to get her attention. "Lady Crestwood, I must speak to you in private."

"I am busy, as you see." Lady Crestwood shook off Mary's hand.

"It is about Lady Lucy. It is about Lady Lucy's *problem*. You see, she thought you would let her borrow the emeralds for a time." Mary spoke with earnestness, feeling it was necessary to emphasise her words in order to convince Lady Crestwood, but from the mother's frightened glance Mary saw that the idea had already occurred to her.

"This has nothing to do with her," the noblewoman said, her tone insistent, but new wrinkles sagging at her eyes.

"It *does*." Mary's voice was small, still timid under the weight of shouts and laughter rolling all around her, but she knew the firmness in it would affect the mother. "Let them save face and walk away with the emeralds now. The captain will get them back and return them to you later. Will you, Captain?"

He nodded, his eyes darting back to Lady Crestwood.

"No. I will have them off her neck this instant." Lady Crestwood insisted on uncoiling the necklace from Mrs White's throat, and from the disappointment flashing across the mistress's face, Mary had to agree that perhaps Lady Crestwood's demand was wise. When she had secured the necklace, the noblewoman turned to the group of onlookers with a queenly air. "There is nothing more to see here. I am sure a better drama will unfold onstage."

Few women could have induced such a crowd to return to their seats and wait for the curtain to rise, but Lady Crestwood's demeanour showed she had every expectation of obedience, and she received it. Her bold stride led Mary back up to the opera box to retrieve their belongings, and then the entire party sailed out, Lady Lucy stalking with as firm a step as her mother as she approached the Crestwood carriage. Apparently the young lady had no intention of going home to her lodgings, and her mother accepted her company without a word.

"Heavens!" Lydia gasped as she settled into her own carriage, Mr Wickham ensconced beside her while Mary sat on the opposite side. "That was the most exciting night at the opera I have ever had! Did you see Lady Lucy's face? She will not return to the captain after that, I vow."

"She might have lied to save Lady Sarah, but she refused to lift a finger for Mrs White." Mary shook her head.

"Well, I would not have lied to save either. Mind that, Mr Wickham. Any ladies you bestow jewels upon must take their chances." Lydia's smiled showed no real concern for such an eventuality.

"I have only one lady at whose feet I desire to lay treasures." Mr Wickham's charm had not suffered from his pecuniary difficulties, apparently. Lydia beamed back at him, and they began to banter in friendliness.

Mary sagged against the side of the carriage, exhaustion draining the last flickers of anger and fear from her body. *I was brave again. Well, it was a problem I helped create, so perhaps there is not so much virtue in it as all that. But at least I spoke up.* The memory of the jeering crowd made her arms and neck tingle. Of course, they had not been jeering at her, but the sensation still felt raw. *Will I ever be able to endure such things in an unflappable way, the way Lady Crestwood does?* She doubted it, but the small changes she had undergone still satisfied her.

"How courageous you were, wading into that *contretemps!*" Lydia said, as if echoing Mary's thoughts. "Not even I could have done it, and I have the audacity of ten woman, have I not, Mr Wickham?"

"Twenty, my dear."

"And so it is rather odd to think of your doing it, Mary. I suppose I really must not call you 'Mouse' anymore after that. Cannot you be some other little creature?"

Mary thought of an owl, silent in its flight, hidden in the night, but able to strike with force when necessary. She would always be on the quiet side, but she hoped she could now be bold enough to capture what she wanted or hoot in warning. "How about Owl?"

"Because of your interest in science, you mean? I suppose it will do." Lydia lost interest as she spied a woman in the carriage stopped alongside theirs. "La! Mrs Reddings always has the choicest gowns. Look at that lace! Two layers thick, at least. Oh, when will this carriage *move?* We shall be stuck in front of the opera house for all eternity, and I shall perish of envy staring at Mrs Reddings's lace."

"There is quite a crush on the road, to be sure," Mr Wickham said, "but it will clear up. Besides, if you perish, you will not be here for all eternity."

"That shows all you know about it!" Lydia tossed her curls, but no one could fully appreciate their glistening in the murkiness of the carriage. "If I die, I shall become a ghost and haunt this very spot, unless I decide to haunt that ghastly drawing room instead—"

The squabbling continued, but somehow it did not ring the same way in Mary's ears. Where before it sounded grating and threatening, now it sounded almost...merry. *Did they change? Do they have a new rapport after all these months of jealousy and rebellion? Or was their bantering always cheerful, and it is I that have changed, able to hear closeness in what sounded like danger before?* Mary did not know, but she let the banter wash over her, feeling undisturbed. *Do I even have reason to feel peaceful? Mr Wickham seems to be stirring up trouble of some kind, bad enough he may have to leave England. The Crestwoods are in chaos. And yet...*Her shoulders relaxed against the padded seat. *I feel a kind of peace any way. I cannot make everyone live the sort of life I would have, quiet and orderly. I have done what I could, and they must make their own lives now. I have my own future to look after.*

Mr Wickham proved right about the crowds thinning eventually, and the carriage wheels squealed into motion. The thrum of wheels vibrating against stone went through the vehicle and up through Mary's body, contrasting with the smooth sheen of silk brushing against her hand as she moved her reticule on her lap. At first, she simply leaned against the velvet-lined side of the carriage, her mind drifting in a void. But as her energy renewed, the sensations of the world outside caught her attention: the acrid scent of smoke from half-blocked chimneys, the creaks of nearby dray-carts, the sharp shadows falling through the window and then being sliced by lantern light in turn. Mary drew closer to the open air and breathed it in, gazing upward at the dark smudge of sky. *No owls here. But I imagine there are some on the Cole estate.*

She would fit right in.

Twenty-Nine

"That looks very well, Mary." Lizzy nodded with approval at the arrangement of hothouse flowers Mary had constructed. It felt strange to bend stalks and position flowers while snow churned outside the windows of Pemberley, but apparently the Pemberley gardener was very proud of his floral accomplishments, and Lizzy liked to use them when company was expected for dinner. "Perhaps you had better get ready now."

Mary removed the apron from over her gown with reluctance; the fire in the grate did something to banish the winter cold, but her arms still prickled with goosebumps from the chilly air. She wondered if it had snowed harder on the Cole estate than it had in Derbyshire. *Mr Cole will be able to tell me today.* The thought sent more goosebumps along her skin, this time in delight. His family had invited Mary to visit in June, shortly after Mr Cole's triumphant lecture for the Informed Ladies of London Association. The visit had broken forth a flood of emotion, like ice breaking up in a spring river. Mary's emotions had been part delight at the comfortable house and spreading fields and part shy reassurance from Mr Cole's parents, who welcomed her with an affection she strove to deserve. Mr Cole's emotions had been more mixed.

He was proud of Mary and happy to be with her, but at first, he had cringed at every mention of his brother's name. Mary had to admit that some of the comments levelled at his replacing Thomas Cole as heir were cutting and insensitive. But each time, Mr Cole cringed a little less, and by the end of Mary's visit, he endured the discussion of his brother's virtues and death with equanimity rather than pain.

Mary had come back to London at the end of June, expecting to stay with the Wickhams, but apparently Mr Wickham had realised business matters required his attention abroad sooner than he thought, and he and Lydia had decamped without notice to Mary—or their creditors. Luckily, Mr Darcy had been willing enough to come to the rescue, and the Darcys had invited Mary to stay with them for a few months. *Now that was a solace for the loss of Lydia's company, indeed!* Though Mary loved their scamp of a sister, it was much easier to feel at home with Lizzy's kindness and Mr Darcy's quiet courtesy. Lizzy had been delighted with the success of her scheme; though the reputation of the Wickhams had descended again after their flight to the Continent, at least Lydia had not been too great a scandal while they were there, and better yet, Mary had blossomed into the woman Lizzy had guessed she might become. Lizzy was all too happy to invite Mr Cole to make frequent trips to Pemberley, and Mr Cole divided his time between learning the ways of managing an estate from his father and taking his recreation in Derbyshire examining geological samples with Mary. Once, the Darcys even took Mary to a site in between the two places, remarkable for its rock formations, and Mr Cole had met them there. The pleasure of indulging in their hobbies while solidifying their attachment was not one Mary was likely to forget. *And soon he will be back again, to take me home for good.* A new home, with new parents, new duties, and a new husband. November weddings might not sound as poetic as some, but Mary felt sure neither snowdrifts nor icicles would detract from her enjoyment of the event.

In the meantime, she studied geology, read letters from Jane of her new-born Lizzy Bingley, and wrote to Lady Lucy. The peace of Pemberley was a welcome shift from her London adventures.

As Mary returned from arranging her hair and changing her gown, Lizzy looked up and smiled. "You always had a prettiness of your own, Mary. I am glad to see more of it now, though."

Mary flushed. Her sister must have recognised her discomfort, for she changed topics. "You have had a letter from Lady Lucy, have you not? Does she still sprinkle all her statements with 'Mama says,' the way she used to?" The wry twist of Lizzy's lips showed she still savoured the frailties of humankind.

"She is getting much better now. Most of the time she simply states her own opinion." Mary gazed out at the thin layer of snow silvering the Pemberley lawn. She hoped it would not deter Mr Cole.

"I would think living with her parents, she would be more inclined to mimic Lady Crestwood than ever." Lizzy adjusted a curtain, taking a moment to watch snowflakes pirouette.

"Oddly enough, I think she has become more independent, living with them. She chooses where she goes a bit more now." Mary's wistful smile acknowledged the change. It had been difficult rebuilding her friendship with the young lady, despite Captain Roarke's removal to the Continent and Lady Lucy's remaining with her parents. Though Lady Lucy no longer wanted any part of her husband, she still resented the forced revelation Mary had pressed upon her.

Lizzy could not resist the humour of it. "Perhaps Lady Lucy found filching her mother's jewels a bolstering experience."

Though Mary winced, she had to chuckle as well. "In a way, you may be right. It was an act of defiance, and Lady Lucy is part ashamed of it but part proud, too. I do not think Lady Crestwood ever thought her daughter would do something as daring as stealing the family emeralds. She probably feels she never knew her and should have. At any rate, Lady Crestwood is a little less...dictatorial over her, and Lady Lucy is a little more self-assertive." Mary smiled. "Lydia gave her their dog Prince, you know, before they made their mad rush to the Continent. He was a little bored at the Wickhams', I think, and was tearing up things. Now he lives with Lady Lucy, and she dotes upon him."

"It cannot be the same as having her husband."

"No." Mary remembered the clinging need Lady Lucy had had for Captain Roarke, the affection hopeless of a genuine response but eager to receive any pretence of love. Though the separation was doubtless painful, she thought it probably meant something good for Lady Lucy. *She is learning to care for herself, as I did. And though having Prince is not the same as having a baby, I am sure it does her good.*

They turned to other matters: Jane's new baby, Mr Bingley acquiring enough treats and dainties to make a host of new mothers ill, Mr Darcy's plan for the northern fields of the estate. But the whole time Mary chattered with her sister, her gaze drifted again and again to the doorway, waiting for the butler to bring forth the visitor she longed for.

At last he appeared. Mr Cole's hat had protected most of his head from the snow, but flakes had moistened the chestnut hair at his temples and neck. The glow of warmth in his smile belied the frigid air outside and the ice rimming the tops of his boots. Mary rose. Her feet passed along the carpet as if she had no control over them, and she had only the vaguest sense of Lizzy discreetly withdrawing from the room. Her gloved hands were captured by Mr Cole's, and she found herself smiling up at him as if a summer sun had suddenly emerged into November.

"A few days more," Mr Cole murmured, lifting one of her hands to kiss. "A few days more, and you shall be home."

But as she gazed into the welcoming depths of his dark eyes, Mary knew she was already there.

Epilogue

Mary glanced at her pale blue silk gown in the mirror, checking to ensure it was as gleaming and flawless as it had been when she first descended from her rooms. Though it was hardly her first time as hostess for the neighbouring gentry, she wanted everything to go perfectly.

"Mama!" Thomas ran up to Mary, crushing her skirts in a hug as far as his ten-year-old arms would allow. "Tell Jane she must not dress up Hercules in her cap and ribbons. He is an old dog, and deserves some respect."

Jane pattered to them, her little shoes scraping the well-polished floor. "He likes it," she said, a hint of insistence in her tone that would have ill befitted her aunt and namesake. Her hair was too dark to be much like Jane Bingley, but the beauty blossoming on the little girl's face promised other similarities. Their cousin, William Darcy, hung back behind her, and though he was the same age as Thomas and the two were fast friends, his reserve made him appear much older. He was spending his holidays with the Coles, and Mary prized the trust Lizzy placed in her.

"Hercules was probably just being patient with you, Jane," Mary said, caressing Thomas's head and reaching out to pull Jane into the hug. Though William looked askance at the procedure, she pulled him into the hug as well.

"I only was dressing him because you have not made me a patchwork doll yet." Jane tilted her head back to look up into her mother's face as William politely disengaged from the hug, wearing a half-pleased, half-disgruntled expression. "You promised you would make me one just like the one you had as a little girl."

"I did not promise that," Mary said, hiding a smile.

"You did! Tell her, Thomas—you were there—"

"I promised that *we* would make a patchwork doll." Mary gently stepped back and stooped to Jane's level. "We will do it together, tomorrow. Now you must both go back upstairs. You know your father and I have an important dinner to give this evening."

"I know that." Thomas grinned at his little sister in triumph. "I told Jane not to bother you, but then she bothered Hercules instead, and I could not let that stand, you know, so I came down here…" He peered past his mother to scout the dining room. "Are they really all coming to honour Papa for his rocks?"

"Some of them are geologists, Thomas, but most are just our neighbours." Mary felt a swell of pride at the reminder of her husband's success. In the first few years of marriage, when the older Mr Cole had passed away and Richard had been still learning the ways of managing an estate, he had not had much time for dilettante geology. But once he was more familiar and Thomas and Jane were a little older, Mary had pressed him to return to his old pursuits of crawling over hillsides and comparing samples in his study. She had had enough time to help him then and although Richard could not add her name to the paper he presented at the Geological Society of London, he had openly admitted his wife's contributions to his work to all who would listen. Now some of the members of the society were staying with them for a visit, and Mary had planned an elegant dinner for them and the neighbouring gentry to enjoy on the last day of their stay. She had hopes they would announce that Richard would receive a special commendation from the Geological Society.

Not that he needs awards and accolades the same way now. Her husband had grown happy with his life on the estate and proud of his children, dogs, and most of all, his lovely wife, now returned to geology with a sincere love for it, rather than one tainted by needs of praise or reassurance.

A nod from the butler suggested the guests who were coming by carriage were arriving, and Mary gave her children and William a last hug. "Run along upstairs. I must greet our guests."

Thomas and William dashed up the stairs, vying for who would get there first, while Jane trailed and sang a nonsense song to herself. Mary smoothed her skirts as best she could. In the past, the slight crumples from a child's hug might have disturbed her need for tidiness and made her worry about how she would appear, but now she simply gave a rueful smile and let the matter drop from her mind. Two children made adjustments in one's need for perfect order, and Mary had learnt that she had other talents and enticements that made a slightly crumpled gown slip by others' notice.

Richard joined her to greet the guests. His blacksmith's shoulders still filled out his coat admirably, and though his skin was a bit rougher from days of scrambling into gullies under the hot sun, the warm smile he gave Mary was just the same as it had always been. He took her hand and squeezed it between arrivals, and his bow and her curtsey dipped in perfect time, as well matched as the rest of them.

When the guests had all arrived and marched into the dining room, Mary seated herself and began conversing with the gentleman next to her, one of the geological members staying with them. The dinner proceeded with all conviviality and decorum, and Mary found herself gazing at the talkative ladies interrogating the experts and the cut glass dishes arranged in delicate refinement before her with an appreciation that almost felt dreamlike. *I really did it. A dinner this large —and this important for Richard!—and it is all harmony.*

Almost all, at least. Sir Reginald Colton, his white hair thinner than it had been when she first knew him, still managed to rile up his competing scientists, and a quarrel in the servants' hall grew venomous enough to require a moment's setdown from Mary, but she accepted the former and smoothed out the latter with a fluidity that would have shocked her younger self. It helped that their new housekeeper was Hannah Cupp, who had remained loyal to Mary and kept in touch with her through the trials of motherhood and a country lifestyle. Hannah said she had married a young man there and been widowed shortly thereafter, and Mary permitted the story without too much investigation. Though she had had to bend when Mr Wickham insisted Hannah's pregnancy made her unfit for service, now she had command of her own household, and Hannah—or Dawkins, as Mary called her now—had proven herself hardworking and sensible, both as housekeeper and mother to her John. Dawkins and Mary restored harmony to the dispute among the servants, and Mary found herself brimming with confidence as she returned to the table, despite the lady guests expecting fluster and embarrassment. *That is something I could not have done so serenely before.* And when Mary found the braised trout more delectable than she had expected, she bid the footman come round and bring her a second helping with perfect nonchalance.

"To Mr Richard Cole," Sir Reginald said, lifting his glass, "and his exemplary contributions to science. And to Mrs Cole, without which neither his work nor this lovely dinner would have been accomplished." As the others toasted, Mary saw a smile exchanged amongst the members of the Geological Society, as if other announcements were to come.

I will have good news to write to Pemberley tonight. Mary wished her sisters could have been here for the moment, even Lydia, who still roamed the Continent with Mr Wickham in a marginally respectable lifestyle. Most of the Wickham fortune had been lost in whatever suspicious manoeuvres Mr Wickham had been agitating in London, but the couple had enough to keep them afloat in watering places abroad, and the occasional gambling windfall made a welcome addition to Mr Wickham's pocket. No doubt he stirred up schemes for greater patronage and wealth in foreign places, but the Wickhams dared not return to England without a fortune large enough to quash any accusations of wrongdoing. Mary doubted she would see Lydia in person again anytime soon, but in the meantime, she wrote to her whenever she knew an address for them. At the moment, the old address had fallen through, and Mary would have to wait until Lydia had leisure enough—or felt desperate enough—to write to her with a new one before she could tell her news.

Mary would have to settle for long letters to her other sisters and perhaps one to Lady Lucy as well, who now patronised an orphanage of her own design and was aided by a saucy but grateful sixteen-year-old Betsy. Captain Roarke still flitted over the Continent, but Lady Lucy seemed satisfied at their estrangement now, and Mary had the feeling the captain would have to lower himself indeed and greatly change his behaviour to ever win his way back into her good graces. *Thank heaven I have had better luck with my husband.*

Richard's debate with a colleague was too avid for him to spare many glances down the table, but he did throw one meaningful look at Mary in between courses, and she felt the same giddy rush of love she had felt all those years ago. *Such happiness! Though I am sure he is wrong about where that granite came from, and I shall have to tell him so when I get a chance.* The dispute would prove interesting.

Peace and disputation, harmony and conflict. Though she still preferred quiet days and calm, Mary had grown equanimity enough to weather the other times—and sometimes, enjoyment in them enough to seek them out. She could foresee a long line of days of both kinds ahead of them.

The thought made her smile.

THE END

Quills & Quartos
PUBLISHING

The author and Quills & Quartos Publishing thank you for your purchase of this book. We hope you will consider leaving a review.

Subscribers to the Quills & Quartos newsletter receive advance notice of sales as well as bonus excerpts, deleted scenes and other exclusive content. You can sign up on our web site at www.QuillsandQuartos.com. Thank you!

ACKNOWLEDGMENTS

Special thanks to Jan Ashton, Amy D'Orazio, Debra Watson, Carpe Librum Book Design, and the whole Quills & Quartos team.

ABOUT THE AUTHOR

After acquiring a doctorate in philosophy from the University of Arkansas, Elizabeth taught philosophy in the United States and co-taught English in Japan. Now she and her husband live in northwest Arkansas, the 'garden of America'. (At least, she has only ever heard Arkansas called so.)

She dreams of visiting Surrey (if only to look for Mrs Elton's Maple Grove), Bath, and of course, London. When she has a Jane Austen novel in one hand, a cup of tea in the other, and a cat on her lap, her day is pretty much perfect.

Elizabeth Rasche is the author of *The Birthday Parties of Dragons* and her poetry has appeared in *Scifaikuest. Flirtation & Folly,* published in 2020, was her first regency romance and *A Learned Romance* is her debut Austenesque romance.

ALSO BY ELIZABETH RASCHE

Flirtation & Folly

Marianne Mowbrey is a responsible country rector's daughter who longs for the novelty and excitement she reads about in novels. When her crusty Aunt Harriet agrees to give her a Season in London, Marianne vows to dazzle the world, win a husband, and never go home again. But the Londoners who determine social success are inclined to pass over plain Marianne in favor of her beautiful, reckless younger sister.

In a world of ambition, fashion, flattery, and deceit, how can Marianne stay true to her real self—when she is not even sure what that real self is?

The Birthday Parties of Dragons (as Lisa Rasche)

In the strict society of dragons, becoming an adult means everything. For only adult dragons are fearsome enough to dazzle human minds into forgetfulness, thereby keeping dragons safely within the realms of myth and mystery.